BANISHED
The Long Road Home, Book One

BANISHED

THE LONG ROAD HOME, BOOK ONE

AN AMISH ROMANCE

LINDA BYLER

New York, New York

CHAPTER 1

THEY RODE THE TRAIN INTO BLYTHEVILLE, ARKANSAS, ON A hot spring morning when the wild plum trees were an explosion of blooms, the cherry trees were blushing with their flagrant display, the dandelions and wild mint were nodding in agreement to the frenzied chatter of the grosbeaks.

Obadiah and Merriweather Miller were still children, half-grown and long-limbed with wide, frightened brown eyes and hair the color of new wheat. Clutching the canvas drawstring bag the neighbors had given them and licking the grainy soot off their dry lips, they remained in their seats while the cars clanked to a stop behind the hissing, snorting beast that had powered its way for too many miles, dumped them at some nondescript station or other, only to be herded onto a new car with more strange faces staring down at them from various heights. They knew they were meant to sit still and wait till the conductor gave them instructions, so with the resigned air of the world-wise, they looked at one another and nodded.

The city of Blytheville, Arkansas, with Uncle Melvin and Aunt Gertrude Amstutz living on a farm not too many miles away, would be their new home—a word and place as questionable as it was alarming. The only spoken word about it had been in hopeful whispers from the time Lizzie Bontrager had packed the change of clothes and cold corn pone with the assurance their relatives could barely wait to have them.

Eliezer and Veronica Miller were dead. Eli and Fronie, their parents, both drowned in the silent, roiling floodwaters of the Apple Creek in Ohio on a night when the flickering kerosene lantern attached to the side of the carriage sputtered in the driving rain and they could only have guessed at the depth and power of the current or the power of icy needles. The carriage had been rolled from end to end, the snorting bay mare's lungs filling with the floodwaters, the same as Eli and Fronie's.

The rescuers searched for days before they found the horse washed into the roots of a willow tree, pieces of her harness snagged on limbs that hung above the current. They all said Eli and Fronie looked young and peaceful, as if they'd fallen asleep together, but Obadiah knew they hadn't done that, they would have struggled and cried out with no one to hear until the dirty water filled their lungs and there was no more air to breathe. He'd seen a cat drown in a flooded creek, and it had been nowhere near being peaceful.

His own lungs filled with a rebellion against God and the fact that He allowed this to happen, his heart beat sullen and angry in his chest, and he stood beside his parents' coffins during the funeral service and hated everyone, including the bold-headed preacher who read a German poem in a nasal twang that made him sound as if he swallowed the words before he spit them out.

Merriweather—May for short—stood beside him with her black bonnet and her black shawl clutched around her skinny frame, her head bent as tears washed over her cheeks with a small trickle that never stopped. Obadiah allowed that girls cried easily, everything hurt them more, including the death of both parents, but when none of the family offered them a home and no one knew what to do with them, it hurt him more than anyone would ever know.

Grandfather Miller had hardening of the arteries, which made him abnormal in his way of thinking, so Grandmother Miller had her hands full with him, just shook her head, and said Melvin would take them. Everyone else had big families with small houses and barely sufficient income to keep everyone fed and clothed, and with the pioneering Melvin having made a fortune in cotton somewhere in Arkansas along the Mississippi River, well, he and his wife could raise Eli and Fronie's two children. And they said they would. It was their Christian duty.

Obadiah hated Melvin before he knew what he looked like. He hated the stench of black smoke and soot that constantly filtered through the half-open windows of the train, and he hated the fact that no one wanted them back in Apple Creek, Ohio.

The hatred felt manageable, whereas the instant welling of weak tears that appeared the minute he let go of it was too much for his young heart to handle. To turn into a sniveling, pathetic little boy would be worse than glaring out at an unfair world through dark, sullen eyes—eyes that refused to allow any sign of life and certainly no fragility.

Merriweather was named after a close neighbor, one who had predicted this second child would be the coveted girl, so when she came howling red-faced and healthy into the world, Fronie was overcome with gratitude to the pompous neighbor, tradition being what it may, and promptly gave her a namesake. Obadiah was the firstborn son, which called for a regal name from the Old Testament, but his name had been shortened as well. He was known as Oba.

The train clanked at the couplings, jerked and slowed as the brakes were applied, hissed steam, and threw off flakes of soot like some belching, flame-throwing dragon. The folks around them gathered cardboard boxes, valises, and paper bags of half-eaten sandwiches, smoothed their hair, and ran hands discreetly along wrinkled skirts and crooked belts.

Some rotund gentleman of unknown nationality bent over with his bulging eyes and yellow teeth and sprayed saliva across both of them as he asked where they were bound, which terrified May into silence, but Oba told him this was their stop, then watched with his flat, lifeless stare until the man brought the conductor, who told them to follow him out of the railroad car, down the iron steps, and onto the asphalt as hot as their mother's sadiron, the sun blinding in its intensity.

"Someone here for you?" the conductor asked.

Oba looked around into the sea of moving limbs and rattling carts loaded with luggage and containers before saying they'd be along shortly, which left the conductor free to perform more pressing duties.

"It's so hot," May whimpered, her tongue as dry as peach fuzz.

"We'll go inside," Oba told her, and turned in the direction of the brick railroad station.

Inside, it wasn't much cooler, with the milling crowd, but the shade was welcoming. They found an empty bench, slid onto it side by side, the canvas satchel clutched in Oba's lap.

"I'm so thirsty," May whispered.

"I don't have money," Oba told her, his brown eyes flickering with empathy. It wasn't his sister's fault they were in this mess.

"I know."

Oba watched the crowd, his straw hat perched on the back of his head, the rounded crown like a bowl made of straw, the brim turned up the whole way around, with a black band tied around the base. His shirt was long-sleeved, the collar buttoned to the top; cracked brown leather shoes were on his feet. May wore a blue cotton dress with a blue pinafore-style apron to match, a white bowl-shaped covering on her head, black stockings, and slightly worn black shoes on her feet.

Their blond hair was the color of new wheat, the eyes large and dark in golden faces, which caused more than one passerby to take a second look, then hurry on, leaving the siblings with a burning thirst and growling empty stomachs that had not seen food in more than eight hours, the last of the corn pone eaten somewhere in Missouri.

"Samwitches! Samwitches! Get your chicken samwitch!"

Oba swallowed back the rising saliva as a portly black gentleman wove his way through the crowd, a wide wooden shelf hanging from a band around his neck and containing a variety of white-bread sandwiches that were cut in triangles and wrapped in waxed paper.

He swallowed and shook his head when May lifted hungry eyes, questioning. The man was so black his eyes appeared blue and there was a satiny sheen to his skin; his hair was in tight curls as dark as everything else. When he smiled, his teeth were a flash of white in his face, his eyes crinkled with kindness.

"Yo'all got folks comin' to gitcha?"

"I think so."

"Yo sure?"

"Yes."

"Yo had yo dinnah?"

Oba shook his head, terrified to feel the prickly tears forming. He wanted to tell the man he had no money, but the lump in his throat pushed back the words until they disappeared and made his stomach burst when they growled and rattled around with the rest of the emptiness.

"Here. Yo'all take this samwitch. It's on me."

It was incredible, this hand reaching out to them, a proffered treasure thrust within reaching distance. They both tried to restrain themselves, but both grabbed quickly.

"Thank you," May said first, and Oba repeated it immediately.

"Hey, hey, it's alright. Reckon youse is both hungry. And over there?"

They turned to follow the pointing finger.

"S'water there."

"Thank you."

"Hope yo'all's folks shows up. I'll keep an eye out."

Oba nodded before they slid off the bench and slipped through the crowd to find the water that bubbled up from a strange sink when they turned a handle; they didn't even need to use a cup. They drank so greedily May became a bit sick, but they felt as if they could face anything now.

They unwrapped the sandwich and ate it in ravenous bites, relishing the chicken and celery and mayonnaise. They licked the tips of their fingers, then licked the waxed paper.

And they waited.

May fell asleep, her head on Oba's shoulders, her breathing soft and slow, rhythmic, like a butterfly on a milkweed pod. Oba glared out from his seat on the bench, his large eyes flat with the sense of holding out the increasing sense of desertion, the bitterness he felt prematurely toward this unknown relative who would be taking them in, propelled by a Christian duty and the knowledge of free labor that was sure to follow.

Oba figured all this out, his mind reeling from the cavernous fact that no one wanted them back in Apple Creek. Looking for love was a lot like exploring caves: the way every new passage turned into a dead end or threaded its way back out to the original room, which was a huge black hole in the earth. But he didn't tell May any of his thoughts, mostly on account of her being so sure everyone loved them, despite the fact it didn't suit the rest of the family to take them in.

"Hey."

And there he was. Melvin Amstutz.

He was dressed in traditional garb, his wide straw hat clamped on his head like an oversized lid, his jaw wide and firm and sprouting scraggly hairs stained with tobacco juice, his earlobes as big as apricots separating the thick strands of greasy hair into gleaming sections.

"You Eliezer's kids?"

Oba blinked, caught unaware.

"Y . . . yes."

"Well, come on then. Time's a-wasting. I had an option to send Israel, but he had work to do. Come on. That your satchel?"

Oba did not give him the satisfaction of an answer.

The Arkansas countryside was viewed from the bone-rattling perch of the high seat of the wagon, looking down on the back of a brown horse who stepped nervously, jumped when a burlap sack rolled along the side of the road, flicked his ears constantly, and took off like a scared rabbit whenever the whip sizzled through the air, which was frequently.

There were hills covered in trees, potholed red dirt roads with plenty of stones to spit out from under the wagon wheels. The sky was still blue in late afternoon, with fragments of wispy white clouds with lavender tints along the edges, same as home in Ohio. The sun was hot on their shoulders, the horse working up a white lather where the leather harness rubbed along the side and around his haunches where the breeching hung.

It was comforting to know the exact same sun was shining in Ohio, and the same blue dome of sky was there as well. He thought, things couldn't get too bad here in Arkansas if the same sun and sky watched over them, could it?

They came to a long, steep incline, one that took his breath away. Melvin yanked on the cast iron lever that applied the brakes, but in spite of it, the horse sat back into the leather breeching, hunched up, and wrinkled like a newborn colt. May slid off the seat, hit the dashboard with a soft, embarrassed thud, her eyes going to Melvin's face immediately.

There was no response, so Oba reached down to help his sister back on the seat, then placed an arm across her thin legs to keep her there.

Down, down, until even Oba admitted to a queasiness in his stomach. The road turned right, then eased into a left turn, which turned gently onto a slight grade, the forest on either side thinning as they emerged from the shaded road that brought them to level ground. All around them, the world opened into brilliant light, revealing a flat plain devoid of trees except where they were clustered along fence rows that divided one property from another.

Oba couldn't make sense of the crop growing in these fields. The plants were unlike any corn or soybeans he'd ever seen, and certainly it wasn't alfalfa, which they raised back in Ohio to feed the dairy cows. He looked at Melvin Amstutz, his new benefactor, with the question on his lips, but decided against it as the man pursed his lips in a peculiar pucker and let loose a stream of brown tobacco juice that arced out across the wheel to an amazing distance.

He blinked, swallowed the question.

The sun was getting lower now, the heat on their shoulders less punishing. The wagon rattled along the red dirt road, spitting small stones as the horse's hooves unearthed them. On either side, this strange crop stretched out in long, seemingly endless rows. White farmhouses with weathered barns dotted the countryside, but there were no silos or corncribs, only the occasional shed or chicken coop. He became aware of bent figures with hoes, dark faces, women in long skirts, some of them with babies tied in a sling on their backs.

Before he could stop himself, his natural curiosity took over, and he blurted out, "Do people still own slaves?"

"No. Of course not. They're paid workers. We Amish would never break the *ordnung* like that."

Oba took some comfort in the fact that the man cared about the *ordnung*, the Amish book of rules. Although personally Oba thought some of the rules were silly, their shared faith made Melvin seem more familiar. Satisfied, Oba's eyes darted everywhere, taking in the length and breadth of these fields, the endless level land like a huge flat blanket covered with these strange plants, the sky a dome of blue above it. The only ruffle was an occasional line of trees, or a fence built of rails that zagged its way from one point to another for no apparent reason.

On they went, the horse throwing his head up, then down, the way a tiring horse will do when he wants to rid himself of the rein attached to his bridle. The whip hissed over his back, and he lowered himself, increased his speed yet again, flecks of white foam raining off the breeching.

No words passed between them. May sagged against Oba, her body pliant with weariness, so he kept his arm across her to prevent her from sliding off the seat. Melvin slanted a look at them but said nothing.

A single pine tree was the marker for the long lane that led to the farm. On either side, the straight rows fell away, the rich reddish hue changed to a deep black, the soil unlike anything Oba had ever seen. In the distance, a house and barn came into view, the trees around it the only thing that kept it from appearing lonesome. As they approached, Oba could see the peeling paint on the barn, the blackened lumber telling him no one cared or there was no money to remedy the oddness of old lumber with tendrils of white paint like fish scales. Doors hung open on broken hinges, windows sprouted cracks and fissures like broken ice.

The house was set a good distance from the barn, the white siding peeling layers of paint. A pair of brown and white goats raised their heads to stare at them with bulging eyes like wet marbles, then ran in their odd gait to a safer distance. The lawn fell away on either side, cut unevenly into the tall grass to whatever the goats had consumed. A wire fence in various forms of direction—straight, leaning to one side or another—sagged into a gate that was tied shut with a stout rope. The yard was littered with tin cans, a rusty brown wagon with one wheel missing, a brown barrel. Dairy cows dotted the barn yard, lowing.

The horse slid to a stop by the barn door, its sides heaving.

Oba looked around, unsure. He was aware of a deepening sense of lost hope, of captivity.

May whimpered tiredly.

Oba bent his face to hers. "We're here, May."

She nodded, looked around with frightened eyes.

Melvin instructed, "Get down. You can go in till I get the horse put up."

Oba looked at the house, the yard fence and the goats, the rope holding the gate into position, and said they'd wait.

"Go on in. I have to get the cows in."

So there was nothing to do but let himself off the seat, help May down after him, grab the satchel of extra clothing, and set off toward the house and the formidable goats. The trees stood silent, the leaves still, ushering them to the gate and the knot of stout rope. Oba set the satchel down. His fingers worked at the rope till he pulled it apart, then let them both through. Instinctively, he reached for May's thin fingers, twined his own through them.

Both goats raised their heads, their jaws working like small grinders. The darkest in color stamped a small hoof, glared as if he had a personal grudge toward both of them, then went back to his dandelion consumption.

A skinny cat slunk around the corner and disappeared into the weeds at the side of the house, tail like a bottle brush. The black wing of a bird lay on the wooden porch step, along with bits of twine and a beat-up galvanized bucket.

Oba stopped, looked at the closed door, unsure. Wasn't someone supposed to come to the door the way his own mother used to do? The fear that rose in him gave rise to the only emotion he knew that could outrun it. Anger coursed through his body, gave him the courage to step up and knock firmly.

"You don't need to knock. Just come on in."

So he did, an arm across May's back, pushing her along.

The woman who was their aunt looked much the same as all the other Amish women they were used to. White head covering, wide strings on either side, a navy blue pinafore across her chest, and a gray apron pinned around her waist. She was of average height, not too thin or too overweight. An average face, plain, not unkind.

"So you're Eliezer's children?"

She walked over and peered into their faces. Oba saw the mole at the side of her nose, the yellowed teeth like a broken comb.

He nodded, his eyes glued to the fascination of the protruding mole.

"How old are you?"

"I'm eleven; May's ten."

"Well, you should be good little workers. You'll be able to help a lot around here. So your Mam drowned? Your Dat, too? Well, it leaves you without parents, but the Bible says the Lord giveth and he taketh away, so you may as well get on with your life. Are you in school?"

"We were. School's over."

"So it is."

There was an awkward silence. Oba became aware of a small child in the corner, asleep on a pile of blankets, his thumb in his mouth. Two pairs of eyes watched from the sagging sofa in the corner.

"This is Ammon and Enos, our boys. Leviticus is asleep."

There were no words to affirm the meeting of cousins, only stares that sized each other up. Oba didn't like them or dislike them; he merely accepted them as being there, hoped they'd stay out of his way.

What kind of a name was Leviticus?

They stood together now, him and May, thin arms dangling, unsure of what was expected of them. The house was dark, strange, with sour odors and unfamiliar faces.

"Your satchel there. I'm assuming it's clean clothes. I hope so, because I don't have time to sew."

Oba nodded, didn't meet her eyes.

"Well, is it or isn't it?"

"What?"

"Clean clothes."

"Yes."

"Alright then. Say it."

Off to a bad start, a vague, unsettling sense of impending animosity crept into his young heart. Bewildered by the lukewarm welcome, unsure how May would survive, he resorted to his usual helper—anger. He refused to answer again, and instead stared back with a challenge in his eyes. She looked for a moment like she might rebuke him, but then turned away, perhaps deciding it was too much trouble.

"So, if it's extra clothes then, I'll show you where you'll sleep. Come."

Up the steep narrow staircase they went, into a room rank with wet sheets, unwashed and slept in repeatedly. Oba swallowed, felt sick.

"May is the only girl, so it won't be fit to have her sleep with the boys. Enos and Amos won't be parted, so you'll sleep with Leviticus. Ach, the bed's wet. He's a bed wetter."

In one swoop, the acrid sheets were off the bed, flung out the window, the lower half smashed down to secure them.

"There, they'll be dry by bedtime."

May was shown to her room, and then they went back down the stairs to stand against the wall and watch Melvin return from the barn. "Hurry up with dinner," Melvin ordered, not speaking to anyone in particular. "The cows are waiting." Gertrude sloshed something from an iron skillet into a granite bowl, barked at Enos to set the table.

Enos never budged, so she let it go, then threw soup plates and spoons on the crooked, greasy tablecloth.

"May, you may as well make yourself useful now. Get the water glasses. Water in the pump out by the stoop."

Oba was proud to see his sister open cupboard doors till she found seven aluminum tumblers, set them carefully by the plates, look around till she found the pitcher, and let herself out the door.

"She learns quick, right?"

Eyes flew like darts to Oba's face. He made no further comment.

The stew smelled of goat, the vegetables a mystery, but it had been a long time since the chicken salad sandwich, so they both cleaned their plates, scraped them well with the side of their spoons, then sat expectantly waiting for the remainder of the meal. They were used to finishing off dinner with cake or pie, cornstarch pudding or canned fruit. When none was forthcoming, they bowed their heads for the after-meal prayer and watched warily to see what was expected of them.

"Come along, both of you," said Melvin, toothpick dangling, belches rumbling from the slapdash intake of food.

They followed him to the barn and were introduced to the dark confines of the dairy, where they both listened to instructions about the proper procedure of extracting milk from a cow's udder.

Oba had tried his hand at milking at home but was too young, so his father had laughed, said he'd try again a year from now. Oba remembered the whitewashed stone walls, the floor swept and limed, the manure removed on a daily basis, the milking stools hung in neat rows from wooden pegs. His father's laugh, his constant whistling.

A sense of dread welled up but was quelled by his anger.

"Here's your bucket. Stool over there."

Oba looked at the floor of the barn, the gutter heaped with old piles of straw and manure, the fresh stench of liquid. He watched as a cow humped her back and let loose a strong runnel of steaming urine, then swung her wet tail to rid herself of the hordes of barn flies.

"What are you waiting on?"

Oba did as he was told, sat on the stool, placed the bucket beneath the cow, grabbed the two back teats and pulled, his mouth set in childish determination.

"That ain't the way. You want to get kicked? Just keep that up. Squeeze, don't pull so hard."

So Oba obeyed, his fingernails biting into the delicate udder, resulting in a well-aimed kick from the cloven hoof, straight to his forearm, upending his seat on the milking stool, the bucket clattering into the manure, a purple bruise flowering on his arm. He gritted his teeth, dodged the barrage of outrage from Melvin, and tried again.

He went to bed hungry, lay on the dried sheets with a howling individual named Leviticus who fell asleep eventually and promptly soaked the sheet again. He lay with wide-open eyes, watched the stars through the curtainless window, and was comforted by the crescent moon that hung in the sky like a sympathetic slice of kindness.

He couldn't know that May's slight figure on her narrow bed was heaving with suppressed sobs, tears pooling on the rough muslin of the pillowcase, the balled-up sheet pressed against her mouth to keep him from hearing.

CHAPTER 2

THE FIELDS THAT PUZZLED OBA WERE COTTON PLANTS. ROWS of cotton grew in the fertile valley, sprouted up from the dark, porous soil, and spread healthy roots nourished by spring rains. He learned quickly that Melvin's disposition was ruled entirely by the weather, which in turn pertained to the long stretches of cotton rows that fell away from the buildings and the cow pasture.

Melvin spoke only about cotton now. He told Oba it wasn't as easy as it looked, after planting. Weather was critical. They had to contend with boll weevils and armyworms, both pests that could almost destroy a good crop. They needed rain, plenty of it in spring, but come summer, the dry was good, as were the sweltering days and uncomfortably warm nights. If the nights were too cool, the cotton was suffering.

With no newspaper or radio, Melvin scanned the sky worriedly, tested the direction of the wind by wetting his forefinger and holding it aloft, shaking his head and muttering to himself.

Melvin was driven, obsessed.

Cotton was in his thoughts, ran through his mortgage payments, controlled his temper and his rare moments of happiness. He owned six mules: brown, big-eared, and ornery, but necessary. Like goats, they survived on the worst hay and scrubbiest pasture, drank muddy water from potholes in the soil that was as thick and sticky as gumbo. Where a horse would sometimes kill himself by working too hard in the unrelenting heat of the delta, a mule would go all day at a steady pace and no faster, no matter how Melvin applied the whip or wore himself to a frazzle by hopping and shrieking.

Oba was given a team of affable creatures, thin-necked and lop-eared, their winter coat hanging on in untidy swatches, as if shaven in spots.

Pete and Kick.

He learned how to hitch the two to the long-tongued cultivator and set out for the cotton fields in front of the house that stretched all the way to the river. The hot morning sun lay heavy on his back, the mules' ears wagged with every step, the harnesses slapped and jingled in time to the plodding, and a stone of cold fear lay in Oba's stomach.

He was told to cultivate the lower forty, with no assistance from Melvin and dire threats if he damaged the cotton plants.

He stood on the platform of the cultivator, stopped the mules at the end of the row, looked longingly toward the house, then the barn. If he'd only helped him to get started. Unsure how to work the lever exactly, he experimented by playing with it before he had the mules situated between the rows, which in itself was an impossibility. Sweat broke out on his forehead. He swiped his hair away from his face, his hands shaking.

Tentatively, he drew back on the lever, amazed to find the prongs of the cultivator lowered. The mules' ears flicked. The signal to start was the raps on the iron lever, so they stepped forward as obedient as well-trained dogs.

Oba was caught off guard, grabbed the reins, and yelled, "Whoa!" But the mules heard the lever clank into place and saw the rows of cotton ahead of them, so they plodded straight ahead, the double-tined cultivator following, straddling the row of cotton plants expertly.

Oba yanked on the reins, yelled, and hollered, then sat down and grinned sheepishly. He was shaking all over now, but the worst was past.

Pete and Kick new precisely what they were about and went ahead with it, which was to walk between the rows without touching the cotton.

Slowly the knowledge of the simplicity of it all settled into Oba, and he hunched his back in relaxation, allowed his senses to take in his surroundings, and absorbed the sights and sounds of the Arkansas Mississippi River Valley.

It was steaming hot. The kind of heat that is cloying and wet, drenches man and beast in a matter of minutes. The sun laid a steaming cloth of heat across the low, level land and pressed it down until perspiration appeared, ran in rivulets, and disappeared, only to be replaced.

The clear, bright, windy days of Ohio were a thing of the past. This Arkansas valley, this flat steaming delta fed by the river, was where he was placed by uncaring relatives and a cruel act of God, the drowning of his parents.

He was here now, so it was up to him whether he'd sink or swim, seeing as God didn't care or had forgotten him and May. The air was heavy, laden with smells and no wind. He found nothing to break the monotony of the plodding mules and vast acreage of cotton, but he could always watch the birds that sailed and cavorted like acrobats. He cringed when the high squawk of a huge gray bird erupted above him and looked to find massive wings slowly beating the air, what he guessed to be a heron or fish crane. Busy mallard ducks quacked their signal as they propelled themselves through the humid air on their way to the river.

No one had offered to take them to the river, so he could only imagine the breadth and volume of it. He wondered if he'd ever see it.

He wondered, too, if this farm and these people were where he would be expected to stay for the rest of his life or until he'd get married.

But at eleven years of age, the future is never thought out completely—a child's survival kit—so Oba lived from one day to the next, keeping himself as invisible as possible and as willing to work.

He blessed these mules. He loved their bony backs and their list-less eyes, the long ears, and large ungainly hooves. They took away all his fears of cultivators and long rows of cotton, the apprehension of being unable to do what Melvin required.

Gertrude, or Gertie, as she'd told them to call her, had packed a paper bag for his lunch, saying Melvin didn't like to unhitch the team at lunchtime, it took too much unnecessary time. So when Oba's stomach began to growl and the sun was directly overhead, he stopped the mules by the fence row and opened the sack.

Glad to find two pieces of bread with meat in the middle, he unwrapped it to find butter and strips of ham. But what was this? White dots. Oblong ones that were, in fact, moving.

Maggots. The ham was infested with the larvae from flies' eggs. He flung the ham to the ground, but held the coarse bread and but-ter, searched for more maggots. He swallowed hard, but finding nothing else in the brown sack, he folded both pieces in half before stuffing them into his mouth. He willed himself not to think about what he'd just seen.

He became aware of a burning thirst, a dry desperation on his tongue. Had Gertie really expected him to stay on this cultivator in the heat without water? He walked around, finding pine trees, holly bushes with red berries, weeds, and white flowering trees, but no stream or brook. The afternoon seemed like an eternity, stretching before him with this thirst.

He thought of his mother, the kindness with which she would hand him a glass of cold tea. He felt the sweetness of it slide down his throat.

He shuddered with thirst.

Fronie Miller was small and blond, the kind of woman people called petite. Her large brown eyes were as soft and gentle as a fawn's, her hands made to pat a baby's soft cheek, to touch her husband's shoulder when he needed encouragement. She read her Bible to the two children in the evening, sent them to bed with verses from Matthew, Mark, Luke, and John.

She taught them to love Jesus, told them he was God's own Son, and only He had the power to save. She told them He loved little children especially and blessed them every one. She was the light of Oba's life, the flame that kept him and May growing in love and stature, the mother every child deserves. She loved her husband in the same way but enhanced by a deep respect bordering on reverence. And so Oba and May spent the most tender years of their life without knowing cruelty or deprivation, loved and nurtured like tender plants.

Some of the family thought they were coddled. Aunt Magdalena, on their father's side, thought it would do them good, going to Arkansas. No use *fa-buppling* (spoiling) them. They were like hothouse flowers; let a little cold wind or rain enter their lives, and they'd wither away.

But Oba knew none of this.

He only knew he was placed into this strange place among people who could hardly be counted as blood relations, and he had to make the best of it. No use crying about something he couldn't change.

He doubted if he'd actually die of thirst, remembering how he'd read somewhere that it took three to five days for a person to succumb, taking into account the conditions surrounding him.

He jumped when he heard a loud rustling in the underbrush by the crooked split-rail fence. He froze when the brown ears and bright eyes of an inquisitive dog burst through the holly, then retreated, only to appear gain. Oba held very still, but when he appeared the third time, he snapped his fingers and called softly, "Come here, dog. Over here."

The dog was of medium build, no specific breed, lop-eared and short-haired, obviously attracted to the ham.

"You can't have it," Oba called.

The mules lifted their heads, blinders from the bridles flapping.

"Go away, you can't have it. The maggots'll make you sick. Shoo."

The dog stopped, sniffed the air, wagged his tail and smiled. Oba recognized the smile. A dog greeting. He smiled back.

A straw hat appeared above the rail fence, followed by a dark face the color of good chocolate, a white set of teeth, and two huge brown eyes, the whites like crescent moons. They sized each other up, one wary, the other as friendly as a drink of water.

"Hey dere, my fellow!" the dark-skinned boy called out, his voice velvety and soft with a kind curiosity.

It was the first stroke of kindness Oba had experienced for many days, and he found himself tearing up before swiping at his eyes with the back of his hand.

"Whatcha up to?" came immediately after, seeing as he got no reply from the white boy on the cultivator.

"Just . . . just sitting here. Resting."

Up came the straw hat, followed by bare shoulders, a patched pair of overalls, and bare feet. One leg was thrown over, followed by the other, and the boy stood abreast of the cultivator.

"I'm Arpachshad. Arpachshad Brown."

Oba nodded, smiled a weak hesitant grimace.

"What's yours?"

"What?"

"Your name? Everybody has one." His voice was still kind; it had a burn in it, like water tumbling over stones, but smooth, with a level delivery and a lilt at the end of his sentences.

"My name is Obadiah Miller. Oba."

The boy shook his head, then laughed out loud.

"We straight out of the Old Testament, ain't we? Mama would be proud."

Oba acknowledged this with a nod, another half-smile.

"Nobody call me Arpachshad. Not even my mama. Everybody call me Drink."

"Drink?" Oba repeated, thinking of his awful thirst.

"Yeah. I was two, I fell inna river, and they fished me outta the drink."

Oba laughed now, genuinely, then ran his tongue across his parched lips. "That's funny."

Arpachshad was so pleased to find this sober boy laughing at what he'd said, that he stood beaming up at Oba with eyes like stars, teeth as white as snow.

"Drink's a lot easier to say than Arpachshad, ain't it?"

"Sure is."

"So, Obadiah Miller, how come y'all here?"

"If I told you, you would think I'm lying."

"Really?" Drink squinted, grimaced. "Try me."

So Oba told him.

Drink shook his head, took pity on him, said Melvin Amstutz was his father's boss, basically. They were sharecroppers, meaning they picked cotton for a share of the crop, which was a step above being slaves, but wasn't much different a lot of the time, the way some of them beat them out of their fair share. When Oba kept glancing uncomfortably toward the barn, Drink understood and said he'd have to move on. The dog had eaten the ham and the maggots with neither one of the boys noticing and had fallen into a midday nap immediately after.

"You best get back to cultivating. I'm on my way to the river."

"Doing what?"

"Fishin' fish every day I can. Mama needs fish for supper."

"Where do you live?"

"Just over the way."

He called to his dog, hopped the fence, and left, leaving Oba with a deepening sense of loss. He hadn't realized how lonely he was until Drink showed up.

That evening, Oba had his first lesson in being caught in the crosshairs of Melvin's hawkish vision.

"I don't want you talking to that black boy."

Oba's mouth fell open, snapped shut. There was no way he could have seen him down in the lower forty, unless he was God. Or had been secretly spying on him.

"Those black people are trouble. As long as they pick my cotton, that's all that's necessary. Stay away from them."

Oba stuffed his toe into the dirt, shrugged his shoulders, and didn't say a word. Down came Melvin's fingers, clamped like a vise on his shoulder, squeezing until Oba fought tears.

"Y'hear me now? Don't give me that silence. You'll learn to respect what I have to say. You're just a greenhorn from Ohio. Never forget it. I catch you with that black kid, you'll be thrashed."

Later, when Melvin wasn't around, Oba asked Gertie what a share-cropper was, just to see what she'd say.

"Oh don't bother your head about it. It's just what it sounds like. Negroes are no good, so stay away from them."

It was different, being around Gertie, so he asked why. What was so bad about them? He thought of Drink's happiness, the melodious voice, the kindness.

"Oh, because, Oba. We don't socialize with them. We're Amish. We stick to our own kind."

May was scrubbing the milking pails in the washhouse, her sleeves rolled above her elbows, her thin arms red from the hot water and the lye soap.

The heat had been unbearable all day, the temperature climbing to over a hundred, the humidity like a heavy cloak.

When he asked May the question he'd asked Gertie, she said maybe skin color had something to do with it. She didn't know.

Oba looked at the dark circles below the soft brown eyes, the chapped skin and broken nails on her hands, and asked if Gertie was good to her.

"Yes." But she looked away from him.

"Do you want to go to church on Sunday?"

May shrugged her shoulders.

"You should. You could make friends."

"I don't really want any."

"I know how you feel."

Up to this point, Ammon and Enos stayed on the outskirts of both their lives, eyeing them as intruders but returning to their play and largely forgetting they existed. Leviticus followed May around like a faithful pet, always filthy and reeking of the previous night's bedwetting, sucking his thumb, and asking slow questions whenever he removed it.

May was always patient, but the hard work was taking its toll.

Oba thought often of Drink, unwilling to accept what everyone else said about why he had to stay away from black people (*schwarzen leute* in German). He could hardly stand to hear Melvin say those words, in the nasal condescending tone of voice, as if he was so far above any of them. Him with the unwashed hair and chewing tobacco habit, splattering the nauseating juice all over the farm. Picking his nose and kicking animals, worrying himself sick about the cotton, the weather, and back to the cotton.

He often wondered what his parents would say about Melvin.

But the farm had improved somewhat, since their arrival. May kept the yard clean, and most everything else, taking orders from Gertie in a meek and quiet spirit. Ammon and Enos were the biggest problem, messing things up after they were cleaned, but since Gertie never seemed to notice, she never said anything.

On Saturday night, they each took a bath behind the curtain in the galvanized washtub, went to bed early, and got up even earlier.

They milked the cows, heard Melvin grumble about the weather, ate the sticky oatmeal, and were dressed in their Sunday best.

Oba wore an old white shirt that had been Melvin's before he was married to Gertie, so of course it was too big, but no one seemed to notice, so he didn't say anything. Black trousers and a vest were his own, as was the straw hat. Bare feet were perfectly acceptable, and he was ready to go.

May looked a bit off-kilter in the misshapen cape and apron, pinned crookedly, but she didn't know. Two bright spots of color showed on both cheeks, color that showed her excitement, which made Oba feel better. She was so small, so thin, and seemed like a much older person, not a child of ten. As always, he felt protective of her, wanted to make her life easier, but had no idea how he could ever accomplish it.

The spring wagon had not been washed or swept. They merely climbed into the filthy mud-splattered wagon, watched Melvin rein up the horse, and rattled away, bits of twine and clumps of mud jostling along with them.

The morning was thick with the smell of wild plum trees and jasmine, heady scents that made them all breathe in deeply, savoring the startlingly delicious odors. Lady slippers curtsied by the side of the road, as if to usher them to God's service. Quail called from the roadside, then flew up in a flurry of wings when they approached.

Even Melvin was in a jovial mood, an unexpected turn.

Oba found he disliked his silliness even more than his normal brusque manner, the way Gertie simpered at his side, giving him the occasional fist bump on his skinny upper arm. Ammon and Leviticus began a quarrel over a dead butterfly, until Oba reached over and threw it across the wheel, then threatened them with his eyes.

Ahead of them, there was a group of black people dressed in Sunday finery. Melvin drove past without acknowledging their presence, but Oba lifted a hand to wave, told May to do it also.

"Dat, Oba and May waved *an die schwarzen leute*," Ammon yelled.

"Oba. For shame," Gertie called back.

Melvin turned in the seat and fastened his glare on Oba's face. "You do that again, you'll be going to the woodshed with me, and it won't be cutting wood, either."

A hot fury threatened to choke him. He trembled with suppressed rage, thought he could throw up with the unfairness of it. He wasn't going to follow Melvin's way of thinking about black people or anything else. No one could make him. He was fiercely glad he had waved.

Church services were held in a small white house set between cornfields; there was a large chicken coop between the house and the barn. Melvin stood with the boys between the ages of nine and twenty-one, but stayed a bit separate, scuffling his toes into the dust self-consciously, his hands clenched behind his back.

No one spoke to him, but they spoke to each other. A few of the older ones puffed on corncob pipes, sank their hands into their pockets, and tried to look nonchalant. A boy of about twelve threw a rock at a barn cat and howled with glee when she took off unharmed but frightened out of her wits.

They were seated in the stifling house on hard wooden benches, a black *Ausbund* (hymn book) shared among two boys. They lifted their voices as the slow rhythm of the hymn rose and fell, then sat soberly as the minster brought the first sermon in a rousing voice, his beard rising and falling.

Oba's nights spent with Leviticus kept him in constant need of sleep, so he fell into a stupor followed by a slumber so deep he could not remember where he was when he blinked awake. Embarrassed, he looked around, but found no one eyeing him with distaste.

The long prayer, the closing song, and the boys were released from the heated vacuum of the still rooms where not one puff of air entered.

They ate lunch standing along a lengthy table with large bowls of bean soup scattered along it. Plates of sliced bread, bowls of jelly, and sliced cheese, pickles, and red beets completed the meal. As was the custom, the bean soup was eaten from the bowl, every spoon dipping in with his neighbors, to signify unity. Oba found himself exchanging glances with a boy of his age, curly-haired and freckled, his eyes shining with adventure.

After dinner was eaten, the boy sidled over, cleared his throat, and asked who he was.

"Oba Miller from Ohio," he said solemnly.

"Rufus Hostetler. I live here."

They each stuck out a hand, clasped, let go, and became self-conscious. After a few awkward glances, they developed enough nerve to begin a halting conversation based entirely on curiosity. Oba left the church services on the back of the spring wagon with an increasing sense of having found a reason to live beyond the overwhelming despair of his first few weeks. He had a friend named Rufus, who he would be able to see every two weeks. He also had a friend named Drink who he fully intended to see whenever he had an opportunity.

The remainder of the Sunday was spent under the oak tree, trying to find a comfortable spot in the heat. At bedtime, there was no respite, which left Melvin rubbing his hands together at the prospect of a perfect cotton crop. Cotton shot out of the ground like bamboo in this weather, he claimed as if he had already made thousands of dollars.

Leviticus tossed and turned, howled in misery on the rancid sheets. Perspiration formed in pools around them. Finally, Oba lay on the floor with his pillow, which seemed much more comfortable, woke during the night, and thought he must be suffocating. There were no fans and no possibility of sleeping outside. Melvin and Gertie would not allow it.

He dreaded every night, every day as summer came on with its blazing sun and life-sucking humidity. The flat delta of the Mississippi that flowed into Arkansas, with the long narrow strip of hills called Crowley's Ridge like the sides of a wide flat bowl, retained heat like an oven. The cotton grew, and it grew well, which gave the whole family a rest from Melvin's nervous temper. Like a dog licking its chops in anticipation, he roamed the fields, checked for quality, kept an eye out for the enemy boll weevils, and exulted in his own good fortune.

Gertie's garden was a source of constant sweat and labor, harvesting peas and beans and red beets. They ate so much boiled cabbage the house was rife with the result: roiling stomachs, belching, and gas.

There was fresh lettuce, onions sharp with spring flavor, rutabagas, and finally, sweet corn. Oba lowered his face to ear after ear of yellow corn, sprinkled with salt and spread with the butter May had churned, her thin arms turning the handle in the awful heat, which husky six-year-old Enos could have done as well. Or Ammon.

Not once did Drink show his face, even when the cultivator clanked across the fields and Oba was sure Drink would hear it if he was on his way to the river. And not once was he allowed to go to the river, in spite of asking repeatedly.

He was told idle time was the devil's time, and they had no time to sit and fish. Seething with resentment, Oba bit his tongue to keep from saying what he thought, buried his eagerness to learn how to fish the way Drink did, and went ahead with his work, through every sweltering day and night.

CHAPTER 3

May wept silently at night, but during the days she kept her thoughts to herself, already shored up with a tremendous will to survive and a sunny spirit to make the best of a bad situation. She went about her work without complaint, carrying the memory of her mother deep within her.

She found Gertie to be a poor substitute, didn't count on her for much of anything, and so found resilience from loneliness and isolation.

She never told anyone, not even Oba, of her deep and abiding fear of the goats in the trash-strewn yard. They were like the devil, sneaking about with their malevolence, their glass eyes that missed nothing, tails twitching like pinwheels to keep the hordes of black flies away.

She soon discovered the glee Ammon and Enos displayed if she showed her aversion to these creatures. The boys would chase them to the wash line when she pegged clothes to the sagging line, struggling with wet towels and tablecloths, watching for any sign of the goats driven mostly by Enos.

A boy big for his age, Enos was left mostly to his own devices, his father being obsessed with the weather and the cotton fields, his mother slogging through her days resisting the heat and longing for Illinois, where she had been born and raised, taking out her frustrations on her three offspring, especially Enos, and now, the girl

Melvin's relatives sent for her to raise, as if she didn't have enough with the three rowdies she already had.

As for May, there had been no more children for her own parents, on account of her difficult arrival into the world and the subsequent sickness that left her mother in a weakened condition. And as children often do, May benefited from this, being seated for hours at a time beside her sweet and patient mother, being nurtured by stories from the Bible, taught how to embroider, how to write in a fine hand, how to crochet a doll's scarf in brilliant colors.

To have this wellspring of love and caring removed at such a young age was painful, but May had her mother's sweet disposition and, as some children will do, carried on with no visible scarring.

She carried out her duties as quietly as possible, took Gertie's scolding and complaints as a step up to better herself, so before long she was performing tasks well, as much older girls would do. Most of the cleaning was left to her, given that Gertie did not like to take upon herself any duty that involved too much self-denial. She liked to sew, especially knitting and embroidery, so when the summer's heat began to show its force, she shrank in the face of it, sat on a padded rocking chair in the most available breeze and did what she liked, leaving May with the work and the care of the three boys.

Leviticus, at four years old, found a little mother in May. She sang to him, told him stories, showed him a nest of chipmunks beneath the old stone wall, allowed him to reach into the chickens' nests to find the warm brown eggs and never smacked his hands when one broke.

Smackings, paddlings, whippings were meted out with regularity to all three of the boys, and it wasn't long before May felt the sting of the hickory switch, the sweating red face of her benefactor above her.

It was punishment for allowing Leviticus to go to the creek without Melvin's permission, so May took the administered blows without crying, nodded her head in agreement when he told her never, ever to allow the young boy to the creek. Ammon and Enos sneaked off to the creek on a regular basis, but somehow, they could get away with it.

It was a bright June morning when Gertie told her they were going to town. She'd best get the dishes done and the kitchen swept, so she could braid her hair. May looked at Gertie, scraping the last of the *ponhaus* (scrapple) on her plate, belching, and wiping the grease from the corners of her mouth with the edge of the tablecloth.

"Yes."

"Alright then, make it quick."

She slid the teakettle over on the hottest part of the wood stove, put the dishpans in the sink, added a piece of lye soap, and began to clear the table.

"Are Oba and Melvin going?"

"No. Just us, with the boys. We need supplies. And I thought maybe a piece of fabric to make a Sunday dress for you."

May was pleased, but she said nothing, simply worked faster as Gertie finished her coffee. She held very still as the stiff bristles from the brush raked through her tangled hair, blinked back the tears as Gertie's hard fingers pulled dreadfully as she began to braid.

The sun was already a white orb of pulsing heat in the sky, the air thick with moisture and whining insects. Black flies crowded around the tired horse's ears, lay thick around his eyes and nostrils. Mosquitoes sang. Bumblebees and wasps flew drunkenly from one nectar-filled petal to another.

Melvin came out of the barn, pushed his hat back on his head, and looked them over.

"Where's her bonnet?" he asked.

He never said May's name, only "her."

"She doesn't have one."

"She shouldn't be going to town without her bonnet. Stop at Alphus Yoder's and get Sarah to make her one."

"I can make her a bonnet."

"Yeah, yeah. But you won't get around to it. Ammon, keep your hat on. Boys, you behave yourselves. Don't stare at the black people."

"You know they don't do that. They're used to them working in the fields."

"I will speak to my boys however I decide to, and I won't be second guessed." Melvin's voice thundered.

Gertie didn't answer, as Melvin handed her the reins. She kept her eyes somewhere above the horse's ears and chirped.

The horse leaned into his collar, and they were off, the high wagon bouncing over the many holes in the level driveway, a teeth-jarring klunk that could have been avoided had the driver been more aware.

May wondered at the lack of goodbyes. The lack of smiles or well-wishes, the conversation like sandpaper to her senses—rough, abrasive. Her mind could not always fathom the absence of everyday kindness, so she closed her ears when Melvin berated Gertie, which was almost every day.

She tried keeping sunshine in her life by showing kindness to the boys, but they did not always respond the way she expected, so her sunny spirit had dulled after a few months. Each morning, her hope burned brightly as she told herself today would be different, today someone would be kind, but they never were.

She sat stiffly, aware of the lack of a bonnet. Her tender conscience was like an unfolding rosebud, keenly aware of right or wrong, and Melvin berating the fact that she was not wearing one made her head feel exposed, naked.

She so wanted everyone to like her, to be obedient, so happiness and especially kindness would follow her like a protective cloud.

The day was beautiful, if warm. The cotton fields stretched away on either side, the wide level fields interrupted only by lines or groups of trees that surrounded the zigzag of the rail fence or a small meandering waterway. Swallows raced madly across the sky snatching mosquitoes and other droning insects to feed the babies housed securely in the mud nests built with exquisite precision in the rafters of the barn. Tiny baby rabbits peeped from the culvert, where the wild strawberries grew in a profusion of color.

May took a deep breath, clasped her hands in her lap, glanced at Gertie for any sign of conversation. But Gertie was staring straight ahead, as if some malevolent thought rode somewhere above the horse's ears, her mouth pinched and unhappy.

May thought of her own mother, sitting in the buggy with her smile that was like a permanent fixture, the hand that would reach over and squeeze an arm, a knee. Her mother had been affectionate, always touching her, smoothing back the strands of blond hair, straightening an apron, kissing her cheek. They would always sing when they went away in the buggy.

They sang "Komm, liebe Kinder" (Come, dear children) and "Heaven My God to Thee," her mother's voice rising and falling in a beautiful cadence, one May heard now, sitting beside the austere Gertie.

"It's warm," May offered.

"I hate Arkansas. At home in Illinois the heat was never like this. I will try to get Melvin to leave as long as I live."

With that dire statement, a new responsibility was planted in May's young heart. To ease Gertie's unhappiness, to bring Melvin to see what he needed to do to have a happy wife.

As if that statement opened the gates of a dam, more bitter words poured forth from Gertie about how much she struggled to accept everything: the heat, the cotton, the sharecroppers, the other Amish people who lived and worked among them. The snakes and lizards, even the air she breathed was tainted with the stink of the Mississippi River.

"See, I told Melvin I didn't want to move. My parents and all my sisters and brothers live in Aurora, Illinois. We had a good life, milking cows, growing corn and hay. I wasn't always sloppy like I am now. I kept a nice home in Illinois."

May wondered at her words, pictured Illinois as some far-off promised land rife with milk and honey, the land God gave Moses and the Israelites in the Bible. She felt a deep, sincere empathy for the unhappy woman beside her, vowed to do everything possible to ease her situation.

"I write to them, but it's not the same," she said, suddenly.

"No, I guess it wouldn't be." May thought, *if only I could write a letter to my mother or my father.*

They rattled along in the old wagon, the boys prattling among themselves, the horse working up a lather under the hot morning sun.

May spied a few houses ahead, built by the side of the road, automobiles chugging toward them, spitting exhaust and loud popping noises. Gertie shortened her grip on the reins as the automobile approached, but the rangy horse never missed a beat in his gangly stride.

"Guess he's used to automobiles. Now there's something that shouldn't be. Those black people driving cars. They shouldn't have all that money. They belong in the fields, not driving around on the roads like that."

May stared ahead, blinked with confusion, and questioned Gertie's statement. How could one person be less in God's eyes than another? Her mother sang a lovely song about Jesus loving all the little children in the world, red and yellow, black and white, which surely included these brown people from Arkansas.

She said nothing, took notice of her surroundings now, as they came upon more houses crowded close together, the way houses were built in a town. May had gone to town with her parents when her father accompanied her mother for supplies at the general store in Kidron, Ohio, where she had learned the delights of licorice, lollipops, root beer, and ice cream that melted on her tongue.

"Mam, we want molasses candy," Enos called out.

"Hush. Someone will hear you."

"Well, we want some."

"Hush."

May turned, the smile on her face evaporating as she saw the tongue protruding, flapping obscenely at his mother's rigid back. Enos lifted his face and howled, finding this bit of flagrant disrespect funny indeed. Ammon twirled a finger in May's direction, telling her to turn around, mind her own business.

The interior of the store was dark, so it took a while to adjust her eyesight to the many items piled on shelves and along the wall. She walked behind Gertie at a respectful distance and listened to the exchange with the portly gentleman at the counter, her eyes missing nothing as Gertie followed him to the shelves of fabric and chose a dark blue cotton, then a card of black buttons.

She shrank back as a buxom Amish woman strode up to them, her black bonnet hiding most of her face, her bare feet slapping the wooden floor.

"Vell, Gertie Amstutz. Imagine seeing you here."

Gertie turned, her eyes unwelcoming, no greeting forthcoming.

"Who is this?" The woman asked, pointing a sausage finger at May.

"His sister's child from Ohio."

"Oh. I heard about that. You took them in. Well, I'm sure there is a *sya* (blessing) in what you're doing. *Au g'nommany* (adopted). She's right pretty, so she is. What's her name?" The woman continued as if May had no eyes or ears of her own; even so, she stood quietly.

"Her name is Merriweather. May for short. What possessed them to name a child such a heathen name, I'll never know. It's not in the Bible. There's no excuse for something like that."

"No, certainly not. We need to stay with the plain names. I fear she'll think she was not meant to be Amish, *gel* (right)?"

"Vy, sure. Sure." Gertie nodded in a sanctimonious manner, as if her choice of names for the three boys had been steeped in righteousness and carried the promise of ingrained tradition that would ensure them a seat among the saints.

They moved apart, each one to her own business, the children following Gertie in various stages of circumspect. The fabric was measured, cut, folded, and handed over without a word of conversation. Gertie turned, handed the man behind the counter her list of items, and stood, eyes missing nothing.

Enos asked for molasses candy. Ammon echoed the request.

"Hush."

When no candy was forthcoming, the boys sauntered away, their hands shoved into their pockets, glowering. Leviticus began to cry, soft wet sounds accompanied by rattling sniffles.

A firm "*Shick dich*" (Behave yourself) was followed by a hard grasp of loose skin from the child's forearm, a twist that resulted in a horrible wail of agony, followed by a shrinking away, palm clasped to the bruised forearm.

May's heart beat in her chest, a dull fluttering of sympathy, wondering why a penny's worth of candy was simply not allowed. She curled a hand around the thin, heaving shoulder, offered her yellowed handkerchief, but was met with a defiant stare and a slap from the small hand.

They strode from the store, a tight group of unhappiness, cast covert glances at passersby, and returned to the wagon where the horse was whipped into compliance and turned on the road to home.

May caught sight of a large building constructed of graying lumber and corrugated metal. Odd barrels and crates, fences with various gates. It was all strangely silent, the rutted lane showing the emergence of growing weeds that lay unkempt along the sides.

May tried to gauge the mood of the woman beside her, wanted to ask a few important questions. At that moment, Gertie turned her head to say, "Cotton gin."

May nodded. Emboldened, she pointed a finger. "So what does it do to the cotton?"

"Cleans, sorts, bales. This whole region is overrun with the stuff. Melvin thinks we'll be rich, come fall, but I have my doubts. He has to pay his help, so we'll see."

"Who is the help?"

"You'll see."

May took an interest in the long rows of cotton growing by the side of the road. They were so neat, so orderly, growing in low clumps of healthy green plants, one melding into the other to create the uniform rows. She wondered where the cotton would appear and when, but knew she had asked enough.

"We didn't get any molasses candy," Ammon whined from his seat on the dirty straw in the back.

Gertie's thoughts were far away, so she didn't respond.

"Mam!" A loud, impertinent call.

"What?"

"We didn't get molasses candy."

"No, you didn't. And you're not getting any."

"I want some."

"Hush."

Only the rattling of the wagon, the clomping of the horse's hooves broke the stillness after that peculiar exchange, leaving May searching for any sign of humor, anger, amiability, anything. But Gertie sat like stone, her mouth turned down in the usual grim manner, the straight pins keeping her cape from sliding down her rounded shoulders.

How different one human could be from another. How varied their dispositions. To compare her mother to this outraged, inwardly seething individual brought only a vague despair, a fear of the future coupled by a child's sense of prayer. For May knew God sat on a great white throne in Heaven, looked down on her as a loving father does, and seemed to accept the fact that He would see to her safety, even in the face of so much adversity. She would try to make life happier for Gertie. She would.

And so the winsome child did her best, bowed her bright head to mean tasks that Gertie might well have taken on herself. She learned to peel potatoes thinly, to scrub floors with a brush followed by a cloth wrung out in hot, sudsy water. She started a blazing fire in the outdoor boiler, heated water, and did great piles of reeking laundry— the result of seven days without a bath, a change of clothes only on the third day. In the wet heat of the Mississippi delta, with perspiration-soaked clothing like a second skin, the laundry was nothing May looked forward to, ever.

She poked a stick in the boiling hot tubs, shaved the right amount of lye soap, rinsed in vinegar water, and cranked the handle of the wooden clothes-wringer with all the strength of her young shoulders.

Gertie saw to it that there were three meals a day, sparse and tasteless, but cooked food that kept them all with full stomachs, and for this, May was grateful. She was, after all, not quite eleven years old and had never imagined learning how to cook, with her own dear mother bending over the stove, singing low, then humming, turning to tell May they were having *oya Dutch* (egg omelet).

Often, when May stood on tiptoe to peg the clean clothes on the sagging line, she would sing low, like her mother, only to find tears coursing down her thin face, sorrowing when she remembered the same song her mother frequently sang. Tears ran with the perspiration, her face reddened from the steam, and so she allowed the healing tears to run their course, until she could hum without them.

"*Yesus liebt die kleine kinder. All die kinder in die velt.*" (Jesus loves the little children. All the children in the world.)

And sometimes, she imagined the beat of angels' wings, the way she imagined her mother in a flowing white gown with a bright halo surrounding her, a spiritual being sent from the glory land to brighten her days.

She wished Oba could peel off the suit of anger, lay it aside, and accept his life here in Arkansas, but he never did. His walk was like a fighting rooster, his dark eyes sizzling with resentment, his young mouth set in a grim line of determination. May hardly knew the brother she had once had.

She was folding the washing, heating the sadiron on the cook stove, the afternoon Gertie fell off her chair by the window and lay in a swoon on the floor, her white legs with the dark hairs exposed, her purple dress twisted beneath her. May ran crying to Melvin, who laid down his lathe and hurried to the house to stand over his unconscious wife before delivering a blow to her cheek.

"Come on, wake up. Gertie!" He had no time for weak, unhealthy women. If she didn't spend all her days on that blasted chair with her mindless embroidery and went out and got some exercise, she'd feel better.

When her eyelids fluttered and she rolled over to heave up the remains of her dinner, Melvin rolled his eyes and wrinkled his nose in disgust before taking his leave. Enos stood and stared at the strange spectacle on the floor, but it was May who helped her to a seated position, brought her a drink of water, and wiped up the gelatinous mass she had deposited.

Gertie had simply been overcome by the heat, she said, lying in a weakened state the remainder of the day, leaving May to serve something for the men's supper.

"You can make milk toast. That's easy. Scald milk and pour it over toast. There are melons in the garden."

Melvin snorted at his serving of milk toast, asked Gertie how she figured a man could keep up his strength on this slop. May felt her face burn painfully with shame. Oba looked up from his plate, said there was nothing wrong with it.

"I didn't ask for your two cents," Melvin threw back, ready for a fight from this young upstart.

Leviticus laughed out loud and said "Two cents? Two cents?"

Oba bit back a fiery retort. May told him she was glad, with her eyes. Just keep everybody happy. Keep tempers from flaring and everything would be manageable. Angry words were like pounding hailstones to the sunny May, and she would do almost anything to appease a boiling temper.

Dishes had to be finished after milking, without Gertie's help, so it was past the usual bedtime when she hung up the dishcloth and helped the small boys wash their feet before sending them to bed.

Gertie wanted three poached eggs on buttered toast before she went to bed, so with precise instructions, May cooked the eggs, made the toast and brought it to her on a tray. She watched her wolf it down like a ravenous dog, with snuffling sounds and solid belching afterward. Melvin had fallen asleep on the hickory rocker, his mouth hanging open and emitting all sorts of rattles and wheezes. The smell of buttered toast and succulent eggs must have awakened him, as he sat up, blinked, and said something smelled good.

He wanted his eggs fried, though.

So with eyes drooping with weariness, May fried his eggs, buttered his toast, and set it on the table.

"No, bring it in here."

She obeyed and was rewarded by a gap toothed smile from him, a soft "You're really worth something, you know that? You're a good cook."

Her face was shining with the first praise she had received from anyone since her arrival. She fell asleep with a smile of gratitude on her sweet face, even more determined to fulfill her role as guardian of everyone's temperament, including Oba's. If she did everything they asked of her, it would surely make a difference somehow, she reasoned.

She awoke with a start, suspended between dreams and reality. She lay very still, without knowing exactly why she was awake, then became aware of the bed sheets soaked with her own perspiration. The lone window could not provide an inkling of a breeze, the night still and almost unbearably hot. May rolled onto her back, flung her arms wide and listened to the call of a barn owl in the hawthorn tree by the garden.

He wouldn't have to fly out of the barn at all, there were plenty of mice in the hayloft where he slept throughout the day, but she couldn't tell Mr. Owl her thoughts. She smiled to herself. Maybe it was Mrs. Owl.

She remembered Melvin's praise, and a warmth spread through her body. Things would change. God would look down on them and fix Melvin and Gertie, take away Oba's bitterness and turn it into the smiling face, the sweet personality of his former self.

And then, really, everything would be fixed.

Gertie felt well the following morning and cooked the grits and fried the sausages with her usual plodding strength. The morning was uncomfortably warm, especially with a fire in the cook stove. Melvin yanked irritably at his collar, his face creased with peevishness, but regained his sense of good humor when he thought about the cotton.

"We'll have a bumper crop. Three hundred bushels to the acre. I bet you anything. A bit of sweating never hurt anyone, never will."

His wife favored him with a bitter glare, opened her mouth, closed it again, then spat out, "In Illinois, you can make a good living without all this heat. I tell you, Melvin, I can't take it. I'm warning you. This heat will be the death of me. I didn't pass out like that for nothing. I'm not well. But do you care?"

"Blame me, why don't you? Of course I care. I know it's hot, Gertie, but the summer will soon be over, then you'll be more comfortable."

From Melvin, these words were very kind, a more caring dialogue than she had ever heard. Her spirits soared. Yes, she could make a difference. Hadn't it worked already?"

"Oba, the cotton will be setting to burst out after a few more weeks of this. We have to go over to the sharecroppers' homes, see who we can line up to pick cotton. They have their own share of cotton, but a bunch of 'em work for me. So much a pound." Though he didn't say how much.

May watched Oba's face, sensitive to all his expressions that crossed his features. Anger meant a set jaw and steely eyes, indifference meant a slack jaw and a small, barely discernable lift of the shoulders. Approval and willingness were fleeting, barely even on display, so May learned to be accepting of any sign of life from the silent Oba.

"I can go along?" he said, looking at Melvin intently.

"Why not? You're gonna work with them. Black as night, lazy as a new moon. Your job is to help me keep them on their toes."

Oba nodded, but May knew the only reason he wanted to go was to see if he could find the boy named Drink.

To find a friend in the miserable heat of this Arkansas hole.

CHAPTER 4

WHEN THE COTTON FIELDS BURST INTO AN ARRAY OF white, the blossoms like clumps of snow, Oba could not imagine how anyone would ever manage to pick all of it. The cotton plants had already seemed to be innumerable, but now, covered in white balls of the stuff, there seemed to be millions of pounds that would have to be picked, packed in containers, and hauled off to the gin.

Melvin was in a near state of hysteria, shouting at Oba, bellowing at the mules, threatening to shoot the cows, the way they never learned to stand at the gate when it was milking time. He should never have brought the dairy cows and wouldn't have if it wouldn't have been for his wife.

Gertie depended on a milk check, but in the heat and humidity of a Southern summer, milk production dropped, so he was tired of prodding the dumb things into their milking stalls.

Oba thought, he never did the milking anyway, what was he complaining about? He cleaned the cow stable himself until sweat ran off his face like water, him and May did most of the milking, so what sense did it make?

Oba liked the cows, the only gentle creatures on the farm, besides his little sister May. He was increasingly amazed at May's ability to do all the tasks he knew she did, especially now, with Gertie's failing health, which he chalked up to laziness.

On the first morning of cotton picking time, the wagonloads of hired men and women arrived at daylight, before the milking was finished.

There were old men, bent and wizened with accumulated years, and young strapping men who appeared to be able to lift a mule, then the wagon. Women with shy glances, ready smiles, turbans in bright colors like dark parrots. Young girls in bare feet and torn blouses, walking with the grace of a cat.

Oba stood beside Melvin, listened carefully as he gave orders, told them where to start, how to be careful of the plants, and he'd be along with the wagon. He introduced Oba, who kicked at the dirt and avoided all the dark faces with the curious black eyes. He was only slightly afraid of them, unsure of what they would do to him, especially the young men with muscles bulging like glistening brown melons.

Oba eyed the crew of ten, evaluated the fields of cotton, and thought of the impossibility of it all. They'd never finish, and Melvin would return to his bizarre howling of frustration, but he kept all this to himself and gave the group of workers the benefit of the doubt.

They talked among themselves, lifted large burlap bags that were slung across one shoulder, hung loosely along the opposite side, then walked off and bent their backs in the morning sun with the ease of anticipation, the years of practice. Oba couldn't help but walk with them, stand mesmerized as the strong dark hands grasped the milky white clumps, pulled gently and dropped them in the sling. The hands worked fast, seemingly without effort, raking in the puffy balls of cotton so quickly Oba could not believe it.

They talked in a buzzing tone, a liquid velvety sound of contentment, almost like the purring of a cat. Bits of song broke out among the women and girls, laughter rippled like flowers in a breeze. Oba experienced a strong desire to stay with them, to be a part of this easiness, this lack of pain and anxiety. Here was the closest thing he'd found since his arrival, the closest thing to his own father's view of a world that was good, that had handed him good things and would likely continue to do just that.

An older man stopped picking, watched him stand as if in a trance. "Sonny?"

"Yes?" Oba lifted his face to meet the kind eyes like a burnt chestnut and as black.

"You wanna try pickin' along wi' us?"

Dumbly, he nodded, was given a bag, and shown how to wear it. The man gave his name as Hector, showed him how to pick the cotton clean, how to find all of it beneath the stalk, and told him to pick alongside him, so he could help if he needed it.

It was so strange, touching the soft white clumps that grew from the cotton plants. He had picked plenty of vegetables in a garden, but they were all edible, round, oblong, hard objects that ended up as part of a meal.

This was a plant grown and harvested to be made into articles of clothing, which he could not imagine.

"So where you from?"

"Apple Creek, Ohio."

"That right? 'S far way."

"Yeah." He kept missing the opening of the bag, throwing the clumps of cotton on the ground, so he bent to pick it up and replace it before moving on.

"So how come yer here?"

"Long story." He averted his face, heard the soft chuckle, but missed the raised eyebrows and small shake of the head. Missed, too, the old face with the sunken eyes going soft with sympathy and understanding.

"How long's this story?"

"Too long."

"Okay, okay," in a high voice, followed by a soft laugh. "Here now, you fallin' behin'. Let me get this."

The hands warped with arthritis, the nails thick and yellow, worked with measured speed, almost too quick for Oba's eyes to follow. He sighed as he bent to pick up another ball of cotton, insert it into the bag.

"It's harder than it looks."

"I bin doing this for a long, long time, and my daddy and granddaddy before me. My granddaddy was a slave seventy-some years ago."

"A real slave? No wages?" In awe, Oba watched the old hands threading through the cotton plant, the long sleeves worn thin at the elbows, the threadbare seams of the denim overalls.

"Yas, he was. God brought him out, freed him. Now I'm a free man, can do what I like, and what I like is these cotton fields. Sun high in the sky, birds atwitterin', family working along with you, there ain't no place on earth sweeter. Now, we stop at noon, make us all something to eat, get paid by the pound, make enough to keep us a'going, so it do."

Oba considered this speech, thought of the sun like a sweltering furnace, the misery of his half-bent back, the thirst that raked its claws along his throat. He could think of a hundred places he'd rather be.

"Yessir, Obadiah. I got me a nice little house on McKinley Street. My missus, my daughter and three chilluns, and my nephew all lives wid me. Only two bedrooms, but the nephew, he sleep good onna couch. My daughter, she sleep wid' her chilluns. She ain't got no husband. He was hanged."

Shocked, Oba straightened, stared at the old man. "Hanged? You mean, hanging from a rope?"

"Sho' nuff, Sonny. Sho nuff. They never gave him a chance, after he stole a automobile. Now, he shouldn'ta done it, but he did, gittin' desperate to leave town on account of a feud goin' on wid his landlord. Kind of a hothead, quick to speak, quick to fly off'n the handle."

"Why didn't he just go to jail?"

"Well, Sonny, like you just said, it's a long story. He got in trouble before this . . ."

His words were interrupted by a shrill call from the end of the row, where Melvin stood hopping from one foot to the other, his face as red as a pickled beet.

"Oba! Oba! Get yourself over here. I told you to drive a team of mules. What are you doing? You don't know how to pick cotton."

"Madder 'n a nest a hornets," the old man chuckled. "You best be off."

Oba hunched his shoulders and hated Melvin with a raw, primal hatred he realized was wrong, but didn't care. To be cuffed on the head was indeed painful, but to be yelled at in the presence of the workers was even worse.

"Come on. Hurry up." Melvin was walking as if a snake was after him.

Oba didn't try to increase his speed, knowing Melvin wouldn't know the difference, he'd just yell to make himself feel better. All these workers amid the sea of cotton had his nerves in an uproar likely.

The mules were on high alert, their ears pricked forward, their large faces like watchful servants. Oba could hitch them to a wagon by himself, so he got to work, grateful to see Melvin stalking off to attach his own mules to his own wagon.

The mules were jumpy, nervous, so it took twice as long to get them between the traces and fasten everything before hoisting himself up to stand on the wagon. By that time, Melvin was already out the drive, his mules trotting at a brisk pace, the steel wheels bouncing over the potholes.

"I'd rather help pick," he told Melvin.

"You can't pick cotton. Who will help me load it?"

"You don't have enough for a load, and certainly not two."

"Don't tell me what I have and what I don't have."

One day twined into the next, creating a tapestry of heat, cotton, and mules hitched to wagonloads of cotton and driven off to the cotton gin on the north end of town. The cotton was piled on the high-sided wagons like loose snowballs, all packed together to form a mound of the downy stuff Oba could never quite get used to. At the gin, wagons stood in rows, the mules resting in the heat of the sun, waiting for their turn to unload. Men stood around in groups, visiting, the talk all centered on cotton. The quality, the price, the best hands.

But Oba formed his own opinion, didn't like Melvin's, and waved it off like a bothersome fly. He felt nothing for him, couldn't see how or why anyone worked for him at all, wondered what he paid them.

He learned to ignore thirst. He took up the old man's offer of having a meal with them, until Melvin found out when he wasn't seated at the dinner table, stalked down to the edge of the cotton field, and hauled him home by his ear. Oba walked around for days after with a crick in his neck from being marched along with his head bent sideways, resentment riding on his back like an invisible monkey.

Gertie shook her head, asked if he didn't know Negroes ate raccoon and groundhog. They were dirty, so was their food.

"I had the best thing I ever tasted."

Gertie glared at him.

"A biscuit so light and fluffy it was like a cake, spread with Martha's blueberry jam."

"Martha? What? Now you know them by their first names?"

Oba swallowed his swift retort, ate the thick stew with beans and infrequent chunks of salt pork, thinking how Gertie would do well to take cooking lessons from Martha. She was the matriarch of the group, the cook, the one who led all the songs and told the stories. She was everything Oba's heart sought. She was soft and funny and motherly, kind and caring and genuine, to list only a few of her good qualities. Oba had found a way to spend time picking cotton in the fields—when Melvin lingered too long at the gin.

Oba learned quickly, absorbed talk like a dry sponge. He learned that life held goodness and contentment meted out in small doses. A little house, a large garden, plenty of canning jars, a pig in the sty in the back yard. That was all a blessing. Church, relatives, family get-togethers were also an added bonus. A banjo and a guitar with plenty of pies on Sunday was enough to keep them happy for days on end.

He learned that life could be relaxing, smooth, like clear sailing on a calm day. Money, whether you had some or whether you didn't, was not what created lasting happiness. It was the other stuff. Exactly everything Oba didn't have at this point in his life. Laughter saturated the dry earth of his existence. Laughter and jokes told along the cotton rows, a lighthearted view of heat and hard work.

There would be a remittance at the end of the month, which was far more than their ancestors had, praise be to God.

Praised the Lawd, Praise Him. Praise Him for His goodness and mercy to the end of our days.

And so forth.

Oba found fleeting moments of joy among these people. He dreamed of escape, of living like this, but he knew it wouldn't be acceptable. He was the property of Melvin and Gertie Amstutz, and no one would ever change that. He asked about the boy, Arpachshad.

"Yas, yas, lives a block down. Drink, they call him. Roy Brown's boy. A right busy kid, that one. Catches more fish than most of the men. S'all he does is fish." Hector laughed heartily, thinking of the nickname. "They sure had fished him out of the drink that day."

Oba's barren existence, then, was nurtured in the company of these people. He wanted to eat with them, sleep in their homes, go to church with them, be there when Martha wrung a chicken's neck and fried it in butter. He wanted to go fishing with Drink, did not want to milk Melvin's cows or eat Gertie's indigestible food.

When cotton picking came to an end, he considered running away, planned it every night, but knew deep down he had to stay for the sake of his sister.

When Gertie developed swollen feet and chest pains, she was taken to the family doctor in Blytheville and pronounced ill with heart problems. She sagged into the hickory rocker, gasped for breath, and told Melvin she would die here in Arkansas. Melvin took a sort of absent pity, said they'd go back home to Illinois with a portion of the cotton money, which seemed to perk her up for a few days.

Oba and May offered to stay, milk cows, and look after the place, their faces tense with hope and longing. It was Gertie who allowed it, glad to have only the three boys to get into decent Sunday clothes for the long train ride, and not two more. Melvin was not happy about the arrangement but settled on a long list of dos and don'ts, said he'd wallop the tar out of them if they got into trouble. They both had a hard time concealing their anticipation of being alone for a week, but they managed to keep somber expressions and trustworthy gazes.

When the Amstutz family was taken to the train station, they had no more than disappeared from view before Oba lifted his face and roared, pumped his fist to the ceiling, and hopped like a toad. May simply twirled silently in the middle of the floor until her skirts ballooned around her.

They laughed and talked, baked a shoofly pie and ate it all the first day. They made mint tea with too much sugar, baked oatmeal cookies, and ate every last one with glasses of milk.

Then they drove the horse to town to find Oba's friends on McKinley Street. They were welcomed with open arms by Martha and her husband Roy, who introduced them to so many members of the family they couldn't remember everyone's names.

The houses were small, but most of them were clean. There was plenty of food to go around, and they were loved and doted upon, cared for in a manner they had not been since they lost their parents.

They drove home in the starlight, the crickets chirping in the clumps of grass along the road, foxes yelping excitedly where the woods bordered the edge of a field. A barred owl gave off its weird, twittering call, but the night seemed friendly, free of strife.

Every day, they faithfully milked the cows on time, and tonight had been no exception. Only two more days and the family would return.

"Do you really mind living with Melvin and Gertie?" May asked quietly, her shoulder rubbing comfortably against his.

"Of course. I hate both of them. When I'm sixteen years old, I will leave and never look back."

"You shouldn't hate, Oba. I worry about your soul. Hell is a place for people who hate."

There was only silence. May slid away, to separate herself from the nearness of him.

"You see, we're growing older, and I'm afraid one day you'll do something you'll regret for the rest of your life. You must learn to forgive."

"Melvin is hard to like. I can't like him. He's not a Christian. All he cares about is money, and making more of it. He's mean to his wife and children, to us, to his animals. The only reason he's half-nice to Hector and Roy and all them is because he couldn't make money without their help. He doesn't like us, either. He doesn't even like his own children."

"Oh, but . . . Oba, we need to try and do everything in our power so he will like us, and perhaps he'll change."

"You really think that?"

"Yes."

"You can do it without me then." He heard a small sob, reached for her hand. "Don't, May."

And so they rode together through the star-riddled night with the quarter moon like a perfect slice of light, the only sound the tired clopping of horse's hooves and the rattling of the steel-rimmed wheels.

"May, I'll do my best. But I'm not like you."

"I know, Oba." Then, "Don't go without me when you're older, okay?"

"See, you don't like it here."

"Who would?"

A low laugh. "You're right, little May."

They were up early to do the milking. They cleaned the cow stable, mowed the grass with a scythe, cleaned the house, and did the washing. They had a picnic by the creek, with pork on bread and another batch of oatmeal cookies. They were surprised to see a horse and buggy drive up to the house at a brisk pace that evening, surprised even more to see Leonard Yoder climb down from the buggy, followed by his portly wife, Sadie.

"Hello, children. We heard about Melvin's going to Illinois and wondered if they hadn't left you two in care of the farm. I brought you some bread and a blueberry pie. How is everything going for you?"

"Alright. We're doing okay."

"You have the milking and all?"

"We do."

A clucking of tongues, a "My my."

"The place hardly looks the same. You must both be hard workers."

They didn't know what to say to this, so they stood together with eyes downcast, shuffling their feet uncomfortably.

"They treat you well?"

"Yes."

"You're sure?"

"Yes."

"If you ever need anything, don't be afraid to let us know."

"We won't."

"Well, goodbye, then."

They lifted hands politely, watched them drive away.

The next day, of all the most unreasonable happenings, one of the best milking cows went down, laid in the pasture like some huge pile of flesh and bones, seemingly without muscle or will to gather her feet beneath her and stand on her own. Oba tugged, pushed, coiled, tried everything he knew, but the cow's eyes sagged in her head, her tongue lolled with thirst as the sun beat down in the middle of the day.

May stood beside her brother, her thin arms dangling at her side, and offered to go for help. Oba looked at his sister, then looked at the cow, watched the sky as vultures circled overhead, and felt sick inside. He imagined the terrible anger of his uncle, the bone-rattling, teeth-jarring kick he would receive, the screeching of a blame that would rain on his head.

He nodded, then stayed with the cow while May swung off down the road.

Perspiration ran off the side of his head, tickled his neck as it disappeared beneath his collar. He swiped at it with the palm of his hand and turned to the cow, who seemed to be in misery, her udders grotesquely swollen, her sides heaving sporadically. Oba felt his irritation replaced with a distant pity.

All around him, the land fell away, as level as a tabletop, with houses and barns like stilted intrusions that ruffled the monotony. He hated the land, hated the occupants of this farm, hated the cow that lay here. He ground his teeth, the muscles on the side of his face working. For the thousandth time, he knew he'd risk his life as a runaway if his little sister would not be sharing his fate. He could not put her life in danger or ask her to accompany him on a foolhardy flight.

If this cow was dead when Melvin returned, there would be consequences, seeing how Melvin was given to blaming everyone when circumstances spiraled out of control.

Oba paced and watched the road, the circling vultures; he lifted his face and yelled anything he could possibly think of, wished for a gun.

The cow heaved and groaned, gave a resigned snort and stretched out her neck, looked dead.

"Come on. Get up. Up!" Oba shouted, which did absolutely nothing, so he sat on the grass, crossed his legs, and rested an elbow on his knees.

He willed himself to stay calm, to detach himself from the worst thing that could happen, which was a dead cow and Melvin's wrath.

A crow cawed from the top of the buckeye tree, then lifted itself to preen below a great black wing. Little brown birds twittered from the rail fence, hopping senselessly from one post to another. Mulberry bushes rustled with more small birds, chirping anxiously, likely fussing about a meandering box turtle or a garter snake.

He remembered the box turtle he'd found by the creek, brought home, and proudly showed his father, who admired it, traced the markings on the shell with his forefinger, showing Oba how old the turtle possibly could be. He wanted to make a pen, put it in a dishpan of water, but his father discouraged it, saying the turtle would not be happy away from his friends at the creek.

How could so much kindness and understanding be contained in one person, when someone like Melvin didn't posess any at all? And how could God drown the kind person and leave Melvin unharmed? He didn't know if he liked God at all, wasn't sure he believed in Him. To leave him and May completely motherless, fatherless, with relatives who didn't give two hoots about their well-being was not the kind of thing a loving God would do. God didn't care about him and May, and any idea of prayer and goodness she carried along with her was all imagination.

His thoughts roiled along with the circling vultures, the raucous cry of the crow, which raked along his ears, setting his teeth on edge. He screamed out his frustration, got to his feet, and threw a stone in the direction of the black invader.

And still May did not make an appearance.

Thirst was his biggest matter, so he left the cow to get a drink from the tin cup by the pump, allowed the cool water to dribble off his chin and down his shirt front. He cupped both hands under the last gush of water from the pump, lowered his face, and splashed it over everything; he raked wet hands through his hair and felt better, hopeful.

But when he returned, the cow was no longer breathing. May returned with Leonard Yoder, to find an irate Oba pacing the pasture, kicking at clumps of grass with his bare feet, berating them both for the delay.

Leonard took hold of Oba's shoulders, told him to calm down, there was likely nothing anyone could possibly have done, the way her eyes were sunken in her head, the distended stomach, the swollen udder.

Oba told him to get his hands off him, to go home and leave them alone, then burst into tears of rage and sorrow, leading Leonard to see that the situation here at Melvin Amstutz's was not good. He turned to May, who watched her brother's display with eyes large and dark with wretchedness, the white blond hair like a shining halo of light, the thin, defeated stance. She was a beauty, a diamond thrown into the muck, coupled with the weight of a very troubled brother who was saddled with rage and the inability to accept his lot as an orphan.

"I'll stay," he said then.

There was only the sound of Oba's choking sobs, the cawing of the crow, and twittering of the birds. May stood as if made of stone.

When there was no reply to his offer, he told them the cow had to be removed, would bloat in the heat and humidity, then walked to the neighbors to call Tom McGee, who would bring a truck and take the cow to the rendering plant at the hide and tallow company.

He comforted the children as best he could, went home and told his wife they had better keep an eye on the Melvin Amstutz place, and was rewarded by a look of total agreement and a quiet nod.

Though neither one would see the ensuing homecoming, the faltering courage when Oba told Melvin about the dead cow, or the pain of the whip coming down on Oba's bare legs until welts like red worms crisscrossed them and he lay on his stomach as flies buzzed about his bed for days.

He walked painfully, sat on the edge of a chair, ate sparingly, and festered with hate and the longing to get away, to leave this place ruled by horrible punishment and swept clean of love or understanding.

Oba's heart had been shattered at the death of his parents and now was glued haphazardly by unbelief, hate, and rebellion.

CHAPTER 5

THE INCIDENT WITH THE DEAD COW LEFT MAY WITHOUT THE foundation she'd come to adopt as her own: seeking approval of everything she did, believing it must be sufficient to light all the dark places. When Oba received the whipping and stayed in his bed for days, she wasn't sure anything could smooth over so much cruelty.

She no longer spoke unless she was spoken to, kept her eyes averted whenever Melvin was in the house, tried to appease all of Gertie's discontent.

Out in the garden with a hoe, hacking away at a new growth of thistles, she watched a goldfinch light on a thistle stalk, as light and colorful as a flower, the bright dark eyes mirroring her own before taking flight.

She felt visited by an angel, delighted.

Ammon was squatted in the next row, piling small stones in the dark soil, talking to himself. Leviticus wandered over, bent down to see what he was doing, curious, and was sent off with a ringing smack on the cheek.

Leviticus was surprised but walked off without a tear, simply gave Ammon his space and found something else to occupy his time.

May lifted the hoe, brought it down, over and over. The thistles were high, the sun was merciless, but she wanted to please Gertie by finishing the bean rows before milking time.

"May!" Ammon screeched. "Watch out!"

May stopped, froze when a brown snake with black markings slithered out from under the beanstalks and came within inches of her bare feet before disappearing. She screamed, threw her hoe, and ran blindly, followed by a screeching Ammon. When they reached the yard, they turned, wondered which way the snake had gone, laughed shakily. May did not want to return but knew there was no choice. To ask Gertie or Melvin for a respite would only result in swift denial, so she walked back to the bean rows, her eyes darting from left to right before retrieving the hoe and resuming her work.

Ammon came up behind her, quietly.

"You know, snakes are the devil," he said, inserting a finger in his left nostril and turning it, retrieving the contents for inspection before popping it into his mouth. "Boogers are salty," he said.

May suppressed a shudder. "You shouldn't do that. Nice children don't pick their noses."

"Don't they?"

"No. It's not clean or polite. God doesn't want little children to do that sort of thing. If you feel like there is something in your nose, you should get out your handkerchief and blow."

"I don't have a handkerchief."

To remedy that situation, May learned to hem squares of muslin fabric on the treadle sewing machine, a Singer, after Ammon told his mother what May had said.

"Well May, if you want to put fancy notions in the boys' heads, I suppose you'll have to learn how to sew, huh? A few boogies never hurt a child."

May swallowed, nodded, and learned to sew, without taking offense. In the way of a child, she was forming lifelong habits, creating an aura of servitude and devotion, no matter the situation. She gladly handed over her opinion for one of Gertie's, believing her willingness to comply would remedy even the worst situation.

Except for Oba's whipping.

She could see no solution for Melvin's unfair act or her brother's private rage. She watched Oba's jaw set, his shoulders stiffen, his walk become jaunty, the way he put his weight on his heels. If there was one thing she wanted more than anything else, it was the healing of Oba's heart.

As the broiling summer turned into fall—a warm, steamy autumn that allowed no crisp breezes, only a coloring of leaves and a fading of foliage in the garden—May learned to accept her lot, with Gertie becoming steadily more conscious of her ailing heart, frequent trips to the doctor's office in Blytheville, and heated arguments in the kitchen when the adults thought everyone was asleep.

Gertie refrained from any physical exercise now, choosing to spend her days in the hickory rocker or lying on the sofa, covered with a sheet so the flies would not bother her swollen legs. She ate prodigiously. Potatoes, ham hocks. She gnawed on chicken bones, sucked out the marrow, cooked cornmeal and sweetened it with molasses. She taught May to bake bread, ate half a loaf with churned butter, but scolded her for not kneading sufficiently.

By the time May was thirteen years old, she was running the house efficiently. She took orders from the now obese Gertie, cooked and baked, cleaned and washed, learned how to sew trousers and shirts, and found favor in Melvin's eyes as he watched her grow into a young woman.

Enos and Ammon went to school now, which left only young Leviticus and Oba, who lived in a constant state of withering rebellion.

The neighbors, including Leonard Yoder, liked what they saw and reasoned among themselves that things were going better there at Melvin's.

Even Gertie seemed content, if obese.

The whippings, the beatings, and threats were all hidden away.

No one spoke of it, no one inquired or noticed, so May accepted it as a parental right and thought nothing of it. One week melted into the next, seasons came and went, until Oba turned fourteen and was taken to town and told to get a job for the winter.

May listened as Oba gave his report in the cow stable.

"I'm supposed to learn a trade."

"What does that mean?"

May, her head covered by a cloth, leaned up against the cow's flank, her young, rounded arms browned from the sun, muscles underneath appearing and disappearing as she milked, the sound of milk hitting foam.

"I don't know. I guess learn how to do something. I'm not doing it. These Arkansas people don't like the Amish, and I don't like them."

May knew he didn't like anyone anymore, really. Amish, English, black, or white. He'd never been able to develop a friendship with anyone, no matter how he longed for one, so now to be sent to town to learn a trade would be painful indeed.

"The people like the Amish," she said hopefully.

"No they don't. I've seen people spit at buggies."

May shook her head. "Oba."

"It's true. They don't like us. Make fun of us. We're like the Negroes. They don't treat them right."

May thought how bitter Oba was, really. How prickly. Like a chestnut burr, all spikes and pain.

"Maybe you'll like it," she volunteered, always cheery, attempting to instill hope.

The doorway was darkened by Melvin's bulk. All conversation ceased.

"Aren't you done yet?"

"Two more," May offered brightly, soothing any trace of an outburst.

"Hurry up. We got corn harvesting. You can both pick."

May got up, lifted the heavy bucket of foaming milk, bent to pick up the three-legged stool, then stepped across the gutter. She felt Melvin's presence, stopped, looked up to find his eyes on her face.

Bewildered, she tried to push past him, felt a hand on her shoulder, a squeeze.

"You're a good milker. All that foam says you milk fast."

She nodded, got away, her cheeks flaming, unsure if she should be pleased or put off by the affectionate squeeze, then decided anything, anything was better than anger and the resulting terror of the whip. She must remember this. Keep trying to instill this value in Oba, to prevent the punishment he so often received.

She lifted the bucket of milk, poured it through the strainer into the galvanized milk can, thinking eagerly about a day of cornhusking with Oba. Another chance to talk, to share, to try and change him.

The milking done, May hurried into the house to start breakfast, which would be eggs, milk gravy, and cornmeal mush. She got down the cast iron skillet, threw in a rounded tablespoon of lard, and sliced the mush.

"May!" The whining, bloated voice broke through her thoughts.

"Yes? What do you need?"

"I don't have any clean stockings."

"I will wash some for you, after breakfast."

"My feet are cold now."

"Wear Melvin's."

When there was no reply, she figured Gertie would find something, then turned to set the table. First, a clean tablecloth, then seven plates with utensils and water glasses, a pitcher of milk, a smaller one of cane molasses, and salt and pepper. She poured milk over browning butter, made the gravy, then got down another pan for the eggs.

She stiffened when she heard footsteps on the porch, the sound of boots being removed in the washhouse. She was accustomed to the sound of silence, the lack of conversation, often Oba coming in alone, or Melvin late for a meal, but somehow, today was different.

Her hands shook.

Her shoulder tingled where he had squeezed it, as if waiting for the hand to descend, the grip of an unclean talon. Instead, while Gertie fumbled in the bedroom for something to warm her feet, Melvin gave

May a resounding smack on her backside, with an accompanying laugh that seemed more like a childish giggle.

May dropped the metal turner, fumbled the eggs, felt the heat in her face as she placed the dishes on the table. She kept her eyes lowered but was aware of Gertie's presence as she folded her vast form into the heaving chair, breathing hard as they bowed their heads in prayer.

The meal was eaten in near silence, punctuated only by the off-beat chatter from the three boys.

"May, you need to fry the mush harder." This from Gertie, who viewed May with distaste.

"What's wrong with the mush?" Melvin asked, his gaze going to the downturned face, the bright hair parted like the sleek wing of a canary.

"It's not crispy. You know that."

"I'll fry it longer next time. It does seem soft." May replied, trying again to agree with everyone to keep the peace.

"I don't have clean stockings."

"I'll make sure I wash them before I go to the field."

"Yes."

After dishes, May swept the floor and hurried to don a light coat and scarf to spend the day with Oba out of earshot from anyone, even the cloying Leviticus. It was a luxury that she could only imagine.

The day was overcast, as fall days often were, with wedges of geese honking their peculiar song as they flapped through the air, intent on some southern destination only they recognized. The ash and basswood leaves rustled their dry anthem, heralding the approach of cold weather. The spiked glossy leaves of the holly bushes flaunted their decorative red berries.

May breathed deeply, took in the flopping ears of the mules, the flapping harnesses and jingling traces. The wooden boards of the wagon creaked as the steel wheels hit mud holes or hidden stones.

"This will be like a vacation, Oba. Just you and I."

A nod. A squint of his eyes.

They positioned the mules between the rows, then ripped off the dry husks of the heavy, waxy ears of corn and threw them on the wagon with an expert flick of the wrist, a dull thud as they bounced on the wooden wagon bed.

When Oba remained quiet, May's sensitive spirit sank. She checked his expression, dismayed to find his face white, like alabaster. A statue.

"Oba?"

"Hmm."

"Tell me what's wrong."

The outburst that followed was not what May had expected.

She was the only reason he didn't run away, but he knew if he stayed here with Melvin, he would begin to fight back. Just the other day he had run into Arpachshad and decided to go fishing with him for an hour. When Melvin found out, he gave Oba the worst beating of his life. Next time, Oba thought he might fight back. He could feel his muscles developing, feel the hot strength that flowed through his veins, felt his rounded fist connect with that lecherous face.

He saw only disaster if he stayed. If he went, there might be disaster there, but at least he was master of his own destiny.

"We are never master of our own destiny. God is," May said, speaking in a voice barely above a whisper.

"I don't believe in God."

Anguish spread through May's heart and soul. "Oba, please, please don't say that. Jesus is the way, the truth, and the life. Jesus is God's Son. He died for us."

"I don't care. Melvin says he's a believer, sits in church as righteous as a woodpecker, the most pious of all men, and look what he does. He lives like a heathen."

May said nothing. There was no room for words around the lump in her throat. Finally she spoke. "Don't go, Oba. I can't bear being here without you. Gertie needs me. There is Enos, Ammon, Leviticus."

"You're not responsible for them. Melvin and Gertie are."

"Where would we go?"

"To the colored people. To Roy and Martha and Drink."

"Oh, come on, Oba."

"I'd do it tomorrow if I could. You are the only reason I don't." Oba chirped to the mules, called *whoa* when it was time to stop. The faithful creatures swung their heads low, shifted their weight on one hip, and fell asleep as the cornhusking continued.

"You could tell Leonard Yoder. He'd bring Melvin to the ministry."

"He'd do no such thing. Beatings are a form of discipline, upheld by church members."

"Not the kind of beatings you receive."

"May. You have no idea how bad it is. The backs of my legs and buttocks are like the slats of a corncrib."

May gasped. "Oba, surely you're not serious."

"I am. If you weren't a girl, I'd show you."

There was a long silence broken only by the rustling of cornstalks, the clunk of ears of corn, the occasional snort from one of the mules, the jingling of harness buckles.

"So when will you go?"

"I can't go without you. I won't, ever."

"I'll never go. I think we can change them. Look how Melvin told me I'm a good milk maid." But she couldn't bring herself to talk about the other incident.

They talked of the past, snatches of remembering. They laughed, kept talking most of the day, till Oba's facial expression was molded into a softer version of his former features.

"I think we can do this, Oba. With God's help, we can conquer our enemies. We'll be Christian soldiers fighting for Christ. After we're twenty-one years of age, we can leave, live on our own."

"I'm not staying seven more years. And just shut up about God."

The day ended on a bitter note, leaving May even more distressed at her brother's inability to confess, to be a believer.

She threw herself into her work, stayed out of Melvin's range, became a young caregiver to the passive Gertie, and tried being a mother to the three boys, who were growing like wild weeds, unchecked and unloved.

Enos, for one reason or another, was clouted on the top of his head, smacked around or pinched, sometimes kicked or whacked with a board.

He was called a slow, stupid, *ungehorsam* (disobedient) ox, a Mama's baby, while Ammon was approved of, no matter what he did. Leviticus bumbled between the two, sometimes approved by his father, sometimes mocked for his efforts.

But always, there was May.

Leviticus knew she would tell him a story, read to him from Unger's Bible storybook, or sing *"Yuglie vill net been shiddla"* (Yuglie will not shake pears), a song that always produced a pleasant sensation of humor and ruptured into an infectious giggle. When Ammon pinched him, he ran to May and received justice.

Gertie watched all this with a distant view. She visited the doctor's office frequently, then even more as winter came on. A mild slushy snow was followed by days of north wind, followed by a cold slanting rain that melted the wet, cold mixture. Gertie sat inside beside the stove, called to May whenever she felt a mixture of cold feet and icy chills up her spine, watched as she replenished the wood in the firebox of the cast iron stove, her supple young body no longer the ungainly tangle of skinny arms and legs with feet and hands like overgrown appendages. Gertie's eyes narrowed as shapely calves showed when May emptied an armload of firewood into the box.

She'd have none of this, the sightly young girl being an attraction to Melvin. Not that he wasn't trustworthy, but still. She knew she was doomed to live inside this unattractive mound of flesh, with her heart condition and low metabolism, her raging appetite and need to fill the void of homesickness for her family.

Gertie glared at May and told her the white underwear needed to be boiled longer, they were gray along the seams.

Leviticus was playing with his wooden wagon and corncobs for logs, humming to himself while the clock ticked on the wall, the acorn-shaped pendulum swinging in time to the ticks and tocks. The kettle on the back of the stove hummed in a homey way as Gertie dozed off, her feet propped on the hassock provided for that purpose. May stood by the ironing board, her strong arms wielding the iron back and forth, lifting the white shirts before upending the sprinkle of water from the Mason jar with holes poked in the lid.

She never heard the door to the washhouse open or close, never realized Melvin had entered the house till she felt him behind her, felt the tickle of his beard on her neck.

She gasped, moved to the side so swiftly her foot caught on the leg of the ironing board and threw it to the floor. The sadiron crashed against the side of the cast iron range, the Mason jar splintered as it hit the linoleum, dousing Leviticus, who screeched like a scalded cat.

Gertie awoke with a high, wild cry of her own, lumbered to her feet with a hand held to her heart, the thumping inside like the harbinger of death. Her face was chalk white, her mouth in a snarl as she pointed a finger at Melvin and told him to get out of the house and stay out. If she caught him slinking around May again, she was going for the preachers.

Duly chastened, Melvin became absolutely docile, repentant to his wife, although liberally peppered in self-defense, crawled into bed that night, and vowed total devotion to her for the remainder of his life, if God so willed.

They knelt side by side, asked God to bless their small family, bequeath wisdom and strength to raise the boys in the way they should go, repeated devout "Amens," and lived up to it for exactly three and one half days, till there was a knock on the door and Melvin opened it to find the minister and the deacon standing in the light of a kerosene lantern.

"Good evening, Melvin."

"Nice evening," echoed the deacon.

Melvin found nothing particularly nice about the evening, especially since they were there, but found enough graciousness to invite them inside, where May remained with the boys around her, reading from the Bible.

Gertie had already retired for the night, which both the deacon and the minister found a bit strange, but nothing was said.

May looked up, placed a finger between the pages as her voice fell silent. She knew instinctively that a measure of respect was required, and so held a finger to her lips to shush the boys chattering.

Melvin resigned himself to asking them to be seated, but they both remained standing, shifting their weight uncomfortably. May thought perhaps they were waiting to speak till there were no children to hear, so she rose and ushered the boys up the winding staircase and into their beds.

There was a low drone of voices from the kitchen, but May paid them no heed, washed her face in the porcelain sink, got into her nightgown, and crawled into bed. Still the voices droned on, sometimes rising to a level that kept her from drowsiness and sometimes lower with less punctuation.

An hour passed, then two. May still had not fallen asleep.

Finally, the front door opened and closed, buggy wheels crunched on stones, and the house became very quiet, with only the sound of the wind sighing in the trees.

But something had changed after that evening.

May felt an electric current of suppressed rage whenever Melvin entered the house. Gertie withdrew into a tightly woven shell of misery and pain, real or supposed, the boys quarreled and went to school sniveling with sore throats and watery eyes.

The days were gray and gloomy, with no snow. May tried to keep a song in her heart, her naturally sunny spirit shining through for most of the day, but when Gertie asked her to take out the letters to the box at the end of the drive, she was more than happy to obey.

She donned a light coat, no head scarf, and started off, lifting her eyes to the scudding gray clouds that raced by like dirty cotton.

The holly bushes were thick with red berries, clumps of Indian weed dotted the side of the road, bright cardinals and their ordinary mates flitted from branch to branch. The level land was enveloped in brown, the cotton bedraggled and molding into the soil. Trees had lost their leaves a month ago, the dark branches etched against the sky like thin arms. But the air was fresh, the day was young, and May could spend some time away from the constant whining from Gertie, the smoldering irritation from Melvin.

She watched his approach without seeing him, and suddenly he was there, straddling his bicycle before it came to a stop. He was the color of a new pecan, neither brown nor white, a rich tanned color, with a map of tight ringlets as black as night matching his almond-colored eyes.

He was very tall, a magnificent man, one that seemed to have been sculpted by an artist who most certainly had been God.

"Good morning, Missy."

May nodded, dumbfounded.

"I ain't exactly sure whereabouts I is."

May blinked, found her voice. "Um, Melvin Amstutz. This is his driveway."

He gave a short laugh. "Not the place I need. Who're you?"

"I'm May. I live here with Melvin and Gertie."

The man nodded, looked at the huge brown eyes in the heart-shaped face with the hair like new corn silk, and wondered. "I take it you ain't the daughter."

He pronounced it "dotter," and she had to think twice about the meaning. "No. No, I am not."

"You say it like you is glad you ain't."

"I didn't mean it that way."

He watched her face, thought she was little more than a child, but the most intriguing combination of child and young woman. "So how come you live here?"

"I am a niece. My parents died, so we were sent to stay."

"Okay. Good. Look, I'm looking for a boy named Obadiah. Oba. My brother Arpachshad—Drink —is looking for someone to help skin coons."

"Oba is my brother. He lives on this farm."

"Oh well, then. I'll continue on my way."

He leaned on the pedal of his bicycle and was off, leaving May in the middle of the lane, watching him with an unfathomable expression.

All at once she was hit with the realization that there should be more to life, and she experienced the first stirring of discontent, a vague longing to be released from the endless rounds of servitude. Something about the chance encounter seemed to wake her up and she was filled with a confusing feeling that was equal parts pain and pleasure. Unaware of what she was doing, she moved very slowly, taking as much time as she could to the mailbox, lingering there, and finally turning back.

So when the man came back, she was still in the driveway. She smiled, and he slid to a stop, shook his head, and asked if she was sure she wanted to stay in that house, that Melvin was clearly an unhappy individual. "Ain't no way he's letting Oba out to help Drink with his coon hunting," he said, shaking his head. May was glad he didn't seem offended by the counter.

They stood in silence for a moment, each drinking in the sight of the other to take out and examine over and over in the weeks and months that followed. May went on with her life, entered her fourteenth year without seeing the young man again, but if anyone would have asked, she could have told them in perfect detail the contours of his face, the color of his almond eyes.

CHAPTER 6

HE WAS BEING SUCKED INTO A VORTEX OF REBELLION. HE felt the oxygen of life being drowned out of his soul, felt the hatred spread like cancer, knew he was anxiety-ridden and poxed with fear.

The most recent beating had put him down; the edge of the board caught his collarbone and snapped it like a piece of chalk. He lay in bed, willing himself to stay motionless, until the pain was bearable after a few weeks.

When he wasn't in church, the men asked if he was sick, and Melvin feigned concern, saying he'd injured himself falling off the hay wagon. Everyone nodded, believed the smooth story, and no one asked any more questions. Gertie believed her husband's version; May knew better, having crept to Oba's room where she was told the truth, reluctant tears squeezing out from the corners of his eyes.

"We have to leave," he groaned.

May bit her lip, torn between loyalty and servitude, the need to prove that she could make things better. "You can leave, Oba. Just go without me."

"I can't do that."

Yet he could not stay. Collarbones healed, life went on, but the ruination of the heart would never mend.

"Are you sure none of it was something you could have avoided?" May asked, still in the same frame of mind.

Oba asked how could he have kept the mules from running away, wrecking the cultivator in the process? A doe and two fawns had exploded out of the line of trees, raced away on thin, springy legs, and left the mules with no sense in the tiny brains God had given them.

May reminded him of his unbelief and took heart that no matter how he boasted of not believing in God, he did. He did.

He was up and back to work in a month, went to church hiding the stiffness of one shoulder, his face white with a grim slash where a boy his age should have had a laughing mouth, a white set of teeth. He sat on the hard bench with his aching shoulder, listened to Melvin lead the singing in a clear, strong voice that never wavered, knew the congregation admired his voice deeply, depended on him to teach the young men. With his attentive face tilted toward the visiting minister, his face as smooth and unruffled as a baby's, Oba felt the ripples of unfairness, the cluttered hatred in his soul. And for the first time, the uncomfortable sense that perhaps it was all his own fault, the beatings and whippings were deserved. Perhaps he was so far in the devil's lair that the anger was directed well, Melvin's wrath the fruits of his own rottenness.

And so, like May, he tried harder.

He worked from sunup to sundown, milked cows, wrestled milk cans to the cooler, slung heavy harnesses across the mule's backs, chopped firewood, and planted, cultivated, picked, and drove cotton to the gin where he lifted bales of it on wagons alongside strong black men.

Melvin began to watch him with a wary eye. He noticed the bulge of muscle beneath the too-tight shirt, noticed, too, the thighs that strained against trouser legs. Feet like slabs, hands as big as a small pie.

Yet there was another time when the whip flashed and sizzled, caught Oba off guard and threw him to the ground, where he rolled into a tight ball, his hands over his head to protect himself. He felt the back of his shirt give way, felt the sting like the slice of a knife, knew the warm blood was soaking the shredded fabric. The hot sweating face above the whip was contorted with savagery, and something else.

Oba slunk away, into the haymow, where he spent the night in an agony of pain, fresh blood matting the hay with every move, his tongue thick with thirst, his eyes pulsing with rage.

He could not have prevented the cow from kicking Melvin, no matter how he'd tried. She'd lashed out after he twisted her tail. And yet, perhaps he could have; who knew?

At sixteen years of age, he was crosshatched with self-hatred, scoured by too many whippings and beatings, unfit to be cast into a group of *rumschpringa* taken with wild ways and soaked with alcohol.

He stayed with Melvin for May's sake, unwittingly laid down his life for his sister, took every whipping, every foul word, all the roiling self-blame and doubt, for her.

Gertie took a mild interest in Oba's clothes, ordered a few yards of fabric and had May create a new shirt, some Sunday trousers.

"My," she said, "we have ourselves a *rumschpringa*," and giggled behind her swollen fingers.

Oba was a strapping young man in every sense of the word. He was all sinew and muscle, tight-working jaw, intense dark eyes, with a disconcerting thatch of blond hair, the ruined remnants on the inside all that remained of the once winsome, loving little boy.

The first Sunday evening proved disastrous. Intimidated, belittled by his own demons of self-hatred, his view of those around him distorted by his false sense of bravado, the first swallow of whiskey was like setting the whole sordid cauldron of wreckage on fire. He smoked cigarettes, learned how to swear and spew words meant to impress; he staggered and felt full of importance for the first time in his life. He lay behind the barn, gagged, and vomited, the self-hatred magnified a thousand times with sobriety.

He awoke to the sound of the jangling alarm, wished himself dead. Melvin took one look at the pasty white veneer on his face and laughed so hard he almost fell into the gutter. May watched, terrified, afraid Oba would lunge at him, but he walked away.

Oba realized a new step had been taken, a new horizon had opened. When he forced that alcoholic liquid down his throat, he had friends he could talk and laugh with, and he could joke and carry on with the best of them.

There was Amos Hostetler, the leader of the pack, the one handing out cigarettes, the one who sat with him in the one-seated buggy, hiding the bottle away from the ones who didn't drink any of it.

Amos was an amazing friend, one who took him right under his wing as if he'd known him all his life. There was the possibility of belonging now, a sense of place he hadn't known existed among other Amish people. So let Melvin laugh, he didn't care. Melvin no longer mattered, now that he had friends he was allowed to spend time with.

On Tuesday, he felt better. Excellent in fact. He carried Leviticus on his shoulders, teased Enos and Ammon until they ran after him for more attention, then asked Melvin if he could go along to the horse sale in Blytheville.

"It's not a horse sale, it's a cattle sale. And no, you can help pick cotton. We need all the hands we can get. I'm asking May to help, too."

So that was alright with him. At least with Melvin gone, he could visit with Roy and Martha's family, his favorite time.

He no longer minded the hot sun, the heat of the Arkansas delta. After five years, he was accustomed to whatever Mother Nature threw at him, had even learned to enjoy picking cotton, the actual labor involved no longer an impossibility.

He saw May leave the house, saw her stiff gait, but thought nothing of it; he realized more and more that May had changed from the sweet light-hearted girl to one who said very little, and if she did speak, it was with a low voice, penitent, as if anyone who might hear would correct her.

She'd had trouble with her back, she said, pain that centered around her spine, but there was nothing Oba could do to change the amount of work she took on herself. Still convinced she could change the situation if she tried hard enough to please everyone, she kept hope alive inwardly, but her young body was tempered with servitude and tasks too hard even for a grown woman.

But Oba could only watch from a distance, keep his fierce loyalty and love to his sister in check, told himself there was nothing he could do.

Hector, the patriarch of the group of sharecroppers, was only becoming older, his gnarled hands twisted with knobs of inflammation, his back bent as if permanently picking cotton. There was always a light of gladness in his eyes, a twinkling that made Oba feel blessed to be in his presence.

And they talked.

Hector told him the young man named Drink had gotten himself a job at the cotton gin, that perhaps if he drove a load to town, he could talk to him. He knew Oba had never been allowed to go fishing or develop a friendship with the youth, and he took pity on the young Amish man.

The next week, Oba was in no mood to pick cotton. The heat pressed on his shoulders, the headache he'd carried with him since Sunday night was excruciating, his tongue felt swollen and dry, his eyes narrow slits of pain. He soon lagged far behind the group of people who worked as if the heat and the cruel sun was only a minor annoyance.

"I am in the gloryland way-ay.

I am in the gloryland way."

The song erupted so suddenly, Oba straightened his back to squint through the brassy light. All around him, the song was taken up, voices blending like the ripple of water, hips swaying, hands clapping as the old favorite was sung in praise.

Oba pressed his mouth into a hard line, noticed the delicate curve of a young girl's hips, the one named Meredith. Merry.

He knew another girl named Laura, whom he had spoken to, but only in passing, her dark eyes correcting him for being bold.

He could not help himself, it was natural that he would take notice of young girls, but he never worked up the courage to have a serious conversation with the Amish girls that were always on the outskirts of the well-behaved crowd.

He watched the strong young arms lifted in praise, clapping; he felt a stirring, a longing. The skin on her arms was like dark polished mahogany.

Oba had no one to explain the facts of life in a Christian way, no one to guide or nurture his growth, so he fell prey to the natural way of a man, found himself swept up with a fervor that matched the intensity of his survival, his hatred for Melvin and all of Arkansas.

He became bold, arrogant, did stupid things to win the attention of the young women, until Roy put a stop to it.

"You know, sonny, you better back off a li'l bit. You get in trouble carryin' on dis way. De womenfolk don't take kindly to yer overtures."

Oba cast him a dark look, felt his face redden, hated himself and Roy.

"White folk keeps to theyselves, when it comes to it."

"I wasn't doing nothing," Oba mumbled, bending low enough so his flaming face wasn't visible.

Roy chuckled. "You can't climb under that cotton, so you may as well straighten your back and look me in the eye. Look, I know you don't get much help when it comes to this stuff, but yer treadin' on dangerous ground."

"Shut up."

Roy shook his head. "All that anger, sonny. It ain't gittin' you nowhere."

When no answer was forthcoming, Roy turned away and continued picking, the silence between them sizzling in the heat of the day. Oba glanced up once, saw the bent back like an impenetrable wall, and figured he'd be better off without the man telling him what to do.

As if he'd heard his thoughts, Roy turned, straightened his back, and continued the conversation. "You need somepin', an I ain't zackly sure what it is."

No answer.

"How about you think on de Lawd. Our Savior, Jesus Christ. You goes to church. Don' you hear how he lived and died for you?"

The only sound was the rustling of cotton stalks, the low voices of the women, the chittering of sparrows hopping from stalk to stalk like anxious children.

Without warning, Oba threw down his sack of cotton, turned and shouted, "I don't need to hear you preaching to me, negro man. What do you know about anything? Your parents didn't drown and leave you to fend for yourself. So don't start with all that stuff you know nothing about." He threw a few words in his face and stalked off, all sizzling anger and rebellion.

Roy watched him go, his dark face lined with hurt and worry.

When Melvin came looking for Oba, Roy shook his head, said he'd not been feeling well; he wasn't surprised when Melvin brought him back and watched Oba pick up his cotton sack and continue picking.

Melvin was breathing hard, his face the color of a ripe persimmon; Oba was white-faced, grim. Roy turned his back and could only see looming disaster.

He'd been taken by surprise this time, lying in the haymow, out of the sun and the shame Roy had brought on him, doubling the self-hatred that dogged his existence. He felt a crippling humiliation for having allowed himself the flagrant display of a young man's longing, so he hid away from other perceptive eyes and told himself the time had come to leave this horrible place, strike out on his own. He didn't hear footsteps or the opening and closing of the barn door, only the cooing of the pigeons from the rafters, the rustling of small creatures in the hay.

There had been no tears.

Only a squeezing of his eyelids, the trickle of sweat down his back, his mouth pulled into a grimace as if in a silent howl. He felt a presence, heard the whistle of the bullwhip before the slicing of the knotted end across his shoulder, into his back. Before he could leap to his feet, it hit him again, throwing him like a rag doll on the floor of the barn.

With every whipping, he never cried out but went into a place deep inside himself, a place where the searing pain and brutality were tempered by his strong will, buoyed by a dull acceptance of his fate. It was only later, when the broken skin leaked water and blood, that his anger reasserted itself and ran rampant in his veins.

"Get up!" Melvin ground out, his voice like a rasp.

Oba tried, got to his hands and feet.

"Get up. I said. What are you, a baby? A weakling?"

Oba got to his feet, his head hanging, his shirt cut into strips, his feet wide, legs trembling.

"Get to the field. I catch you playing hooky again, it will be worse. And don't go to those black people for pity. You won't get any. They know respect, okay?"

Why did he follow Melvin to the field? What cowardice propelled his feet to move in Melvin's wake? The sun on his shredded shirt was unbearable, and yet he bore it. Why did he continue picking cotton?

A broken will is sometimes only broken enough to produce jagged edges that constantly wound the soul. Each and every beating produced another shard that produced more pain and anger, that drove home the fact that he was a coward. A sniveling baby that allowed Melvin to whip him.

Every jagged edge mutilated the lining of his goodness, ripped and tore at every thought and action, until his large dark eyes, fringed with the heavy lashes so characteristic of the Millers, were hot, burning coals of bitterness and contempt.

The suffering he endured that afternoon was beyond anything he had ever experienced, and he had been through more than most people have endured in a lifetime. Most of them had never come close to the required stamina and determination Oba conjured that day.

Melvin was wily. He knew he couldn't send the injured young man to work with the sharecroppers, so he assigned him a row on his own.

At suppertime, he his hid back from the three boys, but May caught sight of it, gasped a small sound of dismay, sought him out after milking, and asked him to go to his room, she'd attend to his wounds.

Gertie saw him creep upstairs, saw May follow soon after with a dishpan of water and the Rawleigh's salve; she plied a toothpick between her teeth to dislodge the pieces of ham and let them go. Oba was a hard nut to crack, she thought, so this might be the one that finally did the job.

Upstairs, Oba groaned as he stripped off his shirt. May took one look at his back, crosshatched with red welts like blood veins, and caught her breath.

"Oh my," she breathed, quick tears stinging her eyelids.

"Oba, you have to learn to obey, then this would all stop."

A vehement denial behind closed lids.

"Oba, listen to me. If you would only learn to respect Melvin, he's really not that bad. It's our fault if we don't do what he wants. You can't go on this way. Just remember to serve him fully, and you will have a different life. Jesus wants us to be good servants for Him, it says so in the Bible. We hear it at church. Whoever cannot lay down his life for Christ, take up their cross and follow him, is not worthy of Him."

He felt the cool washcloth, her soft hands as she spoke, laying before him the path of impossibility. How could one person hold total control over another? This was not God's way, if there was an all-seeing God up there somewhere like everyone said.

"May, our father was not like this. There is so much wrong with the way we are living. I am not staying much longer. I can't."

"No, no, no, Oba. Don't go. You're all I have."

Amid the pain of her administering to his wounds, the terrible, suffocating heat of the small upstairs bedroom, the buzzing blowflies that smelled blood, and May's soft whimpering cries of resistance, a plan developed in Oba's mind, stronger than his wounded heart.

He knew their differences, knew May was sincere, but he could never follow the road she had set for herself. To discuss this with her would only weaken his own resolve, break down the small amount of courage he had left.

He promised her he would stay and was rewarded by a smile of such gratitude it broke his heart. Somewhere in the remains of his spirit, there was still a tender spot for his sister, who was growing into a beautiful young woman before his tired, disoriented eyes.

She was not tall, as if the trauma of losing both parents had stunted her growth, but remained short and petite, a blond wisp of a girl with huge brown eyes that never quite exuded what she felt. A veil covered the bright emotion Oba saw in other young girls, an indistinct smokiness of sorrow and suffering, and something he could never quite name.

So he promised to stay.

The promise remained in place till Saturday evening, when he hitched the young, restless horse to the one-seated, roofless buggy, stored a change of clothes beneath the seat, and drove off as any normal teenaged boy would do, without saying goodbye to anyone.

He never looked back.

He drove into Blytheville, tied his horse to the hitching rack at the railroad station, grabbed his bundle of clothing, and sat in the dimly lit interior of the high-ceilinged brick building, without a penny to his name.

The advantage of leaving on a Saturday night was well-established. No one would know he was missing till the following morning, which gave him a distinct advantage. He simply needed to walk into the rail yard and watch the coupling and uncoupling of the trains, find out which one had an accessible baggage car, and find his way into it.

But first he needed to sit here in the cool interior to gather courage, to get his runaway legs beneath him. His heart banged in his chest, destroyed his clear thinking. Like cobwebs, he needed to brush aside fear of Melvin, the inevitable search party he would launch, along with thirst and hunger, and the unknown dangers of riding the rails.

He thought of the men who did this on a regular basis, thought of his mother's kindness to tramps who came knocking in the middle of the day, down-and-out men who needed a cold drink and a meal to sustain them.

Would he turn out like one of them?

For a long time, he'd considered going to Leonard Yoder, but he knew Melvin and Gertie were in good standing in the church. They were respected members of the Amish community that thrived on the rich soil of the Mississippi delta plains. Mistreatment, harshness, excessively hard work—these things were not talked about, but hidden away as efficiently as if they'd never been.

Melvin kept himself and his family in the *ordnung* (rules) of the church, presented a respectable citizen to the world, and if he was given to bouts of anger and disciplined his nephew, well, then, he was following the Bible to keep from sparing the rod and spoiling the child.

Oba knew he was up against a formidable mountain, Melvin having the clear advantage with his shine of righteousness.

Better to disappear, in spite of May's hurt and disappointment.

He did not want to attract attention, so he wandered out, followed the cement walkway to a chain link fence with a bold black-and-white sign that warned everyone to keep out. Below the concrete wall was the rail yard with a crisscrossing of track laid to accommodate the vast amount of hissing locomotives and stopped cars. He counted sixteen.

He caught his breath as one of them released a quick hiss of steam. Black smoke belched from the smokestack like a monster's breath, then moved slowly down the short track, drawing a string of three cars. His fingers gripped the wires of the fence, his breath came in short gasps of excitement. He watched the sky as the last of the sun's rays painted the evening clouds with hues of ocher, lavender.

A dog barked, followed by the sound of a child shouting. Automobiles rumbled along the street behind him, horns tooted as tires screeched.

How to get into the rail yard without being caught? His eyes lifted to the top of the fence. Ten feet, maybe twelve. He waited, watched, all his instincts alert to any danger. He turned from the fence, felt the first pangs of hunger.

He wondered about his horse, being tied loosely. He hoped the horse would easily free itself, find its way home. Let Melvin think what he wanted, let him think he was dead and gone. Who cared?

But the thought of May brought a pang.

"Hey!"

He jumped, gritted his teeth, and turned to find a middle-aged man wearing a battered fedora and an old pair of overalls, his face creased with goodwill.

"Find the trains interesting, do you?"

"Yeah, I do."

"That your horse parked by the hitching rail?"

"Yeah."

"He ain't tied too good."

"He'll be alright."

He was relieved when the man nodded and walked off with an unhurried gait. Hopefully, darkness would cover him before his attempt at scaling the fence.

The stars were excruciatingly slow in making their appearance. Lights from below created an aura of semi-darkness, and Oba knew he had to be quick. He still had his eyes on the hissing engine with the three baggage cars. The door on one was wide open, revealing a stack of wooden packing crates and an odd assortment of baled cotton and fifty-gallon drums.

He bit the inside of his lip till he tasted blood, lifted his eyes to the darkened sky that showed pinpricks of emerging stars, then moved to grip the fence. It would have to be now. That locomotive would not be idling on its sidetrack forever. The stench of sulphur. There was no breeze, only the heart-stopping sense of danger, of being caught climbing this fence.

He was underage, not yet eighteen years old, and would be handed straight back to Melvin, placed in his possession to face a beating that might actually kill him.

Now.

Quickly, he slid out of his shoes, tied them with shaking hands, slung them across his neck, stuffed the bag of clothes below his elbow.

The wire dug into his fingers, into the underside of his toes. The bag of clothing slid out from under his elbow, but there was nothing to do about it. Spurred on by a crazy fear, he became catlike, scaled the fence with ease, and dropped to his feet on the other side. His face burned. He looked from side to side, lowered himself to a hunch, and dashed for the safety of a rail car, then to another.

From the ground, they were so much higher than he'd thought. How could he hope to enter one? He swallowed, heard the dull thud of his pulse in his ears. To have come this far, only to return in defeat was unthinkable.

He found an empty, rusted-out fifty-gallon drum, rolled it through the semi-lit area, uprighted it, and swung himself on top of it, then hoisted himself onto the solid firmness of the floor of the baggage car, his breath coming in ragged gasps, sweat pouring off his face in the heat of the night.

He wriggled between two packing crates, felt as if the air around him was dissolved into water, and found himself gasping and crying in sloppy sounds that were a release from pain and anger, humiliation and despair.

CHAPTER 7

THE DAY MAY WAS SENT TO PICK COTTON AND WATCHED HER brother flirt with the working girls seemed to be the entry to a dark corridor of events that spiraled out of control very quickly. Waking up on Sunday morning to the sound of Melvin bellowing like a wounded buffalo would forever be etched in her mind.

A numbing fear kept her in its grip, even as she dressed and went downstairs as quietly as possible, with Melvin yelling to a disinterested Gertie about Oba's team arriving home without him, the dangers of a horse running loose during the night, and now where in the Sam Hill was Oba?

She milked the cows desperately, doing Oba's share, answered Melvin's onslaught of inquiries with respect, until he sat down to milk and stayed quiet.

When the cow he was milking sensed his agitation, she brought down a clumsy foot and stepped on his toes, shifted her weight before preparing to bring up a succulent cud to chew, was surprised by a roar from beside her, and promptly lifted the erring hoof and whacked wildly at the bucket of milk, sending it rolling away with a trail of creamy milk that picked up bits of straw, bird droppings, and manure.

Melvin hopped and yelled, sat in the middle of the cow stable and peeled off his shoe, then his sock, watched the blood seep out from beneath the toenail on his big toe, and roared on.

He stayed home from church but sent May with the three boys. Gertie had a bad case of the stomach flu and stayed home as well, close to the back door for hasty access to the privy. Melvin soaked his foot in Epsom salt water while the sun climbed into the sky and baked the roof of the house efficiently, leaving the occupants sweating out their own misery individually.

May loved driving the small Morgan horse named Lacy, a rare treat, one Melvin allowed only on the occasion that he was in good humor. This morning the air was heavy with the scent of blue lobelia, verbena, and wild hydrangea, a heady mixture of perfume that took away some of the sting of her morning. The loblolly pines shaded portions of the road, the scrub jays darting from branch to branch like bright bits of blue cloth.

Lacy lifted her feet daintily, brought them down lightly, drew the courting buggy with ease. May's spirits lifted as she watched the delicate ears, the proud lift of the black mane and tail.

Where was Oba? Had he stayed at a friend's house? Would she see him in church?

But she knew with the intuition of a woman that he had been whipped for the last time, had broken free from the prison of his uncle. A fierce gladness muddled with heartache and anxiety, fear for her own safety, and a prayer to God to keep him in the palm of His hand. She felt a sort of pride in Oba's strength, his strong body and quick mind, but feared the bitterness he wore like a second skin.

"Why do we hafta go to church?" Ammon whined beside her, kicking the seat with his bare heels.

"It's too hot," Enos echoed.

"It's not hot this morning. Look, boys. There's a fish crane flying over the woods."

She pointed to the right, a smile on her face as she watched the slow movement of its magnificent wings.

The boys watched it go, eyes alight, then smiled at May with a rare display of approval.

"Why didn't Dat go?"

"The cow stepped on his toes. He'll probably lose a toenail."

"Why?"

"Nails come off if they're pressed too hard."

"Does a new one grow?"

There was a long beat of silence as the bright summer morning turned into the gray and white of unreality. "I don't know."

"You were dreaming," Leviticus snickered.

"I was not."

It was a mercy when the subject changed to the litter of pups found in the haymow, two dead and five of them alive.

"Dat doesn't want them," Leviticus chirped.

"We do," Ammon said.

"We sure do. He better not do anything to them." This from Enos, the set of his jaw already a portent.

May swallowed her fear of the boys' veering off to the previously mentioned events, drove the horse well, and arrived at church on time, where the boys took the horse and carriage, unhitched, and tethered Lacy in a stall, while May walked into the house to stand with the group of girls that were not much more than church acquaintances.

Melvin and Gertie rarely attended social gatherings, and May was content to stay home on most Sundays, so she never developed any real friendships the way most other girls did. She was viewed as quiet, withdrawn, not interested in girlish prattle, having aged far beyond her years. The girls always greeted her warmly and included her in their plans, but she remained on the border of their conversation willingly.

That she was not like other girls was an acceptance, one that grew into her conscience as she grew older. There was a hidden quality of maturity, a level of womanhood coupled with days of hard work, the ability to maintain a garden, can vegetables, cook meals, and wash clothes. She could keep a house clean and in order, while catering to the unwell Gertie, who sat on her hickory rocker and pined for Ohio, comforting herself with an ever-increasing amount of food and attending doctor's appointments to check the state of her weakened heart.

The fact that her husband harbored a level of disdain for her didn't bother her at all, merely caused her to justify her actions. She asked May to read to her from the Bible, listened to the soft voice, and thought it was a good thing she'd been the one who had generously offered to take on these two children; look how it had turned out, with her health and all.

May's eyes searched the room for Oba, watched every man and boy that entered, each one not the one she was searching for. She listened to the sermon, helped with the hymn singing, prayed in desperation for Oba. She kept her tears in check, her back rigid with the effort.

She was stopped in the washhouse by Elam King sie Annie, a thin, hawkish woman with a caring heart and the spirit of perceiving a troubled mind when she saw one.

"May?" A hand on her sleeve.

May stopped. Fear in her eyes. Fear that was like a caged animal. Fear that should not have been there, should not have been in any young girl's face.

Annie trembled, righted herself, and smiled. "Are Melvin and Gertie ill?"

"Melvin's foot was stepped on by a cow, and Gertie has stomach flu."

"And Oba?"

A flicker of indecision, an intake of breath. May's eyes lowered, as her fingers grasped at the long sleeve of her dress.

"May?"

"He's . . . he's . . . I'm not sure."

"What do you mean?"

May's fingertips came to her mouth to still the trembling. Only for a moment she felt the iron control slipping, the kindness in Annie's eyes the hardest thing to resist.

"His . . . the horse and buggy he drove last night came home this morning without him, so I think he's likely at a friend's house. He became drunk, perhaps." As good an excuse as any.

"My. I hope he'll be alright. And you, May? Are things going well there at Melvin's?"

"Oh yes. Yes."

"Does Gertie do any work at all?"

"Yes. Well, no. I mean, she embroiders things."

"May, you shouldn't have to shoulder those responsibilities."

Annie could never know how many responsibilities she had taken on, so she wiped all expression from her face and said that she must be going, that Enos had the horse ready, which he didn't.

Annie gave her one more piercing look, as if to uncover the top of her head and find the truth written in plain letters, but both parted knowing everything had been said that could be brought out and examined in the light of what was proper and acceptable.

As they drove home, dark storm clouds gathered on the horizon along with the impending gloom of May's thoughts amid the boys' happy chatter.

Leviticus said his friend Sammy ate hay during services, chewed it over and over like a cow, lifted his face, and howled with glee. Ammon told him he'd get the worms from eating hay, and Enos said everyone had the worms.

"What does *harta vasser* mean?"

"Hard water."

"No," May corrected them. "It was sacred water, or some special water at the end of Moses' journey."

"Hard water is ice."

"There wasn't no ice in the desert."

"You don't know."

"How could there be ice in the desert when it's hot?"

"Jesus can do miracles."

"Jesus wasn't living back then."

"He is now."

"No, he isn't. He died."

"He rose again, boys. Don't you know he did not stay in the grave?"

"I know. He went back to Heaven."

May loved the boys, loved to sit among their talk, the views they decided on their own, the amazing facts they discovered among themselves. These three boys were actually the one thing that kept May from absolute hopelessness, the way they freely accepted her as the one who saw to their needs, as their own mother retreated further into her own cave of misery and self-pity.

May rested beneath the basswood tree in the backyard as the boys played a game of "Lotta" beside her. She found it difficult to keep her thoughts away from Oba, wondering if he was safe, where he was, or whether he'd appear on Monday morning. She considered the beatings, the injuries on his back and shoulders, and wished away the hope of reconciliation between him and Melvin.

Was one cruelty worse than another?"

She went for a walk after the heat of the day had mercifully folded its wings and allowed a cooling, if sultry, breeze. The thunderstorm on the horizon had shifted away to the west, leaving the valley steaming with oppression, the heat and humidity like twin torments.

May wore only a light dress, a washed-out colorless one that had been a feed sack scattered with printed flowers, which Gertie had showed her how to bleach, cut, and sew. It had turned out to be almost the color of her hair, so she had to keep it for an everyday work dress.

She had no idea how innocently attractive she was, swinging along amid waving grasses that contained shy salamanders and hovering dragonflies, the air thick with the wonderful scent of magnolia flowers.

She stopped to pick a few, tucked one behind her ear, since she was out of Melvin or Gertie's sight.

The crunch of tires.

She slowed her walk as the bicycle approached. She couldn't help the smile from forming at the sight of him.

"Imagine seeing you here," he said, his dark face alight with welcome and gladness.

She couldn't stop smiling, so she held it in place, her eyes never leaving his.

He stopped, got off the bicycle, tapped a foot to the kickstand, and turned to find her standing close. He filled his heart with the sight of her, the white magnolia flower enhancing the lovely sheen of her delicate face.

"How are you?"

"I'm okay. And you?"

"I'm doing alright. Still haven't found your brother."

"You won't. Not now."

"Where'd he go?"

"He left. Probably for good."

"Why's that?"

May shrugged, unable to say what she knew.

"Look, my name is Clinton Brown. Thank God they named me before they got started on Arpachshad. What's yours?"

"Merriweather Miller. May for short."

"And you ain't for real Melvin Amstutz's offspring? Is that correct?"

"His niece."

"And how come you're here?"

"My parents drowned. Melvin and Gertie are our only relatives who'd take us in. We're Amish from Apple Creek, Ohio."

"So you're like these folks around here?"

"Yes."

"My turn. Clinton Brown. From here, born and raised. My daddy ain't the same's all the others. He's a Mexican from Texas who ran into my mother somewhere along the way between here and there. He ain't around, never met the guy. Got a good father now, though. We live on McKinley Street with the rest of the coloreds. I got a job cuttin' cane. I'll be leaving here in a coupla weeks."

"Where will you go?"

"Over toward Eudora. El Dorado. Along the coast. I done it last year, so I'll keep on with it, when the harvest lasts."

"Do you like it?"

"It gets into your blood. Hard work. The cane's heavy. You whack along with this big curved knife, pile it in bundles."

May thought it explained the physique, the muscles pushing from his arms and legs. She found herself wishing he did not have to go. She smiled again.

"So we've run into each other again."

"Looks like it."

They smiled at each other again, then became self-conscious, aware of a certain forbidden attraction. He reached out and slowly removed the magnolia flower, flattened it to his gray T-shirt, held it out to her.

"Smell it now."

She sniffed deeply, her eyes closed, then opened them to find him staring at her with a soft expression in his dark eyes. She would never be able to name what passed between them, but she knew she would always remember this time and place.

He blinked. "You're beautiful."

No one had ever told her that. She had never thought herself pretty, had never viewed herself as someone of worth on her own, but rather as a person who was born to serve others, to give her life for others' needs.

She turned her face away, gave a low laugh. "I'm not beautiful."

Clinton made a soft sound, mesmerized by her profile, the soft bulge of her downcast eyelids, the delicate curve of long lashes. "You are the loveliest girl I have ever seen."

"No, no. I'm not. You don't know me."

He saw her agitation, wondered. "We can't feel this, you know. I'm black. You're white. Your religion ain't same as mine. So we're done right there, right?"

"Yes. I suppose we are."

"No blacks marry a white girl."

"No, they don't."

He searched her face, found a question. "Could they?"

A shrug of the delicate shoulders.

"You wish so, too, huh?"

"I can't say. Look. I have to go. It will be time to start supper before

I get back. Melvin and Gertie would not want me talking to you, I'm pretty sure of that."

"Where'd your brother go?"

"He ran off. I think. I doubt if he'll be back."

"When can I see you again?" he asked.

"Probably never. We can't."

He sighed, looked off into the distance. She saw his profile, and knew she would always keep the memory locked somewhere deep inside of her.

"So then, what are we going to do?"

She knew what he meant, feigned bewilderment. "Nothing. I guess."

"Look. I'm going off to cut the sugar cane in less than two weeks. When can we talk again? When can you get away?"

"I can't . . . except maybe on Sunday. About this time."

An invitation, an agreement. Ah, but why not?

May found her days colorless without Oba but splattered with glittering anticipation when she thought of one more Sunday evening in Clinton's presence.

She learned to dodge Melvin's rants, listened to threats of punishment when Oba returned, but not once did she truly wish him back. It had been inevitable, his leaving, and she had to learn to trust God with her brother's well-being. She kept a mental photograph of him in her heart. She knew his love was with her and threw herself into her work until she dropped into bed at night.

Gertie's flu turned into a severe gallbladder attack. She cried and rolled in the bed with pain so intense it drove her mad. The doctor recommended surgery, but she said there was no way she'd go and let someone cut open her stomach. She'd rather die.

They summoned Sadie Yoder, Leonard's wife, who was a midwife and self-proclaimed botanist. She told Gertie to drink only cider for a day and follow up with a cup of olive oil and lemon juice afterward, go to bed, and lie on her right side until morning. Melvin was dispatched to Blytheville with all due speed for the necessary items and brought them back straightaway, the fear of losing his cotton money to a hospital bill goading him on.

She carried out Sadie's instructions, thought surely her time had come, but passed an unbelievable number of gallstones and felt better in a few days, whereupon Melvin urged her to get off her rump and get some physical exercise, which brought a hot color to her cheeks, eyes that snapped like a shorted wire, and the dire declaration of going back to Ohio herself.

But she seemed to take her husband's words seriously and, for a short time, washed clothes and ironed them.

That Sunday afternoon Ammon begged to go along for the mail, but May persuaded him to stay and she'd play baseball when she got back. She then walked down the road with so much guilt that she found her anticipation dampened.

When she saw him approach, the gladness returned, but it was subdued by her keen sense of right and wrong, coupled with her own sense of worthlessness.

"May!"

"Hello, Clinton."

"Why don't we go down to the creek?"

"Alright."

He pushed his bike, and she walked beside him. She was so small, so slight, he asked if she wanted to ride the bicycle. For a moment, he thought she would, the eager light in her eyes giving her away, but in the end she shook her head.

The creek was a lively little stream of water that tumbled between the banks of a meadow, wound its way through a small patch of willow trees and under the roadway, babbling and tinkling its way to the Mississippi River. Clinton sat on the soft mat of grass, reached for her hand to pull her down beside him. They shared their lives easily, each one given to storytelling, to listening with interest, so the evening flew by with neither one aware of time.

"Clinton, do you believe a . . . a person should . . . uh . . . uh?"

He waited.

She bent her bright head so low he could barely hear the sound she made in her throat. "Oh, don't mind me."

"Tell me, May."

"No, I can't."

When he asked if he could kiss her goodbye, a look of pure terror slid over her beautiful features, contorting it into a mask of herself, the horror so real he looked behind him to see if some slimy river creature had heaved itself out of the creek.

She ran, then, blindly, ran and ran until she fell down in the road and cut her knee on the sharp gravel. He caught up to her and called her name, got down on one knee and begged her to tell him what was going on.

She sat back and pressed the skirt of her dress to the injured knee, her head bent over it as hoarse, dry sobs escaped her throat, her blond hairs stuck to her perspiring forehead and tears made gray trails down her cheeks.

"May. Please, May. What is it? I won't kiss you if you don't want me to. I'm sorry. I'm just so sorry. I didn't mean to hurt your feelings." He thought he'd rather have his hand cut off him than cause this lovely girl such unexpected anguish. He had a nagging doubt, a feeling something was not quite right. Perhaps it was her being Amish, the strict rules that would forbid her to be with him.

"It's alright. Goodbye, Clinton. Just . . . just goodbye."

"I can't leave like this. Not without knowing what caused you to run."

She would not raise her eyes, simply stayed huddled by the side of the road like some bruised and broken animal.

"May. Look at me."

She would not.

"May. If it's okay, I'll be back in the late fall. Maybe winter. Can I see you then?"

She shook her head. "I don't know. I just don't know."

He placed a hand on her thin shoulder. "Goodbye, then."

She shook her head no.

"Why do you say no?" he asked now, bewildered.

When she finally raised her face, he hardly recognized her, for the raw torment hidden deep within the brown eyes, the ravaged look that took his breath away.

"Don't come back to me. Just forget you ever met me. I'll forget about you, and I'll stay with Melvin and Gertie. They need me."

"Is that what you want?"

"Yes."

There was a long pause. Finally he replied, "Alright."

He extended a hand to help her to her feet, and she took it. When he thought she would let go of his hand, she unexpectedly gripped her small slender fingers into his, her eyes going to his face.

"I have a friend."

"Yes."

They parted; both felt the pain.

May walked home to the place she had known for all these years, an eternity. She kept memories of her mother and father alive, but as the months had turned into years, any former happiness seemed blended with the years here at Melvin's, turning bright thoughts into tarnished ones.

She yearned for Oba, to see his face, to know he was alright, but knew she might never see him again.

That night, she knelt beside her bed in the steamy room, folded her hands and laid her forehead on them, before turning her thoughts to God. She had no one to talk to, no one who cared, and the one whom she could name, this Clinton Brown, would never be allowed to be her friend. So she spoke to God, asking for courage and strength, the will to go on, and to please watch out for Oba.

He was all she had, and now he was gone.

A sense of being imprisoned became overwhelming, cut off the gentle prayer as she got into bed, the curtains hanging motionless in the still night air, the bed clothes soon soaked with her perspiration.

Outside, the moon hung in the sky, the cotton grew in the heat of the night as Melvin reveled in the perfect cotton-growing weather, counting his profits and the cost of doing without Oba.

CHAPTER 8

H E HAD NO WAY OF KNOWING HOW LONG HE WAS SUSPENDED between two packing crates, his head swimming with nervousness and exhaustion. The dark space had no beginning and no end, only strange lights that sometimes stabbed the darkness, sounds of the rail yard, clanking, hissing, men shouting.

Fear of discovery kept him awake all night, the pre-dawn bringing lurches, metal against metal, and then the sound of more voices, the dull reverberating of a truck, and someone on board.

Footsteps.

"Over here. Over here."

He couldn't breathe. His heart pounded. He shrank back between the narrow space.

He heard the creak of wood, a teeth-rattling clunk as more wooden crates were set on the floor of the rail car. More shouting and thumping. The smell of cigarette smoke, the squeak and rattle of the heavy iron doors closing, the bars in place, locked.

Slowly he let out a long breath, felt the relaxation settle across his shoulders as the lurching began; the undercarriage of the cars clanked as they were pulled forward. Then, mercifully, the steady pull of forward movement, the clack of steel wheels against track, steadily increasing as the massive locomotive picked up speed.

He fell asleep to the song of the rails.

Hunger awoke him, but it was the thirst that clawed at his throat, raked it dry until he could barely summon enough saliva to swallow.

He was completely closed in on all sides, so for a moment he fought a clenching sense of claustrophobia, broke out in a cold sweat as he fought panic.

He looked up to the thin bar of light above him, evaluated the distance to the top, before realizing the futility.

There was no food or water anywhere on this rail car, so he'd only have to hope, take the chance of being able to survive.

He could not go back, ever.

He moved his legs to a more comfortable position, tried to let sleep claim him, but the hunger growled in his empty stomach, his throat burned with the desire for water, so there was no reprieve.

He allowed his thoughts to wander, back to his years with Melvin, clenched his fist at the innocence with which they first rode up to the house, their fate sealed, the wide-open curiosity and the sense of optimism that got them through the first month.

He had tried, had tried hard, but in the end, he knew his hatred, anger, and rebellion had taken first priority. He had been whipped in innocence as well as in rebellion, but not once had he ever deserved the brutal damage he received.

Even harder to tolerate was the pious display Melvin produced, sitting on the hard bench in church, his face a smooth mask of godly observance, the advantage of being a respected and well-liked person in the Amish church. The passion of his anger, the greed with his growing cotton, the treatment of his sharecroppers all added up to a hidden hypocrite, a person who portrays the devout, *gehorsam* (obedient) spirit but lives a life rampant with ill temper and greed.

A growing distaste for the Amish church was planted the day he bore that last whipping. There was not one member in all of Arkansas that would believe his story, not one person who would expect these atrocities, this outrageous behavior inflicted on him at increasing intervals.

He suspected a lot of it had to do with Melvin's frustration at his wife, the now bulbous Gertie, who languished on the hickory chair, rocked, embroidered, and declined in mental clarity.

Alcohol had loosened his tongue, but even in that state of drunkenness, never a word had passed. It was too horrible, the inflection of evil etched on the reddish purple face, the eyes glittering with the power to correct, subdue, control, while thinking himself pious, devout, on God's side, breaking the will of the errant young man.

Oba gritted his teeth with the pain of remembering. Better to shrug it off, better to forget, and still waves of memory assaulted. As the train wound along Crowley's Ridge, carrying him out of the Arkansas Delta, his mental state was in disrepair. Humility, shame, rejection, loss, bitterness—all cocooned into a poisonous vapor that ruined his soul.

He thought he might be on the St. Louis–San Francisco Line, called the Frisco, although he could not be certain. He suspected he was headed west, west into a land away from the drenching sweat of the delta.

He had no destination, no contacts or timeline; he only knew he needed to get away, remove himself from any danger of Melvin Amstutz's presence.

Day, night, hunger, thirst—he was unsure now which one blended into the other until he woke from a weakened stupor to find an absence of noise or movement, a creepy stillness that brought him to his senses.

He froze when the grind of iron on iron sounded through the railcar, the wide doors slid open to reveal a patch of light, a squiggle of light now snaking between the packing crates. Voices, the sound of a motor running, then the removal of items. Wood creaked, barrels scraped. Like an unwanted rodent, he was trapped, discovery imminent by the removal of the crates in front of him.

Light blinded him. He raised a forearm to shield his eyes against it, shrank against the side of the crate to his right, hoped they'd miss seeing him.

"Stowaway!" The yell of discovery.

A face above him, dark, grizzled, cracked yellowed teeth.

"Git outta here. Git."

A hand like a bear paw latched to his forearm, hauled him up, and dragged him across the filthy floor of the railcar. He was thrust out the door like an unwanted cat, flung into air rife with the smell of sulphur, coal, steam. He fell hard on one shoulder, then his hip; his neck cracked as he hit the ground. He scrambled to his feet, found his legs would not support his body, so he crawled on hands and knees, cinders cuttings into the palms of his hands, blackening his trouser legs.

A light drizzle was falling from the dark sky. There was no moon, no stars, only the black night interrupted by yellow light from the rail yard, piercing white lights from the monstrous locomotives, the hulk of the corrugated metal cars.

He tried getting to his feet, then tottered unsteadily to the inevitable chain link fence.

He realized he had to get out of the railyard, had to come into contact with human beings, some merciful occupant of this city, or wherever he had been deposited. Without human aid, he actually believed he would perish, so enormous was his thirst. He opened his mouth, pushed his tongue into the falling drizzle of rain, contemplated licking the fence, a rail car.

He walked in what he felt was a western direction but couldn't be sure. He followed the fence, found a narrow opening, and slipped through it, only to find more cinders, tracks, cars, and the stench of sulphur so strong he gagged. The smell of rotten eggs, he thought, but knew it wasn't that.

He was hungry enough to eat them.

He walked on, meeting only dark, wet, stinking railyard, but now a silhouette of tree tops appeared, lights winking like fireflies, and he realized he was on the outskirts of a large town, sprawled along the basin of another ridge.

If there was a town, there were people, and to find someone who would give him food and water was the most pressing of his needs.

He could walk right out of the railyard, the gate to the chain link fence having been left wide open—a stroke of good fortune that lifted his spirits tremendously.

Brick buildings like squat towers, four or five stories high. Cracked sidewalks, tufts of weeds scraggled from curbs, brown and limp. Tin cans, paper bags. A skinny mongrel dog slunk under the gate to a park lit feebly by yellow lights.

He stopped when a door was yanked open from the inside, a container heaved into a metal garbage can, the lid replaced with a loud bang.

"Hey!"

Desperate, Oba stepped forward.

"You scared me."

"Sorry. I need a drink of water, please?"

"I don't have a drink of water." The man took his container and disappeared, the solid door closing after him with a final thud.

Oba couldn't believe the refusal. Who would refuse a young man a drink of water? Did people in cities actually do that?

He crept silently to the garbage bins, lifted the lid, and instantly replaced it, the smell of rotting vegetables, blowflies, and maggots momentarily taking away his burning hunger and thirst. He walked on and turned a corner to find himself under a striped awning, a plate glass window beneath it, with the words "Spacey's Diner" written in an arc of fat blue letters across the glass.

A blue door with a worn knob.

He reached out, turned it, found it locked, stepped back, and squinted at the hours written on a black and white paper: 6:00 a.m. to 9:00 p.m. all week long. So it was after nine, he supposed. Nothing to do about that, so he moved on, his stomach as if it were scraping his backbone.

More pole lights, more awnings, places of business closed for the night. He stopped, leaned against a crumbling brick wall, his hands thrust deep into his pockets, his shoulders slumped. He looked up to find two men, dressed in jeans and white strap T-shirts, their eyes bold in the light from the corner, sneers, cigarettes dangling.

"Well, if it ain't a country boy."

Oba stayed quiet, his heart pounding weakly, his head spinning.

"So, what's up, Pumpkin?"

"Nothing much," Oba creaked quietly, then cleared his throat, ashamed of the gravelly sound.

"You lost?"

"No."

"That's a lie."

Oba said nothing.

"Where you from?"

"Blytheville."

"You know where you're at?"

"Not for sure, no."

"How'd you get here?"

"A railcar."

"I figgered. Skinny little guy. Bet you anything you're about a week away from starving."

Oba nodded, tried to hide his eagerness.

"You know, we could beat you to a pulp, take all your money, leave you in the ditch over there, but it ain't our night to do that."

One looked at the other, laughed a short, harsh sound.

"You're in Sulphur Springs. Almost Oklahoma. Look, if you're desperate, keep going, turn left on Castor, right on Broad, and you'll come to a place'll take you in."

Oba mumbled, "Thanks."

"See ya 'round, Pumpkin."

He sighed with relief, walked fast, carefully, following the directions until he came to another door in a seemingly endless row of brick, with black letters etched into the front: Soup Kitchen.

Afraid to try, he pulled on the knob and was relieved to find it open.

Slowly, he drew it toward him, then stepped into a sort of vestibule with another door to the side. He tried that knob, gratified to feel it open, then stepped into warmth and a delicious smell of hot food.

A large man in a clean white shirt approached him, sized him up with the eyes of experience. He was not smiling, but his eyes held a kind of curiosity, an acceptance.

"Good evening."

Oba nodded, would not meet his eyes.

"Is there anything we can do, young man?"

"I'm hungry."

"Well, you've come to the right place. I'll be right back. Have a seat there by the table."

Oba found himself shrinking away from the unsavory characters in various states of repose, draped across the table top or slumped in their chairs.

An elderly lady kept up a lively repertoire, answering all her own questions, her hands waving dramatically. He found this array of derelicts so unsettling, he forgot about his hunger, until a bowl of soup, saltine crackers, a cup of tea, and a peanut butter sandwich was placed in front of him.

"There. I'll bring your water."

The water was like an elixir, pouring life and spirit into him. He drank a few mouthfuls, remembered to go slow, then bent to his soup, tore into the peanut butter sandwich like a ravenous dog, and did not care.

He sugared and drank his tea under the man's watchful gaze.

"More?"

"If you have it."

"Of course."

Oba could not fathom such kindness, such generosity. He felt a lump rising in his throat, hated the weakness, and set his mouth in a hard line.

More soup, the absolute delicious aroma of corn and bits of chicken.

He looked up when he heard, "You can call me Ralph."

"I'm Obadiah Miller."

Ralph raised his eyebrows, taking in the haircut, the broadfall trousers. "We have a few beds available if you would like to stay."

Oba nodded. His throat clenched.

He fell asleep, hot tears soaking his pillow. To treat a stranger with such kindness was simply not understandable, and he came so close to believing there was a God who showed His face.

In the morning, after a dish of steaming oatmeal and an egg sandwich, he made his way back to the railyard to find an opened door, the same as he'd found before, but with a lone occupant sitting on the floor of the car, legs dangling down the side. Oba stopped, took a long look.

The man was older than him, certainly. A long brown beard, lots of facial hair, a fedora that rode low on his forehead. Patched overalls. A companion?

He had to force himself, but he walked up to the railcar, stopped, looked up.

"Yessir."

"Hello. I'm . . . you know, wondering if I could ride?"

"You want a train ride but ain't got no money, is what you're sayin?"

"Yes."

"Well, you may as well come aboard, sonny."

Oba grinned, reached for the extended hand, and was swung aboard; he scrambled to sit beside his smiling benefactor.

"Well, since we're up here together, we may as well become acquainted. Name's Larry, okay? That's all you need to know. Just Larry. I came from there, and I'm going nowhere. That, too, is all you need to know."

"I'm Oba."

"What fer name is Oba?"

"Obadiah."

"Straight outta the Bible. Hmm."

"Yeah."

"You ain't some plain sect, are you?"

"I was."

"You ain't now? Cause I don't like to travel with the Jesus people."

"No, I'm not."

"Okay. You know you're on the Frisco line?"

"Am I?"

"You are. If you want, you can go clear to California." He pronounced it Californ-eye-ay.

Oba grinned, cast him a sideways glance, saw the slash of his mouth buried in facial hair, but his eyes crinkled to slits when the smile reached them. His cheeks puffed up.

"You got some destination?"

"No. I'm . . . from Arkansas, leaving my uncle's cotton farm."

"You a runaway?"

Oba shrugged. "If you want to call it that."

"Don't make no difference to me. Look, sonny. You don't make no trouble for me, and I won't make no trouble for you. We'll enjoy the ride, and I'll get you a fine education, let you find out what this world's about."

When the car was loaded, he merely got up, stepped aside, and allowed everything to be put in place, then stood and chatted with the forklift operators before joining Oba on the floor of the car.

"They'll leave this door open for us. They ain't supposed to do it, but it's hot, so they will. Ain't much on this here car anyhow, so we may as well enjoy the view."

Oba nodded; his eyes sparkled.

The morning sun glinted off the night's light rainfall, the sky as blue as a robin's egg, wisps of cottony cloud riding high. The air was crisp, but the decided smell of sulphur was in the air, overriding the smell of the railyard. They moved out of town slowly, past rows of houses with peeling paint and small sagging wash lines, derelict cars succumbing to their weed-strewn graveyards. Near-naked children hung on rusted fences, waving and yelling at them, shouting words they could not hear. Dogs ran from one end of fenced-in yards to another, their mouths open, barking.

As the train left town, it picked up speed, the slow rhythm of the wheels on the rails turning into a frenzied clickety-click until it all ran together into a gravelly humming. The wind in his hair, the sun on his face, having eaten and slept, Oba felt the first thrill of freedom.

A river meandered lazily among groves of trees, tractors moved like toys among rows of knee-high corn. Green squares of pasture were dotted with Holstein cows. Automobiles raised dust on country roads.

There was no need for conversation; merely the fact that someone would know how to procure a meal, to lead him in the ways of the world, was hugely comforting. Here was a man who'd ridden the rails for many years, so he would not let him go hungry.

The sound of the wheels were like a lullaby, so he stretched out on his stomach, folded his arms and fell asleep, to awaken to Larry's still form beside him.

At first, he felt anxious, disoriented, as if he had to hurry to accomplish something, till he realized he was free, had no schedule, and none to answer to except himself. So he rolled over and let sleep overtake him again.

Larry laughed when he sat up and rubbed his eyes, then offered him a slice of bread with margarine, salt, and pepper, which Oba found surprisingly tasty. He ate three slices, drank gratefully from the jug of lukewarm, sulfurous water.

"Now we're in Oklahoma, sonny."

"We are?"

"You bet. Interesting country."

Oba paid attention, looked around, but it seemed exactly like Arkansas, although he kept this bit of observance to himself.

"How far is it across Oklahoma?"

"I couldn't say. I don't keep track of miles."

Oba nodded.

Larry began to talk then, in a quiet singsong way that filled in a longing to hear about other's lives, the assurance he needed to feel he was not alone in the world. So Oba listened intently, nodded his head while receiving bits of news.

Larry had a wife and two children. His son had leukemia when he was eleven years old and died. He never got over the loss but took up drinking himself into a stupor on most nights, until his wife couldn't deal with it, took the girl, and left. He lost his job, tried several more, then collected his savings, quit the drinking, hopped a train, and never got off.

It was a way of life, a hobby, a culture he enjoyed. There were hundreds, thousands just like him. They had their meeting places and get-togethers, worked for a while in certain towns, some farms, then moved on.

Without responsibilities, life took on a certain quality, he said. An easiness. You didn't have to answer to anyone, only yourself.

But he'd loved his wife. Remembered her. Hair like spun gold.

A temper though. Look out when she got mad. A tiny waist. So small he could span it with his hands.

Oba thought of Gertie's huge mass of flesh, her unwillingness to do any type of manual labor. He couldn't dwell on May; it brought too much pain.

"Tell me about you," Larry said.

So he did. He placed the story of his life in this stranger's hands and was rewarded with a low whistle, a hand wrapped around his shoulders, a tug till he was pulled against him.

"You poor kid," he said in a voice choked with emotion.

Oba looked up, marveled at the fact that Larry was genuinely struggling to control his tears, his face working into all manner of contortions. The hand on his shoulder tightened, drew him even closer.

"Poor kid. You got a bad rap. No one deserves that."

Oba said nothing.

"See, that's why I have a hard time with this God stuff. Why'd he let my son die? He could have stopped it. And your parents. Why'd he allow it?"

Oba shrugged.

"Yeah."

But Oba thought of the goodness since he'd been on the road. He thought of Leonard Yoder and his concerns, but the politeness of not being too curious, the sad fact that so much was hidden away for the sake of respectability. The hypocrisy of Melvin, the sickening display of godliness.

"Yeah, well. I can take it better, thinking of my parents, if it . . . If I could move past Melvin."

"That the uncle?"

Oba nodded.

"I don't know that he'll get away with all that, eventually. Stuff doesn't stay hidden very long, most times. He's got three boys? He beat them?"

"No. Not that I was aware of. Sort of ignores them, as if they were not really there."

"Yeah. I know the kind. It'll come back to bite him in the backside. These things do."

Too young and inexperienced to know if he meant it, Oba lost interest in the conversation, so he half-listened to Larry's philosophies and half-remembered the good times when his parents were still alive. There was a certain truth in Larry's questioning, and yet, he knew he believed, or he would not have questioned God's actions. He simply was not spiritually advanced, in having faith that God knew what he was doing. Like himself.

His father had had a premonition, a bad feeling about the coming storm. He had dreamt of a swollen creek and flooded pasturelands but went on his way, thought nothing serious of it.

Not that Oba didn't.

He'd lain awake for many nights, afraid of his father's dream. Well-versed in Bible stories at his mother's knee, he knew plenty of instances where God warned people in dreams and wondered why his own father had hitched up that team when he knew the water was dangerously high.

By late afternoon, they reached the town of Tulsa, or so Larry said. Oba wondered aloud if he'd been here before, which of course he had.

He said they'd stay a while; he was getting low on cash.

Here in the city of Tulsa, Oklahoma, Oba was introduced to the world of skilled labor, the fact that no one, not Larry or anyone else, looked out for you, ever. It was each man for himself. Sink or swim, he said.

He was hired on with Larry at sawmills on the outskirts of Tulsa. He took boards from a long roller table, mostly white or yellow pine, stacked them in neat rows, over and over from seven in the morning till five in the evening. If he was lucky, he had bread and margarine for lunch, but on many days, there was nothing till evening. He loved the smell of sawdust, the hum of the saw, the roar of the diesel engine, but his back became tired and sore till evening, even as his shoulders and arms developed muscle.

He was teased without mercy about his long blond hair, the men naming him Cathy, so he spent his first paycheck on a haircut and a change of clothing. He felt fine, walking along the streets of Tulsa without the usual Amish appearance that set him apart. He was just another youth, mingling with hundreds of others, strolling the Tulsa sidewalks.

He ran a hand through his short blond hair, loved his reflection in the shop windows, felt a keen sense of abundant life. He made forty-two dollars in three weeks, hopped the Frisco line once more, and was off to the freedom of California.

CHAPTER 9

SUMMER TURNED INTO EARLY FALL, WITH MAY'S LIFE TAKING on a quality of unreality, times when the morning sun seemed brassy before breakfast, the day turning ominous by noontime.

Gertie had taken a decided turn for the worse. The buildup of excess fluid, coupled with inactivity, obesity, and her air of negativity and frustration—all took a bitter toll on the unhappy woman.

The family came from Ohio—all sorts of cousins, sisters, sisters-in-law, and brothers-in-law, as well as a few anxious aunts who were stuffed into black Sunday dresses and arrived in Arkansas with rings of perspiration like dinner plates below massive armpits, reeking of body odor and onion sandwiches they had brought on the long train ride.

They brought news of home, salt-cured hams, fifty pounds of red potatoes, live chickens in crates, and heads of cabbage in burlap.

They took stock of the situation, routed poor Gertie out of the rocking chair, and told her there was nothing wrong with her heart, it was all in her head. Wide-eyed, sweating profusely, Gertie made an effort but fainted in the pantry, and they had a most alarming time of it, dragging her out with shelves and door intact.

Then there was the situation with the now beautiful May. How could Gertie have her at her beck and call like that? The place was much improved over previous years, and they guaranteed Gertie herself had nothing to do with it. That May was being treated unfairly.

And what did they say happened to Oba?

He ran off. Well, it happens. The *ungehorsam* (disobedient) eventually joined the tide of other slaves to the devil and lived their lives without fear of God, so that was that. Melvin played the victim with sheep's eyes and artificial reverence, and every last one of them swallowed his story.

Except Aunt Sarah, a buxom middle-aged widow with a heart of gold. She watched the boys' disrespect; she watched May's veiled eyes that held nothing in them, her work-roughened hands, and slight figure; she watched Melvin's eyes follow May's quick movements through the house and could not leave before she cornered her by the garden shed.

"Well, May, this is our last day. You'll be glad to see us go, with all the cooking and washing."

May smiled, a small turn of her full lips that never reached her eyes. "Oh, you were no trouble. Gertie needed you."

"Yes, I know. Of course, she did. She simply is not feeling well. Tell me, May, do you enjoy your time here with Melvin's family?"

"Yes."

"Are they good to you?"

"Yes. It's my home."

The lack of girlish things in her room, the double bed with no nice quilt, no china or pretty dresser scarves, no extra shoes or clothing, gave away the true family life. She was not the loved daughter, neither was she a maid, but a station perhaps worse than a sharecropper. The poor people at least had homes of their own; they had love and laughter, fun, a circle of family and friends far above the price of money.

"Are you telling me the truth?"

"I am."

But was that a flicker of indecisiveness first? Had she almost told Aunt Sarah the truth? Such a beautiful, wan face! So bereft of human kindness.

"Would you prefer coming home with us? Starting a new life?" Sarah's round blue eyes were filled with so much caring, so much kindness, May almost broke down and poured out the detestable truth, but she could not face the consequences of revealing so much.

She was alone in the world, alone with her sordid secrecy, and so it would have to remain, for the sake of conventional decency. She had the boys, she reminded herself. She had love and companionship, especially with Leviticus, the youngest. He had been a neglected, sniveling bed-wetter, and now, with all the friendship of May's lonely heart poured out on him, he was developing into a friendly, open little person with a knack for reading and writing far beyond his years.

"May, please tell me. Does Melvin treat you right?"

"Yes."

For all Sarah's concern, she could not ask the unspeakable question, and with May's hurried yes, she put her fears to rest. These things were not spoken of as it should be, and if things were not right, well, God would eventually bring justice. She gave May the benefit of the doubt that day, which sealed the young woman's fate and delivered her into the path that was hers to travel alone.

She stood bravely, grouped with the remainder of the family, and lifted a hand in farewell before they embarked on their long train journey. She turned to go back to the house, carrying a dejection so heavy she felt the buckling of her knees. Torn between her own fierce loyalty to Gertie and the boys, undecided about trying to break away, the loss of Oba pressing on her spirits, it was almost more than anyone could bear.

She cleaned the house that day, scrubbed floors, and washed bedclothes and rugs, telling herself someday she would be free to choose. Someday God would hear her prayers and deliver her from this farm.

She rallied again in time, as the heat turned into the freedom of autumn breezes, of frost in the morning and earlier evenings. She brought in every last head of cabbage, dug the carrots, and banked the celery with newspaper and soil. She canned pumpkin, made applesauce, stored turnips down cellar with the potatoes.

They found Gertie unconscious, waved smelling salts to revive her, but she took to her bed and never recovered her health. She was swollen and miserable; they had to employ a nurse to help with her care, a dark woman of great height and capabilities. She hefted Gertie from bed to chamber pot and back again, massaged her swollen feet, and made her food without salt.

Her name was Tessa. Tessa Chamberlain. She lived on McKinley Street with the rest of the black people, took no nonsense from Melvin, collected her weekly wages without comment, and appraised the situation there with a keen eye and no fear of respectability.

"May, honey chile, you'll sit down. Sit down. You are so tired dis mawnin', and I brung you a pineapple cake wid buttercream icing. No, don't give me dat look. Sit down."

Her starched white dress rustled as she swung from kitchen cabinet to table, brought a small plate, and proceeded to cut a hefty chunk of cake and set it unceremoniously on it.

"Eat. I'll bring you a cup of tea."

May protested, then sat back and savored the rich cake, the strong, hot tea. Tessa watched the color return to her cheeks, watched her eyes light up when she talked, and nodded in understanding.

"Bless yo' heart, yo' po' chile. Yo is too young fer dis all." She waved a hand, included the entire house and beyond. She watched May finish the cake, watched as she moved about the house, watched Melvin as he entered the kitchen and decided there was a skunk if she ever saw one.

Tessa was black, which sharply curtailed her rights, so she kept her mouth shut but never stopped watching, never stopped building her case.

Something was off. Not right.

Gertie passed away on a dark, rainy night, with Melvin, May, and the boys by her side. She spoke endearing words, set her sight on Heaven, and whispered goodbye with her last breath. Melvin sobbed at her bedside.

May bent her sweet face and prayed for strength, donned her black funeral attire, and met the neighbors when they came to prepare for services.

She comforted the boys, then sat quietly as women of the community came flocking into the house, beating eggs and milk, producing loaves of homemade bread, pies, soups, and casseroles.

The house filled with friends as Gertie was brought back from the undertaker, the coffin opened for grieving family. They came from Ohio and Indiana, the funeral services delayed on account of the long train ride.

Melvin was the picture of the devastated husband, quietly blowing his nose into his snowy white, ironed handkerchief, saying over and over how he didn't expect her to leave him alone with the boys. So glad he had taken May when she needed a home. Oba was never mentioned, however, as a runaway child was shameful.

The boys cried genuinely, wept copiously beside the coffin, clung to May who kept them by her side through the time of the viewing.

How she would dislike being buried on Arkansas soil, May thought, as she stood with Melvin and the boys, her black shawl wrapped around her slender frame, the black bonnet hiding her face well. She wept for Gertie's sad life, wept for the motherless boys, but did not weep for Melvin at all.

His sister stayed on, the one who refused May or Oba. She stayed to set the house in order, and to tell Melvin of his own duties in Ohio. There were only a few of them, and with his parents all but bedfast, it was time he considered returning. It wasn't fair to the rest of them, wearing themselves out taking twenty-four-hour shifts.

Melvin heard her out, told her he was well on his way to paying off the mortgage with his cotton, so no, he had no plans of returning, ever, and she may as well put that thought out of her head. She hadn't wanted Eliezer and Fronie's kids, so he took them in, now it was her turn.

She seethed with thinly veiled rage.

Rachel was a woman of means, her husband having done well for himself in Ohio, managing the farm with a tight rein and a keen eye for profit. She was his right-hand helper; she drove a team of horses like a man, hefted forkfuls of hay, and carried five-gallon buckets of water with ease.

She detested Arkansas, could see no reason for a respectable Amish man to bring his family into this wet delta that was like living in a bowl of chicken noodle soup. Hot, steamy, and miserable.

Now, when late fall was upon them, the days could seem like August, and she had no intentions of staying longer than necessary. Her refusal to take Oba and May as small children did not bother her in the least, seeing how the girl managed the household well, a blessing to Melvin when he needed her most.

The harvest was in, so they cleaned house. Rachel carried galvanized buckets of hot water up both flights of stairs to the attic, instructed May in the art of scrubbing filthy oak floors, splattered with bird droppings and bat guano.

She railed in front of Melvin like a great flapping crow, exhorting him to get the cotton out of his head and look around. No attic should have missing windows; now look at the damage these flying creatures had done.

Melvin was busy burning fence rows, so he took no heed, let her flap her arms and went off with the boy. Rachel watched him go, before hitching up a horse, telling May to get her shawl and bonnet, they were going to town for windows.

She'd taken measurements, counted the cash in her wallet, pinched her mouth into a straight line, and brought the reins down on the horse's back with efficiency. The air was brisk, a heavenly chill after the smothering heat of the long summer, and May wrapped her shawl tightly, watched the fields and farms with interest, her large brown eyes sparkling at the unexpected treat of riding into town.

They met more teams, men sitting high on buckboard seats, children piled in the back. Automobiles chugged and lurched across the lunar surface of unkempt roads, the drivers watching as horses shied away from the sputtering engines.

The town was closer than Blytheville, and much smaller. A general store, a feed mill, cotton gin, a few businesses lining the wide street, along with houses like building blocks set against each other and encased in red brick. A few church spires reached into the sky, as if to remind the residents of the town that God was looking down on them, and they were expected to show due respect.

May watched a woman dressed in a pink suit, her shoes matching her purse, and the small, round hat perched on top of her blond curls. She was walking beside a well-dressed gentleman in a navy blue suit, the red tie against the white shirt like a banner. A young black woman, lithe and beautiful in a swinging skirt, turned toward them with a bouncing step, carrying a cardboard box by one handhold in the side.

May bit her lip as she watched the girl who did not break her stride or step aside as she came face to face with the well-dressed couple.

They passed, and May turned in her seat to see the drama unfold, was not surprised to see the couple stop, deep frowns telling the young woman to step aside, which she did only at the last moment, a proud mockery in the way she allowed them minimal space.

She thought of Clinton Brown.

As if Rachel could hear the forbidden thought, she pulled her bonnet even farther on her head, turned her face away, and feigned interest in the opposite side of the street. May felt the spirit of the young girl, felt the obligation to conventional servitude when her whole being cried out against it, and wondered at the irony of it.

Had God designed one person to be lord over another?

The color of your skin, the situation into which one was born. Yes, she was white, but she was held by convention to obey every wish of another, with no freedom to command the direction of her own life. The first light of her own conscience revealed a sordid picture of the truth, her future pockmarked with the tangled web of being held to a situation against her will.

Her breathing became hurried, her eyes large and dark with the knowledge of what was right or wrong, but the moment of courage passed when Rachel pulled up to the hitching post, told her to watch the horse, she'd be back.

To do as she was told was not a question; it was an answer. So she got down from the buggy and went to stand at the horse's head.

She heard the crunch of tires on gravel, watched as a young man leaned into a turn, and knew it was him before she turned her back, the black shawl and bonnet effectively hiding her identity. She heard the bicycle come to a stop, heard the kickstand being released, heard the light footsteps, but could not turn or call out a greeting.

For a young Amish girl to be seen with a strapping young Negro man was a blatant display of *ungehorsamkeit* (disobedience), and so she shrank into the black safety of her shawl and bonnet.

She watched a group of sparrows squabbling over the pickings of half-digested corn in a pile of horse manure, thought of her own inability to fend for herself. Always on the outside, looking in, watching others who lived by their own rules, never taking what was rightfully hers.

She wondered about Oba. Was freedom a good thing for him? Would he remain true to his teaching?

When Rachel returned, she laid the brown paper-wrapped parcel in the back of the buggy, told May to get in, she'd back the horse, which she did, drawing on the reins until the bit tore at the corner of the horse's mouth and he sat down against the breeching.

When she clambered hurriedly into the buggy, when the wheel screeched against the metal roller attached to the side, May looked over to find him watching the procedure.

Their eyes met.

He leaned forward, walked a few steps, lifted a hand as if to retain her, but as the buggy moved away, he let the hand drop and stood as one in a trance, never taking his eyes off her until they turned a corner, out of sight.

Rachel said if she had to live here among these blacks, she'd likely go crazy. They gave her the willies. Seriously, they did. When May did not respond, she turned her face and slanted her a questioning look and realized agreement was missing somehow.

"You don't like the coloreds either, do you?" Her voice like thrown gravel.

"I have met kind ones."

"Puh."

From the depth of the black bonnet, came the small voice. "They have a mighty faith. They are satisfied with far less than we."

"So what you're saying, they're on your side, and you're on theirs. I hope you know, May, that kind of thinking will only lead to the path of destruction. You stay away from them."

What, really, had possessed May to say what she did? It was only later that she trembled.

"God created us equal, no matter the color of our skin. Gertie's nurse was the kind of woman I would be proud to call my mother."

A gasp of indignation. "That is not the way we are taught, and you know that, May Miller. If your mother were alive today, she would firmly bring you to task. The very idea."

With another self-righteous huff, she brought the reins down on the unsuspecting horse who was already traveling at a good clip. The wheels bounced furiously over loose gravel, the springs on the buggy squeaking in protest, as the horse lunged against his collar. They rounded the turn on two wheels, the back of the buggy sliding along as the horse continued his headlong dash. May found herself gripping the edge of the seat, wishing she had not spoken her mind.

But Rachel seemed to have taken out her disagreeable mood on the poor frightened horse, unloaded her windows, and proceeded to divest herself of shawl and bonnet before marching up both flights of stairs with May carrying the hammer and parcel of nails.

"There now," Rachel chirped, as she pounded the final finishing nail into place. "No more birds and bats in the house. Melvin needs to see to these things. Not that he's ever done it before." She glanced sharply at May. "You better be prepared to get along with your new stepmother, seeing how Melvin won't wait very long. I don't think Gertie had been a wife to him for a while already. I would certainly hope he keeps his hands off you."

Without so much as a glance in her direction, she rambled on. "Not that it hasn't happened before, mind you, but Melvin is not the type. He may be a bit harsh, but the man is a godly, upright member of the church. He fears God, does what is right, except for counting all that money after the cotton is sold. Greedy, that's what he is. But you know, if he ever does behave unseemly toward you, remember to keep yourself covered, never give him reason to lean toward lustful thoughts." She pursed her lips. "A man without a wife is not always responsible."

May went down the stairs ahead of Rachel, a thin bent figure who could convey much necessary information if there had been a sympathetic recipient, which there was not. And so she went about getting the wash off the line, thought how little anyone could know what occurred under God's realm.

Rachel was in a combative mood.

She told Melvin how much time they'd spent in the attic, the long afternoon going to town, and he owed her four dollars and thirty-two cents. She had no plans of paying for those windows.

Melvin wrinkled his nose, took a bite of his fried pork, and said this stuff wasn't done, pink in the middle. Who fried this?

"I was talking to you about the attic windows. Melvin."

"What? What about them?"

"You owe me money. You should have installed those windows years ago. It was a mess."

"Yeah, well. A couple birds in the attic never hurt anybody."

Leviticus speared a chunk of pork, bit it off with a tearing motion, chewed, swallowed, and glanced around. He thought how strange it was that Rachel didn't answer, looked at May and grinned, before returning to the business of pork ingestion.

"Who fried this stuff?" he repeated.

"I did."

"May's pork chops are much better."

"Is that right?"

And so forth, through the entire meal, until Enos and Ammon began to make humming noises, kick their feet against the bench legs, anything to divert attention to themselves.

"Quit that, Enos," Melvin barked.

"Ammon's doing it, too."

"Quit it, Ammon."

"As I was saying, if you don't like these pork chops, I guess you'll have to fry it yourself. And you owe me money. I'm not paying for your attic windows."

"You should, Rachel. I'm a poor widower, with my wife laid to rest such a short time ago."

Here he bent his head and made gasping noises. May looked up in time to see his face crumple into a pitiful caricature of himself, the tears already creating wet runnels down his lined cheeks.

"Ach Melvin. Yes, yes."

Rachel got to her feet, in passing, clapped a hand on his shoulder, gave a small rub of comfort. "I do sympathize, of course. But you still owe me four dollars and thirty-two cents. I plan on staying another two weeks, so you may as well come up with it."

A large handkerchief was routed out of his oversized denim trousers, a honking of great velocity into it, before he repeatedly rubbed his nose and replaced it. "Rachel. I would never have replaced those windows, but since I am a Bible reader, I will remember the words of our Lord when he said if a man smite thy cheek, turn the other also. Or if a man takes your coat, give him your cloak, too. I'm sure the charge for unnecessary attic windows comes under that admonition."

"Well spoken, Melvin. So you'll reimburse me?"

"I would imagine."

Satisfied with his answer, Rachel brought out the pumpkin cake and the canned plums. The cake being frosted with a delicate seven-minute frosting and eaten with the purple plum juice was a feast in itself.

Melvin ate a second piece, asked for more.

He smacked his lips and told May the cake was the best one yet, whereupon Rachel gave him a piece of her mind, saying she had nothing to do with the pumpkin cake and, if this was how he was going to be, she was leaving for home early.

They continued the housecleaning, on into the second week, until May's hands were chapped and reddened by the strong lye soap. Her shoulders ached as she made her way upstairs to her small room that contained only a bed and a dresser.

She prayed to God for strength and sometimes for deliverance. She kept the memory of Clinton Brown's beautiful face alive by reliving the times in his presence, moment by moment. The reality of her aunt's attitude toward his people only made the impossible even more so.

She could see no way out of her life here on the farm, except if an Amish youth would ask for her hand in marriage, which was highly unlikely, given her nature, the reclusive hiding behind lowered lashes, her refusal to join the goings-on of the *rumschpringa* (youth who were coming of age). She harbored a secret aversion to all Amish men, unbeknownst to even herself.

What had possessed her to speak to her aunt in that manner? Was it the knowledge that he, Clinton Brown, was back in town after following the sugar cane along the coast? Was there a possibility of seeing him again?

To harbor those thoughts would disappoint, and she knew it could only bring bitter unhappiness. She had to stay true to her calling here at Melvin's but could only toss ideas, like juggling five balls at once, watching helplessly as she dropped one, then another, and another, always coming up empty-handed, with no plan and no future.

After Rachel left with Melvin on the spring wagon, driving to the train station in Blytheville, May experienced a sense of doom so strong she could do nothing but sit, staring at the opposite wall.

She wanted to end it all. She never felt such a desire to stop this merry-go-round that had spun out of control, the darkening clouds of her own existence threatening to extinguish her will to live, to destroy her faith and hope.

Where was God, if she prayed so earnestly for a light to see along this dark road of suffering? How long would she be expected to continue? The thought of Melvin bringing home some strange woman was equally frightening.

Oh, Mam, Dat . . . Why did you have to die and leave me here without Oba? Are you angels in Heaven? Can you see me?

She felt crazed by indecision and fear, the hopelessness of being caught like a rabbit in a snare. She had no money and no courage, too much fear, and a sense of duty that was being questioned as she grew older. Life without Gertie's stolid presence was even more frightening than knowing she was there, spreading a weak protection from her creaking hickory rocker.

CHAPTER 10

BY THE TIME THEY REACHED THE STATE OF CALIFORNIA, OBA felt old, experienced, and world-wise. The rules of the hobo life on the rails had been embedded like a piece of lead, carried beneath his flesh, and chafed constantly.

After getting into a fight with another youth over five dollars, bloodied and beaten, he learned to hide money or be willing to share.

Keep your mouth shut, he'd been told.

But a new Oba was emerging, one who was confident, swaggering almost, light on his feet, his sharp brown eyes missing nothing. He stored knowledge, kept the sights and sounds to dissect later, watched and listened to the ways of survival.

Larry took on the role of a fatherly figure, taught him when to enter a rail car and when to exit. The rushing of wind in his ears, the constant music of steel wheels on rails became a way of life.

On a bright, sunny morning when there was a new freshness to the air, Oba woke in his sleeping bag, stretched, sniffed, then burrowed deeper, his nose cold, his shoulders taut with goose bumps. He wondered how cold the temperatures were in California in winter, remembered he had no money, no job, no home. For only a fleeting moment, he felt thrust into a world rife with the unknown, steeped in danger. He rolled over, opened one eye, to find Larry sitting at the opened door of the rail car, his shoulders hunched with the cold.

Oba was hungry, his stomach growling with emptiness. Larry had miscalculated the amount of food for the duration of the ride and was surprised to find the package of cookies and the hunk of cheese already gone, which made Oba feel an anger he hadn't experienced in a long while. Simply the fact that Larry, at his age, had not taken responsibility for something as necessary as food irked him. He rolled out of his sleeping bag, thumped his stockinged feet to alert Larry, then began the process of rolling it into a tight and manageable bundle.

He cleared his throat, watched Larry, who eventually said, "Hey."

"Yeah."

"Cold."

"I'm hungry."

A raised eyebrow. "Yeah. Well, there's no food."

"So when do we get off?"

Some vague answer, a wave of his hand in a southerly direction.

"I'm hungry," Oba repeated.

"Get over it. It'll be awhile."

To spend his day lolling on the cold floor of the rail car took away any charm of riding the trains, his stomach actually painful now.

He thought of May's fried eggs, stewed saltine crackers, and a side of ponhaus, crispy and greasy. He thought of his mother's shoofly pie, the way the brown sugar and vanilla bottom gave way to the moist cake and the crumb topping.

He swallowed, glared at Larry.

"I need a coat," he called out.

"Quit whining," Larry growled.

"I'm cold."

"Look, if you're gonna ride with me, you'll have to disperse of creature comforts. It ain't always gonna be a soft bed and food handed to you on a tray. Either you're in or you're not. I'm sick of babying you."

Ashamed, Oba said nothing.

"I thought you had more in you than this."

But I'm hungry, Oba thought. Hunger separated things, made you feel despair and missing your parents that were dead and gone, made you remember every good morsel of food you had ever eaten, the times you clasped your hands below the table, bowed your head with everyone else, and never once remembered to thank God for the steaming bowls of food. Hunger brought irrational thinking, like jumping off the fast-moving train or trying to open the packing crates in your search for one item of food to stop the misery.

He sat cross-legged, his elbows on his knees, his back bent.

The air was sharp, the leaves on the trees colored with the brilliancy of changing seasons. Used to the steaming summer months of the delta, he shivered, then got up to unroll his bedding.

It smelled. Everything reeked of dirt and rust and cold metal, of unwashed clothes and a body that had not been bathed in weeks. Hunger took away any sign of confidence, any swagger he might have accumulated in his weeks of riding in cars, of meeting up with others who lived this lifestyle.

So Larry thought he might not have it in him.

Well, perhaps he didn't. Perhaps his childhood spent in a stable, Christian home, with loving parents who lived among family, lived in peace and unity, attended church services in homes, and drove horses and buggies was no foundation for this kind of rambling, this blissful lack of responsibility.

At first, it had been delightful. The absence of Melvin was a healing breeze to his scarred and battered body. His soul had been revived by the scenery, the whole beautiful adventure of finding who he really was, but after a few days without food, everything darkened, turned bitter.

This is not an option, he thought.

I am better than filth and hunger, than lying in a stinking bedroll with socks stiff with an accumulation of sweat and grime. He watched Larry's immovable back, his willingness to take cold and hunger and misery for the sake of deserting work and responsibility.

Oba felt faint with hunger, hated Larry and railroads, then hated himself for being dragged wide-eyed into this situation. He should have been smarter, should have thought ahead. Just like the rest of his life, things had gone wrong, yet again.

And still the train moved on.

After Nevada, this seemed like a new country, with rich forest land, rivers and valleys, deciduous trees, a land that seemed fit to support life. He made a decision to get off this train, find a job, a place to live, but kept the terrifying prospect to himself. He was like a leech, clinging to Larry, without a thought of who he wanted to be.

And who did he want to be?

He didn't know. He only knew he'd been raised in a particular lifestyle, the approved way of the Amish. And that was okay with most of them, who stayed and kept the tradition of being separated from the rest of the world through clothes, transportation, and way of life.

But with all his newfound confidence, his swagger, and distilled sense of direction, he was a scared Amish youth with a scarred body and a twisted sense of what was right and what was wrong. To trust parents, to have them taken away by a cruel God, to be shunned by relatives whom he believed to be kindly, then beaten, whipped, and cursed by another relative who was Amish as well, to make this break, a clean splice down the middle of his accustomed way of life—he had endured all this, only to attach himself to a ruined man. It was in itself an act of reliance, the way he had been dependent on Melvin and Gertie.

He had needed someone, no matter how devious, to care for him. And look where he was now, miserable with hunger and loneliness, hurtling along to who knew where.

He had to summon more courage, had to break away from Larry.

The sense of awakening to an unwanted situation kept the despair at bay, as he lay huddled back into his bedroll, making plans, taking stock of his choices. His first priority was finding something to eat. He would sit with Larry after the sun warmed the earth, take his chances, and exit the train. If he was killed, then so be it.

If he was injured, he'd find a way out of it.

He dozed fitfully, then went to sit with Larry, who still had not moved from his spot by the opened door.

Larry turned, smiled, lifted an eyebrow. "You're awful jumpy."

"Hungry."

"Yeah."

"If a person jumped off a train at this speed, would he be killed?"

"You thinkin' about it?"

Oba shrugged.

"Don't do it."

Oba shook his head. "Maybe I will."

"Wait till the train slows."

"When is that?"

"Couldn't tell you."

Oba breathed deeply, felt as if his navel touched his backbone.

He knew if he didn't jump soon, he would never do it. He waited, waited for a patch of grass, then got to his feet.

Larry looked up sharply.

"Sit down. You're not thinkin' about it, are you?"

Oba nodded, and stepped off the fast-moving train. He felt a rush of air, an impact that exploded into his senses, and a merciful blackout.

When he awoke, it was in searing pain, followed by a realization of his own weakness, the quick decision to jump. He vaguely remembered Larry's hand reaching out too late to draw him back. He lapsed into another bout of unconsciousness, being drawn out of it only by the pain in his left shoulder.

He was aware of grasses waving around him, a sky smeared with red streaks, before retreating into the dark world of his subconscious.

When he came fully awake, he was so cold his teeth chattered uncontrollably, his whole body convulsed with shivers. The night was pitch black, the stars obliterated by a dense cloud cover. He smelled cinders, lifted his head to find himself close to the railroad tracks. He moved his fingers, then wriggled his toes. Everything was intact.

Sitting up was excruciating, his left shoulder as if it was on fire. He felt blood on his cheek, tasted blood in his mouth. But he could move, without the hindrance of broken bones, so he felt giddy with accomplishment.

He was too weak to get to his feet; he thought of injured dogs who crept under a porch or corncrib where everyone thought they would die, only to appear a week later. He'd heal. If he didn't, death would be an accomplishment, as would his daring leap off the train. He thought of May, the only thin tie to his existence; he had no way of knowing it was almost the same hour she sat and stared into space, contemplating the end of her own existence.

Before streaks of dawn appeared in the black night sky, the rain began to fall in cold plunks on the back of his head. There was nothing to do about that either, so he stayed inert, the bed of grass the only available resting place. Thirst ravaged him, much worse than hunger. The pain in his shoulder was dwarfed by the need for water.

The duck hunters on the lake were disappointed at the early rainfall, shivered and complained, then decided to build a fire to fend off the chill.

Tom Lyons was the one who offered to gather twigs and set off along the railroad tracks where the grass and bushes had withered in the summer's heat. He thrashed his way through thorny undergrowth to find himself staring at what he thought was a corpse.

"Dear God," he muttered low, a gasp coming from his old chest. His heart pounded so strong that he thought of his own demise, but he walked up to Oba and shoved the toe of his boot underneath one leg. "Hey there."

Oba's eyes flew open, looked into the grizzled face with the brown cap with earflaps pulled over his ears, the rain falling steadily between them, and he knew he would not die. He struggled to sit up, reached for the extended hand, before laying the side of his battered face on his knees. The world slid sideways as his senses spun, throwing him into a vortex of blackness before he rolled back in to the wet grass.

Tom was seventy-eight years old, would be seventy-nine come May, and knew his heart had been acting up of late. So he took it easy getting back to the duck blind on Cameron Pond, which was actually a small lake, surrounded by a lush stand of ash and oak trees, white pine, and smaller conifers, spruce and hemlock.

His son Thomas Jr. and his buddy Bill were huddled inside, drinking tepid coffee out of a thermos bottle and glaring out between branches of the blind at the cold rain that seemed to be increasing. When a white, perspiring face appeared at the doorway, stuttering the news of having found a person by the railroad tracks, they got up immediately, followed the old man to the spot where Oba lay curled in a fetal position, the rain soaking into his thin clothes and matting the slivers of blond hair to his scalp.

"He ain't dead," the old man breathed, his breath coming painfully now.

"We got him."

No other words were spoken as they hefted him onto their shoulders, carried him like a gunny sack amid weak groans that gave way to even weaker sobs.

They started a roaring fire, duck hunting forgotten. The rain changed to a soft drizzle as they stretched a tarpaulin on branches stuck into the ground, brought an extra camp blanket and wrapped him into it, then propped him up like a rag doll and gave him sips of coffee.

After he was revived to the extent that he could talk without passing out, his teeth clacked like castanets as he struggled to tell them who he was.

The old man listened, shook his head, caught his son's eye. For once in his life, Bill was bereft of speech, his florid face as red as a tomato, his eyes popping in disbelief.

Oba ate a sandwich in small bites, washed it down with lukewarm coffee, and thought himself extremely fortunate to be among humans. He didn't say much, but the men got the sense that here was a young man who had suffered, had come through more than most.

"Well . . ."

A long pause, a quizzical look.

"What'd you say your name is?"

"Obadiah Miller. Oba."

"Strange name."

"Yes. It's Amish. From the Bible."

The old man nodded. "I don't know Amish, but I know the Bible."

So he'd fallen among Christians. A safety net. Why was it? Why, if he barely believed in a loving God, and when he knew people like Melvin read the Bible, was it comforting to know he had been found by an old man who was a believer? A Bible reader.

He was taken home to Tom Lyons's residence that day.

Tom's wife, Mathilde, had passed away fourteen months ago. Overtaken by a sad loneliness too difficult to manage on his own, he had turned to his only son for help, who had agreed to build a small ranch house by the side of the road on his own ten acres, the curved driveway close to the north side, where his kitchen window looked out over their comings and goings. How often old Tom Lyons had thanked God for his one son—only one, but he and Mathilde had endured many barren years before the sweet boy arrived, who they aptly named Thomas Junior.

So he'd dwelt in the new house only a few months, his loneliness eased by the frequent visits from his two grandsons, Randy and Brian. And now here was this strange boy, Obadiah Miller, who jumped right off the train and into his life. Well.

"First off, young man, will be a bath. I'll get you a clean shirt. I called Elaine for undershorts and T-shirts, a few pairs of jeans."

Oba nodded, felt like an imposter. He had never thought to feel grateful for a hot bath, every Saturday evening in the galvanized tub by the cook stove, a line strung across the corner of the room to hold the sheet, the only divider between privacy and exposure.

Here was something altogether different.

The bathroom walls were tiled with smooth, glossy blocks that ran the whole way around the small room. Oba reached out to run the tips of his fingers along the wall, marveled at this wonder. He wondered what the tub was made of, the way it looked like glass, like one of Gertie's white serving dishes.

The commode was the same, sleek and white and filled with clean water. The floor was tiled, but with a darker, swirled pattern. He had never imagined a room like this, never knew anyone built these in an ordinary ranch house.

He glanced at himself in the mirror, the ceiling light fixture illuminating his lanky, filthy hair, his face discolored with dirt and bruises. He hardly recognized the angry brown eyes that glared back at him, the growth of facial hair sprouting like weeds. Unkempt, unclean.

Was this who he really was?

Here in this old man's house, taken in like a wounded dog, would he find what he was searching for, whatever that was?

He felt revived after the long hot bath, the water gushing from the spigot. He luxuriated in the smell of the soap, of clean soft towels and a change of clothes. He buckled the provided belt in the last notch, and it still hung loose.

Old Tom Lyons was a man given to generosity, to a deep and abiding kindness for his fellow creatures, man or beast, so having Oba in the house filled an empty space he hadn't known existed. Grieving for Mathilde had eased off, although never vanquished, loneliness an accepted lot. He moved through his days with the unhurried pace of the elderly, thought nothing of spending a few hours cooking dinner, with no other duties to take up his time.

So when Oba reappeared, he looked up from the cake batter he was stirring with a wooden spoon, pushed the bowl aside, and took a long look at the skinny kid he'd rescued.

"Sit down. Make yourself at home," he said, waving a hand in the general direction of the table.

Oba shuffled his bare feet self-consciously, looked at the smooth linoleum patterned in marble swirls, wished he wore socks.

When he hesitated, Tom looked at his feet, clapped a hand to his forehead, and said, "Socks."

Oba smiled, a small elongation of his normal scowl.

"I got plenty. Socks are all the same—an old man's or a young kid's, huh?"

He returned from the bedroom carrying a pair of white socks, which Oba donned immediately, ashamed at the fact that hiding his feet was so important.

His time on the railroad had not prepared him to get along in the real world, the world of people who lived in nice houses and did not know of his own ruined soul.

"So, we'll get this cake in the oven, then we'll get started on the meatloaf. You like meatloaf?"

Oba nodded, forgetting Tom had his back turned.

"Yes or no?"

"Oh. Yes. Yes I do."

Oba felt awkward, ungainly in the man's presence.

"Alright then. You can chop onions."

"I don't know how to cook."

"Time you learned," Tom said, his head inside the door of a white cupboard that was as smooth and glossy as the bathtub. He brought out a package wrapped in white paper, laid it on the table, and proceeded to undo the brown tape.

Oba watched as he unwrapped a pile of ground beef, red meat with flecks of white. He could have eaten it raw.

"Cooking is women's work," he offered quietly.

"Not if you live alone," Tom laughed.

Oba thought of Gertie's slovenly body slapping corn cakes in hot lard, the smell of burning fat hitting the stovetop, the sizzling of *flitch* (bacon). Now, May, serious, pale-faced, her too-thin body moving from stove to table like an older woman, learning through trials, Gertie yelling from the hickory rocker that seemed to become smaller as the pounds increased.

He couldn't think of May.

An onion was placed before him, with a wooden cutting board and a paring knife.

"Just cut the onion crossways, both ways."

Oba looked at the onion, the knife, and decided he would not be learning how to make meatloaf, not now, not ever. He had been a puppet for Melvin Amstutz for too long, jumping when he pulled the strings, he had succumbed to Larry's woeful life, and now here he was, being told what to do.

A shot of swift anger drew up his hand, raked the cutting board, knife, and onion to the floor in a clatter, followed by the kitchen chair that crashed on its back. Tom watched silently as Oba stalked across the kitchen and through the front door, slamming it against the doorframe so hard it rattled.

Tom shook his head, then sighed. So he was one of those. Well, heaven only knew what the boy had been through. He didn't get the sense that the kid was dangerous—just a little unhinged. Good food and a warm bed could do wonders, he knew. And he went on cutting the onion himself.

Oba didn't return, so Tom ate alone. The meatloaf was quite tasty, he thought, as were the sweet potatoes and applesauce. The cake could have used another egg or more butter, being on the dry side, but with a cup of coffee, it was good.

He stopped to turn on the radio, hummed along to the songs on his favorite station as he washed dishes, watching a pair of cardinals in the oak tree by the driveway.

If he got hungry, he'd be back, Tom reasoned, and didn't allow the incident to ruffle his peace.

Oba walked swiftly. He found himself sniffling yet he remained dry-eyed, the violence raging inside of him keeping the tears in check.

He couldn't trust that old man. To bow down and obey was only another trap, a snare that would leave him dangling high and dry, allowing everyone to see his pitiful dependency.

When he'd had plenty to eat, he'd finally felt like his own person. No one to boss him around. He'd felt impressive, walking and talking the way the railcar hobos did. He'd be there still, if it wasn't for the hungry times and Larry too stupid to plan properly.

He found the macadam roads confusing, the air crisp and cold. He had no sense of direction, no idea where he was headed; he only knew he was still hungry and had no place to turn to, so he retraced his steps and found himself back on the front porch.

Tom looked up from his book, placed a finger on the page, then dog-eared the corner.

"You're back."

When there was no answer, Tom laid the book aside, uncrossed his legs, and leaned forward. The lamp on the table beside the green sofa cast a pool of yellow light across the darkening room. His white hair formed a ring around his balding head, his face lined and tanned by the years of sun and wind.

"Sit down, Oba."

There it was again. An order to do something, like a well-trained dog.

He remained standing, which Tom chose to ignore.

"We need to have us a little talk, if that's alright with you."

Oba nodded, agreeable now that he'd asked his permission.

"If you're planning to stay with me for a while, we can't have you flying off the handle. I only asked you to chop an onion for the meatloaf, okay? Why did that make you so terribly angry?"

Oba shrugged, kept his eyes on the floor.

"You seem to have a bit of an anger problem."

The silence stretched on.

"I didn't always," he said, finally.

"So why now?" Tom asked, his face giving nothing away.

Another shrug.

"Well, regardless of your situation, we can't have that. So when you're ready to talk, we'll talk." He pushed himself off the sofa and beckoned with one hand. "Come on. I have a plate for you in the kitchen. I could handle another piece of that cake, but I better not have a cup of coffee this time of the day. I'll be awake all night."

Oba followed him into the brightly lit kitchen, watched as Tom removed a plate from the oven. He swallowed as he watched the steam rise from the large square of meatloaf, the sweet potatoes dripping brown butter.

Tom set the plate on the table, went to the shining white cupboard, and brought out a pitcher of water, added a knife and fork.

"There you go."

He did not tell him to sit.

As he watched Oba fall onto the plate of food with an appetite like a starving dog, Tom silently brought a loaf of bread, some butter, and jam, and watched in amazement as he devoured five slices of bread, everything on his plate, before eating three pieces of cake.

CHAPTER 11

SHE SAT IN CHURCH WEARING HER YELLOWED, TOO-SMALL white cape and apron, with the navy blue dress she always wore on Sunday. Her covering was well past the stage where it should have been worn, the streaks that muddled the limp fabric a testament to her brave efforts of attempting to starch it.

Her blond hair rose above the perfectly tanned forehead, light and glossy, with her huge brown eyes that seemed like a vacant canvas. There was nothing to give away any inner emotion of happiness or even the slightest interest. There was no unhappiness either, only the disconcerting flat stare of a soul that has been injured too many times.

The girl who sat to her right was chewing gum, popping it loudly as she scratched at her inner arm with a straight pin, and leaning forward to whisper things to the girl on May's left, Lizzie Yoder, Leonard's daughter.

May knew who the teenaged girls were, as in being acquainted with them every two weeks in church, but chose to remain at home on Sunday, always being the outsider, on the fringe of all social gatherings.

Her clothes did not allow her to fit in, neither did her communication skills. May knew she was inferior, not like other girls; she was unable to identify with their carefree youth and laughter, their giggling about young men and planning who they would accept and who was a "dud." Some of the girls spoke of dressing in skirts and blouses, going to see a movie, and sneaking out at night with Amos Hostetler—all a part of life that did not include her.

Leonard Yoder's wife, Sadie, sat in the back of the room, the door to the kitchen on her left, where the light poured through to illuminate the sad state of May's covering. Sadie crossed her arms and pursed her lips, thought something had to be done. The women of the church simply were not doing their duty, letting that young girl carry on alone in Melvin Amstutz's house. She had far too many responsibilities for one so young, it wasn't right.

After services, she cornered May as she carried a tray of red beets to the long table set up for lunch.

"May, you set them down, and I need to talk to you."

May nodded, subservient as always.

"How is everything?" asked Sadie, who looked like a bubble of fabric with her rotund figure.

May fastened her expressionless eyes on Sadie's, and Sadie shuddered inwardly. Those eyes. They gave her the creeps. Like a dead person. Something was so wrong there, but what? Well, some children simply never got over the death of a parent, and here was one who'd lost two. Both parents gone at once, when she was at such a tender age, it stood to reason, she supposed.

May's answer was slightly above a whisper, her voice hoarse, low, as if it had been bludgeoned into submission. "Alright. Good. We're doing good."

Her eyes fell before Sadie's, the long lashes sweeping her cheeks.

"That's good. I'm glad to hear it. Listen, I saw your covering is old. Should a few of us church ladies come over to help you sew? Your *halsduch* and *shots* (cape and apron) need to be replaced with a new set. Would you like that?"

Sadie watched for the gladness, the spark in the dark eyes, but there was nothing, only the muted darkness of the brown eyes, a lifting of the corners of her mouth, as fleeting as a moth in near darkness, before she said yes, that would be alright.

"I'll bring the organdy. I thought maybe Sarah Weaver and her sister Louise would come."

A flicker passed over May's features. "Maybe you should ask Melvin."

Sadie pursed her lips. "I will."

She was invited to go along to the hymn singing. Leonard's daughter Salome asked May if she could be ready at seven o'clock, but May shook her head. She'd stay home, she said. The boys enjoyed playing Parcheesi.

"Parcheesi? Really? That's nice." She pushed out her lower lip, blew a strand of hair off her forehead, then shrugged her shoulders before flouncing off, her hips swinging.

May watched her go but had no wish to accompany her or anyone else, absolutely no desire to attend a hymn singing with all those young men watching the girls discreetly, looking for a wife.

She would never be anyone's wife, never give any man the opportunity to know her well, never risk the uncovering of her life here with Melvin and Gertie, never subject herself to the humiliation of having obeyed.

Clinton Brown was the only person she could honestly feel an attraction for, and he was a black man, although lighter-skinned than most.

No one would ever allow them to nurture this temptation, because she was white and he was black. It was *verboten* (forbidden) by the Amish, looked down on by society in general. She shuddered to think how close she had come to divulging her painful secret, to actually allowing him to see how worthless she really was.

She had wanted his kiss, wanted to explore the idea that kisses were meant to convey true and gentle love, to evoke feelings that were right and honorable, designed and approved by the Creator. But she could not bring herself to examine this idea, this sweet innocence—not while also knowing the things locked up in the darkest region of her being.

The certainty with which she led herself to obey seemed to be questioned as she grew older. More and more, she kept dreaming of a getaway, escaping this sordid existence which was bearable only because of the three boys. Especially Leviticus.

She sat beside Melvin in the buggy, a stiff wind causing her to shrink inside her shawl. There was a repeated smattering of conversation in the back as the boys discussed their day, repeating heroic accounts of the ducks shot on the riverbank, a bull that had escaped and gored Rufus Hostetler, but not seriously.

Melvin snorted. "Shouldn't have a bull."

"Can't do without one, Dat. Not if you want calves," Ammon said.

"You need to shut your mouth, Ammon. We don't talk about these things."

"I wasn't talking. Just saying."

A quick twist of Melvin's shoulders, an arm reaching behind the seat, and Ammon received a stinging blow to his mouth. May shrank against the side of the buggy as she heard Ammon's head hitting the back of the seat.

"I said shut your mouth. If you don't listen, I'll shut it for you."

Silence descended like a suffocating blanket, May's breath coming in hurried puffs, her heart pounding so that she was afraid he would hear.

She spent the afternoon in her room, reading her Bible, praying to God for direction. With each violent punishment he doled out to these boys, she felt tied to the farm, a sort of guardian, not necessarily to prevent the abuse (that was what it was) but to administer some sort of healing afterward, a word of approval, a kindness, even a pat on the shoulder, to let them know the world was not made up of cruelty alone.

She could so easily slip away some dark night, go to Leonard Yoder or Perry Mast's house, anywhere an Amish family lived in peace and harmony. She could open the dark place inside her and allow the plain community to see everything, but it was too shameful. Perhaps she would be a sniveling coward, or worse yet, she would be labeled a loose girl, it would be all her own fault, which in her darkest hours, she accepted as the wretched truth.

She thought again of ending everything, ways in which it could be done. Wouldn't Heaven be a wonderful place? To walk with her mother and father on streets of gold, into the mansions God had prepared for them.

Jesus was there, and thousands, no, millions of angels.

And there was no pain nor hatred.

She couldn't take her own life, knowing it was wrong to do so, knowing you had to obey God and wait till He was finished with your work here on earth. *But oh God! Why me?* she would groan. *Why me?*

She felt the coming days would crush her with the weight of a boulder.

How long, Lord, how long?

And always she rallied, wiped her eyes, and went downstairs; she cooked a pot of bean soup with canned tomatoes and ground beef, made a pan of cornbread, and served it after the milking was done, when they all had worked up an appetite.

There was canned peach cobbler with milk for dessert, and Melvin smacked his lips, ran his hands over his stomach, pronounced it a satisfying meal if ever there was one, winked broadly, and smacked her arm possessively. May endured the praise with a stoic air, bowed her head for the after-dinner prayer, and washed dishes as one possessed.

The Parcheesi board came out with its colorful circles and columns, the little tokens that would travel around throughout the game.

Enos and Ammon were subdued, but Leviticus was in a fine temper, joking and laughing, cutting up with his brothers, until May's shoulders shook with laughter.

"I go first," he shouted.

"Not so loud," from the sofa in the living room, where Melvin was stretched out.

"I go first," he repeated quietly.

"Well, go ahead then," Ammon said sharply.

He proceeded to shake the dice with a flourish, a grin of wicked glee on his face. "Whoever goes first always wins."

"No, they don't. You're just talking big."

"Blowing off steam."

"Yeah!"

"I will win. I always do," Leviticus answered, full of assurance.

May made a bowl of popcorn, sprinkled it with salt, poured warm butter over it, and for one evening, reached the closest thing to happiness she had felt in a long time. She decided she could be brave, be courageous, learn to dwell on the good times, learn to love and not to hate, to accept the inevitable, and do the very best she could.

For Jesus's sake, amen.

The women descended on the house like a colorful flock, carrying pies and cakes, ham and potatoes, and lima beans and canned corn.

They measured and cut and sewed. Two of them cleaned the kitchen cupboards and the windows, carried on a lively chatter, made pots of coffee, and drank it all.

Melvin came through the door at dinnertime, his frown turned to a quizzical smile that was pasted on his face with great effort.

"No one told me you were coming," he said in an oily tone as he restrained himself from glaring at Sadie Yoder, Leonard's fat wife, who he guaranteed was the cause of the invasion on his privacy.

"Really, Melvin? Don't you remember?" Sadie asked.

"You didn't say anything to me, did you?" All innocence and righteous questioning.

"Of course I did. You remember." Sadie left no room for denial.

Melvin gave a short laugh, a nodding of his head, as he realized his cornered position. "I'm getting old, I guess. That, and having lost Gertie has taken its toll. Some days I feel as if I can hardly place one foot in front of the other. I miss her so."

Clucks of kindly sympathy went all around.

"I'm alone, yet not alone."

"Yes," Sarah Weaver offered. "Indeed. You have May and the boys."

"Oh yes. I do. But what I meant to say is that I have God. I am never alone." Melvin's face was downright sanctimonious, his eyes as helpless as a newborn lamb.

The women's simple hearts swelled with pity, and they plied him with one hot dish of food, then another, which brought tears to his eyes at all the time and trouble they had gone to, for only him.

"It's for May, too. We're sewing clothes for her. She needs coverings and a new white cape and apron. This one should last until she's married, at least, which I suppose won't be long."

Melvin looked at Sadie, choked on a mouthful of coffee, and had to go to the sink for the dishcloth to wipe away the residue that had spewed from his mouth.

"My goodness, must have gotten something in my Sunday throat." He waved a hand in front of his face as the coughing subsided.

Sadie wanted to tell him he likely didn't have a Sunday throat, but she knew her wit was too sharp and her tongue unbridled. She kept getting herself into trouble, so this time she'd practice caution.

May was grateful, glad to have the women fuss over her; she allowed herself to be measured, stood still with her arms raised as the belt of the apron was brought around her waist.

"You certainly are thin," Sarah remarked.

"She works too hard. Right, May?"

"Oh, not harder than a lot of other young girls." She blinked her eyes rapidly, blushed to the roots of her blond hair.

"She works harder than my Emma, I can tell you that. She is one of the laziest girls I have ever seen. I'm ashamed to say, it's probably my own fault, her being the youngest and all. She'd sit around with her nose in a book the whole solid day."

"Make her work," Sadie said, around a mouthful of pins.

"You better get those pins out of your mouth."

Melvin exited the house as quickly as he could, fumed to himself as he stalked to the barn. The idea of May being married did not sit well with him. He needed her here. He had no intention of asking some old maid to be his wife if May was capable of running the household as well as she did.

Among other things. And she was good with the boys.

The Arkansas winter was mild, with a fire going in the cook stove on most mornings. May was busy every day but welcomed the longer evenings now that the light disappeared at five o'clock.

She was clearing the table, alone in the house, when there was a knock on the kitchen door. Carefully, she left the pile of dishes on the sink, then turned to open the door. She thought of Melvin and the boys gone to help a neighbor stack wood; she was alone in the house.

She turned the knob, opened the door slowly.

She looked at the pockets and shoulders of a gray wool coat, then up into Clinton Brown's dark face, framed by the tight black curls, his brown eyes alight with his joy of seeing her.

"May! It's me, Clinton."

"Oh!" May was so taken aback, it took a moment to gather her wits. Then, all at once, she realized the danger of her situation should Melvin return sooner than expected. "You can't be here," she said, hating the words. "Melvin will be back."

"Melvin? It's ok. A little rudeness won't kill me."

"It's not just that. He will not allow me to speak to you. Please, just go. I beg you."

"May. I miss you. I want to talk to you. When can I see you?"

"Never. Oh, please. We can't, Clinton Brown." She was trembling now, her knees felt weak. She clung to the door handle for support as the blood drained from her face.

"Listen, May. Listen to me. After ten o'clock tonight, I'll be waiting at the end of the drive. Come to me. I just want to talk to you. That's all. Can you do that?"

His face. His dear, remembered face. Her heart roiled in her chest.

Her conscience said no. Tradition and upbringing said absolutely not. Their different races forbade it. And still she hesitated. Just once more. Only this one time.

She moved to close the door, refused to listen to temptation.

He prevented it by placing himself solidly in the frame.

"I'll be there. Please come to me."

"Go, Clinton. Go, please."

This time, he stepped away as she closed the door firmly, the click of the latch like a gunshot.

He slipped away through the semi-darkness, disappeared from view like a wraith, a dark ghost that was swallowed up by the darker ring of trees around the buildings.

May washed dishes with shaking hands, bit her lower lip to keep the tears of fright and refusal at bay. *Oh, dear God, what have I done?* Was God watching down, keeping Melvin and the boys away as she stood at the door? The punishment that would be hers was unimaginable, if Melvin found out she had allowed a black man to step up on the porch.

This was all wrong.

But, oh, how she longed to be with him! He was the only person in her lonely existence that she wanted to be with. Was that a sure sign that she had lost her mind, had simply thrown away good reasoning? She felt a heretic, one who renounced her religion, gone the way of the heathen. Where only hell awaited.

Was that really true? Was Melvin and Gertie's lifestyle an example of true religion? Of carrying on the tradition of the Amish way of life?

Melvin and the boys clattered into the house, threw coats and hats on hooks, in high spirits after doing a favor for a neighbor. May was quiet, straightened the house like a wan image of herself, was careful not to let on that her mind was swirling.

Relieved when bedtime arrived, she bade everyone goodnight and disappeared to her room, washed herself and brushed her teeth in the porcelain bowl with the matching pitcher of warm water, then stood, trembling, her teeth chattering in the cold.

She was crying, then begging God for mercy on her soul if she stepped out of this house to meet Clinton. It seemed truly wrong. It did. And yet, it wasn't right to live this way, to live with a heavy burden like a stone that weighed her down, down, down, until she did not want to go on living.

She steadied herself, took deep cleansing breaths, then went to the old armoire and chose a clean dress, one of the three she owned. She combed her hair with shaking hands, then lay in her bed and prayed that she could somehow make it down the stairs. She knew Melvin retired early on most nights and had never heard him awaken after he fell asleep, not even when Gertie needed his help, so tonight, she could only hope for the best.

Stay with me, Lord Jesus.

And then she felt tied into knots, the guilt of this wrongdoing making that whispered prayer seem blasphemous. And still she knew she would go, propelled by her loneliness, her hope of . . . of what?

She could not imagine a life with Clinton, could not see herself as his wife. They would be mocked, stoned with words of harsh accusations, chased out of Arkansas by their own shame.

And would that be worse than her own paltry existence?

When the house ceased to reveal any movement, when the damper on the stove clapped after being banked and the silence hung restful, she placed one foot, then the other, beside her bed and slowly leaned her weight on the edge of the mattress before easing herself to a standing position.

She held very still, every nerve straining, straining to hear the loud snoring that meant Melvin was asleep.

There was no breeze.

May would have welcomed the banging of shutters, the shifting of branches on the roof, but she could be very quiet, as light as she surely was.

One step, then two.

To open the doorknob took a very long time, so afraid was she to hear the offending click. When she was through the door, she had to close it again, which was as time-consuming and even more frightening, now that she was standing in the hallway.

She moved slowly, stopped at a creaking floorboard, listened for Melvin's breathing, the great, ragged snores.

All was quiet.

Oh no. Please don't let him awaken.

The snoring resumed, so her downward flight continued. Across the kitchen, past the cook stove, and into the washhouse, where she lifted her coat from the hook by the door.

Melvin coughed, and May was stung into decisive action, opening the door to the outside in one firm motion, closing it behind her before running.

She ran blindly in the dark, not caring if she tripped and fell; she just needed to be free, away from that house and its inhabitants, away from the chains that kept her in their grip. If the alternative to her life was this, if this was a form of guilt that differed from the guilt of shame and self-hatred, well, there was no decision anymore.

And so she ran.

The sound of her feet on the red soil pounded in her ears. The air was crisp and cold, smelled of cows and frosted brown weeds and the muddy scent of the Mississippi, the sharp scent of holly bushes with red berries.

Then he was there.

She stopped, her breath coming in sharp gasps. He closed the gap between them. She went into his arms gladly, wrapped her own around his waist, the whole solid width of him. She laid her head on the prickly wool of his coat and breathed in.

He held her away for a moment, then cradled her face with his hands. He gazed at her small sweet face in the starlight, shook his head as if in disbelief, then slowly lowered his dark face to hers.

When their lips met, she did not pull away, but stayed where she found a gentle love, a new sensation of unspeakable gratitude and wonder, an acceptance and promise beyond anything she could ever imagine. Healing poured from him, healing with the hope of a new and better way, of fully realizing that her life did not have to continue in this manner.

"May," he said brokenly and wept.

She gave him her lips gain, felt his warm tears mingling with her own. When they finally parted, she was smiling. Smiling with the assurance that life was about to begin, that everything else was dwindling in importance.

"What are we going to do?" he asked.

Both were trembling with the magnitude of discovered love.

May laughed, a sound like music to him.

"We're going to stand here in the dark at the end of Melvin Amstutz's driveway and try to figure that out."

He hugged her to himself, held her so close it was almost painful.

"You're happy," he said.

"I am happy."

"Thank God. Oh, thank God."

"We will simply love a day at a time. I know now that I can break free. I just don't know how or when." Unable to contemplate it just yet, she changed the subject. "Tell me about your summer. I want to hear about the sugar cane."

He told her, haltingly at first, as if ashamed of the adversity he'd met head on, a fire breathing dragon of epic proportion. It was terrible hard work, along the coast where the heat and humidity made Arkansas seem like the North. The cutters were mostly black, some of them a mixture like himself. "High yellow," he'd been called. And picked on.

He had to prove himself, which wasn't easy. There were fights, blood was shed, but in the end, he'd found his place, learned to cut with the best of them.

"How do you cut sugar cane?" May asked.

"You bend over, grab a stalk, slash with a special knife, and repeat over and over till you have a bundle. Tie it. That takes practice.

"Then cut more, just slashing through the cane as fast as possible. Mosquitoes are terrible. Snakes, lizards, crocs, any old reptile you can think of. At night, we stay at sugar camp, sleep in cots with mosquito netting, after we're done bandaging our hands. Our legs.

"The cane can cut like a knife. Blisters and calluses pop open. Hurt like crazy. Your back goes out, your feet get blisters, but after a few months, you're a genuine cutter, with hands like leather and a back made of steel. You just keep cutting, tying, cutting, for twelve, fourteen hours."

May was very quiet.

"May?"

"Take me with you," she said hoarsely.

"My lovely girl," he said and held her close.

"I must get away. I must. I'm afraid for myself if I don't."

"What are you talking about?"

In answer, she merely shook her head.

"Tell me."

"Someday."

"May, listen," he said, his voice urgent. "I get a bad feeling when I think of that house. Something isn't right, and yet you won't tell me. Does he beat you? I'm not going to let you go back until you tell me why you need to leave."

"No, he doesn't beat me. And that's the truth." She couldn't bring herself to tell him the rest, the other things that happened when the boys weren't around. It was too horrid. A pause, then she asked, "Do you think God's love is greater than being Amish or being black?"

For a long moment, he was quiet. When he spoke, his voice was rife with emotion, his words thickened and slurred. "Your question is like a tightrope between two cliffs, the fear of falling into the chasm makes me afraid to speak. I don't know anything about the Amish. I know everything about being born with black skin, but I have been taught that God's love is the same for everyone except for the unbelievers, the sinners who don't do what is right and accept Jesus. But, I'll say this, to be born already labeled with skin color, makes life a bit more difficult. I don't know about you."

CHAPTER 12

Oba awoke with the winter sun on his face. He looked at the green walls, the curtains with roses printed on them, the brown carpeting that was like a soft pillow on bare feet, the framed prints of ducks and hunting dogs on the wall, and remembered where he was.

He rolled over, drew up his knees, winced at his sore shoulder, and went back to sleep, luxuriating in the wonder of a soft mattress, two fresh pillowcases, and warm blankets.

When he awoke a second time, the sun was high overhead, the room was in shadow, and he was ravenously hungry. Only for a moment did he hesitate, allow the old shame of imposing on someone enter his head, then he stepped into his trousers, pulled on his shirt and socks, before opening the bedroom door.

Everything was quiet, too quiet. No water running or the old man's shuffling footsteps.

There was a note on the kitchen table, propped against a box of Kellogg's corn flakes: "Oba, have a doctor's appointment. Be back at two."

Oba blinked, felt a sense of belonging, then felt the sting of tears. He grabbed the box of cereal, ravenous now, and began opening cabinet doors until he found a bowl, a spoon. He tried the shining handle on the strange cabinet that stood separately, stepped back in surprise when a waft of cold air greeted him.

Wow.

So this was a refrigerator. A real refrigerator, with meat and vegetables. It was cold. He pulled on a smaller door and found it to be even colder. A freezer, with ice cubes.

Wow.

The milk on his cornflakes was fresh and cold, so he ate two bowlfuls with a sprinkle of sugar before going to look for something more satisfying, like eggs.

It seemed as if his stomach was an empty fifty-gallon drum, like the ones on railcars, that would never be filled, no matter how much food he put into it.

At 2:15 p.m., Tom Lyons came in from the garage and found Oba sitting self-consciously at the kitchen table, his stockinged feet flat on the floor, his hands clasped in his lap.

"There you are, Oba. Sleep well?"

"Yes."

"That's good. Glad to hear it. I had to visit my heart doctor. He doesn't like the sound of the old ticker, but if you're almost eighty, you're living on borrowed time, so we'll see. Supposed to watch my salt."

Oba didn't know what to say to this, so he said nothing.

Tom Lyons had lived a full life, being the town of Bridgeport's pharmacist, owning the pharmacy along West King Street that lay between a florist shop and a green grocer. Fresh out of the University of California in Berkeley, he'd married his high school sweetheart, Mathilde Tyzonesky, and went to work for Zeigler's Pharmacy, where he'd stayed all his life, except for duck hunting, forays into National Forests, and teaching troubled kids at a summer camp in the El Dorado valley. He'd thought God was surely finished with him at his age, and here he stumbled on this kid who was clearly not a normal, happy adolescent, more like a few of the worst ones who'd always escaped on foot or had some lowlife buddy come pick them up.

The pharmacy had been his life. He loved the drive from his house in the rural countryside surrounding Bridgeport, traveling through lush green forest until he broke out along the river, then followed the winding road beside it till he came to town. Some men would have chafed at the restrictions of the four walls of the pharmacy, but he loved the scent of powders and pills, the goodwill of customers who greeted him regularly, the lunch counter along one wall with its line of stools.

He sold all kinds of medicines and home remedies, supplies for the aging, greeting cards, first-aid necessities, and various other sundries.

He'd employed many people over the years and enjoyed them all. His main cashier was still there. Old Margaret Kreit. She was in her thirties when he hired her and was now approaching her seventies; she knew everything there was to know about the goings-on at the pharmacy. Her husband passed away in 1929, so she'd been a widow for quite some time. There were those who thought she should set her hat for Tom Lyons now that his wife had passed away, but she told them all she had no hat to set out, it was gone and buried with Arnie the day he died.

Tom Jr. owned the pharmacy now, but old Tom still went in on most days, sat on a barstool, and ordered a malted milkshake, then spoke to customers or teased the soda jerk, young Don Fortney. Don was red-haired, freckled, and had about a hundred and twenty pounds on his six-foot frame. Snaggletoothed, his eyes peering from behind thick lenses that made them look like green marbles, he had a good smile and an even better sense of humor.

Tom had a few great employees in his time, boys just like Don and a few women who'd done their jobs well. He never could place his finger on what separated the excellent workers from the good ones, but at the very least, they were willing to learn, focused, and never shirked any duty, no matter how hard.

He watched Oba, wondering what went on in his head, knew Tom Jr. had a sign out. HELP WANTED. But he had misgivings about this one, for sure.

He'd hate to have him in close proximity to any of the customers, with that lean, hungry look and the perpetual scowl.

"Would you like to do something this afternoon?" he asked.

"Not really."

"You're still pretty stiff and sore?"

"Yeah."

"Why'd you jump off the train?"

"I was hungry."

"If you don't mind my asking, what were you doing on that train?"

"Getting away."

"Away from what?"

"It's a long story."

"I want to hear the long story."

Oba eyed him with all the anger he could muster. Nosy old man. That was the trouble with old people. They didn't have a thing to do except sit around and be curious about everything, ask stupid questions that was none of their business. This old man was getting on his nerves.

"You don't want to talk, you don't have to," he said.

"I don't want to."

"Okay. Here, give me that shirt. On me, it looks great, but its three sizes too big for you. I got a couple T-shirts from Tom's boys."

He got up, handed Oba the folded shirts, and waited.

"Mind if I go to the bedroom to change?" Oba asked, blinking rapidly.

"Not at all."

When he returned, he looked much better, more like a normal teenaged boy.

"So if you don't want to talk about your past, do you think it's fair for me to take you in? I mean, you could have killed someone, running from the law. You could be a dangerous criminal or worse. I have no way of knowing whether this was a smart move on my part. You know you'll have to find a job, right? Or go back to school."

"I'm done with school."

"Oh, how's that if you're not eighteen?"

"I am. Almost."

"You didn't graduate."

"Amish kids don't go to twelve grades."

"How much schooling did you have?"

"Eight years."

Tom pursed his lips, arched his eyebrows. "That enough?"

"Yeah."

Tom poured himself a cup of coffee, offered one to Oba, who shook his head. He brought out the rest of the cake, two plates and forks, and cut a sizable chunk for Oba and one for himself.

"Okay. So if you're not a criminal, where are you from?"

"Ohio. My parents drowned in a flooded river."

"The truth?"

"Yes."

Tom gave a low whistle. "That's tough."

"It was."

"How old were you?"

"Ten."

"That's hard."

"Yeah. So we went to my uncle and aunt in Arkansas."

Tom waited.

"We. My sister May and I."

Suddenly he got up, lifted his arms, and pulled the T-shirt up over his head, an unexpected gesture that caused Tom to sit up straight in his chair. Oba was almost as surprised at himself as Tom was. What was he doing, already sharing his secrets with this old man?

Oba turned his back, waited, then said that's what he ran away from.

Tom was used to hearing sad stories, even gruesome ones, but he had never experienced a sight quite like this. He drew in a deep breath to steady himself but said nothing.

"My uncle didn't like me," Oba said.

The thin young back was sinewy with muscle, the skin tanned by days in the blistering Arkansas heat. It was a beautiful back, on a strong young boy, hopelessly lacerated and disfigured by the uncle's weapon of choice.

Tom was deeply moved. Taking another breath, he steadied his voice and said, "I guess you won't be wanting to go back."

"No. Not for me. But I care about May. I deserted her."

"Your sister?"

Oba nodded.

"Does he beat your sister?"

"If he did, I didn't know about it."

Tom said nothing. Hoped it wasn't the other. Then he asked, "Would you go back to get her if you could?"

"Of course. If she'd come with me."

Tom looked up. "She might not?"

Oba shrugged. "She thinks if she gives in and obeys perfectly, Melvin will change, become a better man."

"Melvin is the uncle?"

"Yes."

"Do you think so?"

"No."

"His wife is alive? They have children?"

"Yes. Three boys."

"Would you return, then, to help your sister?"

"I would. But first I need to make some money. I don't want to ride the rails again."

Next thing he knew, Oba was brought before Tom Jr. and introduced to his two boys, Randy and Brian.

He secured a position at the pharmacy, stocking shelves, cleaning, carrying customers' orders to their cars; he was told to greet customers only when they addressed him, to use the string mop after hours, and to help someone find an item on the shelves when they asked.

Tom Jr. was a replica of his father, except for the well-rounded stomach and a different pair of glasses. The boys were still in school, and his wife Elaine had her own cake-decorating business she operated from her kitchen. She was very pretty, much too young-looking to have two sons, and the first time she smiled at him, Oba blushed like an idiot, then felt all the shame and self-hatred start anew.

He was still Oba Miller, the orphan who deserted his sister, who was whipped and beaten until his back looked like the railroad tracks he'd escaped on, and now he was shamefully attracted to pretty girls and young women, which was a sin—one he would have to overcome or go to hell, the way Melvin told him.

He learned to turn his back without ogling the girls when they came in. He kept a tight rein on his wandering eyes, wished for blinders even, but he finally came to realize most of this was normal. He observed a group of boys hanging out of a slowly moving car, whistling at two girls who seemed to be flattered, putting their hands to their mouths and giggling, flouncing their skirts like umbrellas.

He was glad to be like other people, no longer chained to the long hair, the straw hat, the patched broadfall trousers, the muddy bare feet, and the fear of being mocked. Here in Bridgeport, California, he would get his start in the world, make something of himself. He would learn how to save money, how to better himself, if he could.

He wondered, sometimes, if he should be afraid of having left the Amish way of life. He'd had only dead parents, uncaring relatives, and a violent uncle to teach him that lifestyle, although there were others. Leonard Yoder and his wife had done their Christian duty, but they had never really dug deep enough to uncover the cold, hard truth. But then, it was the way of it. These things were not to be spoken of. If a man chose to beat his children then he was entitled to that, the Old Testament agreeing with him. Steeped in the law, to spare the rod was indeed shameful; a spoiled child was an ill light to the community, so corporal punishment was meted out with regularity.

But to be whipped and beaten till the scars crisscrossed his back could hardly be justified by any scripture, no matter how old. Neither could he put out the flame of his consuming hatred toward Melvin.

Oba never read his Bible. Even before fleeing, he questioned a loving God who cared about him; he refused to attend Tom's church.

No matter how pretty the church, no matter how many stained glass windows colorfully portrayed Christ in Gethsemane or Christ on the cross, he wanted none of it.

Tom in his old age was filled with wisdom and did not push the issue, knowing he could not force Oba to accept Christ, allow His forgiveness to heal the hatred.

Oba immersed himself in the fascinating world of pharmaceuticals. He took an avid interest in the powders and potions that were mixed at the back of the counter. He read textbooks from the library, studied medicine and healing methods of old, kept to himself through that first winter in California, when the nights were cold but the days surprisingly pleasant. He loved the little ranch house, the freshly painted walls, and the gleaming kitchen floor after he polished it with wax.

He still had moments of terrible temper, but mostly he was slowly learning to trust Tom, day by day, as he realized he was always the same. He was kind, friendly, but if the need arose, he could be firm.

Oba was not allowed to run with the town boys that drove fast cars and drank beer. If he wanted to do that, it wouldn't be while he lived under Tom's roof, which so far, Oba had respected.

The younger Tom's house was just across the road from the older Tom's place. It was set on a picturesque angle against a backdrop of deciduous trees, an incline of gentle rolling land falling away on either side. It was painted white, with heavy black shutters on either side of large many-paned windows, yews and arborvitae planted in neat rows around the perimeter, cut to attractive globes. The front porch pillars were sturdy round posts that flared to a greater circumference on the bottom, where they rested on a stone foundation. In winter, great, heavy wreaths were hung from every doorway, ropes of juniper and spruce were wound around the porch pillars, and candles burned in every window.

Oba had never seen such opulence, such flagrant generosity of money and presents and spirit. He shrank at the gaily jostling crowd, the happy voices calling "Merry Christmas!"

All the waste, the strange food and drinks bought and stock-piled, created an unrest, a certain fear that none of this was meant to be.

He took to his room, refused to help with the cookie baking, rudely told Tom it was women's work, slammed his bedroom door, and stayed in his room. He couldn't understand his own sense of helplessness in the face of all this good cheer, the merry-making like an overdose of an over-sugared drink.

He felt left out, alone, wished Christmas to be past. He could deal with sadness and disappointment better than he could deal with this abundance of joy and goodwill.

By the time New Year's Day arrived, Oba seemed to have drawn himself out of his dark place. He'd kept up his work at the pharmacy, and Tom allowed himself to relax, thankful to see he'd returned to his normal self. But when Tom mentioned the evening's party at his son's house, the dark cloud that obscured the light in Oba's eyes was too obvious, so he allowed Oba the luxury of declining. Tom went to the party alone, but he couldn't enjoy the celebration, worried as he was about the boy.

Many troubled young men couldn't experience joy the way other people could freely give and receive, wish others well, accept praise and congratulations, but he had never seen this level of gloom at the holidays.

Oba sat on his bed in the room that had become a haven, a place where he was locked up, safely hidden from prying eyes and smiling faces, from expressions of cheer and good wishes that strangled him.

It was all he could do to stay in the room, the room that swarmed and hummed in his ears like hundreds of fire ants, a sound that made his heart beat twice as fast, the panic pushing the pounding into his head until he thought he might explode. Wracked with a painful sense of foreboding, he had the idea that he would surely die a wretched, miserable person, and it kept him isolated on New Year's Day.

An increasing sense of being misplaced occupied most of his thoughts. The pharmacy was the only place he could forget the feeling of imposing on others, of being in the wrong house at the wrong time, wearing someone else's clothing, and eating someone else's food.

How did one go about securing a future?

He needed to be on his own. He needed his own place, then send for May. If he could have May with him, everything would be right.

None of this was possible without money, of course, so his first resolution was to keep working all the hours he possibly could. He would keep every dime in the top drawer of his dresser and wait until he had enough.

He opened his bedroom door, took a breath of much-needed air, and walked slowly down the hallway to the kitchen. He walked over to the sink and gazed at the lights from the windows of the big house where the New Year's party was going full swing. He thought of the food and drinks, the decorations and stupid party hats, the laughter and dancing, and wondered how these people could manage to be Christians when God would surely disapprove of such luxuries.

Melvin had often told him to be hardworking, sober, dressed in plain clothes, and to turn away from all manner of lusts of the eyes and the flesh; he was to stay on the straight and narrow path, the one to Heaven. Broad is the way to hell, full of excess and pleasure.

Even as the whip came down, he'd extolled this mantra, over and over, the rebellion in Oba refusing to accept any of it. And yet, when he was alone, these sayings were like signposts in his head, black-and-white warnings that glared at him like the great yellow eyes of a crow. Confusion warred with unacceptance of Melvin's words and the obvious love and cheer so grandly displayed at the big house. These Christians that reveled in Christ's birth, that laughed and hugged and kissed and piled into automobiles to celebrate Jesus' birth at their church with smooth wooden pews and carpeted walkways.

For Oba, it was easier to draw away from God, deny His existence if he had to. For which God was the right one? The exacting God who would cast one into hell for any sin? Or the God who smiled down on people with benevolence and grace?

Better to let it go.

He turned away from the window, stood in the middle of the kitchen, and felt the tightening in his chest, like a strangulation. He struggled to breathe, felt the nausea rise in his throat. He felt a strong inclination to get away from these four walls that pressed in on him, the ceiling that would pop and creak, a crack appearing, then elongating until a jagged portion fell in, then another. The ceiling joists would tear loose from the walls, the nails pulled out with a high screech, before crashing on his head. The electrical wires would be torn, igniting, turning the ranch house into an inferno in which he would be trapped.

His anxiety mounted until he sat down on the edge of a chair, his head clasped in his hands, his breath coming in rasping sounds, pure terror keeping him from fleeing into the cold night.

This was how Tom found him before the clock struck the hour after midnight. Pale, sweating, his eyes dark pools of misery, his hands clenching and unclenching, he was obviously in a state of distress.

Slowly, Tom pulled out a chair and lowered himself into it, before leaning forward to address him. "Oba."

Between ragged breaths came a quiet "What?"

"Is there something I can do to help?"

"No. I don't know."

"Can you explain?"

"No."

"Perhaps you want to try."

"I don't."

Tom waited, then got up to heat milk in a saucepan; he added cocoa powder and sugar, then brought a mug to Oba, who looked up with frightened eyes.

"Drink this."

Oba shook his head, pushed the cup away.

So he waited.

Finally, with an air of resignation, Tom drew himself up and said the hour was late, he was beyond weary and bade him goodnight.

"Wait."

Tom stopped, but did not turn around.

"I can't stay here. I shouldn't be here. I need to go away, find my own place."

Slowly, Tom turned, waited before more words tumbled from Oba's tortured spirit.

"I want to find a place I can afford, then find my sister. I have to find her, don't you see? I can't be here with all this . . . this pleasure and stuff, this undeserved goodness from people who have no idea how rotten I am. I'm horrible on the inside, leaving May with Melvin and Gertie and that awful farm."

His words became garbled as his handsome young face was twisted into a grimace of the most intense despair, his eyes closing as the tears were squeezed out against his will.

"I shouldn't have done it," he ground out. "I should have stayed. May will never stand up for herself, and I'm afraid for her."

His sobs continued as Tom stood quietly.

"I've told you before, we can take a train to Arkansas," he said finally.

"No, no. We can't. I can't do that. I can't ask you to pay. I'll save my money."

Tom knew what he was being paid, knew, too, the amount of time that would elapse before Oba would have enough to even have the hope of beginning the journey.

"Oba, you've been through this before. Why don't you accept if you feel your sister may be in danger? We could just go and see. Maybe she's already found a way to leave."

Suddenly, an outburst from Oba put the whole picture into perspective. No, she wouldn't leave. That was the point, he shouted. He stalked the perimeter of the kitchen like a caged lion, waved his arms, and shouted obscenities, until Tom was afraid for the suffering young man.

When he slowed and sat in his chair, panting, Tom put a hand on his shoulder and told him to get some rest, things could be worked out in the morning.

Chapter 13

After her night with Clinton Brown, May seemed to experience a surge of energy and hope. She laughed at Leviticus when he showed her a frozen snowball packed tightly to ambush Enos, she hummed below her breath as she ironed Melvin's shirts. She took to gazing out of the kitchen window, the paring knife in her hand falling into the potatoes she had been peeling, as she relived her time with the one she loved.

Yes, loved.

She loved Clinton Brown with every fiber of her being; she loved him with a freedom of expression that had bound them together as they shared a magical conversation of discovered and acknowledged love. In her short life, May had never imagined the joy of physical touch, the glorious surge of happiness that was like the ripples along the river when the ferry passed through. Over and over, the happiness rose in her heart. Nothing could take it away; nothing could ever undo the realization that God had prepared this love, that not all men were cruel and possessive.

Oh, Clinton, my beautiful man, she thought to herself.

Beneath the cresting waves of her own secret paradise began the undertow of her upbringing, the beliefs and traditions of her elders, the lengthy church services that instilled in her the fear of God and respect of men.

To be with Clinton meant leaving the group of Amish who knew her, leaving Melvin and the boys. To be with him would be a black mark on both of them in all of society, this she knew as well. When she felt sure, she was giddy with happiness, only to be dragged down by sound reasoning.

They had promised each other to stay apart.

It was not safe to be seen. They would be wise, give it at least till springtime, if she felt it was alright to stay with Melvin. May had taken her time but gave him an answer that seemed to satisfy him. Yes, it was best, and yes, she could certainly stay. Hadn't she done it all these years?

Melvin watched her with narrowed eyes, noticed the heightened color in her cheeks, the unusual sparkle in her eyes as she moved on feet as light as a feather, moved from room to room with a song on her lips.

He no longer praised her cooking, told her he didn't like his eggs fried as hard as she had been frying them. When that didn't subdue her the way he had hoped, he cornered her in the washhouse when the boys were at school, pinned her against the wall with the palms of his hands on either side of her head, his face just inches from hers.

She lowered her eyes, refused to look at him. She knew all too well the greasy strands of dark hair that fell below his ears and over his cheeks, the scraggly beard that was always uncombed and unwashed.

"Miss High-and-Mighty these days, aren't we?"

She kept her eyes lowered.

"Look at me."

She would not.

"Look at me, I said."

When she obeyed, her eyes were half-open, her dark gaze penetrating the distance above his shoulder.

"You dare disobey me, May, you will regret it. Now tell me, what's going on with you these days? Did someone ask you?"

She shook her head.

"I don't believe it."

Again, she shook her head.

"Tell me."

"No. No one did."

He lowered his face even farther, until his breath wafted across her face, the smell of yellow teeth and onions fried into his breakfast potatoes.

"Just make sure no one ever does. You are my maid, and I have no intention of setting you free."

She nodded, a wave of revulsion so strong it required all the effort she could muster not to retch at his white, pockmarked face.

He left her then, trembling against the wall, but a new spirit of strength rose in her, buoyed by the knowledge that there was something better, something new in her life, that even Melvin could not destroy by his control of her.

She was sent to the feed mill with only Leviticus to accompany her, Ammon and Enos having chores of their own. Seated on the high spring-wagon seat, the cold wind whipping the edge of her shawl away from her gloved hands, she felt a sense of optimism watching the red-tailed hawk gliding on drafts of air overhead. The holly trees were filled with brilliant red berries, picturesque against the blue winter sky with the fluffy white clouds that changed patterns and shapes according to the wind's direction.

Slivers of ice formed a pattern in the mud holes, the horse's hooves separating them easily, rearranging other hoof prints in the cold, red mud. The sun was shining. Leviticus was beside her, and Clinton Brown's love was in safekeeping, to be taken out occasionally and remembered with a reverent awe, something too close to worship, she knew.

"The horse has to pull hard, the way the mud sticks on the wheels," Leviticus observed.

"Yes. But not much to do about it."

"Dat says they need to pave more roads."

"I imagine they will someday."

"I'm not going to grow cotton when I'm old."

"You aren't?"

"No. I'm going to move to Ohio."

"And what will you do there?"

"Raise hogs. I love our pigs."

May smiled to herself, then looked down at Leviticus, with his straight brown hair and torn felt hat smashed down below his eyebrows, his cherubic grin with the deep dimple in his chin. Somewhere in his lineage he had acquired a sweet disposition and a quick mind that seemed to decipher a situation with the wisdom of one much more advanced in years.

Suddenly he asked, "How old are you?"

"I'm sixteen."

"That's old."

Oh, if he only knew how old those sixteen years were, but she smiled.

"Not that old."

She pulled on the right rein to draw the team to the side of the road as an approaching vehicle came chugging through the mud. She lifted a gloved hand in response to the driver's friendly wave, then drew on the left rein to return the horse to its position.

"Why don't Amish people drive cars?" he asked, buttoning the top button of his overcoat.

"Oh, they're too worldly. Too modern. We should always remember to keep the *ordnung* our ministers lay before us. It is for the good of our souls."

"Is it? Well, I'm going to drive an automobile."

"Oh, now, Leviticus." She smiled at his pronunciation. Audomobeel.

"I'm going to drive a Dodge, white and silver."

"Really? Why is that?"

"I don't know for sure."

At the feed mill, May placed her order and waited, her back turned to the men that normally inhabited the front room. They were seated on wooden barrels with a checkerboard between them or sprawled across bulging bags of feed, a variety of tobacco being smoked in corncob pipes or chewed in plugs. Spittoons were placed at handy locations, although May had never seen anyone actually hit them, only heard the "whit" sound of the projected stream of tobacco juice.

She said a quiet hello to Albert Troyer and two of his daughters, nodded to the feed store owner in acknowledgement of her purchases, then turned to leave, her eyes searching the circle of men, resting longer than usual on the colored men, longing for the sight of Clinton Brown.

But, of course, he had no business at the feed store, living in town the way he did. What was the street called?

McKinley. Or was it Ash?

For a moment, she wanted to drive the team through the town, find the street, search for the house.

But she knew it would not be wise.

After her display of inner happiness and well-being, Melvin took it on himself to ferret out the reason, waylaying her at the slightest opportunity, making suggestions, and when she would not comply, he became withdrawn, bitter.

Her inability to divulge any secret, real or imagined, seemed to create frustration to the point of distraction. He did not want this new May, the glowing face that radiated an inner light, one he had not devised by himself.

So he made an effort at reducing this strange glow.

"Aren't you just the ticket, walking around here with your head in the clouds?" he said to her at the supper table.

Ammon and Enos grinned, then watched her face with shrew eyes.

When she didn't answer, they relished the outcome, watched their father's face for signs of anger.

"You might come down to earth and fry these potatoes with more lard."

Still no answer.

Then, "Cat got your tongue?"

Titters from the boys.

"Well, you may as well get off your high horse, young lady. You'll be here till you're twenty-one, no doubt about that. Unless you disappear the way Oba did. You ever hear from him?"

"No."

"That's good. He better not set foot on this property again, or he'll wish he hadn't. He never could give up to authority and still can't, likely. That attitude will land him in jail, sure as nothing. You mark my words, boys. Disobedience brings a curse."

Leviticus swallowed his bread, watched his father's face with frightened eyes. May watched him, gave him a reassuring smile, before biting off a corner of her own slice of bread; she tried not to think of five more years of this. She often wondered about Oba, prayed for him every morning and night, but remained in a state of resignation—but only for lack of courage.

She sat by the fire on a cold, rainy day in February, a few months after her meeting with Clinton Brown, shelling ear corn after it had been roasted in the oven. The aroma of the roasted ears always reminded her of home, the times when she helped her mother shell the corn, preparing it for the grinder to make cornmeal. They would sing songs, talk about the day spent at school, and sometimes she would teach her to whistle, to imitate the sounds of the birds that twittered and chirped around the birdfeeder in the yard.

It all seemed so far away, so distant now. She couldn't conjure her mother's face anymore, not really, and for this, she was often sad. After Oba left, there had been no one to love, no one who made her feel cherished, so she spent her own affections on Leviticus, the darling of the family.

Whether she missed Gertie had never been a question, but still she tried to remember her as a stepmother who took them in when no one else would.

She supposed her life had been as good as it possibly could be after they were sent to Arkansas—except for Melvin.

And now there was Clinton Brown, the one person she longed to see, to hear the lovely velvety voice lilting his phrases. She loved the way he sometimes rolled his Rs and sometimes eliminated them alto-gether, and she loved his long slender fingers with the callused palms from cutting the cane.

Why was it so wrong? Why was it forbidden when he was the kindest, most gentle person she had ever known? Over and over, she dwelt on this question, searched her Bible continuously for answers, but always came away with the unsettled question like a wound con-stantly chafed.

Why did a set of rules that set you apart from most people matter so much? You could no more help being born into the Amish culture than you could help being born with dark skin. Did that mean you had no choice but to remain under that certain set of rules, being born into them?

She cut her finger on the sharp edge of a knife, blistered her thumb on a hot ear of corn, her thoughts whirling around in her head as restless as the sea. She knew what her mother would say, knew the kind words of her father.

But what a horrible example in Melvin, one who was devoutly obedient to the Amish church but held Christian clause as mere after-thoughts, who twisted the Scripture that was holy into a set of rules written by his own burning wants. She felt contempt, a deep loathing; she was trampled and downtrodden by the hatred that ran rampant if she allowed it.

And how not to allow it?

By the time she would reach the age of twenty-one, she would be eighty-one in spirit, still knowing she must forgive, must for-get, and never being able to accomplish it. A deep depression often showed her ways to end it all, another consequence of her existence, being obedient, always hoping for change, never facing reality, ever.

But there was nothing to be done about any of this, no matter how her thoughts roiled within her. She read her Bible often, with a need to find grace and purity and forgiveness. She searched every book in the New Testament for ways around the restrictions where their—hers and Clinton's—relationship was concerned, but she always came away with an inner sense of doom.

How could she, one lone young woman, go up against the elders, the entire ministry in Arkansas? She couldn't, not without condemnation.

She would be labeled from the day she left with Clinton. The *ungehorsam* (disobedient). The loose girl with no moral compass, given over to the world as a deserter of the faith. An outcast of society.

She knew she could not face the consequences yet. She was legally too young, too inexperienced with her love, there were simply too many obstacles in her way.

And yet, Oba had accomplished it. He had broken away, made a life of his own. Or so she thought, hoped, but had no reason to believe this was true either. She missed him with an almost physical ache.

When an early spring was heralded by the warbling call of the red-winged blackbird, May threw open the attic windows and began the spring housecleaning, plying broom and rag with bucket after bucket of soapy water. She washed walls and windows until they gleamed, watched the fish crane flap its insolent way past the house on its way to the swamp to find its dinner. Bluebirds twittered as they carried bits of hay or twine to build a nest in the bird box Enos had made during the winter.

She showed this to him, which brought a smile to his face, a genuine moment of pride and understanding between them. The apple trees blossomed, giving off their heady aroma, and May gathered armloads of the flowers to put in a vase on the table in the living room. She decided to mow the yard down by the apple trees, using a scythe and finishing up with the reel mower, then stood to survey her work, satisfied with her efforts.

It was the time of day when the sinking of the sun casts a warm sheen like liquid gold over everything, making the white apple blossoms appear yellow, turning her gray dress into a golden color as well.

From the pine trees, a sharp whistle.

Her head turned quickly, she caught sight of his dark face.

Without a thought for her safety, she abandoned the mower and the scythe, ran straight down the row of apple trees ablaze with the fiery sun and into his arms.

"Clinton. Clinton."

"My May. My lovely girl."

How many forbidden kisses? How many weeks and months of thinking of this moment? No matter they were in their work clothes, their hair uncombed, bodies unwashed. They were together in the safety of the dark pines, night was coming on, and they would be safe.

The floor of the pine forest was perfect for sitting side by side, the scent of the needles pungent with every move they made.

There was so much to say, so much to talk about.

"I'm leaving in two weeks. There's jobs in Louisiana, planting. After that, I follow the cane."

May sighed, a deep resigned expulsion of breath that signified far more than empty words.

"You'll miss me?"

"You know I will."

"I'll be back."

"Will you?"

"You say that as if you don't believe me."

"I do believe you. But even then, nothing will really be changed."

The darkness obscured his face, but she felt him stiffen, draw back. "You don't believe we can ever be together?"

"I want to say I do, Clinton, but how can it ever be right?"

"How can it be wrong? If two people love each other, doesn't love trump everything?"

May pictured books stacked with rules and traditions, more books filled with dark skin and African culture, both histories of the past, both steeped in rights and wrongs; another stack of books that was the prevailing white authority handed down through the decades. She wanted to believe what he said, but how could she when her stack of books meant so much?

"But how do we know there is any right in this? We can't. I am definitely not following the way of tradition, neither am I being true to myself. I could never make a good wife, with all this guilt hanging over my head."

"You just don't get it, do you?" he asked finally.

"I guess not," she said, in a small voice.

"You'd rather listen to your sense of duty, right? You'd rather stay with a man who is . . . well, I won't say what he is. Look. I was going to ask you to go to Louisiana with me, but I can see you won't. So I'll go, save my money for you. So we can get away. Someday, if God wills, we'll be together. I have never once put you out of my heart since the day we met, and I won't let you go until I have no choice, which is you telling me you won't go with me."

"I don't know if I can ever do that."

"I'll give you a long time to think about. It will be late fall when I come back."

He gathered her back into his arms, where she stayed until the night creatures scurried through the pines and the barred owl's eerie calls echoed weirdly from branch to branch. He sighed and knew everything he had ever given up had been nothing compared to this.

Almost, she simply walked away from the farm, slipped through the pines and stayed with him, knocked over every stack of books in her way. The desire to do so was so close she could feel her breathing accelerate, listen to the pounding of her heart. Their last embrace, their last kiss mingled with both of their tears, the salt taste like a healing balm.

"I can't let you go," she whispered brokenly.

That proved to be the hardest trial of all, simply letting go, letting God control the long hot summer months, all the unexpected dangers of cutting cane, and for her, a different kind of danger, but no less ominous.

He clung to her, and she to him.

Finally, it was she who broke away, who turned away blinded by her tears, and there was nothing left for him but to find his way back to his bicycle in the black night, as black as the hole in his heart made by her absence.

In the morning, May was unaware of the danger they had so narrowly escaped until Leviticus innocently mentioned the person he'd noticed close to the apple trees in the backyard.

They were seated at the breakfast table, the morning sun bringing early light to the white tablecloth, the simple white cabinets and the gleaming floor that was chipped and dented, but perfectly cleaned and waxed. There were fried eggs and liverwurst, stewed crackers, and stewed tomato gravy, which had all of Melvin's attention as he buttered a piece of toast.

May looked up sharply, her eyes dark with fear, then quickly lowered them when Melvin laid down his butter knife, his glance going around the table, eyes drawn in dark suspicion. May felt his eyes on her, felt the buzzing menace like the hovering of an angry hornet.

"What?" he asked.

"I think it was a colored person, really."

"What? You mean to tell me that there is someone lurking around our property? Likely a thief. Some person who is too lazy to work, figures he'll nip a couple tools and sell them down at the pawnshop."

His view of Clinton's people was her saving grace. He esteemed them far below himself, his children, or May, never imagining the forbidden meetings she had accomplished. Besides being sharecroppers, laborers, turning a good profit for himself, he deemed they were all worthless. Thieves, lazy slackers.

"I better replace the lock on the tool shed, if some darky is lurking around here. He ever shows his face, he'll be peppered with buckshot."

May finished her tea, bowed her head for the after-breakfast prayer, then slipped to her knees with Melvin and the boys as he read the morning prayer from the small German prayer book. She listened as his voice rippled along the words, sacred words in the language of the forefathers, and thought there must be some good in every person, no matter how vile, to be able to kneel by his kitchen chair every morning and evening as regularly as the rising and the setting of the sun.

She rose, finished packing the tin lunch buckets, setting them in a row on the cleared table before setting the dishpan in the sink, running the cold water and adding hot water from the teakettle.

She washed dishes methodically, wiping her cloth across a plate long after it was clean, weighing her love for Clinton Brown on the scale of right or wrong. She knew what was right.

The right thing to do was to send him to the sugar cane with a flat, stern refusal to see him ever again, to return to this house where she had been placed by her elders. This house that was infused by so much that was wrong, so much completely out of anyone's knowledge, except her own bitter, broken existence.

Was one wrong so much worse than the other?

If one chose the better of two wrongs, did that make it right?

And there were the boys. How would they ever manage without her?

She wrung out the dishcloth, hung it on its rack by the door, smoothed the apron down over her slim hips, and sighed. There was ironing, a stack of denim trousers to be mended, but she was no good at that, the Singer sewing machine constantly eluding her efforts. She longed for a mother to sit with her, guide her along as she plied the patches beneath the device where the needle came up and down as her foot pressed on the treadle.

She imagined Sadie Yoder, Sarah Weaver, anyone, to come sit with her as she patiently learned to maneuver the fabric the way she'd watched her mother expertly turn at the corner, lift the small lever along the back to raise the needle. She found herself weeping quietly, longing to see her mother one more time, tell her about her life here with Melvin and the boys. Perhaps Albert Troyer's wife, Suvilla, would agree to come do the mending, would sit and listen as she poured out her sordid tale of servitude and the all-encompassing loneliness and betrayal. To have someone, anyone, to talk to, to give advice, to care would be such a luxury.

So she let go of the thought.

Troubles were hidden away. The mark of a strong character was to bear whatever it was that life threw at you, no matter how hard. She had read it in her Bible only the night before, how Jesus would willingly take the opposite side of the yoke you carried, and together, it would become lighter, more easily managed. All she needed to do was to keep the faith, keep the hope of salvation alive. Someday, some glad day, there would be redemption from this world, where hidden sin was brought to light, where the Savior would pardon everything that had been thrust upon her.

Would He pardon the choice she made if it was the wrong one, or would she always reap in sorrow if she chose to leave with Clinton Brown?

But she knew deep within, her choice had already been made.

For a long time, she stared unseeing through the kitchen window, before turning to lift the stack of torn denim trousers, draw up a chair, and thread the needle on the sewing machine.

When the boys came in to pick up their lunchboxes, it was Leviticus who came over to the sewing machine, touched her shoulder and said, "Goodbye, Mam."

She turned to him with a smile and told him to have a good day at school, saw the light of understanding that passed between them, the decision to stay one more day embedded in her heart.

CHAPTER 14

In the morning, nothing was worked out, Oba sullen and unresponsive, Tom hovering uneasily in the kitchen while he prepared scrambled eggs and bacon. Silence seemed to be what was required of him, so he let any questions he had prepared dissolve in the air. Tom was practiced in the ways of kids like Oba, knew time was often the greatest healer. He believed Oba was thrown into his life for a reason, and his prayers intensified as the winter months wore on.

Oba never stopped saving money, and he never forgot about May. His days at the pharmacy filled his head with customer service, listening to all manner of conversations, yet he befriended no one, not even kindly old Margaret Kreit, who brought him cupcakes and chocolate cookies, who questioned him about his church attendance and clucked in dismay when he told her he didn't believe in God.

Tom told her he probably had at some point in his young life, where he was from, and to what religious sect he belonged. Margaret sat on a red barstool at the lunch counter like a prim little hen, her white hair permed and curled around her small face while she slanted a look of incredulity at Tom, then gave a low whistle.

"Now, Tom, you really believe that hogwash?"

"I do. I think the boy is being truthful."

"And what makes you think that?"

She smiled at the soda jerk when he placed a malted milkshake in front of her, then handed her a paper straw.

"Thank you, Don."

"You're welcome."

"I'll have one of those, please," Tom said, nodding toward the shake, which Margaret seemed to be enjoying immensely.

"Oh you," she said, jabbing an elbow into his side.

He smiled into her watery blue eyes and thought they were the color of the larkspur that grew in his garden. Not every woman in her seventies could perch on a barstool with her trim legs tucked under her like a much younger woman.

"So this, this Oba . . ."

"Shh. There he is."

Oba was carrying a stack of cardboard boxes, filled with dental items from Colgate, which he almost dropped when Tom called his name.

"Wh . . . what?" he asked, his eyes wide with alarm.

"Come over here. Don, get another malted for Oba, please?"

"Sit down."

Margaret turned her barstool to acknowledge him as he slid into it.

"You have been working hard," she observed.

No answer, only a stiffening of his shoulders, a lift of his finely molded chin.

Margaret had often admired the young man, with the large dark eyes and the light blond hair, his fine features twisted into a hard demeanor that made him appear ominous. The kind of youth who usually repelled an old lady like her, the kind who would think nothing of snatching a purse out of fingers weakened by age and arthritis.

"I am speaking to you," she said quietly.

He turned, shrugged his shoulders, and started to walk away.

"Hey. I ordered a milkshake for you."

There was a mere flicker of hesitation, before he walked back to the store room, pushed open the swinging door, and disappeared.

Margaret looked at Tom, then swung the barstool and slid off, walked back to the swinging door, and disappeared. Tom thought he should intervene, so he followed her. Don Fortney brought two malted milkshakes and set them on the now-empty counter, looked at the swinging door and shrugged his shoulders.

"Oba!" Margaret shouted.

There was no answer.

"Oba Miller, I know you're in here. You need to learn some manners and be appreciative when someone orders you a drink. Now get out here and be nice."

Tom placed a hand on her arm.

"Won't do any good. Sorry."

Oba crouched behind a stack of boxes, his ears burning with shame and his eyes sizzling with anger. That old lady was coming too close, asking too many questions. There was no way he was going to be seated with both of them, that idiot Don Fortney watching him drink a milkshake he hadn't paid for, knowing he didn't know how to suck up the thick creamy concoction because he'd never had one.

He'd never let Don see the pathetic backwoods Arkansas hick he really was. There were certain lines he wouldn't cross, and to appear inadequate was one of them. No one would ever view the injured little boy who lived beneath the hard crust he used to protect himself.

"Oba!"

This wasn't working. It was time to call her bluff.

"What do you want?" he asked, as irritably as he could, stepped out from his hiding place and turned in the direction of the querulous old voice.

"We got you a malted shake. Now come on out here and drink it."

"I don't want it."

"Sure you do."

"I guess I know if I want it or not."

"Okay, be that way. Come on, Tom."

Tom looked at Oba. Oba looked back at him, and the slightest understanding passed between them.

He went back to work then, wanting the milkshake in the worst way, but never once giving into the fact that he did. He opened boxes of toothpaste and toothbrushes, stacked them neatly in piles, used the palm of his hand to create flawless stacks, and stood back to survey the shelves afterward.

He read labels, shook bottles of aspirin, and wondered how someone went about manufacturing pills and what exactly were the ingredients that actually took away pain. He had never taken an aspirin, had never known about them before the pharmacy.

But he could have used them many times.

The bell above the door tinkled out the arrival of another customer, a middle-aged lady in a brilliant floral dress, her belt tightened around her ample waist.

She greeted Oba with a sniff, walked to the counter, and said hello to Margaret with a honeyed voice, then turned to Tom with sugar fairly dripping from her tone. The conversation found its way into Oba's jealousy, the barren, unloved part of him who hated everyone that ignored him and adored others. The part that floundered on dry banks like a creature of the sea who needed water to stay alive.

Stupid woman. He hated her dress, her wide hips, her obnoxious eye glasses. He hated Don when he called out, "Good morning, Mrs. Wilson. How's Mr. Wilson?"

"Oh well, he'd be in here himself if he could. He eats too many sweets having the diabetes and all, now he's got a sore on his leg. Every step pains him so bad, but nothing I can do about it."

"Tell him I said hello."

"Certainly."

Oba was overwhelmed by longing for the milkshake that sat melting on the counter. He hadn't eaten since breakfast, and it wasn't lunchtime yet, so perhaps he could slip over to the counter and snatch it away before anyone noticed.

He stepped out from the aisle, turned toward the counter, saw the absence of the sweet drink, then watched as Don Fortney lifted it behind the grill and drank it down.

He sat on his bed, counting his pile of cash.

Almost two hundred dollars, not quite. One hundred and ninety-three. He exulted in his stash of bills and recounted to make sure. He wanted to write to May, tell her to be ready on a certain day, but he knew there was no possibility of the letter reaching her without Melvin getting to it first. And who would know the outcome?

He replaced the cash, bit down hard on his lower lip, crossed his arms over his chest, and felt the tingling of his scars. They would always be there, a physical reminder of his past, his rebellion and bad judgment, his exploited innocence when the fault was none of his own.

How to eliminate these times? How did one go about forgetting? If he lived to be a hundred, he would never forget, and yet you couldn't get into Heaven without forgiveness.

Much better to forget about Heaven and God and, especially, to forget about hell. Perhaps none of it was true.

He lay back on his bed, his hands crossed on his chest, and stared at the ceiling. He thought of his existence here with Tom and knew he could never make the grade. At first, he'd imagined himself a pharmacist, perhaps someday a doctor. But who was he kidding?

He has no education and certainly no money for it either. He knew nothing, never would. He felt silly, loathed himself for reading textbooks, propelled by some dash of grand thinking that would never be sufficient.

A soft knock on his door.

"What?"

"Brian wants to know if you'd like to go to a basketball game with him. Over at the Lions Club?"

"No."

"Come on, Oba. Try it. You need to meet other young people your own age. You need to get out more."

"Why would I need to do that?"

"Open the door, Oba."

Oba hesitated; he didn't want Tom pressuring him into anything, but finally he cracked open the door. Tom stood in the hallway, the light from the ceiling casting a sheen on his white hair.

"We need to talk."

"I don't want to talk."

"I think you do."

"You don't know what I want."

"Come on."

Tom inclined his head in the direction of the living room, his arm beckoning him out of his room. Oba followed, reluctantly, determined to let the old man talk if he had to but had no intention of disclosing any unnecessary information.

"You hungry? You want some dessert?"

"No."

Tom settled himself on his favorite overstuffed chair and reached over to snap on the reading lamp. Oba thought of kerosene lamps with smelly wicks and drums of kerosene propped on concrete blocks, the stubborn valve that never closed quite soon enough and the rancid fuel that ran over the side of the lamp and across the hand that gripped it. Electricity was a wonder: clean, efficient, and much better. He never wanted to live without it.

"Look. Oba. You've been here a while."

"So?"

"I've fed you, clothed you, given you a job, and I expect you to give something in return. We need to discuss your lack of communication, your unwillingness to cooperate or make an effort to interact with young people of your own age."

"What I do shouldn't bother you."

"But it does. It isn't normal to pull into a shell like some hermit crab and never come back out."

"Why not?"

"It just isn't, Oba."

"It is for me."

"No it's not. You are not even friendly to Don at work. This thing of refusing Margaret's milkshake is simply not acceptable. It's rude, unthoughtful, and completely uncalled for. Can you explain why you hurt her feelings?"

"That didn't hurt her feelings."

"Of course it did."

"She's a nosy old woman who wants to collar me and get me to church."

"Did she ever mention that?"

"No, but she will."

"And why wouldn't you go?"

"Because I don't want to. It's not that hard to figure out."

Tom sat back in his chair, pressed the tips of his fingers into a steeple. His eyes watched Oba's discomfort now, the twitching in his shoulders, the crossing and uncrossing of his arms, his gaze evading his own.

"But you need Christ."

"What I need is none of your business."

"It is, Oba, as long as you are here with me. I provide for you, and it is done because I care about you. I want you to be happy here, to build a future, but I also want you to acknowledge that you need to attend church, to build a relationship with God."

There was no answer, only the rustling of the sofa as he changed positions.

"Why can't I just be left alone?" he asked finally.

"I don't think being alone too much is beneficial for you. Old remembered things, dwelling on injustices, and allowing yourself to be out of society is simply not healthy."

"I don't know how you can sit there and tell me this stuff. People aren't all alike. I'm happiest when I'm alone. I don't like people. They all make me mad."

"That, precisely, is why we're talking. That subject. You aren't friendly at all, not to coworkers or customers. You have no friends, no acquaintances whom you want to spend time with. It's not healthy, and it's certainly not normal."

"You can't sit there and tell me what's normal. Ever since my parents drowned, nothing has been what you'd call normal."

"And I understand that."

Tom watched the display of reined-in emotion, watched as Oba's mouth worked to contain the softening of his eyes, the window of perceived love that would allow a melting of the iceberg that was his heart.

"But I also want you to know you cannot blame God or folks around you for the circumstances of your parents' death."

"It wasn't the devil that drowned my parents. And who was it that told my aunts and uncles to send me and May to Arkansas? A loving God? One who cares about each of us?"

Tom winced at the bitterness, the knife edge of his battered mind. "We can't explain all that, we poor mortals who are only human. God's ways are not our ways. His mysteries will never be understood, but our faith and obedience is what tells us we are controlled by a Higher Power."

"Look. I won't be preached to."

At this, Tom grabbed the arms of his chair, heaved his tired body out, then winced as his arthritic knee stiffened. "Alright. I won't. You want a snack before bed?"

Oba thought of the raisin cookies, a glass of milk. He also felt a sense of loss, a distant longing for the talk to continue. This abrupt shutting down of all the tortured questions he contained was a disappointment.

So he said yes.

They settled themselves around the kitchen table, Tom with his Ovaltine, Oba with his large tumbler of milk, the container of raisin cookies between them. Under the kitchen light, Oba felt a new sense of awareness, as if too much of him was revealed by the brilliant bulbs, but he supposed there was nothing to be done about that.

"Why do you drink that stuff?" he asked, pointing his chin in the direction of the cup in his hand.

"This? Ovaltine? I like it, that's why. Helps me sleep."

"Should I try it?"

"Here. Have a sip."

"Nah."

"Come on. It's good."

Oba tried it, swallowed, grinned. "Not bad."

Tom laughed heartily, then shook his head.

"Well, if I can't win you to Christ, I can at least convert you to Ovaltine."

Almost, Oba laughed. Tom had never heard him laugh out loud.

Tom went to bed that night feeling just a bit better about Oba, although he knew he had merely scratched the surface of every complicated layer that made up the young man who had been deposited into his life.

He longed for his beloved wife, someone to share his thoughts. He reached over to bring a hand down on the empty pillow, a gesture he had done every night since her death, blinked back the tears of his gathering grief, and began his nightly talk with the Lord.

Months passed before Tom could persuade Oba to give basketball a chance, and then he refused to play, merely sat on the sidelines and snapped his chewing gum in the most irritating manner, his eyes flicking from side to side as he judged the bystanders.

His grandson, Brian, was quite good, dribbling, shooting hoops, always moving; his muscular arms and legs, along with his height that was approaching six feet, were a decided asset. Tom felt a certain pride, knew Brian would perhaps be able to win a scholarship in the coming year.

After the game, Brian walked over, the perspiration beading on his upper lip, the ball held between his hip and his long arm.

"That went well, Brian. You're getting better every week."

"Thanks, Grandpa. I work at it." He glanced at Oba, whose face was turned away.

"Hey, Oba." When there was no answer, Brian tried again. "Hi, Oba."

"Oh, hi."

"How's it going?"

"Pretty good."

"You want to play?"

"No."

"Just practice, you know. Why don't you?"

"No. Not this time."

Tom asked if they wanted to go for a burger and fries, but Oba shook his head. He wasn't hungry, he said. Brian was disappointed and said as much, so Tom drove over to the diner on highway 395 and left Oba in the backseat of the car while they ordered, then sat in a small booth to enjoy their treat.

Oba glared out from the rearview mirror, watched the perfect spring breeze play with the buds and new mint-green leaves on the oak trees, the sun sliding behind the small building with an ice cream cone on the roof. A dog tugged on its leash as a squirrel dashed across a patch of mown grass and disappeared up the trunk of a tree. All around him, there was the golden glow of the setting sun, the happy brilliance of a spring evening.

His stomach growled, he was starved.

But he simply could not sit at the same table with Brian. He wouldn't know how to order, wouldn't know what flavor of ice cream to choose, or how to pronounce it. And he would never play basketball because he would never wear those ridiculous shorts. His Amish background simply would not allow it; the thought of all that exposed skin brought a painful blush. And there was the T-shirt without sleeves.

Someone might see the nightmare that was his past.

No, absolutely not. He couldn't do it.

They brought him a paper container of French fries, something he had never eaten but often heard about. He thanked Tom and ate them silently, furtively, glad to have the back seat so Brian wouldn't see him stuffing them hungrily into his mouth, like the starved hobo he'd been not so very long ago.

He watched the evening scenery, children playing on the sidewalk, boys riding bicycles, girls jumping rope, parents visiting on park benches, all of them free and secure, able to enjoy the evening and each other.

The women wore dresses with gathered skirts; they looked like pretty flowers dotting the playground.

He thought of Gertie, her slovenly purple dress and gray apron, moving from stove to table, bitterly regretting her move to Arkansas, no joy or beauty gracing her house or herself. Obedience and submission rode her shoulders like a cumbersome weight.

And still he missed the orderliness of May's plain dress, the light in her eyes, the glistening blond hair. He had seen the dark side of plain life, had been a victim to one man's cruelty, but he knew it was a rare case. There was good in every culture, as well as bad, he supposed.

He felt mellowed, stable, a strange goodness as he finished the French fries. He didn't hate Brian after all; there was only a mild jealousy to be so good at a sport and to be so praised by a grandfather who loved him.

That night, he lay awake thinking. Perhaps it was a good thing, and perhaps he was turning into an English person without being aware. He was literally living in the world, being worldly, and found the world had caring people who preached at you more than anyone else.

But he had fallen in with churchgoing Christians. Larry had not been like Tom. Not at all. He grinned, thinking of Larry and his friends, floating along on the trains like dandelion seeds, landing wherever and whenever they felt like it, as if an inner wind pushed them along.

It had been better than slaving for Melvin, but he didn't like the hunger, the instability of never knowing what the next day would bring. He'd acquired a level of confidence, knowing his status as better looking and smarter than many of his peers, whereas here in California with Tom, he always felt inferior, an outsider, an imposter.

He wasn't planning on staying, but still.

May was his goal. To get to May, to remove her from the Amstutz farm, no matter how unlikely the attempt to rescue would prove to be.

He thought of her often. He knew the closest thing to real love he had ever felt was all for his sister, the dearest person in his life.

If he had to ride a bus, he would. If he had to ride the railroad again, he would. He would hitchhike, he would walk, somehow he would get to May on his own. He wouldn't depend on Tom or anyone else to get him there. It was his mistake for leaving without her and, in his mind, the only way to make it right was to be solely responsible for her rescue. Plus, he wasn't sure he wanted anyone around to witness what might happen when he set foot back on Melvin's property.

He shivered. A thread of fear threatened to choke out the growth of his courage, thwart the challenge of his planning.

Hold on, May, I'll be there.

The truth of this thought struck him with a blow that took his breath away. He swallowed, choked. Yes, the iron resolve was settled, embedded into his body, his mind, and his heart. The only person he cared about had been neglected, deserted, and all for his own selfish reasons.

But was escape from cruelty really selfish?

Oh, May.

He turned and buried his face in the pillow and allowed a few heaving groans to escape, dry lamentations of loss and confusion.

Help me. Help me.

To whom he asked, he couldn't tell; he only knew that he would need help to come up with a plan to rescue May, and even more help to make it happen.

As the moon played hide and seek behind wisps of clouds, a breeze sprang up in the west, bringing the scent of rainclouds and a low dense fog that rolled in, wrapping the small brick house in its misty embrace.

CHAPTER 15

With the arrival of spring, May sensed an abiding duty to the boys, felt her time to leave had not come. She planted the garden with the meticulous precision of an older person, stretching twine between wooden stakes pounded on each side of the garden, hoeing deep into the earth with the two-pronged hoe, dropping the seeds inches apart.

Leviticus rid himself of cracked leather shoes and darned socks, splayed his bare toes in the moist soil and howled with glee.

"Not a bumblebee in sight," May said, laughing.

"They're flying in other directions," Leviticus said, keeping an eye out for his father.

Enos and Ammon were in the fields, driving four mule hitches, plowing, spreading manure, working like grown men to keep their father's ill temper at bay. Spring meant the planting of cotton, the readying of the soil for corn, and endless farm jobs that looked at Melvin with glaring eyes. They became hunchbacked from forking manure, thin-lipped and bone-weary as the heat of the sun increased, and yet they could not keep up.

Melvin decided it was time to hire a few good men, went to the simple homes of the sharecroppers and asked around. They were all plenty busy themselves, but they would see what they could do.

Whether they liked Mr. Amstutz or not, he was the source of their income, and to those higher on the food chain, you scraped and bowed.

Over on McKinley Street, Clinton Brown sat at the kitchen table with his face propped on his hands, a week's worth of dark stubble like a shadow outlining his face.

The rain beat steadily against the loose-paned window, the dried caulking splintered and warped with age and the fierce summer heat.

It dripped off the crooked eaves, plunked in the ditch filled with water, and ran steadily into the street. A thin cat appeared from beneath a brilliant automobile, sat against the wall of the house, and began a methodical grooming.

"I told you before, I ain't going," he said, in a low voice that spoke of too little sleep.

"You are going, Clinton Brown. If I have to hogtie you, I'm gittin' you off down to the sugarcane. Ain't nothin' here for you. Nothin' can come of your shenanigans wid dat white girl. She got a other religion aside o' bein white."

"Martha, you have to see. I love her, and she loves me. I can't get her out a' my mind. I have to get her away from that place."

"Stop calling me Martha. I am your mother, and you kin jus' call me Ma, not that Martha business."

She was ironing sheets and pillowcases, the electric iron zooming across the expanse of white fabric with the skill of much practice. She took in laundry from two of the big houses, the white three-storied mansions with pillars along the front and windows so tall and deep they appeared to be doors. Wealthy plantation owners had taken the liberty to show off their profits, to impress their acquaintances and traveling relatives with the style and glamour of the well-to-do. Most of these houses were in decline after slavery was abolished, but the servants still did for the house what needed to be done.

Clinton looked up and smiled with so much weariness, it melted her heart. He knew she'd seen it before, clandestine love affairs between different races, and it had never worked.

She'd told him so, over and over, but it hadn't done a bit of good. The boy was so gone on this May, he didn't eat right and hardly ever slept. He'd be sick.

"I done made up my mind, Martha."

"Your mind about what?"

"The sugar cane."

"You're going," she repeated, thinking it would certainly cure him of the girl if he stayed south till the fall came around.

"No, Ma. I'm staying.

"You can't do it. You'll be sneakin' out to that farm and git your backside full of buckshot. Or worse."

"I ain't goin' out there. If I go, it'll be the last time, and she's comin' away with me."

Martha upended the iron, whisked a perfectly white sheet across the ironing board, and began to fold it, tucking corners under her chin, her massive arms moving with precision.

"And where will you go?" she asked, placing the sheet in the basket, smoothing corners.

"Here."

Martha rolled her eyes, lifted her hands with palms outward.

"And when Melvin Amstutz sends the police, we'll be sitting ducks, punished for abducting the little lady on account of the color o' our skin. You know zackly what'll happen. You always bin smarter den dis wild-eyed schemin' you got up yo' sleeve. Now come on."

There was nothing she could say to change his mind, nothing she could bludgeon into his strong will. He was filled to the brim with determination, his brain addled by this disease called love, and she wouldn't give two cents for the relationship to last longer'n a month of Sundays.

When Roy came in, he tried his best to persuade Clinton to go with the cane cutters. It was good money, he loved the hard work, and it would get his mind off the white girl with religion.

May was asleep when she was awakened by the barking of a dog, which seemed unusual, the way the closest dog was the next farm over. Melvin didn't like dogs, said they were nothing but trouble; he put up with the cats that were good mousers, eliminated the rest.

A ping against her window, then another. She listened for the wind that accompanied a rainstorm, but there was none, only the breathless silence of the night.

Another ping, stronger this time. Slowly, so as not to allow creaking of the bedsprings, she got to her feet and went to the window. She jerked back when another piece of gravel hit the pane, then hooked her fingers beneath the pull and slowly pushed it open.

"Hsst."

She froze, suddenly terrified.

"It's me!"

She strained to hear, to see through the thick darkness of night.

"Come down to the pine woods."

"Clinton?"

"It's me. Get dressed, I'll wait."

"But . . ."

And then she understood. He had not gone to the cane. He had stayed behind when the rest of the crew climbed into the truck and drove away.

She put up her hair with shaking fingers, her mouth gone dry. Like a wraith, she slipped out of her nightgown and into a navy blue dress, tied a gray apron around her waist, set the white covering on her head, adjusted the straight pins, and crept toward the stairs. She could feel her heart beating in her ears, a thick pounding at her temples. If only she could escape one more time. If only she could . . .

"What's going on?"

Melvin's rasping voice from the depth of the downstairs bedroom caused her to stop on the stair tread, her breath held, her chest straining to contain the frenzied heartbeat. *Oh, dear God. Not now.*

"Get that mule unhooked!" Melvin shouted, mumbled something unintelligible, then coughed, groaned, and sank back into a state of deep slumber.

May almost fainted with relief and clung to the railing for support before continuing her precarious flight. Slowly, so slowly, she let herself out the door, then ran across the dew-wet grass and into the pungent scent of the pine woods.

She found him soon enough, felt his fierce strength as his arms took possession of her. His lips claimed her as she clung to him.

How long did they stay in the pine woods that night?

Before dawn, there was no longer a shred of doubt left. May was fully persuaded there was a right time for everything, and this was their time.

She would leave with him and never look back.

She cried about Leviticus, wept so softly and brokenly that Clinton told her they would come back for him some day. But she knew. She knew that was a promise that was impossible to keep.

And she was filled with a fierce longing to be free from Melvin, free from the invisible chains that bound her. Fear, submission, loathing—it was all the same thing, an awful hoard of wrongdoing that bound her to him. Her hope of ever changing him would never come to pass, of this she was certain. So there was no point in the slavery she had imposed on herself.

He was a predator without an ounce of kindness, emptying her of even the most basic gratitude or desire to please him in any way. To be painfully honest with herself and Clinton was like a cell door being flung aside, the light of day blinding her by its unaccounted brilliance.

She told him everything that night, left no stone unturned. He remained stoic, but she could feel him trembling, containing the wild anger that consumed him.

To reach his car was not the hardest part, each brush of the dew-infused weeds goading her on. She clung to his strong hand, moved on feet that felt as if propelled by wings, muscular wings of a large bird in full flight. But to be seated in a real automobile, to hear the engine turn over and sputter to life, was almost more than she could bear.

She was riding in a car with her love, an English man who was not white, but the color of a ripe acorn, with burnished copper skin, and the kindest brown eyes she could ever hope to see.

She should not be doing this, her conscience told her. Go back to Melvin and do your duty.

But the car was moving along a gravel road, the headlights prob-
ing the black night with a strong steady light that led them up over
the winding roads of the ridge they had slid down so many years ago,
when Melvin brought them here to the farm as innocent children,
perched on the high seat of the spring wagon without a thought of
what awaited them.

Here she was, escaping her life in a car with a black man, Oba gone
to a destination she could only guess. Suddenly, she was so glad her
parents were not alive to see the soul-wrenching sadness of their death,
the scattering of the seeds they had planted in their lovely children.

May thought they might be scattered by outward appearances,
but most certainly not in her heart. *Just give me a chance, Mam.
I'll not dishonor you. This is a matter of survival*

That first night in Blytheville was a blur of voices, darkness illumi-
nated by the glow of a single electric bulb hung from the low ceiling,
quickly extinguished when the parents caught sight of the trembling
May, her eyes so large and dark in her pale face, her hair like new
wheat.

Martha rolled her eyes, threw up her hands in defeat, called on the
Lord for his mercy. Roy took one look, sat down heavily, and wagged
his great, graying head from side to side. Few words were spoken.
Martha, realizing the foolhardiness of the venture her son had under-
taken, hustled May off to bed in a dark bedroom so small it contained
only a single bed and a narrow dresser. There were no nightclothes
and none offered, so May lay on top of the patchwork quilt and stared
at the darkness around her, searched for assurance and answers without condemnation. A part of her was wildly elated, euphoric beyond
reasoning; another part was stone cold with fear and dread.

She dozed off, entered a fitful state of near sleep and subconscious awareness, was jolted awake by the light that probed the cur-
tained window. She squinted against it, rolled over, and went back to
sleep; she awoke a while later to find waves of drowsiness overtaking
her again.

She remembered wondering how a person could sleep so much for such a great amount of time, before falling into the cushioned bliss of a deep, healing slumber.

She had no idea how often the doorknob was turned slowly, the crack only widened enough to enable an eye to peer through, then closed just as softly.

Whispers in the kitchen.

Martha told Clinton something wasn't right with that poor girl staying asleep like that.

He shook his head, lifted burning eyes to his mother's face but said nothing. Martha gave him a long penetrating stare, then lifted her body off the chair to replenish his coffee cup.

"You know you can't stay here."

"I know."

"Where you going?"

"Well, I have two bus tickets. One for New York."

"You can't both travel on one."

"No. I mean. I'm not sure where we'll go. New York or Ohio. We haven't really talked about it. We'll be leaving in the morning."

"You'll be marrying her?"

Clinton raised an eyebrow. His mother's face softened, remembering the look on his father's face, the profile, the lifting of one eyebrow that could set her heart to fluttering like a silly teenaged girl.

"You will or you won't?"

"What do you think, Ma? Who's gonna do it? Huh?"

Martha shook her head, sat heavily into the creaking protest of the kitchen chair. She looked up as Roy's frame filled the doorway, patted the tabletop to show him where to sit.

Roy fixed Clinton with a grim look, one that did not allow any evasive words or wrong intentions. He followed this stare with low words, spoken barely above a whisper—admonishments, warnings, followed up with a phrase about taking her back today, as soon as possible, save himself and her a lifetime of being shunned.

"I can't take her back, ever. That place is worse than we thought."

There was no budging Clinton, who stuck to that phrase and would not relinquish it, no matter how both parents pleaded.

"Then take her to her people. Simply ask her where she'd like to go and leave her there. I know Melvin Amstutz will obey her wishes. She ain't goin' nowhere if she has a decent place to stay," Roy said, his brow furrowed like a plowed field.

"He'll never let her go. It'll be his word against hers, and I know the church will believe him long before they'll take her word. She'll never tell the elders the truth."

"What is the truth?" Martha asked.

They never did hear what Clinton meant by that phrase, only a stony face and eyes that bored into theirs.

In the morning, they were gone, a note propped on the sugar bowl, the bed neatly made, the table wiped, and dishes rinsed.

Martha arose late that morning, her back giving her a rough night, so she hunched in her chair, rubbing the sore spot as she squinted at the note. Wide awake now, she hurried to Clinton's room, then to the room May had occupied, and found them both empty. She returned to the kitchen and unfolded the note with shaking hands.

Dear Ma,
    Thanks for what you done.
    Don't try to find us. If Melvin asks, tell him nothing.
    We'll try to return someday. If we don't, we'll meet in Heaven.

Love,
Clinton

A shrill keening escaped her lips before she could stop it, the sound bringing Roy from the front porch, his empty coffee cup dangling from one hand, his eyes wide with fright. That sound had only been heard once before, the day Arpachshad had been taken from the dirty water of the Mississippi, thought to be thoroughly drowned.

Martha thrust the note at him, tears coursing down her ebony cheeks, her chest heaving with sorrow.

Roy read it, thrust it angrily on the tabletop, then slapped a hand on top. He raged, he paced, he swore and shook his fist, said that boy had not a drop of common sense in his head and how could he go against everything they'd always tried to teach him, whereupon Martha yelled at him to get him to calm down, asking when he'd ever taught him anything about running off with a white girl.

She fried his eggs and sliced the ham into another skillet, talked around a mouthful of bread crust, and kept on talking long after it was swallowed. "He'd be takin' a risk, but de Lawd was with 'em both. If it's true love, they'd find a way. Love is greater than men's ideas of how it should look. No manmade rules are ever gonna trump true love, and this love is big. So big, in fact, Clinton was sick with it. He wasn't himself, hasn't been himself for so long I couldn't say. And if they was bound and determined to be together, and they'd done the right thing by warning us, then I guess their fate is in God's hands, and not Roy's, so you may as well sit down and eat."

And Roy sat down and ate.

They boarded the huge glistening Greyhound bus in Blytheville, glad to hand over the tickets and find their way to the very back of the bus, enduring open stares as they passed numerous passengers.

A black man obviously of mixed race, called "high yellow," with a very white, very blond slip of a girl dressed in strange religious clothes was an odd sight indeed. The black men and women lowered their eyes, were afraid to comment lest some white person become angry and begin a showdown. An elderly lady in a purple suit and pillbox hat, her hair coiffed into boxy submission, pushed up her glasses and looked to the left in a discreet gaze at her husband, whose neck was turned into a corkscrew, watching the couple move back along the aisle.

"Charles, don't stare."

"Olivia. Something is . . . well . . . out of the ordinary."

"Lower your voice, please."

"You think he's kidnapping her? Should we intervene?"

"Certainly not. It's none of our concern."

"Very well."

And so on throughout the bus, murmurs behind palms extended over mouths, a few bold enough to turn their heads to get a better look, but after the bus rumbled to life and moved down the street, folks settled in and tried to do the right thing, which was to leave them alone.

Clinton reached over to take her small hand in his. She looked at him with gratitude, her eyes large and dark in a small, very frightened face.

"It will be alright," he said.

She nodded, tight-lipped.

But it was not alright. Even as the bus picked up speed on the highway that led from Blytheville, the only place she had known for years, a sense of wrongdoing pressed her into the seat, took away the normal breathing and replaced it with a stone's weight in her chest.

What was she doing? What had she been thinking? For a wild moment, she knew she must escape this bus, run back the way she had come and keep running until she was back in the house where the three boys needed her.

Where Melvin subdued her.

She gripped the edge of her seat, her shoulders stiff with the panic that held her. She opened her mouth, closed it, then opened it and tried to speak, the sound coming from her throat and no less than a croak.

Alarmed, Clinton turned to look at her.

"May. May, it's alright."

Vehemently, her face in a grimace of pain, she responded with swift denial. "No, no, no, no. I have to go back. The boys . . . the boys."

"The boys will manage without you. He'll marry again."

"No, no. Leviticus. He needs me. He's not like Enos and Ammon. He'll miss me terribly. Please, Clinton, I need to get off this bus. Now."

She half rose in her seat, her hands fluttering, helpless in the face of this monumental guilt.

He spoke softly, coaxed her into sitting back and taking a few deep breaths.

"If you really want to get off at the next stop, we will. I will take you back to Melvin and the boys if that is truly what you want. I would never force you against your own will. Is that what you want?"

"Yes, yes. Please take me back. This is wrong. I have not been faithful to my God-given duty. Please take me back. Please."

They spoke in low whispers, knowing the passengers around them were on high alert, suspicion oozing along the aisle.

"May, listen. Is that what you really want? You told me everything. You can't go back. I promise I won't force you to leave, but I don't believe you're thinking straight. You're frightened, you're nervous, and you have every reason to be. Just wait, sit back, and try to relax."

Clinton searched her face, but she would not allow herself to look into his eyes. Those warm brown eyes in the face of her dreams. Her love.

His handsome face, his love for her.

She had lived for this moment, had dreamt of it, and now it was so wrong, so utterly and absolutely forbidden. It was late morning, the time of day when breakfast dishes would be washed, dried, and put away, the water in the boiler steaming already, the piles of sorted laundry waiting to be swirled into the washtubs. She could smell the homemade lye soap, feel the heat of the water as her fingers reddened.

Who would wash the clothes? What had they eaten for breakfast with no one to cook for them? Melvin would be furious, rain his ill temper down on the boys, and all of it was her fault. The boys, especially Leviticus, would be ruined, their blood on her hands. She would be the one responsible if they turned into undisciplined rowdies, rebellious to the core.

She had told herself she would stay till the boys were grown and had broken that promise. God would not forgive broken promises.

She would burn in hell for all eternity. She was a bold, lustful girl, filled with all manner of unrighteousness, and the only way to repentance was to return to the farm as soon as possible. A fear so consuming was the right kind of fear, brought by God at the last moment, and now she must obey.

She had obeyed Melvin, had obeyed all his wishes, and that had been right.

Hadn't it?

The question was like a ray of light that separated storm clouds, revealed the one true thing in her life that prevented her return. It would all resume that first night.

She pressed her handkerchief to her face, then turned toward Clinton to avoid being seen. She allowed the tears to come unrestrained, as Clinton kept his face away from the misery in hers, watching steadily at the Arkansas landscape as it fell away.

After a long while, she whispered, "I don't know what to do."

"Shall we get off when the bus stops?"

She shuddered but said yes.

True to his word, he helped her off the seat and down the aisle, explained his intention to the bus driver, who handed him the required documentation.

May had stopped the soft weeping but was obviously in a state of distress, so he kept her behind him to save her the stares of the curious onlookers.

The station was small and very hot. Aluminum fans whirred on desktops as folks extracted handkerchiefs, mopped their faces, and tried to concentrate.

There weren't many, certainly not a crowd, but enough people that Clinton was not comfortable staying inside, with May becoming so agitated. He led her to a bench beneath a spreading elm, the grass brittle and dry beneath their feet. Traffic rumbled behind them, the squat white cement-block station receiving passengers or expelling them, the sun hot on the flat, black roof, the air brassy with the shimmering heat.

For a long while, neither one of them spoke. May inhaled deeply, then let it go. Her fingers twisted the damp handkerchief around and around her forefinger, until he saw the tip had turned purple.

He reached over and placed his large dark hand over hers.

"You can't go back to Melvin," he said. "I'll take you back wherever you want me to, but never to him. It's not right."

"It's not?"

"No, May. No. You can't go back."

He searched her face in desperation, and this time she met the love in his. She realized it was true. He would do whatever he needed to do to make her happy, but she could never go back to the farm.

Where could she go? She could not go back to the Amish community, but still . . . . The rest of the world was a vast and lifeless place.

CHAPTER 16

He became increasingly restless, prowled the aisles of the drugstore like a cat, jumped in his skin when the bell above the door tinkled, hid behind shelves to avoid talking to customers. He stopped riding to work with Tom, chose to ride a bicycle instead, much to Tom's disapproval, but he won the argument by saying he needed the exercise.

He finally admitted his boredom to Tom, who seemed concerned but didn't comment, merely listened with the usual kindness that was so much a part of him.

Oba went to bed that evening, knowing he needed more than he received here at the old man's house, as he had come to call him. He wanted to purchase a car, he wanted to learn how to drive, and after he did that, he wanted to drive up and down the California coast, see the Pacific Ocean and the land that went to Mexico, see the city of San Francisco and all the wonders it held. But first, he had to get to May, bring her back with him.

They made plans, then, after he disclosed the amount of money in his savings. Tom tried to convince Oba to let him go also. He reminded him that things could get ugly when they reached the farm, and there was safety in numbers. He tried to explain that there were legal ramifications to kidnapping a girl, even if you're her brother. But Oba would hear none of it, so eventually he backed down and turned to discussing the travel logistics. They decided on Greyhound bus travel—less expensive and the most uncomplicated.

Tom took him to town and helped him replenish his wardrobe, which left Oba standing in front of the mirror wondering if Melvin would recognize him at all. His hair cut short, wearing a striped shirt and jeans, there was no trace of his former upbringing. He was wearing *Englishy hussa* (jeans).

His shoes were brown, and there was no straw hat on his head, so he figured he really was not an Amish person at all anymore. It was the clothes that branded you into the community, the clothes and the horse and buggy and growing corn and cotton and going to church in one another's houses.

Inside, was one Amish after being born Amish, no matter where they went or how they dressed? Was it necessary to be identified as Amish or Mennonite or Russian or American or anything at all?

Since he had no answers for that, he'd decided on his own to dress and drive a car like *Die Englishy*. He hated being apart, being odd and old-fashioned and eccentric.

So he boarded the bus with a new level of confidence, knew he fit in with the rest of the passengers, felt Tom's love and approval, knew he truthfully hoped he'd be back with his sister, who he planned on giving a good home to as well.

He kept to himself, though, rode alone and was content to stay that way, watching the scenery, minding his own business, anticipating his first sight of May.

Dear May. He wondered if she'd changed in the time they'd been apart, wondered, too, if she'd accept him this way. She was so terribly conservative, so obedient to her keen conscience. He thought perhaps he'd have to wear his Amish clothes if he wanted her to leave with him. He planned his arrival on the farm, felt his breath quicken at the thought of Melvin.

Melvin could not keep him there, and he certainly wouldn't.

He looked up to find a short, sandy-haired youth standing beside him. His freckles looked like flung sand that stuck all over; green eyes, alight with interest, shone out from the sea of freckles. He wore a look of comfortable curiosity, no more and no less.

"Mind if I sit here? Bus is full."

"Is it? Yeah, go ahead."

He scooted over as if to make room, although there was already plenty of space. The young man lowered himself into the allotted seat, although there wasn't much to lower, just a mild folding of the short, husky body.

A hand came at him sideways. Oba hesitated, lifted questioning eyes to find only curiosity and kindness, then took the hand in a limp, questioning shake.

"Richard Timton."

"Oba Miller."

They assessed each other with an open curiosity, the frankness of youth. Oba found himself approving of this young man, actually liking the way his hair was out flat along the top, so that all the hair stood up and he had no bangs.

His forehead was smooth, except for the splattering of freckles. If Oba looked close enough, he could see a sort of galaxy, like the stars in the sky: large planets, small ones, and a smattering of tiny stars in-between.

What a happy person, though, living in this skin.

"Call me Rich."

"I will."

There was only a short silence before the conversation flowed easily, led and conducted by Richard, of course, but Oba found himself a willing participant.

He was on his way to Penn State University in Pennsylvania, hoping to major in biology, which was extremely interesting to Oba, of course, having worked in the pharmacy in Bridgeport.

When night fell, they had discovered a mutual friend, although Oba withheld almost all of his life's information, embellished a few details, and made up outright lies to make it all sound believable.

Tom Miller (close enough) was his father, he told him, and his mother had died, which was true. He was going to get his sister after she was done with her tenure at Arkansas College in Batesville (Batesville sounding close enough and a college being a place where you learned things . . . May was surely learning in the college of Melvin Amstutz). She was taking human relations and science, which was said quickly and easily enough, without a trace of truth.

They exchanged addresses when the routes differed, waved as they boarded other buses, and were parted as travelers often are.

But Oba was smiling. He had acquired the art of making do. He was learning to others with half-truths and undisputed lies, building an imaginary world in his head and allowing the words to mesmerize, enthrall.

Boy, he thought, *that Richard believed every word I said. He really did. He had no reason to think otherwise.* He could never know the messy existence he had in his past, the sad truth of his parents' death, and certainly not the cruel life he'd lived in Arkansas.

He giggled like a schoolgirl, felt alive. He'd successfully pulled off a series of made-up stories, made a good friend in the process.

So why couldn't he do the same everywhere he went? Another Oba Miller would emerge from the cocoon of his past, grow wings, and fly. There was no limit to the fiction he could spew into the world, the open-minded people like Richard who would be happy to receive it.

He looked up to find a balding middle-aged man with a green satchel clutched in a hammy paw, his cheeks rounded into glistening apples of smooth flesh.

"The seats are all filled. I need this one," he drawled, in a voice like teeth on a comb, setting Oba's nerves to quivering.

"Sit down then."

He turned his head to stare out the window, decided to forego conversation and to attempt to avoid the smell of perspiration and stale talcum powder, laundry detergent and garlic.

Oba twisted his body even farther against the wall.

The green satchel was opened, with a series of breaths exhaled, grunts and stopped attempts. Finally, there was a rustling of waxed paper, the unscrewing of a metal cup. Oba glanced sideways, swallowed his hunger when he saw the size of the sandwich the guy had unwrapped.

Cheese, bologna, onions, pickles, lettuce.

"Want some? I have another."

He had never wanted anything more, so he nodded, said "Thanks," and carefully adjusted his knees to hold the waxed paper spread out like a tablecloth. He was offered crackers and cheese, a doughnut, a cinnamon roll, and a bottle of lemonade, which he accepted as they arrived. There was no name offered, so he didn't share his own, only the fellowship of the silent meal, the appreciation of good food in the small space, the hum of the wheels and the muted throbbing of the motor in the cavity of the bus.

They both fell asleep, another human requirement he shared, and awoke in each other's company, refreshed, relaxed. The man was ready to disembark when the bus pulled into Abbottsville, Nevada.

They parted without further words, and Oba found himself disappointed, having thought up another believable story for the entertainment of this man, who had obviously not been interested at all. Oh well, there was always the next time. He was sure to meet more people who needed to share a seat, and he certainly did not have long to wait.

It was early in the morning, and the other passengers were awakening, longing for their journey's end, a hot bath in a comfortable room, a good breakfast. Oba was making up more stories to tell, reveling in the freedom of imagining a new life. He could be anyone, make up anything.

"Hey, man."

Jolted out of his imagination, Oba glanced up to find a dark youth staring down at him, his eyes glowing in the overhead light. Oba was surprised. Black people were supposed to sit in the back of the bus. He shrugged, looking away and back out the window, eager to work out the details of the stories he'd tell the next person willing to listen.

"Look, man. I got a injury. Seats in back are full. I'm on my way home from France. The war, you know. Give me a seat?"

"Sure." Oba was so lost in his own mind, he hardly looked as the man sat down gratefully, pushed his head against the headrest, stretched, and sighed.

In a moment, the man interrupted his thoughts again, said, "Name's Arpachshad Brown."

Oba coughed, choked, coughed again.

"Everybody call me Drink."

"What?" Oba sat straight up, his eyes going to his old friend's face. He remembered the eyes, the full lips, and handsome nose, all turned into an older version.

He laughed aloud. "Drink? Remember me? Oba Miller? I worked on Melvin's farm. His nephew?"

"Yeah, yeah. Sure. I remember you!"

Oba laughed, genuinely pleased to be reunited with an old acquaintance, even if it would be for only an afternoon.

"So what happened to you? You only came fishing that once."

"My uncle didn't want me to be with the coloreds."

"The black people? Really? And they work in his fields? How come?"

Oba shrugged.

"Well, sometimes being black is all the reason they need."

"Guess so."

"So tell me 'bout yer life, Oba."

This time he told the truth, hinted at Melvin's temper, said he was going to get May. Drink talked most of the morning and the forenoon about enlisting in the army, being shipped to France, receiving two bullets in his left leg, and being sent home, which was only a day away.

He seemed tired, much older, the way his voice cracked and broke; his fingers drummed the arm rest, his shoulders twitched.

"That's an amazing story. I just worked on the farm, was beaten by Melvin, and kicked around like a stray dog until I left."

Drink shook his head, knew what Oba was talking about, had seen it firsthand.

They talked most of the day, sharing life experiences, comparing hurts and heartaches, looking for the good in every situation, or so Drink declared.

Oba stayed mostly silent on the subject of Melvin Amstutz, wondering if he was a rarity, one who had hardly a sliver of good in him.

He was about to find out how much good he actually contained.

He was not coming away from that farm without May.

The day was hot, bright, and still, the early autumn leaves dangling like a tired elderly person, ready to greet their own demise. Oba had a good breakfast at the hotel in Blytheville, bade Drink goodbye when he was taken home by his uncle, but declined the offer of a ride home.

He was not ready to meet Melvin just yet.

As he walked, he took in the remembered beauty of Arkansas, the trilling of swallows and wrens, the high call of the blue heron, the waxy leaves of the tupelo tree.

The red dust on his shoes made him smile, then he thought of drought and times when Melvin had to accept the lack of rainfall and the ensuing punishment as he vented frustration on Oba's back.

How did he feel walking along the same road Melvin had used to convey them to the farm so many years ago? He knew he was not the same as that innocent young boy, but who was? Who had not had adversity and sadness, although he now knew his case was rare. Well, he was here, he had a sound mind, was of legal age to come and go as he pleased, and there was nothing Melvin could do to detain him. He half-looked forward to seeing Gertie, in spite of her slovenly ways and excess flesh. She had merely been a cog in the mighty wheel that had been Melvin, rolling along to whatever he demanded, so how could he harbor ill feelings?

He sat by the side of the road to rest his feet, then drank from the small stream. He inhaled deeply of the wet, humid air, the mud of the delta. He saw Crowley's Ridge in the distance, heard the cawing of a crow, thought of seasons ebbing and flowing.

He broke off a bunch of primroses, buried his nose in the scent. Quail broke out of the honeysuckle that grew wild, choking the split rail fence that hosted it. Arkansas was a beautiful land, and now that he was free to enjoy it, it seemed to fill all his senses.

It was late in the afternoon when his shoes puffed up little clouds of dust in the Amstutz driveway. He was unprepared for the choking sensation that threatened to cut his air supply or the hammering of his heart as his mouth went dry with raw fear.

It was only for May that he could place one foot in front of the other, only for May that he could walk up to the front door and give a resounding knock.

When no one opened the door, he looked around, found the yard weedy and unkempt, but without the strewn garbage or the goats they had encountered on their first arrival. Perhaps the boys had learned from May. He knocked again, stepped back in case May opened the door.

There was no one inside, he had to admit after another knock.

Perhaps they were in the barn.

He found the cow stable as he remembered it. No significant changes.

He turned to find himself face to face with a boy almost as tall as himself. Enos.

"Oh, hi! I . . . I am Oba."

"You're Oba?"

"Yes."

"You better not let Dat see you."

"Where's May?"

"She left. We don't know where she is."

"What? When? When did she go?"

"I dunno. Weeks. Months. In the spring."

"Enos. I have to see her. I came all this way. I have to see her."

"Well, she's gone."

There was a clatter of steel wheels on gravel, the sound of mules running, a clank of chains on traces, and Enos left quickly. Oba peered through the dusty cow stable windows before stepping to the side, rolling his body along the wall until his back sagged against the cement block.

It was him. Melvin. Hauling back on the reins, his feet wide apart, his straw hat wide-brimmed and low on his head, his shirt wet with sweat and grime. He could smell the odor, hear the harsh breathing, feel the whip that sang through the air and sank into his skin. Everything faded, the cow stable as black as midnight. He struggled to stay conscious, then took deep breaths to restore relaxation and lucidity.

Could he walk out there, confront him?

He could, for May, and he did.

The wagon was stopped before the ascent to the upper story where the hay was stored, so here was his chance. He took it. On shaking legs, he made his appearance, didn't flinch when Melvin flung the reins over the post, jumped off the wagon, squared his shoulders with both thumbs hooked in the broadfall trouser pockets.

Oba kept walking.

The mules had worked up a good lather, the harnesses whitened with flecks of it, the hair on their hide darkened by the sweat. Their large ears flung back and forth as the horseflies buzzed around them, their eyes gentle and kind, despite giving daily service to convey crops from the field to the barn, standing for hours in the rows of cotton as their thin tails swung from side to side, keeping flies at bay.

Oba swallowed, lifted his eyes. "Hello."

"Who . . . are you?" Melvin asked, but he knew.

Oba could tell he knew by the wide opening of his narrow eyes, the sharp inhalation of breath. "I'm Oba."

"What do you want?"

"I came to get May."

Melvin's face darkened with a rush of quick fury. "You're not getting her," he ground out.

"Where is she?"

"She's not here."

"Well, tell me where she is."

"I don't know."

"When did she leave? How did she go?"

"I can't tell you."

Enos was joined by Ammon, both boys taller, huskier, older versions of the boys he remembered. They stood splay-legged, with torn trousers and bare feet, their mouths open as they watched and listened to the exchange.

"I'll find her, Melvin. She's not coming back here, ever."

"You don't know if she will or not. She has a conscience, unlike you."

"You will never get the chance to mistreat either one of us again, so help me God."

"Don't swear in my presence."

Oba spat on the ground. "Swear? In front of you? And you whipped and beat me senseless. I'll do what I want as far as you're concerned."

"Get off my property." His breath was coming fast now, his eyes bright with anger. "Get off!"

Oba stood, tall, handsome, and eyed him coolly. "I'll go when I'm ready. Now tell me where May is."

"She ran away, just like you did." With one quick movement, he was on the wagon, the reins in his hands, bringing them down on the mules' backs. They lunged into their collars, headed straight for Oba as Enos and Ammon leaped aside.

He would be run over if he didn't move.

On they came, Melvin bringing the reins down in a frenzy. Oba stood his ground until the last minute, when he stepped aside, the furious hooves inches away. He felt wisps of hay hit his face, watched the dust roll up after the steel wheels, before he realized Melvin would be back.

Sure enough, he made a wide circle before returning at breakneck speed, the mules wild-eyed, the blinders flapping haphazardly as they broke into a gallop.

Oba realized then that Melvin meant to run him down. The man had lost his mind. He would be labeled *vild* (wild), *aus da kopp* (out of his head) and sent away. He had certainly fallen to a new level of craziness, and something had to be done for the sake of the three boys.

He turned to find the mules coming from the opposite direction, the wagon swaying as their speed increased. A large portion of hay loosened and slid off, fell to the dusty lane with a whumping sound.

Again, Oba stepped aside, climbed the barnyard fence, and sat on the top rail as Melvin clattered past, his face white with uncontrolled fury, flecks of saliva flying from his mouth and down his chin. He was screaming unintelligible words, raising his fists as he careened past.

Then Oba ran, then ran and ran, his fists pumping the air, his feet hitting the ground hard. He wasn't aware he was crying until he felt the snot run from his nose, and yet he ran on.

He had no destination, no place to go, but he had done what he set out to do. Or had he?

He believed the boys were in danger. Where was Leviticus? He had always been May's favorite. He stopped running, bent over with his hands on his knees and caught his breath.

Leonard Yoder. He had to see them. If he did nothing, who would? And yet, the thought of Melvin's perceived normalcy, the pious goodness of him, the prestige he enjoyed in the community would be a serious hurdle in Oba winning his case. And if he did present the elders with his stories, who would believe him? Who would help?

An Englisha boo. Ungehorsam. (An English boy. Disobedient.)

Without uttering a single word, he would be viewed with suspicion. Anyone who could not comply with a parent's wishes was labeled a troublemaker. The ways and means exercised by the parent was not taken into account.

He stood in the center of the long, red dirt road, dejection creeping up like evening fog. May was gone, and Melvin was in serious danger of hurting himself or those boys. How could he let them fend for themselves? He had nothing but his words, and Melvin had his.

He set his face toward the road that led to Leonard Yoder, the only man in the community who had ever shown sympathy or taken an interest in his well-being. Indecision turned him back to the farm where he had spent too many years with Melvin, blows raining down like poisonous arrows, blows that threatened to kill his spirit and spread the infection of hatred for all members of any plain sect. Hypocrites, all of them.

He turned again, then began to walk in the direction of the road that led to Leonard Yoder's.

Doubt followed him like a swarm of bothersome gnats, but he kept walking in the only direction he knew he could take. The air around him was filled with misgivings and questions, but he'd forgotten how much he loved the Arkansas countryside, the profusion of verdant plants that were amazing even in autumn. There was a low humid scent of earth and water, the elements creating a bounty of trees, shrubs, and wild flowers that Bridgeport, California, could not match.

The wild cherry trees had already turned yellow; the small leaves swirling through the humid afternoon created a carpet of gold at the base of the tree. He smiled to himself, thinking of the time he'd eaten far too many of the fruit and paid for it with a roiling stomach and horrible consequences, sneaking upstairs behind Gertie's back to change trousers. Where was Gertie? Perhaps she had gone to town or to visit a neighbor.

Poor Gertie.

She'd lived a sad, unfulfilled life but had done the best she could in her unhappy self-absorbed way. She had submitted to her husband, right or wrong, but had never fully accepted her fate, living in the heated delta plains with Crowley's Ridge hovering over her shoulder, longing for Illinois and the family who still resided in the old settlement.

And where was May?

Fear settled like a stomachache, a hard knot that brought a sense of unfulfilled duty, the terrible conviction that he had left her to fend for herself.

Perhaps she had gone back to Ohio, to seek employment and a home with one of the relatives who needed a maid. He could only hope she could survive in a world that could swallow a young slip of a girl, one who had no experience dealing with strangers. She was so innocent, so eager to please, always looking out for others' happiness, and who would take advantage of her?

He shuddered, a cold chill running up his spine.

For the thousandth time, he wondered what his parents would say or do, knowing what they had left behind. Two good people taken out of the world, leaving their children to fend for themselves. How could there be a loving God who truly cared?

Oba felt alone, frightened, unsure of anything. Riddled by doubt and anger, he shouldered his way through a maze of confusion to come upon the sight of Leonard Yoder's picturesque farm, nestled in a grove of basswood trees.

Every instinct told him to flee, to turn around and go back. He was afraid to tell, afraid of the devastating consequence of dealing with the fact that Leonard might not have mercy, that all Amish men were indeed alike, and that he deserved every slice of the whip that scarred his back and his soul.

CHAPTER 17

SHE WAS SO TIRED.

As waves of indecision and fear swept over her, she wrestled with her strict upbringing, the confusion of what was truly right and what was wrong.

She felt suffocated by the ever-tightening noose of one wrong which seemed no different from the former one. How could God have mercy on her soul if she was disobedient?

Obedience to elders was so highly esteemed among her people, obedience to the wishes of those in charge, whether it was the ministers of the church, parents, stepparents, or, in her case, an uncle. To have escaped the bondage of one as deranged as Melvin, the hidden sin of her mortification well concealed, would never be viewed as anything other than wild disobedience, a girl who lusted after *un schwottsa* (a colored person). Melvin, the poor widower, with his sheep's eyes and trembling voice, would sway all authority in his direction, while she remained covered with her own shame and wrongdoing.

She wrestled with her sense of duty, her pride, her past. She would be shunned forever by her people, the kindly women in conservative clothes who lived their lives according to scripture, who lived with clean and unbothered consciences, worked hard, and took great joy in their homes and in their children, their lives unspooling in simplicity and order.

She began to shake her head back and forth, murmuring softly, as if the anguish was unbearable.

"May, my love, what is it?"

Clinton bent low, trying to hear the soft words that fell from her lovely mouth.

"I can't do this," she said, very low.

"Then I'll take you back."

She raised stricken eyes to his. "No!"

The refusal cut across the station with the force of a blade. Heads turned; a few people scowled but kept to themselves.

May trembled with the force of her protest. The truth cut through all her indecision, separated the fact that, no matter what the outcome, she could never go back to her uncle. She knew by Clinton's willingness to let her go that he loved her enough to set her free, had unknowingly shown his noble intention. He would lay down his life for her, let her make the foolish mistake of returning to the horrible net in which she had been entangled.

"I can't," she whispered.

"Then trust me, May. Trust me to provide a future for you. We may have to live a secluded life, but trust me."

When she considered his words, thought of a life lived with him alone in a small house, her love for him was all-consuming, a barrier between her past, her future, her people. She looked at her small, pale hand, his large dark one holding it so tenderly, and nodded her head up and down, her heart singing a constant song of yes, yes, oh yes.

They had arrived in the state of New York in a town called Henderson in the middle of a pouring rain, the kind of rain that rode in on a dark bank of clouds to the east and emptied their contents for days.

The big silver bus had splashed along the highway most of the afternoon, the huge wipers turned on high, sluicing rain away from the driver's vision as they moved steadily north.

May slept in the gray light of the dreary afternoon, awoke refreshed, confident, and glad to follow Clinton's tall form as he disembarked.

The station was very small, an alcove in a high-ceilinged insurance company, but there were comfortable chairs, and it was warm and dry.

She sat alone, her large dark eyes taking in the high counter with the tight-lipped proprietor, the stares and raised eyebrows of the other passengers.

She took a deep breath to steady herself and wondered if this ill-concealed disapproval would follow her wherever she went.

She watched Clinton at the desk, his wide shoulders and narrow hips, the length of him, his dark curly hair, and humble demeanor. She was filled with so much love, so much longing to stay with him all the days of her life. The doubt and fear was pushed effectively to the side, as she kept her eyes on the one person in whom she had confided, the one person who would not cast her aside. He was good and kind, everything she could imagine a husband to be.

Did love trump obedience to the law of her people? Did it truly have enough strength to overcome the law of the land? Marriage was not legal for them, not by the courts, not by all the laws of the United States. He was black, and she was white, a union that was refused to be accepted by society everywhere.

It simply wasn't done.

Bus travel had been a test of wills, the black people seated along the back portion, in which May had settled herself in spite of the other passengers' outward curiosity. She had become accustomed to stares of disapproval as an Amish girl, the general public viewing them as strange, not always wholly accepted. But this, being in the company of a black man, was a whole new level of disapproval, haughty looks like arrows that struck pain wherever they found their mark.

"Separate but equal" was as far as civil rights had come, according to the law. Black people were separated from white people but could still ride buses and trains and eat in restaurants, so long as they obeyed the rules and kept to the designated sections.

The colors of May and Clinton's skins ruled their existence on the long bus ride and would continue to be their biggest challenge as they chose to live a life together.

Yes, she would do this.

They would be husband and wife in the eyes of God, may He have mercy on their souls.

They walked the streets, took leads from one person to the next, were refused boarding rooms and hotels, slept in a church on the hard, cold pews, ate whatever Clinton bought at the small stores that dotted the main street.

May longed for clean clothes and a hot bath, raised a hand to her wretched hair and covering. Clinton told her to stay in the safety of the church, he'd find something, someone. It was better to go alone, brought less suspicion.

She shrank back against the pew and closed her eyes, as he let himself out the back door, closing it carefully behind him. She dozed again fitfully, thought she heard the back door again, but it was only the wind playing with a loose shutter. She shivered, wrapped her arms around her thin body, and waited. She could tell the sun was climbing higher by the light that came through the stained glass window, illuminating the picture of Christ's baptism by John the Baptist, complete with the white dove his Father had sent him.

May marveled at the skill and the hours of labor someone had put into that window, someone who had loved God immensely to give so much of his time. In the Old Testament, the temple had been magnificent, overlaid with gold, built with riches she could not comprehend. And when Jesus came, he drove out the moneychangers and men with greedy intent who had defiled God's temple.

She thought of her own people, who would never worship in a fine church with stained glass windows, who held humble services on hard benches, crowded into small houses, a tradition held over from the days of the martyrs who had gathered in coves and secret barns. Untouched by the world, a people set apart.

But were they truly?

Melvin Amstutz was ruled by his greed, driven to frenzied hard work to produce a substantial profit on the cotton. He whipped and swore his days throughout the week for six days, but on the seventh, he turned into a humble, God-fearing apostle of truth and righteousness, accepted as a stalwart member of the church.

And for the hundredth time, she shook herself free of cloying hatred of one so demented, so driven by strange desires, and she knew he was not the normal plain person. There were many good and loving men, men who abided by the Word of God, were kind and honest and lawful.

She could not judge a large group of people by one man. She realized, then, the sadness of her ruined existence. She would never be free of him. Never. To obliterate the overwhelming wrong of her past was an impossibility. It would always be attached to her skin, like a brown mole or a red, jagged scar, a part of her, same as every hair that grew from her scalp.

When the back door opened, she lifted glad eyes to receive Clinton but was horrified when brilliant lights turned on overhead. She heard voices, one shrill and strident, the other low and modulated. She slid off the pew, rolled underneath, stretched flat on her stomach, and hoped for the best, her heart thumping in her chest.

A door opened in the back. Objects rattled and bumped.

"I told you, Minerva, it ain't right. The way we git our turn two times to ever' bodies once."

"I like cleaning the church, Ruby. I told you often enough. If you don't want to help, well then, I guess you can go on home."

"One of these days. I'm gonna."

"You know, Ruby, you have a problem. You're plumb lazy. If you weren't helping me clean this church, you'd be lying around the house, pestering your little brother, and listening to the radio."

"Hm-mm. I would not."

A bucket rattled, then was followed by the sound of running water.

"Alright, you get the lavatories, and I'll run the dust mop."

There was no further exchange, except for the low sound of someone humming, the banging of the mop handle against wooden pews.

May shrank against the hardwood floor, prayed Clinton would not return.

"Minerva!"

"What?"

She was so close now. May could see the sensible black lace-up shoes, the sturdy ankles encased in heavy beige nylons.

"My rag fell in the toilet, and I ain't gettin' it out, either!"

There was a sound of exasperation, then the heavy tread as Minerva went to Ruby's rescue.

It was now or never.

In one lithe move, May slid out from under the pew, sprang to her feet, and ran to the massive front door, sliding soundlessly across the floor. She fumbled with the latch, until she saw how the heavy bolt slid back, and was out into the brilliance of midday sunshine. She squinted, looked right and left, before making her way around to the back door, where she waited beside a conifer tree, ready to melt into its needled branches if someone arrived.

She licked her dry lips, put a hand to her chest to still the thumping, then kept a practiced eye out for a stranger's approach. Somewhere, a door banged, a child shouted. A car horn honked in the distance, followed by the revving of an engine. It all seemed so foreign, so big and fast-moving, so frightening.

Where was Clinton?

Surely it had been more than three or four hours. She looked for a spot to sit on the ground before lowering herself as far beneath the prickly pine branches as possible, her ears tuned for his arrival.

She was becoming thirsty now and hadn't eaten since the evening before. She put a hand to her stomach when she felt a growling, then merely sat, waited, and tried to harness the thoughts that kept running through her head.

Surely he would not have met danger, been overtaken by men who were overcome with dislike at the sight of a black person.

This was New York, a safe place, wasn't it?

She shrank back when the back door was pushed open from the inside disgorging a middle-aged woman of considerable girth and a young petulant girl in a T-shirt and boy's trousers, chewing gum and popping bubbles as she waited till the key was inserted into the lock.

"There now. Whoever left that back door unlocked will certainly hear from me. An open church door is an invitation to all kinds of vagabonds. Remember that, Ruby."

But Ruby was tapping her feet and snapping her fingers in time, to an imaginary beat in her head and didn't respond, merely followed Minerva with her hips swaying arrogantly.

"Now Ruby, did you hear what I said?"

"Yes, ma'am."

They reached the gleaming black automobile, pulled open the doors, and folded themselves inside before moving off toward the street.

May breathed a long sigh. That was too close, she thought, and hoped Clinton would return with good news.

It was getting toward evening; the sun had already sunk behind the tall two-story garage that sat near the church when he finally made an appearance.

May stepped out from her hiding place and rushed to meet him, closed her eyes, and bit back the tears by compressing her mouth as he folded her against his chest. He rocked her gently, laid his cheek against her hair, murmured sweet words, and would not let her go.

"Clinton, someone will see," May murmured.

"Let them."

She smiled, then looked into his weary brown eyes when he told her he'd found an apartment and a place of employment.

"Really? Oh my. It's almost too good to be true."

"Yes, it is, isn't it?"

She could only nod happily.

"It's not much, but it will do. I met this man when I went to inquire at a gas station. He said to ask over at the grocery store, and that guy sent me to the fish market."

She nodded.

"So, at the fish market, there was a man who owned an apartment and would let me have it until I told him about you."

"Oh, I'm sorry," May said, the light passing out of her eyes at the thought of being a hindrance.

"It's not your fault, believe me. But I realized then that I was going to have a hard time finding something. They all said no, until I was directed to a Mrs. Mary Weinstein. She's Jewish and proudly told me she's eighty-three years old, and she didn't care who I brought into the apartment as long as it wasn't a camel."

They both burst out laughing.

"She said as long as we keep it clean, pay our rent on time, and keep the trash burned in a barrel in the backyard, the color of our skin doesn't mean anything to her."

May laughed outright, incredulous. That God had provided for them was proof that He would watch over them, perhaps love them enough to allow their union. But she knew He likely would not bless them, the guilt like a shield around her.

She said nothing to Clinton, however; she knew she must keep the faith and teachings of her people inside.

The apartment was two dingy rooms with cracked plaster on the walls, the color of the peeling paint neither gray nor green. The window frames and sills had been white at one time but were streaked with another grayish-green color, the paint scratched and peeling like a bad sunburn. The floor was an undetermined color, the tiles missing or broken, but there was a refrigerator, a metal cabinet that contained a porcelain sink, the faucet loose and dripping, the countertop stained and fractured. A small metal cabinet had been installed on the wall above it, and there was an electric stove with strange black coils on top. The kitchen table was sturdy enough, the chairs with missing rungs and chipped paint, but it was there, and it would be serviceable.

The windows had no blinds or curtains, the glass was streaked and gray, and tired flies buzzed around the cracked panes as they sought a way to freedom. A sagging brown sofa, a floor lamp, and a wooden stand beside it completed the kitchen.

May rushed eagerly to peer into the small bedroom that contained a bed and one mirrorless dresser, the adjacent bathroom an alcove with a porcelain claw-foot tub, a small sink, and a white commode. The tile on the wall was filthy, cracked and broken, but it was enough to please her. Yes, this was her home. She would scrub and scour, make curtains, cook and bake, and love her man; she would spend her days hidden away from prying eyes and curious onlookers.

"It ain't much, May, but we'll work on it," Clinton said, so contrite and so humble that she threw herself into his arms and murmured heartfelt endearments, so overcome with the joy of having her own home, no matter the circumstances that surrounded them.

"Oh Clinton, don't. It's perfect. I love it. We'll be happy here. I'm just so relieved to be free of that bus and those stations, and the rain can't get in at all, and we're safe and dry, and you have a job."

"If I can handle it."

Again, she heard the self-doubt, the modest tone.

"You never said what you're doing, exactly."

"Well, this town is on the edge of Lake Ontario, so I guess these fishing boats come in with their catch at the fish market. I'll be learning the art of cleaning fish, getting them packed and ready for the wholesale guy. Something like that."

May told him it might not be to his liking, the way the hard work in the sugar cane fields kept him happy.

"Yes. I thought of that, I did. I love to be challenged, to meet the demands of hard labor, even surpass my own expectations. The cane took everything I had to give, but it built character. There's a competition goes on with those men, see how many pounds you can cut. So maybe cleaning fish will be the same."

"You think you'll be able to bring them home?"

Already thinking of the meals she would prepare, May remembered the golden fillets of catfish she'd fried for Enos and Ammon, the small bluegills she'd rolled in flour and fried in butter for Leviticus.

Clinton shrugged, and May noted the faraway look in his deep brown eyes.

With money scarce, they had to ask Mary Weinstein for cleaning supplies, which was met with a snort of disapproval, saying she hadn't included this in the monthly rent. They promised to repay everything after Clinton received his first paycheck, were met with a wave of her hand and a "yeah, yeah, I hear that all the time." May was upset and took the mistrust and grudging attitude to heart, but Clinton shrugged it off, said it was the way of it when you lived in the world.

They cleaned until exhaustion overcame them, the light bulb from the ceiling lighting the walls only enough to correct smudges. Both were nervous, thinking of bedtime, not knowing what the other was expecting, so it was far easier to keep working, chattering on about nothing. Finally, Clinton emptied the bucket for the last time, stopped, and looked at May.

"If you take the bed, I'll sleep on the couch."

With one sentence, he had cleared her fears from the air. Indeed, there was much to overcome, much that needed discussion, and May was not prepared for what he expected of her.

"I . . . I need clean clothes. I have no sleepwear." Flustered, she passed her hand across her dress front, felt the dust of travel, the time beneath the church pews, the smell of the filthy apartment. "I'm no better than a tramp," she finished.

Clinton looked up from emptying the bucket.

"Well, I never thought of all that. Now you know how lacking I'll be as far as a . . . a husband."

"Clinton, will we be husband and wife with no marriage license and no minister to perform the ceremony?" She almost said *no God to bless us,* but didn't.

"My darling girl, what are we expected to do?"

She turned her face away, shrugged.

He went to her then, took her small reddened hands, and kissed them, first one, then the other.

"Look at me, May."

When she did, there was no denying the strong feelings he had for her, his eyes burning with unspoken love and longing. She exchanged the yearning, the joy of their love with one of her own, her brown eyes softening until a lone teardrop fell on her cheek, where it glistened like a rare pearl.

He reached up to wipe it away so tenderly she moaned and brought her arms up to his shoulders, gripped him with all the strength she felt for this kind and humble man.

That night, the moon rose above Lake Ontario in New York, moved up above the jagged line of the conifer forest, its light shimmering across the dark still waters of the lake, then climbed higher in the sky to touch the window of Mary Weinstein's apartment, its blue light illuminating the old brown sofa without an occupant.

In the morning, May was shy, dressed in one of his shirts and a clean pair of jeans, held at the waist by a large safety pin. There was nothing between them except the true love of two people who had found each other and made the best out of dire circumstances.

Clinton bought a loaf of bread, a dozen eggs, a jug of milk, then found no frying pan or anything to eat with. May laughed, a sound of pure mirth, and felt so happy at the sight of Clinton standing helplessly at the table with his purchases.

They hadn't opened the cupboard doors, hadn't thought of dishes and frying pans.

"How much money is left?" May asked, still smiling.

"Enough for food till my paycheck, but nothing more."

"Well, we'll have to borrow from Mary."

"I'd rather not. She's not real happy to share."

"I'll go."

And she did, tripping down the long stairway with her jeans rolled up to prevent falling, her shirttail flapping, and her face radiant with the promise of something far greater than an existence of dread. Nothing could deter her happiness now, nothing could destroy her warm, secure life with Clinton or ruin a new and promising future of happiness.

She knocked on the door that led to Mary Weinstein's living room, then tilted her head to the right and smiled when the small woman pulled the door open.

"Good morning, Mary."

"Now what?"

"We forgot about dishes. We don't have a frying pan to make our breakfast. Could we possibly borrow one?"

"No, you cannot borrow a frying pan."

"Oh. Well . . ."

Mary looked her up and down, laughed a little, and shrugged. "I'll make you some breakfast."

"No, oh no. We can't put you out like that."

"Why, sure you can. I'll show you what a good Yiddish breakfast looks like, alright? You collect your man and get down here."

May ran up the stairs, burst into the apartment, and told Clinton he would not believe the landlady's invitation. Like two children they were, running down the stairs hand in hand, smiling, talking, laughing, wonderfully in love with each other and the world that stretched before them like a long golden road.

Mary Weinstein was in her element, cooking in her kitchen for two hungry people. She produced a delicious breakfast of fish and poached eggs with a green sauce dotted with spices and herbs, a soft doughy bread that was spread with butter and grape jam, strong black tea, and cups of hot chocolate. She served the food with words flowing as freely as her generosity, words laced with a thick accent once she became enmeshed with stories of the old world.

Clinton listened respectfully but wolfed his food ravenously, watched May with awe—this sweet, delicate girl of his dreams who had followed him all this way, and now his future was woven around her, for her, and by her.

She was his; she consumed his thoughts, his breathing, his spirit.

May nodded at him, sending thrills of sweet and unexpected love into the air around them both, and he marveled that something quite like this could be called wrong.

It was wrong according to society and the law. It was wrong according to the *ordnung* (rules) of the Amish church, disapproved by Roy and Martha's church. They had everything, and yet they had nothing, viewed as strange outlaws and heretics.

When Mary told them Moses of the Old Testament had an Ethiopian wife, they gasped, stunned. When she marched into the living room and showed them from the Old Testament written in Hebrew, May felt as if, truly, her heart could not contain one more drop of joy.

CHAPTER 18

Oba ADJUSTED HIS SHIRT COLLAR, TUCKED IT INTO HIS jeans, ran a hand over his hair, and wished for a pocket mirror. He tried to imagine meeting his old friend—if you could call him that, Oba having met him only a few times—but he was the only acquaintance he could attempt to ask for help.

He found his knees were shaking as he walked up to the wrought-iron gate that was latched, lifted shaking hands to undo it; he watched a large farm dog lift its head from its paws before rising to its feet, eyeing him warily.

He heard dishes rattling, voices from the kitchen. He hesitated, then stepped up on the porch, relieved to find the dog's tail wagging back and forth, a welcoming banner of brown fur.

Before he could lift his hand to knock, a voice from inside called, "Come on in!"

Oba felt strange, opening the screen door, so he stepped in quietly, stood against the door to quiet its closing, cleared his throat, and tried to speak.

Leonard rose from the table, came over to peer at his face, his wife's and children's faces all turned in his direction.

"Are you who I think you are?" Leonard asked, his voice not unkind.

"Oba. I'm Oba Miller."

"I thought so. Come on in!"

Oba allowed himself the smallest smile.

"So, tell me, where have you been? Are you hungry? Sadie, you may as well put on another plate."

"I'm alright."

"But you'll eat. We have new potatoes and peas."

He didn't know if he should. Perhaps they shouldn't eat with him. He was English and no longer a part of them. He'd heard about *bann und meidung*—the excommunication, followed by the shunning, wherein a person would no longer be allowed to sit up to a table and eat with the devout members of the Amish church.

It was an *ordnung*, a rule kept by them all, everyone who had been baptized into the church, who had promised to lead a life for Christ and obey all the rules made by God and man. And here he was: an *Englisha*, dressed like the world, disobedient. He should be shunned, not seated at a table with Leonard, his wife, and children.

He felt unclean.

"Come, Oba. There's plenty." Leonard questioned him with his eyes when he hesitated. "Come. Sit down."

"Maybe I shouldn't."

"Why not?"

"Don't you have to shun me?"

"Why, certainly not. You never took the vows. You were never a member of our church. So no. There's no shunning for someone like you. It's for the ones who make the promise and break it."

A very small "oh" escaped Oba's lips before he sat down and looked around self-consciously. Should he pray? Or should he eat?

Leonard saw his discomfiture, motioned to his family to bow their heads for a moment of silence with Oba. Relieved, he followed their lead, then fell on his plate of food without further words.

Leonard slanted a look at Sadie. She lifted her eyebrows, then held her coffee cup to her mouth.

When Oba leaned back, Sadie brought apple pie and milk. There were canned peaches and shoofly cake.

One by one, the small children lost interest and wandered off to their play. Leonard leaned over to extricate the baby from his highchair and was rewarded by a happy laugh from the little one, who nestled on his lap and promptly stuck a thumb in his mouth. A child who appeared to be two years came to grab the baby's hands, saying "Owen! Owen! *Komm*, Owen!"

Leonard put the baby on the floor, and he took off with the speed of a seasoned crawler, the two-year-old walking alongside, saying, "*Ich grick dich*" ("I'll get you").

All this Oba watched around his mouthful of dessert, the pie sweet and flaky, laced with brown sugar and cinnamon.

He felt full. Filled up with a nameless substance that was good and satisfying. It filled up every empty space he hadn't known existed.

When Sadie got up to wash dishes and Leonard told the boys to get the cows in, he'd be out, and Oba saw one of the girls get the dishcloth to wipe the tray on the highchair, he wanted to be a part of this substance that was family and order and happiness and simplicity.

"Do you want to sit on the porch?" Leonard asked.

"I . . . we could, I guess."

"Want a toothpick?"

"No. I . . . no thanks."

Seated on a wooden rocking chair with Leonard beside him, Oba felt unexpectedly exposed, fragile. He felt Leonard would laugh at him, tell him he needed to forget the past, there wasn't anything wrong with Melvin.

He had a hard time getting started.

Leonard asked questions, talked about the weather, his crops, anything to ease the ever-increasing agitation in Oba. Finally, when he knew the milking was imminent, Leonard got up to ask if Miriam could take his place at milking tonight.

"Really, Dat?" from inside.

"Just for tonight since you love it so much?" Leonard followed this with a laugh of genuine mirth when the daughter answered with an exaggerated groan.

Oba felt another empty crevice filled with the marvelous substance.

"Now, tell me why you're here," Leonard said in a soft voice, his eyes still twinkling from the unexpected answer from his daughter.

"Oh, I don't know."

Oba looked at his brown leather shoes, watched a small black spider weaving a web between the shrubbery and a pair of tall rubber boots, cleared his throat, and wished he could disappear. What would this family know of delivered blows and deprivation, of unfairness and assumed craziness? How could this man understand a young life that wandered from one dry desert to another, without love and understanding and deliverance from pain?

Every whipping was a remembered barren island without solace.

"I don't guess you want to hear it."

"Sure I do. Fire away. Tell me what's on your mind."

"Well, it's Melvin."

"I figured."

"You did?"

A nod, a scowl, and a shake of his head.

Encouraged, Oba plowed ahead, drew the furrows deep and steady, leaving no stone unturned. His past was revealed like the roots of the grass he had overturned in the fields, exposing the hard truth with averted eyes, his soft voice riddled with unshed tears.

At one point, Leonard asked if he was telling the truth, really. He knew Melvin to be a hard man, one given to set high goals for himself, but this? He appeared incredulous, in disbelief.

So Oba stood, turned his back, and lifted his shirt. The evening sun elevated the white scars that snaked across his back, crosshatched his skin like an open book—a book that told of a whip that hissed through the humidity of Arkansas summers, that cut his skin and exploded through his head with blinding pain.

Leonard leaped to his feet, grabbed Oba's shoulder, and turned him toward the light, the evening rays exposing the healed, discolored flesh.

"No, no, no," he moaned, then drew in a breath softly.

Oba heard the sobs, felt his fingertips exploring the ridges, felt Leonard's forehead on his right shoulder, and was baptized by his tears, the warm moisture of them like a healing salve that began to melt the frigid iceberg that was his spirit.

A choked, "This can't be true. Oba, where were we? Where were we . . ."

To be believed was all he had asked for, to be understood. He'd gladly take a part of the blame, gladly agree he'd been disobedient, if only someone believed what Melvin had done. He had not expected this, had never imagined the wellspring of mercy and pity and righteous fury, the self-blame and the incredulity of his suffering.

Oba lowered his shirt, turned to find Leonard openly, unabashedly crying, his eyes red and swollen, his cheeks wet with tears. He reached into his pocket for a handkerchief, blew his nose, and wiped his face, as Oba stood before him, tucking in his shirttail, unsure of what he should do or say in the face of this man's reaction.

"Oba," Leonard said shakily. "Oba."

"Yes?"

"Let me say this first of all. Nothing about this is right. This is wrong. No one deserves what you have received. Why didn't you speak to me?"

"I wasn't sure it wasn't my own fault. And I was ashamed. A person shouldn't talk of these things."

"I know things are kept secret, and if we knew the goings-on among our fellow men, we'd be surprised, likely, but this is not the usual order of the day. I have never seen such scars. This will have to be talked about."

"I came here hoping you can help those three boys. He may be treating them the same way. I think he's really lost his mind."

He told Leonard of the incident with the wagon and team of mules.

Leonard shook his head, sank into his wooden chair with an air of exhaustion, the enormity of what had appeared in his life almost unbearable.

Over and over, he voiced his regret of living just a few miles away yet remaining oblivious to the cruelty of his neighbor, uncaring for Oba's plight.

"You didn't know," Oba said.

"I will make up for my blindness. Melvin will have to be brought to account. This isn't right. It just isn't."

Oba felt the easiness, the soft cushion of redemption.

Someone was on his side. Someone believed in him. If nothing good would ever enter his life from here on out, he had this. This evening on Leonard Yoder's porch. He could still feel the cool air on his bare back, the touch of those callused fingers, the warm tears like an elixir from Paradise. It was so much more than he could have imagined.

Quite unexpectedly, he wondered if this was what it would be like to meet Jesus. Wasn't He the Savior who supposedly took pity on sinners? Chills washed over him in cold waves. He felt the prick of tears, but he could not let Leonard see he was soft inside. So he chewed on the inside of his cheek and averted his eyes, afraid one spark of kindness in Leonard's would break the retaining wall of his own emotions.

Leonard sighed. "Would you go with me to the bishop?"

"No."

"If I took you? If I did all the talking? Would you show him your back?"

"I can't. You know how it is. They'll believe Melvin. He'll have his story, and they'll believe it."

Leonard wanted to deny this, wanted to say Oba was wrong, but he knew that might very well be the case, in the end.

"But your back . . ." he began.

"My back is nothing if Melvin tells them I was disobedient."

"Your scars will not be taken lightly by me and whoever I can round up to accompany me. Look. I know we don't take things like this to the police or get lawyers involved—any of that. That is for the world. But, Oba, if anything like this happens again, I'm not too sure about the *ordnung* (rules) of our people. Someone like Melvin cannot be allowed to continue. What about May? Do you think he hurt her, too?"

"I don't think so. May said he didn't."

"But she left."

"Yes. I wanted to come back for her and was too late."

"No one knows her whereabouts?"

"No one, as far as I know. I fear for her safety. I think about her all the time. She's so young and inexperienced."

Leonard didn't answer, merely gritted his teeth at the mention of her youth and innocence. Well, there was only one path forward and that was to talk to Melvin first, then bring other men and try to persuade him to admit and repent, hopefully before it was too late.

He asked Oba if he had a place to stay or if he was going back to his place in California.

Oba was accosted by the rude insertion into another time and place, the reality of returning to a way of life that he now realized was not his own, never had been, and never would be. He'd been like the chaff, blown away by the winds of his own fear and anger and disgust, thought he hated God and the Amish and certainly Melvin.

But here was a renewal, an arrow on a sign that pointed him in a different direction. Had he ever felt a part of Tom Lyons's family? Had he ever been comfortable with his grandsons, their beautiful mother and benevolent father? And the grandiose notion of college and the high aspiration of becoming a doctor or pharmacist?

Why not?

His smallest ambition had been to drive a car, travel the California coastline, see the wonders of the pounding surf and the redwood forests—do what he wanted, whenever he wanted. But he would have to return on his own terms, not Tom Lyons's or anyone else. He wanted to experience that life, free and untethered, but someday he wanted exactly what Leonard Yoder had: a wife, a farm, and a family.

He wanted to feel the supple leather of a harness as he flung it across a mule's back, wanted to feel the strong coupling as he fastened the traces, wanted to feel the sun on his back as he stood on a wagon hauling cotton to the gin, hear the quail whistling their calls from the hawthorn tree. He knew he loved the land, the changing seasons, and the challenge of growing things in the loamy soil of the delta plain.

All this spread a solid gladness in his heart, a warm river of knowledge that filled every barren void. He had not known any of this until Leonard had unknowingly given him a choice, a choice seasoned and tempered by his mercy, his faith in him.

"I don't have a place to stay. I wasn't planning on it, really. I came to get May is the reason I'm here. I was going to take her back to Tom Lyons, who promised she could stay. I'm too late, obviously."

"Well, listen. You can stay here. I'm going to Abram Hostetler's now, and we'll go from there. You won't go with me?"

"No. I don't really want to."

"Well, alright. If I need you, will you come?"

"I don't know."

"You can spend the night here, why don't you?"

"I guess I could." He felt self-conscious now, the way he'd felt at Tom Lyons's house, as if he was a pathetic creature, a nearly drowned cat, an injured dog.

"I'll go talk to Sadie."

The screen door closed, leaving Oba alone with his thoughts, the scars on his back a newly tempered thing. Inflicted by cruelty, but now . . .

He felt plucked out of a raging river of anger, set on dry ground, given another chance. But he realized the danger of living here if the men of the community could not accomplish with Melvin what had to be done.

The screen door banged, then again, as two girls rushed out of the house and down the path to the barn, their bare legs churning, skirts flapping like petals of colorful flowers tossed in the wind.

"I'm first!" one shouted.

"You had him first last night. It's my turn," was flung over the leader's shoulder, her reddish hair loose from the *dichly* (small bandana) on her head.

They disappeared through the barn door. A rooster squawked, running with its wings spread, to turn and glare at the girls before lifting its proud head and crowing his indignation. A cluster of barn cats sat against the wall of the barn, their pink tongues grooming the multicolored fur on their chests and legs, sated by the generous dish of milk they had been given by one of the milkers.

The girls reappeared, holding the reins of a fairly large pony, as white as new cream, his mane a shade darker, as if there was brown sugar mixed with the cream. He pranced a beautiful light dance on feet that would never stay still for any length of time.

The first girl grabbed a handful of the mane, stood aside, and flung herself on his back, the pony accelerating immediately to a leap, scattering gravel before hitting a flowing gallop that was both beautiful and frightening. No saddle, nothing to hold on to.

He found he could not take his eyes off the poetry of the easy way she rode, the understanding between horse and rider.

Oba had never ridden a horse, save for his time on a mule's back when Melvin needed the garden cultivated. He couldn't imagine owning a horse for the pleasure of riding.

She turned the pony, which brought a toss of his head and another burst of speed, the feet barely hitting the driveway as he flew headlong toward the barn. She wasn't holding back on the reins, merely riding low on his back, laughing as she rode, in perfect unison with the pony and his gait.

When they slid to a stop, the sister hopped up and down excitedly, clapping her hands and shouting.

Oba was pulled back from his entertaining observation when Leonard appeared with his wife, Sadie, her eyes kind but very dark and serious.

"Oba, you're welcome to spend the night, as Leonard said. If you'll come with me, I'll show you to the guest room. Do you have a satchel?"

Oba nodded, followed her through the house, up the stairs to a room at the end of a hallway. She lifted dark blinds, then turned to look at him.

"I hope you will be comfortable. Leonard tells me you have been mistreated and wish to find May. I blame myself. I had too many suspicions about that place but chose to let sleeping dogs lie, so to speak. We'll try and do what we can to make this right, Oba, but I fear for May, and for that, I feel horribly responsible. We let this go when we shouldn't have."

Oba shifted his weight uncomfortably, could not meet the earnest eyes. He tried to speak but could only swallow. He nodded, opened his mouth to say something, anything, but could only clear his throat.

Sadie placed a hand on his arm.

He felt the kindness, felt the profound caring, and knew he had found a friend, perhaps the small beginnings of someone who could be like a mother.

Suddenly he thought of Gertie. Would she take kindly to the men who came to interfere in her life?

Sadie assured him there was plenty of room to roam here on the farm, so if he wanted, he could walk back to the pond, see if he could find deer.

He nodded, then left her company, relieved to be away from her kindness, the eyes that spoke in volumes but could never understand the chaos in his soul.

He spoke to no one as he made his way through the kitchen and across the yard. He was dimly aware of the girls watching him as he walked without knowing where the pond or the forest was supposed to be, walked to get away from the magnetism of this loving family.

How could he succumb to their gentleness and goodwill, if it was bound to run out? Like money in the bank, you spent it, and it was gone.

Every day, he would be using up their store of kindness, soaking it up like a thirsty sponge, just being who he was until they saw it, and the kindness ran out. Everything did. Parents died, sisters disappeared, crazy uncles did whatever they pleased, dreams evaporated.

Being here solved nothing.

Leonard Yoder and his men might go visit Melvin, which provided no guarantee to his own future, no matter how badly he wanted to stay, to become a part of this loving family. He had wanted the same thing from Tom Lyons and his family but never belonged in the truest sense. He'd disappointed them all, in the end, as he would disappoint this family again.

And he had his first duty to May. He need to search for her until he found her, impossible as the task might be.

In the morning, he was gone.

The family searched the surrounding woods and fields, checked his room for any clue he might have left, but there was none. The bed had been slept in, neatly made with the quilt tucked beneath the plump pillows; even the blinds were pulled to the windowsill.

Leonard shook his head, his eyes pleading with his wife to tell him where he might have gone. He questioned the children, who all had the same story. He'd come in late, they heard him go to bed in the guest room upstairs, but no one heard him leave.

Nothing was said about Leonard's visit to the Amstutz place, except to his wife, who was well-versed in the way of secrecy. These things were not spoken of, shameful goings-on that needed to be guarded from the innocent ears of children, the outcome of the visit not meant to float through the community like slanderous fog that would diminish the light of peace and love.

Oba went back to the town of Blytheville, inquired at every store, every place of business he knew May might have been seen. A few acquaintances stopped to inquire of his well-being, but not one of them had seen May.

He stood against the wall of the drugstore, his hands in his pockets, watched the comings and goings of the community, automobiles chugging along the potholed streets, hitching racks becoming filled as poor sharecroppers and Amish alike tied their horses and walked off to attend to business.

He had no destination, no immediate plans, only the desperation to find May or at least obtain some lead to her whereabouts.

He thought of Roy and Martha on McKinley Street, wondered if perhaps there was a chance of their knowing anything, but dismissed the idea just as quickly, recalling the way Melvin forbade them having anything to do with the field hands and May's absolute obedience. He considered returning to the Yoder farm, but his mistrust replaced the longing for the stability he knew would come to an end, the result of his inability to tolerate all the kindness.

He did not deserve one good thing.

No matter that Leonard Yoder cried about the scars, no matter that he'd almost experienced redemption by having one person on his side.

Who knew the outcome of Leonard's visit to Melvin?

And so his thoughts roiled as he paced the streets of Blytheville, never coming to a peaceful solution, his mind roaming amid the hills and craters of his violent past.

Was it chance that sent Arpachshad Brown into the drugstore for a vial of healing salve for a cut on the flesh of his thumb where a fishhook had snagged him? All Oba knew was the fact that he was there, suddenly sprung like a dark figure of welcome, his eyes lit up with the joy of meeting Oba again.

Drink paid for his purchases, then strolled with Oba along Main Street, limping a little on his injured leg.

When Oba told him May had gone missing, Arpachshad shook his head sadly. Said he had never gotten to know her, though his brother Clinton was the one who could never seem to get the girl off his mind.

Oba looked at him, sharply.

"You mean, they spent time together? Do you think . . .?"

Drink tossed his head. "Lordy, no. You don't know much, do you? There ain't a black guy in all of Arkansas who would dare attempt getting acquainted real good with any white girl, an' especially if she got . . ." Here, he made motions on top of his curly black hair. "You know, got religion. No, Oba Miller, they ain't no way. Clinton is smart enough not to try any o' that."

Oba nodded.

"Did he find her attractive? I mean, did you talk about her?"

"Yeah. He told me she was like a vision. Like the vision of an angel they talk about in church."

"Well, she was. Is."

Drink kicked a paper cup to the curb, then stopped short, pursed his lips, and said, "He used to go somewhere on his bike, I remember. In the evening, but I can't say where I don't suppose. Nah, he'd never."

Roy and Martha had never breathed a word of the night Clinton and May spent at the house, glad Arpachshad had not been there. They told him Clinton hadn't gone back to the sugar cane and instead had gone up north to try his hand at some new kind of work, which they figured was true.

CHAPTER 19

SHE LOVED LIVING IN MARY WEINSTEIN'S APARTMENT, LOVED the everyday routine of caring for Clinton, cooking, cleaning, washing and ironing clothes, in spite of having to carry all her laundry two stories down to a dark basement that contained an electric wringer washer and hot water from a spigot on the wall. Nothing could take away her sense of newfound love, the joy of being in love with a man who was kind and good, who spent his days at the fish market, then rushed home as soon as possible for a shower, clean clothes, and a delicious supper May had spent most of the afternoon cooking. They savored an unhurried time spent around the kitchen table, learning to know each other on a deeper level. They spoke of their pasts, their future, where they could go to become a part of a community, when the time would come when society in general would accept them.

They never went out together, or if they attempted it, it became like a getaway, maneuvered as quickly as possible, in an effort to avoid undue attention.

With the arrival of winter, May found no reason to fret. She merely bought a few squares of muslin, a variety of embroidery thread, and a package of needles. She settled herself on the couch with a soft lap robe and created beautiful designs of hummingbirds and flowers, butterflies and vines, all the beauty she remembered on the farm in Arkansas.

There had been beauty surrounding her, and she chose to keep those memories alive. She still thought of Leviticus most. She hoped Melvin would marry again and choose a woman who would exercise kindness, someone who might be better able to shield the boys than she had, or who at least could offer them some affection.

The small grains of ice made a pleasant sound on the window pane as another snowstorm spread its power across the northern part of the United States. Up and down the coast of the New England states into New York and Canada, the snow began as bits of ice, followed by a strong wind that drove the particles into cracks and crevices, causing folks to bend their heads and hang on to their hats as they hurried from place to place. Farmers scurried to round up their livestock, reinforced clattering barn doors, nailed down loose siding and flapping corrugated tin roofs. Cars and trucks slipped and slid, righted themselves and kept going at a reduced speed.

May put down her embroidery, walked to the window, and put a hand to the back of her neck, her fingertips massaging the ache, then stretched and yawned. She stayed there, watching the scene below: the scurrying pedestrians, the traffic slowed to a crawl as folks hunched over their steering wheels.

She thought of winter as a child in Ohio, her mother watching the snowstorms from a window in the living room. She had always loved the snow. She would go to the top cupboard to get down her gray metal recipe box and search eagerly for cookie recipes, saying "Which one, May, which one?"

They would bake cookies and bread, a slew of pies, then put them in a basket and traipse through the knee-deep snow to visit the elderly neighbors, their hands and feet tingling with the cold and freezing wind that threw great gusts into their faces. And they would laugh at the cold, giggle like two children, slip and slide and sometimes flounder like fish in the snow.

May smiled to herself, her eyes misting over at the thought of her darling mother, her soul in Heaven now, a new body walking the streets of gold, singing praises to Jesus and to God on His throne.

May believed her mother and father had departed to be with Jesus when they died, and her fervent prayer was to join them there when her life ended, in spite of living in sin.

Yes, she was doing just that, according to Scripture and all the rules of society and especially so of the Amish church. She was dressed *ganz aus die ordnung* (totally out of the rules) in an English skirt and blouse with her hair cut short in a neat style that rode above her shoulders. She kept her old covering rolled into a ball in the back of her drawer in the bedroom, afraid it would be sacrilegious to throw it out. Often, her conscience pricked her uncomfortably, but only when she thought of other men's rules.

She could not help matters, the way society forbid a marriage between two people of a different race, neither could she have saved herself from a far worse fate with Melvin had it not been for Clinton, the only person who had made an attempt to help her.

She would be forever in his debt, this kind and gentle man who gave up his own life to live here with her in New York. Surely God would understand a love such as this, in spite of society's unacceptance.

And so she prayed, always asking Jesus to have mercy on her soul, on the circumstances that surrounded her, to keep Clinton in His mercies, to keep Leviticus safe from harm.

When Clinton ran up the steps after darkness had stolen across the land, May waited eagerly and was not disappointed, swept up into his strong arms, his lips smothering her with cold kisses that were moistened with melting snow. They moved to the couch together and wondered at the love that only grew more complete with each passing day, the heat that generously surrounded them from the rattling cast-iron radiators against the wall, and the smell of the ground-beef-and-potato casserole in the oven.

They were blessed, they said.

The snow continued to fall, silently swiping the cold window-panes, dancing and careening wildly when the wind moaned down from the jagged mountain peaks, but inside the small apartment, there was a haven of rest and love for May, something she had never before experienced or could have imagined.

Clinton was still shivering after a hot shower, his teeth chattering with the cold as he came into the kitchen where May was removing the casserole from the oven. He crossed his arms, ran his hands up and down his muscular biceps, then went to stand by the radiator to absorb more of the heat.

"Are you still so cold?" May asked, laughing.

"I am. Seems I'm chilled to the bone. Can't get warm at all."

"Come. We'll eat, and you'll warm up. Did you have enough in your dinner pail?"

"Yes, of course. You always pack the best lunch ever."

"Did you get my note?" She glanced at him shyly, a small blush appearing on her porcelain cheek.

"Of course, May, my darling girl. It made my whole day. I simply do not deserve a woman like you."

"But you do, you know. I mean . . . Not that I'm . . ."

He laughed, a loud burst of sound that took her by surprise, then caused her to flounder to explain herself.

"I mean, you do deserve good things."

"Meaning you!" He laughed again.

And so they ate, savoring the food and each other, talking about the everyday goings-on at the fish market, the cold and ice building up on the lake, the ease with which a coworker sliced thin fillets of fish and ate them raw.

Still, Clinton could not get comfortable, shivering as he pulled on another pair of socks. May watched him, then decided he needed a hot water bottle. She reached out a hand to check his forehead. She drew back, alarmed.

"You're on fire!" she exclaimed. "Let me go to the five-and-dime store to buy a thermometer."

"No. No use wasting the money. It's just a chill."

"Let me make you some tea, though. A good hot cup will warm you up, okay?"

She wrapped him in the heavy woolen blankets they'd found at the Salvation Army store for a dollar, brought the tea, and nestled beside him with a cup of her own. Still he shivered.

During the night, his temperature rose even further, his body so feverish it seemed to be radiating more intense heat than the radiators that pinged to life as the room cooled, then hissed and rattled as the steam moved along the copper pipes.

In the morning, the storm had abated, slivers of red and lavender showing through thin gray storm clouds. But the wind was picking up by the hour, which meant the streets would be awash in gigantic walls of loose powdery snow that would effectually obliterate all moving objects, turn buildings invisible, and send any person running for shelter.

May stood at the window in the first rays of daylight, her chenille bathrobe wrapped firmly around her slim waist, her feet shoved into a pair of woolen socks. The heat from the radiator felt wonderful, and she luxuriated in it, thanked God for this blessing that floated from the invention of cast iron and unknown other miracles. How often had she coaxed a meager fire to life in the old cook stove, only to find the dense smoke choking her, coughing and slamming the lid as if the devil would climb out if she procrastinated? She grinned to herself, mischievous now. What was she now? Worldly? Was she enjoying luxuries to the point of living for her own pleasure?

But oh . . . she hadn't always. She had not.

She had lived for someone else's pleasure.

She found herself crumpled on the couch, sobbing hysterically, the shame and the pain crawling over her skin like offensive worms. She could never be free of her past, she realized for the thousandth time, refreshed yet again by the one vile thought of Melvin Amstutz, the uncle, the benefactor, the pious churchgoing member of a religious group so conservative they would not speak of sin. The pain of her past inflicted itself on her when she randomly thought of luxury, a well-deserved comfort in a warm room.

Miserable wretch that I am.

She thought of the verse from the Bible. Someone understood. Someone had written those words, a holy man of God. Then surely there was deliverance for her as well.

As Clinton lay in a feverish state, shivering and moaning, May suffered a sickness of the soul as the virus of memories cropped up like an unwelcome scourge. When he called for water, she did not hear, so engulfed was she in sorrows of her own.

He was fired at the fish market because of his sickness. No one could take off a whole week and expect to get away with it. He begged for understanding, was told he'd already been replaced, so there was nothing to do but move on, be respectful, try not to stir up controversy.

Clinton was a man of color, so he took what he could get, which was the right to seek employment elsewhere, and be glad of it.

May was supportive, told him he'd find an even better job, but when nothing showed up in the course of a week, he became bitter, withdrawn.

Two weeks with no income. The situation was becoming serious. They'd managed to save a little money, even with Oba's meager earnings, but it wouldn't last much longer.

May stretched their food supply with pancakes and corn pone, oatmeal for breakfast, and beans instead of meat. Clinton tried to accept it with a good sense of humor but came home every evening with an air of defeat. When he refused to talk about his day spent searching for employment, she was deeply hurt but kept her distance, tried to give him space, and told herself it was only his way of dealing with rejection.

One night after finishing yet another plate of beans, he burst out in a valley of hateful words against the divide between black and white. Shocked, May shrank against the back of her chair, her large brown eyes black with fright.

"Clinton, no, please don't."

"It ain't right, an' you know it ain't."

As always, when he was frightened or angry, he reverted to the old way of speaking, the Southern phrases, the stilted words May loved to hear. She wished he would always speak in the Southern lilt, the dreamy stops and starts she found so endearing. He was so much a part of her, so huge in her existence, she loved everything about him, even his speech, the way he bounced slightly when he walked. Everything.

"If my skin was white, I'd have a job, and you know it. Every white person that owns a business in this town could use me in their business, I guarantee it. Then they wonder why we got violent, land in jail? I'll tell you why, May. This is why. Because we live in unfair conditions our whole life. We're colored as the day we was born. That very thing takes away our privileges, our right to have what is rightfully ours. It's just wrong."

With that, his big fist came down and hit the table, rattling the dishes and upsetting a water glass. May quietly rose, reached for a linen tea towel, calmly wiped at the small puddle of water, then turned to wring it out. Very softly, she sighed.

Clinton put his head in his hands, his handsome face distraught, his eyebrows lowered to hide his closed eyes.

"You think my life was fair?" she asked, quiet and low.

She saw the transformation before he turned to her, felt his arms drawing her to him, and was held on his lap like a child. He murmured his heartfelt regret at the outburst, and she put a hand on each side of his face and kissed him softly, with so much love, that he laid his head on her shoulder and cried his tears of frustration.

"It's life, Clinton. As long as we are mortals on the face of the earth, we will encounter prejudice, unfairness, evil, cowardly people. We need to remember God wants us to have courage, to face every obstacle with His strength, then we will be able to conquer."

"But I forget, May. I do. I get so mad I want to take the low road and smash my fist into someone's face. I want to yell at the fat man behind his desk and tell him he doesn't have to lie or smirk or give me that triumphant look. He's glad he can't give me a job. Glad! He's happy to see yet another black man get turned away, because he is BLACK."

The word was spat across the room, with every person of color who had been mistreated behind its emphasis.

"Maybe not all of them are so awful," May said softly.

"I'm sorry, May. You're right. Maybe not."

She brightened. "I'll go look for a job. I can cook, clean. I could wait on tables at some restaurant. Or iron clothes for people."

"No, May. I don't want you out there. Please. No."

"We could move to another town."

"You really think that would make a difference?"

"Maybe."

When no job became available until the following Friday of the third week, May felt the fabric of their union beginning to unravel. He no longer laughed or snuggled with her when he came home; he merely threw himself into a kitchen chair, with more stories of outrage and imagined vengeance against the world ruled by the white race. Bitterness erased the laugh lines around his eyes, turned his mouth into a hard caustic line that did not bode well for anyone crossing his path. He refused his plate of cornbread and beans, went to lie on the bed with his face against the wall. When she crept softly to him and began to massage the stiff shoulders, he shrugged her off.

Hurt beyond all reason, she slunk out of the bedroom and out to the cluttered kitchen table, where she threw dishes into the sink without caring if they broke. Such a short time ago, everything had been different. Everything had been filled with love, the very walls vibrated with the power of their happiness, and here was her hero, her whole life, distraught and angry, leaving her helpless in the wake of his desperation.

Courage. She needed it now. She would gather all the courage she could find, the way she used to take the biggest woven basket to the garden when the green beans were ready to pick; she would fill the basket with courage and venture out by herself. She would find a job—perhaps not waiting on tables, since Clinton had forbade it, but she would find something.

She finished the dishes, her resolve spurring her on, then swept the small kitchen with the tattered little broom she'd found in the closet by the door and went to stand by the window to watch the streetlights below. Headlights moved slowly up and down the snowy streets, cars slid to a halt to allow well-bundled pedestrians to cross to the other side.

She had to speak with Mrs. Weinstein before another day went by. Rent was due, and there were no funds. She dreaded approaching Clinton about this matter, which would grow into epic proportions in his addled mind.

Mary Weinstein was in no mood for visitors.

When she heard the timid knock, she looked up from her crocheting, an annoyed snort coming from her mouth, then set the bundle of half-finished blanket aside, rose slowly to her feet, and made her way to the door. She touched the end table, the oak bureau, the back of a chair, till she reached the door and turned the knob with arthritic fingers.

She found May, white-faced and trembling, her eyes like those of a stray dog.

"What?" she asked curtly.

"May I come in?" May asked softly, her hands gathering a thin sweater across her chest.

"I guess you can."

She stepped aside, raked her eyes across the shrinking figure who slipped in like a starved alley cat, all huge eyes and fear.

"Sit down. You may as well, since you're here. Make it snappy, though, 'cause I am not feeling the best. Indigestion, gas, and rifting like a volcano. I think it was the can of great Northern beans I opened. There was something wrong with them."

"I'm sorry," May whispered.

"What?"

"I'm sorry to hear you're not feeling well."

"I'll live. Now, what brings you here?"

May sighed, then fixed her huge brown eyes on her neighbor and told her about Clinton being unable to find work and how she wasn't sure when they'd be able to pay the rent.

May flinched when Mary launched a tirade against her, saying this was the same thing that always happened. A young couple she trusted, give them a couple months, and they turned out to be slackers, deadbeats. He could have kept his job if he'd tried hard enough.

May shrank even further against the back of her chair.

"He was very sick," she murmured.

"Yeah, yeah. They all say that. Every one of them. I'll tell you right now, you have until the end of next month, and that's it. I hope you know, the price will be double, so you better figure something out."

May nodded and kept her eyes on the floor. Disbelief was like a black veil, obscuring her view of the sharp-eyed Mary. Heartsick, she rose to her feet, assured her they would do all they could to come up with the money, and was shocked when the claw-like hand waved away the sincere promise, followed by a belligerent whoosh of air that contained enough caustic mockery to bring a hot wave of shame to May's features.

She let herself out, tried to absorb the change from the once friendly hostess to this. Was everyone the same where money was concerned? Melvin lashed out at her brother, spoke in curt tones to Gertie when the rains did not come or the nights were too cool for a profitable cotton crop. Here was Clinton sunk in despair, now the landlady turned into a whole new person, and money was the reason.

Well, she could fix everything. She'd do whatever it took to make Clinton's life easier and to prove to Mary they were not like other couples. She had been raised on hard work and responsibility, and it would serve her well now.

She ran up the stairs with a new resolve, opened the door and looked for Clinton. He was not in the kitchen or on the couch, so she hurried to the bedroom door, eager to tell him they had more than a month before they had to come up with the rent.

The bed was empty.

She sighed, turned away, walked unseeingly to the window that overlooked the street, crossed her arms, and wondered at the unexpected turn of events. God seemed to have withdrawn His wellspring of blessings, but she would turn this difficulty into a time of growth, assert her rights, practice courage and stamina.

She wandered from room to room, restlessly pacing as she thought. She would have to confront strangers, then learn to get along with people she would work with. She had no experience with the world around her; she could only hope most folks had some small level of decency and kindness.

At eight o'clock, there was no sign of Clinton, so she took a long hot bath in the claw-footed tub, brushed her wet hair, and applied talcum powder to her body. She wrapped a warm robe around herself and went to nestle on the couch with the bundle of magazines Clinton had found tossed out and brought to her. She scanned the ads, cut out a recipe for pumpkin cake, although Lord new she had no idea where she would ever procure a pumpkin, the way she now lived in town.

The second hand on the clock jolted its way around until it was nine o'clock, and still Clinton had not come. She read an article about weight loss and the importance of eating leafy greens, which didn't concern her at all, but Gertie should have tried it.

She stopped reading, stared off into space, thought of the obese Gertie who stuffed herself at every meal, ate cookies and salty buttered popcorn and apple pie, as if the very act of food on her tongue would take away the sting of living a lie. May thought of Gertie masquerading a life, adjusting the mask of normalcy, the mask of well-being and devout Christianity, while sitting on that hickory rocker watching Oba wince as he walked upstairs, his shirt in strips, his face white with pain and suffering.

How much had she known?

She had died with her knowledge of Melvin's cruelty, but had she known more? How could she not have known?

May could only place her trust in a merciful God, a God who loved mankind enough to send His son in the form of an infant in the most unpretentious manner, born in a humble stable, the hearts of proud and haughty men missing the long-awaited event because they were assuming a wealthy king would be born in much grander circumstances. May nodded to herself, wise far beyond her years as she contemplated the nature of human beings, the atrocities one inflicted on another. Her soft heart pitied Gertie and Leviticus, both humble in their own separate way.

At ten o'clock, she fought back alarm, went to put the kettle on for a cup of soothing tea. At eleven, she felt cold tears on her cold cheeks, shivered uncontrollably as anxiety spread its danger through her body.

Where was he? Surely no place of employment was open at this hour. She had to gain control of her fear, quench the rising visions of Clinton being in harm's way.

Why were men of color so beaten back, so visibly set into a lesser section when they had no more control over society than they could help being born? Who had started this idea of one race being superior?

She'd once asked this question of Oba, seeing how only the black people picked cotton. Oba told her that it had started long ago, after his ancestors had arrived from Africa. May didn't know where that was or why they had come to Arkansas from Africa, so she thought perhaps they enjoyed picking cotton, their dark skin shielding them from the relentless sun that hovered over the fields. Somehow, she'd never thought to ask Clinton about the origin of it all.

Here in their New York town, black people were seen only on occasion, most folks as white as she was. Would that be a problem for Clinton, walking down the streets, in and out of the circle of light cast on the sidewalk by the electric streetlamp?

Hatred was not rampant, she reasoned. Most white folks tolerated the black folks, in spite of not always approving of them. She thought Clinton was special, a handsome man with acorn-colored skin and an easy, affable air about him. She couldn't see how he'd have a problem simply walking the streets, especially the way he wore a hat, walked with purpose and pride, a man of ambition.

She got up to go to the window, leaned forward to watch the street from left to right and back again, then looked at the small white face of the clock on the wall.

Almost midnight. A silent scream rocked her body as she stayed by the window, watching.

CHAPTER 20

OBA DECIDED TO STAY IN BLYTHEVILLE, THE TOWN WHERE most folks knew of the Amish and their whereabouts, a place he could keep an eye and an ear out for any snippet of information, no matter how small.

It was not hard finding an apartment or a job. He found a pay phone, dialed Tom Lyons's number, dropping dimes as the operator's voice instructed him, and was rewarded with the raspy voice of the old man who had befriended him.

"Yeah, Tom, this is Oba. I have to make this quick. I'm staying in Blytheville. May is gone, and no one knows where. I have more chance of finding things out if I stay."

Tom asked about his well-being, if he needed money, and that he should call if he needed anything at all. "As soon as you have a telephone, Oba, let me know so we can stay in touch. Or write. The Pony Express is still running."

Oba grinned, felt a rush of love for the old man. "Yeah, guess so."

They laughed, said goodbye, and Oba replaced the receiver, buoyed by the sound of Tom Lyons's voice and the thought that he cared about his life.

The apartment was in a brick building on Cherry Street, up a flight of wooden stairs that creaked and groaned with each footstep. The walls were painted a deep shade of green, or had been once, the paint peeling the way his face and arms had peeled from a bad sunburn that first summer in the Arkansas sun.

That was okay.

Peeling paint and creaking stair treads meant nothing to him. He had a place to stay: two rooms and a shared bath down the hallway. He had an electric hot plate, a refrigerator, a small table and chairs, a few overstuffed chairs, and a green sofa with broken arms like a great wounded bird.

He purchased bedding at J. C. Murphy's five-and-dime store; he bought soap and towels and two bags' worth of food. He moved about the apartment with steps that bounced, he sang under his breath as he plied the broom and wiped down the furniture.

This was just great: a place of his own, a place to be himself, to rest and relax and eat what he wanted and when.

He had never been happier.

Richard Drake was in his seventies and had owned Drake's Sunoco station for over twenty years. A man of generosity and common sense, he was glad to see the youth who turned up at his garage looking for work, especially with the way his back had given him sleepless nights that week. He needed a muscular young man to roll tires and drag heavy tools, to pump gas and wash windshields. It would allow him to wait on customers and catch up on his bookwork.

The gas station was on the corner of Main and Hawthorne Avenue, a squat, white cement-block building with a three-bay garage, a large plate-glass window in desperate need of cleaning, a red-and-white Coca-Cola sign with DRAKE'S SUNOCO written in black letters, the top half of the "S" in "Sunoco" peeling so badly you had to look twice to be sure it wasn't a backward "C," which would have spelled "Cunoco," making no sense.

There was a high counter surrounded by metal racks that held layers of small potato chip bags, stacks of candy and chewing gum; there were small metal trees dangling nail clippers and key chains.

By the door stood great stacks of motor oil and a red cooler containing glass bottles of soda pop. The heavy odor of gas and oil, diesel fuel, and grease hung over everything. The floor was littered with candy wrappers, bottle caps, and stepped-on cigarette butts. Everywhere, there was merchandise, all manner of gadgets and trinkets, and dusty calendars vying for space with racks of penknives and scissors, wrenches, and coils of lightweight chains.

On Oba's first day of work, he arrived a few minutes early, hung his coat on a hook by the restroom door, and turned to find Richard watching him, a half smile on his flat, friendly face.

A man of considerable girth, his gray hair cut short, a navy blue shirt with RICHARD spelled in red letters above the right pocket, he stood jiggling coins in his pockets.

"Good morning, son."

"Good morning."

They stood, sized each other up, then both grinned, found each other likable, and smiled broadly.

"Aren't you the good-looking fellow?" Richard said.

"Oh, I don't know about that."

"Sure are. Well, we'll have those handsome features covered in grease soon enough. This isn't a place for sissies."

"I'm not one of them."

"No, you don't look it. Alright, here we go. I'll show you around."

The garage contained two automobiles, one a metallic green, another with faded red paint and rust corroding every available edge. Two men stood drinking coffee out of filthy mugs, their hands as black as the mugs, in navy blue shirts and trousers with the names TIM and BILL above their pockets.

There were stacks of tires, toolboxes on wheels, tools on tables and strewn on the floor, a dizzying array of metal parts and cast-iron whatnots lying haphazardly around and underneath everything else.

"Good morning, Tim. Bill."

They turned, answered in unison, caught sight of Oba, and went silent. Both scowled.

"Alright, you can wipe that look off your faces straight away. This is Oba Miller. He's your apprentice. You teach him the ropes. He can start from the bottom up, but you better be nice. I know you can take the tar out of these young guys."

"Well, Richard, you know what happened last time," the one called Tim growled.

"Yeah, yeah, yeah. This ain't him. So give the guy a chance."

Bill turned away, banged his coffee mug on the tool bench, and went to work, lowering himself to the floor before disappearing underneath the front end of the rusted automobile.

"Tim sat on a jimsonweed this morning. Grouchy."

Oba smiled, nervous now.

"Don't mind him. He gets this way."

He found the atmosphere of the garage to be entirely different from that of the pharmacy in California. There were no polite exchanges, no quiet, clean environment in which to greet customers or do light tasks.

It was dark, smelly, with heavy objects that blackened his hands and crushed his fingers if he wasn't careful. He took curt orders to get this, replace that, bring rags, discard tires on the pile, was asked if he had no idea where or what anything actually was. He was called names, snickered about, gaffed with all manners of words that described his stupidity and inability to rise to the job. He was cold and hungry by lunchtime, too timid to say anything when the men both continued to work long past the noon hour.

At five o'clock, he was shown how to use his time card and walked down the street in the late afternoon sunlight, his face blackened by oil and dirt, his lunch pail containing everything he had not had time to eat.

He pulled the bill of his cap low as a horse and spring wagon approached and did not lift his eyes to see if he recognized the driver or his wife and children. He merely hunched his shoulders with one hand carrying the lunch pail and the other jammed in his pocket.

By the middle of winter, Oba had won the respect of everyone in Richard Drake's employ. Quiet, learning quickly and easily, he kept up a schedule of doing what he could to lighten Tim and Bill's workload, cleaned willingly at the end of each day, and was rewarded by acceptance he hadn't thought possible.

The men were both in their thirties, more or less, Oba calculated, with wives and children who were often the subject of the conversation as they moved about the garage. Tim was small, slightly built, with the quick catlike movements of the wiry type; he was a good mechanic who took time to teach Oba the uncomplicated rules for beginners. Bill was skinny as a rail but tall, with a loose-jointed amble in his long legs that always reminded Oba of the long-legged herons at the water's edge along the pond. Bill was easygoing, often the buffer for Tim's sometimes heated directions, the impatience like darts Oba did his best to escape.

He made fair wages; he could pay his rent and buy food, the basic needs of clothing and shoes, even a heavy winter jacket when the temperatures dropped. He made few friends, stayed mostly to himself in the apartment, reading books and sleeping deeply and restfully, as he had not slept in years. He was completely alone, with no one to interfere, so when the door of his apartment was locked, he knew he could sleep as long as he wanted.

He ate cornflakes, too—copious amounts of the crispy cereal—liberally sugared, with plenty of milk. He tried Rice Krispies, but always came back to the golden-baked slivers he loved so much. Sometimes he bought ground beef and pressed it into patties, fried them in a pan, salted and peppered them, before putting one between two slices of white bread with ketchup. He learned to drink Coke, ginger ale, orange soda, or cream soda. He drank coffee with Tim and Bill in the morning, learned how to make a good egg sandwich. He thought of how he'd told Tom that cooking was women's work. He smiled to himself a little, grateful that Tom had put up with his anger so calmly.

He always thought of May. He watched every young Amish girl that rode into town, watched as they drove past the garage, but, always, it wasn't May. He didn't know why he thought it could have been her, the way no one knew of her whereabouts. He didn't believe anyone knew he lived in town either, or if they did, they must have written him off as *ungehorsam* (disobedient) and let well enough alone.

Rumors swirled among the Amish, though—rumors and hearsays that traveled from one well-meaning person to the next, curious folks who pitied Melvin Amstutz, to have lost his wife at such a young age, then had his niece and nephew turn against him like that. He might have had his faults in the past, but still. He had a responsibility raising those three boys without a mother.

Sarah Weaver set out to see if it was true, this talk of Oba living in town. She staked herself out at J. C. Murphy's, watched the comings and goings at the feed mill, walked out to the cotton gin and the knife factory, and never once thought about checking the Sunoco station, thereby missing the youth out front, fixing the black "S" in broad daylight. She went home and told her husband she didn't believe a word Millie Troyer said, stretching the truth like a rubber band.

What Sarah didn't know was that Oba had seen her but kept his cap pulled low and continued with his work while keeping an eye on her, the way she loitered along Main Street, going in and out of J. C. Murphy's at least three times. She must have a patient horse tied to the hitching rack, or else her husband had brought her and would pick her up later.

Leonard Yoder and his wife put their farm up for sale that winter. When the evening had not gone well, the fateful event that had led to this decision, Leonard eventually had to shake his head and throw in the towel.

Melvin Amstutz was a master manipulator, a skilled person in the art of deception. He had used every trick in the bag, with quoted Scripture his chief method. Leonard had never given in, even when his fellow men were lured to Melvin's side, the sight of Oba's scars branded into his conscience forever. Melvin had neither denied nor acknowledged them, merely bore down like a highly educated lawyer on the fact that Oba had been disobedient, taken to strong drink, was wild and uncontrollable.

What had God taught through Scripture?

To spare the rod was to spoil the child. Would they rather see him become a juvenile delinquent, a ne'er-do-well who lay on the streets of Blytheville? He had taken these children in, had done his best to train them in the way a child should go. How could it be that he was now being falsely accused?

The righteous blame landed squarely on Leonard and his helpers, and Leonard was the only one left standing. He pleaded his case as the horses' hooves rang on the gravel road and the steel wheels bounced through the ruts and the potholes. He refused to get out of the buggy, even after they threatened him, but asked how can scars lie?

The three men moved off in the night, left him standing on the porch filled with anger and frustration. He talked to his patient wife long into the night, spent many hours in prayer throughout the winter season, but in the end, he could not find it in himself to stay in the community.

God had admonished the budding Christian church through his holy apostles to live peaceably with all men, as much as lieth within you. Leonard decided he could not live peaceably with Melvin Amstutz and put his farm up for sale.

He did try. He went alone to make amends, for hadn't his father warned him plenty of times? Never leave a community with ill will toward the brethren, as no blessing can follow. *Mach dei socha* (Make peace). He came away with the same revulsion he felt for a coiled black snake, prayed for the soul of Melvin Amstutz, the safety of his boys, and left it to God alone.

Winter was mild in Arkansas.

Snow was unusual, although the night could be cold, especially when the wind howled down from Crowley's Ridge and sent shivers up the spines of the pedestrians on Main Street. Holly bushes remained a brilliant, waxy green, with a generous sprinkling of red berries, as picturesque as a heavily colored painting. By the time February rolled around, there was a certain quality of spring in the air, the trilling of an oriole, that liquid cascade of birdsong like tumbling water, the appearance of new green shoots of dandelion and crabgrass by the roadside. The sky was a brilliant blue with shards of long white clouds like broken glass; the horizon turned lavender as the sun moved through the morning sky.

Oba was washing the large plate-glass window with a long-handled squeegee, concentrating on making long even sweeps without leaving a trail of smudges. He jumped in his skin when a voice behind him said, "Hello."

Slowly, he drew the squeegee down, shook to rid it of excess water, and turned to find Leonard Yoder standing alone, his blue denim coat closed with hooks and eyes, his black felt hat set squarely on his head.

"Oba! It's you!"

Oba smiled tiredly, like the hunted being given to the hunter, squinted, and said, "You were bound to find me sometime."

"You never moved out of Blytheville?"

"No. I have a better chance of catching a lead here than any other place. I'm still waiting to find out what happened to May."

"You're brave, Oba, staying here."

"Why do you say that?"

"What about Melvin?"

"He won't find me. I was hoping he'd be . . . you know. Taken care of."

"You mean institutionalized."

"That's a big word. But, yes, I was hoping."

"He's not."

Oba looked up sharply. "Why not?"

Leonard scuffed some gravel with the toe of his boot, then looked up, his eyes mere slits of light. "He's too clever, too sharp."

"What?"

"He denies everything," Leonard explained. "We have our farm for sale. I can't live here without the man being held accountable." Suddenly Leonard's eyes brightened, a new idea forming in his mind. "Oba, come with us! Would you?"

"Where will you go?"

"We're looking in Kentucky."

"I have to find May."

Leonard nodded, then smiled sadly. "I knew you would. I just hope, when you find her, she'll be alright and not . . . Oh, I don't know. I just hope he hasn't inflicted some sort of permanent damage on her."

"I don't think he beat her."

"I know, and that's a comfort."

"What about the three boys, Leonard? What will become of them? I mean, how can you be sure they won't suffer the same fate? How can you move away and leave them to fend for themselves?" Oba became agitated, his voice rose as he flung the questions at Leonard. He set down the squeegee, then picked it up again. He blinked, wiped a hand across one side of his face.

"Oba, I really don't know. I feel responsible, and yet . . ."

"You are responsible!" Oba was shouting now, his hands curled into tight fists of controlled rage. "How can you just leave?" Oba was shaking now, every word catching on the sobs that choked him. "I mean, there has to be something that someone can do. What if he kills those boys, huh? It'll be your fault, because you know the truth!"

Leonard shrank beneath the truth of those words, knew he was shirking a brotherly duty of love. He stood silently, absorbed Oba's outburst before stepping up and grasping his shoulder. "Alright, Oba. Okay. Calm down."

Oba swallowed, choked, and swiped fiercely at his tears, leaving a long black streak of oil as he reached into his pocket for a wrinkled bit of cloth that served as a handkerchief.

"Come with me to show your scars. No one will believe how bad it is without proof." Leonard pleaded.

"I can't go out there. Melvin will surely kill me this time." Oba was serious. He had held this conviction since his last visit.

They parted with the promise that Leonard would somehow see if the boys were being hurt; he left Oba shaken and consumed with something he could not understand. It was almost like the grief he'd felt when his parents died but harder to contain. A deep-searing disappointment that his adolescent years had been taken from him? He couldn't tell for sure. He could only know that it was like being taken off a smooth road and made to travel a torturous route of years and years and years. An eternity of suffering and rage and tears and vows of vengeance.

That was the reason he kept to himself. It was better to feel the quiet, to still the chaos of his thoughts, to bury his whole being in books and the solitude of his apartment.

This was what happened when he was with others, especially those of his past. It was only May who kept him here in Blytheville for months without a lead; it was May who dictated the pattern of his life.

One thought continued to nag at his mind. What if Clinton Brown had not been as smart as Drink said he was?

From inside the garage, Bill called out, "Who was that? You know very many o' them Amish?"

"No. He's a friend."

"Lively conversations going on there. Better watch yourself. You'll be converted."

A snicker was accompanied by a loud explosion of mirth from Tim. Oba turned away. What if he was? He'd never forget his intense wish to live the way Leonard and Sadie did, the children around the table like flowers, bringing joy and beauty into their life, working together in sunshine and rain, cold and heat, in sickness and health. This was the image in his head when he thought of marriage for himself, but he had never felt it was possible, having been an outcast, an *ungehorsama* (one who is disobedient).

His normal stillness taken for the day, Oba found himself ill at ease, restless, with anger seething to the boiling point. He lost his temper at Bill, threw a heavy wrench across the floor, and was thoroughly reprimanded by Richard, who told him one more trick like that and he'd be fired, and he meant every word.

That night, he went to McKinley Street, stopped a man on the street, and asked for Roy and Martha Brown's house. His eyes followed the pointed finger; he took the right turn into an alleyway and found himself at an abandoned house. The windows were boarded shut, the house itself as if it was put to bed for a long night's sleep. He loitered on the back steps, went around to the front, waited till a woman approached.

She was carrying a large sack, a small girl skipping along beside her.

"Pardon me, ma'am."

"Yessir."

"Do you know Roy and Martha Brown?"

The woman wrinkled her brow, put a finger to her lips, and rolled her eyes. The child came to a stop, turned her eyes up to her mother's face.

"I can't tell you rightly."

"Mam, it's Drink's Ma and Pa," the child said.

Oba nodded eagerly, "Yes, they do have a son called Drink."

"They move. They move somewhere. They don't say where."

Oba's shoulders sagged with unexpected weariness. Things would never change. Here he was in his hometown, with no lead except for a questionable one, and now it had evaporated.

"What about Drink? Did he go with them?"

"Now that I don' know. They just ain't no one live here no more."

"Alright. Thanks for your help, ma'am."

He touched the tips of his fingers to his cap and moved on down the street.

The cold settled down into his bones, making him shiver. He walked into the circles of light from the street lamps, then into areas of damp darkness, the odor of wet earth and decaying grass strong in his nostrils. Cars moved slowly along the paved streets, leaving the peculiar smell of exhaust, rubber, and metal. A car horn sounded ahead of him, and he saw a group of boys tumbling across the street like wayward half-trained puppies, shrieking and howling.

The occupant of the car raised his fist, shouted obscenities, and Oba thought of Enos, Ammon, and Leviticus, their shoulders already bent with the weight of the hard labor directed by their father's wrath. Old long before their time.

He imagined himself with the boisterous group of young men, knew he'd had a short bout of *rumschpringa* ("running around" with the Amish youth), but only when he'd been fueled by the forbidden alcohol, imbibed secretly in dark corners of barns and sheds.

He felt the need for it now, but he knew it would be best to stay away from all the places where he could drink the awful liquid that took away his past, his fears for May, the anxieties of living alone and making his way in the world.

He knocked on a few more doors in the neighborhood, inquired at each one about the whereabouts of Roy and Martha. Everyone knew them, but no one seemed to know why they had left quite so suddenly or so unexpectedly.

He always thanked the occupants of the houses, wished them a good day, and came away with the feeling they truly wished him well. No one seemed unduly suspicious or hateful, everyone agreed it was very strange for anyone to leave the tight-knit community on McKinley Street without telling all their friends and neighbors. Especially Roy and Martha.

He tried one more door, the blue of the paint faded to a cracked and peeling gray, the stoop that led to the sidewalk containing a fractured earthen jar filled with dirt, the scraggly brown remains of a few petunias dangling over the side. His knock was hesitant, the exterior of the house giving off a sense of ill portent, as if the owners had no reason to lay a welcome mat for anyone. When there was no answer, he tried again, with a knock firmly delivered.

The door was yanked open, an irritated young woman peering down at him. He stammered his inquiry and was met with an expulsion of fiery words that sent him reeling off the stoop and onto the sidewalk.

"I guess they'd better be moving is all I can say. I seen that Clinton Brown. He thought he could get away with it."

Shaken, Oba held her malevolent stare.

"He was messin' around with some white girl, I don't care what anyone says. No one will believe me. But I seen it."

"You saw him with someone?"

"Not eggs-zackly, no. But he was at it. I know him."

"Where did you see him? Her? Here? Here on this street?"

"They was sneakin' her into the house. I seen it. She's not like us. She wears that white thing on 'er head."

May! He tried to keep his voice steady but found the words tumbling out of his mouth much too fast and far too desperate.

"I have to find her, she's . . ."

"I don't care what she is. She done took my man so I don't have more to say."

And the door was shut effectively in his face.

CHAPTER 21

Sʜᴇ ᴡᴀᴛᴄʜᴇᴅ ɪɴ ᴅɪsʙᴇʟɪᴇғ ᴀs ᴛʜᴇ ʜᴀɴᴅs ᴏғ ᴛʜᴇ sᴍᴀʟʟ kitchen clock on the wall turned to one, then two. Her stomach had a hard knot of fear that would not allow her to rest; her breath was fast and shallow. She could not slow her mind from the frenzied imaginations of what might have happened.

She tried going to bed, covering herself with warm blankets, willing sleep to overtake her. He'd be here in the morning, surely. But what if he wasn't? Her ears strained to hear the familiar footfalls on the steps, the key inserted into the lock, and Clinton wearing the heavy woolen coat, his face alive with gladness at the sight of her.

As the night wore on, her prayers were hindered by the ever increasing knot of fear, the knowledge of some terrible mishap burned into her mind. Clinton would never allow her to worry about him, neither would he stay out all night without some reasonable explanation. When sleep eluded her, she got up, shivered as she drew the bathrobe tighter, then put on the kettle for a cup of tea. Her teeth chattered as she sat waiting for it to give its cheerful whistle. She put one cold foot on the other, trying to warm her toes, then went to the bedroom for an extra pair of socks.

She went to the window with her tea, her eyes searching the dark streets, the weak yellow glow of the streetlamps illuminating puddles of light around them. The uneven line of rooftops jutted into the night sky, the snow like a white foundation around them. The streets were empty, without the usual slow-moving cars or pedestrians wrapped in heavy coats and scarves hurrying by.

When morning brought cruel streaks of light to the eastern sky, she began to cry, the tears of despair weakening her resolve to remain strong. She cried soft, mewling tears at the absolute loss of courage, the overwhelming realization that anything could have occurred to keep him from returning to her, coupled with a stifling guilt that God was punishing her for taking her own path, following her heart when duty to Melvin and the boys had been her lot in life.

Caught in the chains of self-doubt, her tangled thoughts churned into a well of chaotic imprisonment, a deep well where she thought she would surely die.

The sun rose, casting its brilliant hard light into the small apartment, the light bulb from the ceiling rendered useless. Still, she stood by the window, watching the streets come to life, the automobiles crawling along the snowy streets, the people walking briskly to begin their day, to start the work that took up a large part of their lives.

How could life resume without her like this? Didn't they know she was alone, trapped in a situation that was intolerable? She wanted to open the window and cry out for help, to stop the normalcy of everyday life, to have one person come to her door with the promise of his return.

With the realization of her isolation came the will to get dressed, to see the one person she knew, the only person she could share the horror of her night alone. With shaking hands, she pulled on a sweater and skirt, pulled her hair into a ponytail, and stared into the mirror at the white face with red-rimmed eyes and trembling mouth. Then she put on her coat and let herself out of the apartment to knock on the door of her landlady, who greeted her with no amount of morning cheer.

But Mary stood aside to allow her entry, which was something.

May's voice came in a hoarse whisper, so she cleared her throat, then told her Clinton was missing, had been gone all night.

Mary Weinstein had seen plenty in her time and wasn't surprised.

This was often the way of it. The men took to drinking, staying in taverns and bars, removing themselves from reality when the going got rough.

She sat down heavily, patted the couch beside her, and May sank into it gratefully. May turned her large, dark eyes to Mary's face, searched for deliverance, any sign of hope she might offer.

"Well, I can't say where he's at, dear. We know he was looking for a job, so he might have gone somewhere to drown his frustrations with the whiskey or whatever it is these men drink until they get rid of the world they don't want to face."

Incredulous, May opened her mouth, but no words would form. No, no. Clinton would never. No.

Mary Weinstein returned the stare, then shook her head, instilling fear in May's heart, the kind of fear that refused to grasp what had been said to her.

May turned her face away to deter the insinuation of her beloved having stooped to anything so low. "He wouldn't do that," she whispered.

The landlady watched the pitiful young woman huddled beside her, opened her mouth, and closed it again. Then she said, "They all say that."

May's eyes flew to hers. "What do you mean, they all say that?" she whimpered.

"Look, dear. You're not used to the ways of the world. I don't know where you're from, but obviously it's some backwoods place of no account 'cause you sure don't know much. I don't know what your circumstances are, but you aren't very world-wise. It don't matter if your man is black, brown, white, or yellow—if they get into difficult circumstances, you may as well forget it with half of them. Your man couldn't get a job for how long? Weeks. Nothing unusual if you have a skin color that ain't white."

"But why? Why is the world like that?"

"Well, I don't rightly know why, except it's always been that way. The colored people are just coming off a history of slavery, and me being Jewish isn't much better. Look what happened to my people."

May had no idea what she was talking about and didn't want to know. She'd had enough to deal with in her own life, so she said nothing.

"So what do you want to do? Call the police?"

"Could we?"

May's face was immediately turned to hers, lit with so much hope that Mary Weinstein found it unbearable, this childlike trust that burned in her eyes.

"We could. Except don't be surprised if they come up empty-handed."

"Why would they?"

"Well, I don't want to disappoint you, but if it's a colored man, I'm afraid they won't pursue the case the way they would for a white man. They'll question, ask around, but there isn't too much they can do if no one has any information."

She made the phone call, then handed the receiver to May, who did her best to explain the situation and describe Oba's apperance.

The man on the other end of the line was kind but brusque, asking direct questions which she answered to the best of her ability. He promised to do what he could, then report back to her, but Mary shook her head after May hung up, leaving May feeling more despondent than ever.

"The police ain't that bothered by things like this," she said.

"Oh, but surely, Mary. Surely they will do what they can."

"They might. They might not."

Mary Weinstein was not one to take in stray cats, dogs, or people. She wasn't interested in having this pale, skinny girl in her house, so she told her to go back upstairs and get some sleep, then go out and look for a place of employment if she was going to keep that apartment. They were already a month behind on their rent, and she wasn't about to let that go. She patted her back clumsily, sent her out the door, and made herself a good breakfast of broiled fish, poached eggs, and toast.

May stumbled up the stairs, collapsed on the old couch, and cried as if the sobs would literally destroy her, then fell into a troubled sleep where her own cries awakened her, only to fall back into the merciful blackness of slumber.

She awoke to the empty apartment and the realization of the missing Clinton, tears sliding past her closed lashes immediately.

He might have simply boarded a bus and gone back to his family, tired of her and the struggle to support her. Or he could have gone drinking, the way Mary had suggested. Or he could have been accosted on the street by some robber or thug who took his money, beat him, or . . . It was simply unimaginable. She could not dwell on these thoughts, or she'd lose her mind.

Her head throbbed as she raised it from the pillow; the room slanted sideways as she got to her feet. She was weak with hunger and lack of sleep, from the stress of worry and frustration; she was still reeling from Mary's lack of care and the police and all they represented.

Was the world a bitter place, then? A place where each individual had to look out for himself? If neighbors and the law did not do their duty or promise to help, where was the will to go the extra mile?

She drank tea and ate the last crust of bread after removing the blue mold from the edge. The small amount of sustenance enabled her to remove the self-pity, take a deep breath, and make normal, well-thought-out decisions.

She could not stay here in the apartment, and she had no money to board a bus or a train to get away. Where would she go?

Not back to Arkansas, certainly. She had family in Ohio, but would they welcome her? Returning to them was not an option, the way she was dressed and what she'd done.

Clinton. Clinton.

Where was he? Was he in pain at this moment? Had he been beaten, left to die? Or was he on a bus, fully aware and responsible, leaving her here in snowy New York while he returned to Arkansas? No, he would never do that to her. She was so sure of it.

There was only one rational thing to do, and it was going out to look for work. She had to make money, enough to feed herself and pay the rent.

She did her hair carefully, dressed in her best clothes, pulled on a pair of worn leather boots, and made her way down the stairs. She hesitated at Mary Weinstein's door, then knocked, a timid rapping of her knuckles on the door.

When Mary pulled it open, she was met by an instant scowl.

"What do you want?"

May hesitated, ashamed of her question. "Where should I go to look for work?"

"Well how would I know? I've never worked out of my home. Your man back yet?"

May shook her head miserably.

"Well, he ain't coming back, likely. So you best get on down to one of the eating places or the green grocer, see what they say. I expect you could wash dishes or something."

"Thank you."

They stood uncertainly, the Jewish woman knowing she should offer the poor girl a place to stay, May knowing there was no alternative but to brave the cold and the inhospitable doors of places of business. Her entire being shrank from facing another person who might fulfill the duty of greeting her in a civil manner but who had no convictions about turning her away.

She turned, took a deep breath, and stepped out.

Everywhere, she looked for Clinton. Sometimes she saw him in the slope of a man's shoulders or the height of another man, but always it wasn't him. She entered restaurants and taverns, asked about a Clinton Brown, then inquired about employment. Turned away throughout the afternoon, she felt weak and sick with hunger, overwhelmed by the loss of Clinton, but she staggered through one more door, painted green with an old, sagging sign that read O'MALLEY'S.

The room was poorly lit, with the smell of grease and burning food, the powerful odor of (and here, May was transported back to the Amstutz farm) cow manure—the rich, acrid smell of the cow stable that clung to cowman's boots. The clank of utensils on dishes, brown tables covered in oilcloth, the banging of pots and pans were all accompanied by loud conversation and boisterous laughter that erupted from different points in the room.

"Find yerself a table, love." The voice came from a massive woman dressed in a striped dress a few sizes too small, a white apron no bigger than a man's handkerchief around her sizable waistline, the strings buried in rolls of flesh.

"I . . . I'm not here to eat."

"What are ye here for, then?" In the dim light of the room, she appeared absolutely enormous, but her eyes were not unkind, the riot of crimped red curls like a cap on her head, the mouth wide and breaking into a smile easily.

"I . . . I . . . need work."

"You need a job? Well, love, I don't rightly know about that. But here, you look half-starved. Yer no bigger than a soakin' wet chicky. Sit down. Here. Sit down." She motioned to a booth, grabbed a towel tucked at her waist, and wiped the tabletop furiously.

"I'll bring ye some food. You like ale? Water? You want a lemonade or a cup o' tea?"

"Tea, please. But I don't . . . you know. I can't pay."

"We won't worry about that now, hon. You look like a starved cat. I'll be right there, hon."

She moved off with amazing speed, her small feet beneath the stockinged legs propelling her forward smoothly so that she took on the appearance of a large sailing vessel navigating a small canal. She wound her way expertly among the tables, barking orders to the rest of the girls who brought trays of steaming food.

May leaned her head back against the booth and closed her eyes, a great weariness spreading itself through her body as the warmth and safety of the room enveloped her and brought the first real sense of comfort since Clinton's disappearance. She sighed deeply, felt the oxygen to the tips of her fingers.

She must have entered a subconscious zone, a place between being awake and asleep, the way Clinton came to stand at her table, an easy smile of welcome on his handsome face. She struggled with all her strength but could not open her eyes or put out her hand; her arms were held to her sides with steel bands.

"Oh, Clinton, you're here," she tried to say, but no words would come from her mouth.

She was brought rudely back when the heavy woman set a plate before her, then said, "There you go, hon. I'll bring yer tea."

But . . .

Clinton had been here, standing by the table. Where was he now? When the woman came back to her table bearing a cup of steaming tea, May asked her if a man had been here at her table. If she'd seen a black man. A man named Clinton Brown.

She shook her head, her eyes hooded with suspicion.

"Now why'd you ask me that? This ain't no negro place. This is O'Malley's, and all of us is Irish. We don't have anything to do with them. They got their own places where they all flock together." She drew herself up to her full height, which wasn't very much, then lowered her voice to a conspiratorial whisper. "We don't even have them fer our help."

May nodded, confused. Here was kindness, in the plate of steaming food, coupled with the disgusting attitude that hung between them like a foul stench. If she knew why May was seated here, she would never hire her, so she nodded her head in a traitorous agreement. How far did one have to fall in order to secure employment?

But the potatoes were hot and salty, butter sliding down their sides, the flat beans seasoned with pepper and a tomato sauce, the boiled cabbage swimming in a delicious white sauce. The tea was strong, sugared, and life-giving. May found herself eating ravenously, like a wolf who'd endured a week of famine. She washed it all down with the black tea, and felt revived.

Anything was possible, she thought. Anything.

She walked back along too many streets, the cold seeping in under the coat that did not keep out the chill. Her jaw was clenched, her steps hurried, her hand shoved into her pockets to protect them from the bitter cold. When she reached the apartment building, she hesitated at her landlady's door but moved on up the stairs. The food she'd had at O'Malley's would have to sustain her till tomorrow, she knew, unless Mary could find it in her heart to make breakfast for her.

She inserted the key, turned it, pushed open the door, expecting a warm rush of air but was greeted by a wave of cold.

No. Oh no. she'd threatened this, and now she'd done it. She had gone and turned off the heat in these meager rooms. May simply stood in the middle of the cold room, wrestling with disbelief and outrage, the loss of Clinton, her miserable, frightening existence in this strange town.

Why had she done it? Why had she left Arkansas?

She doubted the decision, doubted anything she had ever done, felt alone, deserted. The future rose before her like some bilious monster, raging and spewing all manner of evil threats. She could trust no one. First Melvin and Gertie, then Clinton, and now Mary Weinstein, who had mercilessly shut off the heat. She felt deserted, wrecked on a barren island without vegetation or sustenance.

But had Clinton betrayed her? Had he indeed left willfully, the way Mary had implied? She might never know the true answer. Would it be harder than knowing he had died? She didn't know, not now anyway, with his disappearing so new, so strong in her mind.

Please come back, she thought. Just come to our rooms, here on top of the stairs. I'll forgive you anything and everything. Please.

She went downstairs and talked to Mary, who said that she could not continue to provide the hot-water heat if she wasn't being paid and that May was no longer welcome to stay. Her eyes were hard, and her voice was stilted.

May stood as if the very words from her mouth were actual blows, her intestines twisting into a hard knot until a sharp intake of breath made Mary draw back, alarmed.

"I . . . am . . . I'm sick," May said, clapping a hand to her mouth, before all the half-digested Irish food came spewing out of her mouth.

She was turned out into the street, gripping the sturdy satchel she had purchased at the Salvation Army, her clothes packed hastily, an extra pair of socks on her feet, the cold tearing its claws in cruel, fresh bursts of wind that howled along avenues and alleys.

She had no place in all the world to go—no place to call home and no one to turn to. Darkness kept her from searching the faces of passersby, from asking someone, anyone, for a warm place to stay. She reeled with the knowledge of unkindness, the way the world took what was theirs and didn't worry about the needs of others. Or had she merely been thrown into a headlong freefall of bad luck, meeting folks like Mary, who had once shown kindness but turned against others when they fell prey to unfortunate circumstances?

She was so cold, so terribly cold. The nausea made her head spin, and for a moment, she leaned against a cement wall, closed her eyes, and wished for a merciful end to her life.

She prayed. *Dear God, are you there? Look down on your poor May, who has sinned by following her own lusts, her own desires. Grant me forgiveness, precious Jesus.*

She knew in the same breath that she had loved Clinton, had loved him more than a desire of the flesh. God knew he had saved her from a worse fate.

She had no idea where to go or what to do. Every plan she could possibly imagine eluded her, without one penny to her name. She could not board a bus to find her way . . . to where? Where would she go?

The cold wind continued to buffet her thin frame, with no food to sustain a normal body temperature. She knew she must keep moving, must find some place where she could step inside for only a moment, or she would surely perish.

Most stores were closed, but a few restaurants remained open. She had no desire to step into a tavern, but she might have to if nothing else was available. She walked, hoping she would appear as one with purpose, going to a train station or coming home from traveling on a bus, but when the cold became so excruciating she was swallowing her tears, she merely stopped walking, pulled on the handle of a heavy door that led to the warmth of a tavern, sat in a darkened booth, and put her head on the tabletop, without caring whether she lived or died.

There were few patrons, so she realized she might go unnoticed long enough to warm herself before she set out again. She drifted into an uncomfortable sleep, worn out from the cold and hunger, the terrible jolt of Clinton's disappearance, and the sheer despair that robbed her of her strength. The night was as cold and dark as her spirit.

She was rudely awakened by a shaking of her shoulder. Frightened into wakefulness, she blinked, grimaced.

"Come on, dearie. Sleep it off at home. Time to go."

"Oh, oh. I'm sorry. I wasn't aware that I'd fallen asleep."

"Time to go."

May looked into the face of a thin, middle-aged woman wearing a tight red dress with a row of buttons down the front and said she had no place to stay.

"Yeah, they all say that. If it's that bad, go to the Salvation Army. They'll give you a bed."

"Where is that?"

"What? The shelter? It ain't far. A couple blocks. Turn right on Burd Street. You'll find it."

Without further words, she was ushered back out into the bone-chilling wind. She found herself at the cement-block building with a neon sign above it. She pushed open the door and stood blinking in the bright lights that ran along the ceiling.

The place had a strange odor, but otherwise it was fairly clean and hospitable. A tall man whose clothes hung loosely on his thin frame, his jowls as loose and dangling as his clothes, asked her name, then brought her a sandwich made with white bread and one slice of bologna and one of cheese, a small glass of milk, and one vanilla cookie.

May was grateful. She tried to eat slowly so she would not become nauseated, then sat nervously, wary of the homeless men who shuffled their feet across the floor and kept their eyes averted. An old woman cried out, threatening an imaginary intruder, then began to cry in long, sloppy sobs.

May shivered.

A portly woman with cinnamon-colored skin came to sit across the table from her, bringing with her two cups of steaming coffee and a friendly smile.

May smiled back, tentatively.

"Now you tell me your story, okay? I'm Judy. Maybe I can help you out, but it depends on your circumstances, of course."

May swallowed a mouthful of hot coffee, grimaced, and shook her head. "Oh, if I told you everything, you wouldn't believe it," she said in a very small voice.

"I'm here to listen. Everything is confidential."

May eyed her warily. "Really?"

"Yes. You look so young. What brought you here?"

So Mary told her everything, starting with her parents' death and ending with the disappearance of Clinton Brown, the ensuing eviction from her apartment, and the inability to find work.

Judy showed no surprise, no emotion at all. She merely listened with an expressionless face, sipped her coffee, and leveled a kind gaze toward the face of this slip of a girl. A beautiful girl, really.

"That's quite a story. And how do you plan to continue this story?"

"I have no idea. What should I do?"

The old woman burst into a string of foul obscenities. Judy got up and went over to her, brought a cold drink before hunkering down in front of her chair to talk in soothing tones. She straightened to scold one of the bent old men, told him to leave Bess alone.

May inhaled deeply, tried to calm her fears. She could not stay here with these people. The cold outside was the sole thing that kept her seated at the table.

"So, May," Judy said on her return. "If you have no idea, can I make a suggestion? I find it hard to believe your grandmother would not take you in. If you had the bus fare, would you go? You seem like an honest worker and we need some help around here. It wouldn't take long to earn your fare."

Terrified, May burst out, "No! Oh no. Absolutely not. I have to stay here in this town. What if Clinton returns, and I'm not here?"

CHAPTER 22

Oba's life took on an obsession, a driving need to prowl McKinley Street in the evening after work. He took to watching the old blue door and its unwelcome pot of flowers, hiding as best he could behind the building across the street.

He watched the house's occupants, the coming and going of ordinary family life. There were three younger girls and the one he had spoken to, and as far as he could tell, the father was either dead or had deserted his wife and children. The mother drove an old car that was held together by rust and good luck, which was the only logical explanation. He waited for weeks, months, before he had a good opportunity to approach the girl who emerged from the doorway on a tender spring day when the soft air around him made him feel sad, a weepy longing for something he didn't understand. He just knew the whispery breeze seemed to soften the hard knot in his chest.

She flounced out, looking strangely beautiful in a pale yellow dress that was gathered at her narrow waist. She was a golden brown color with her hair in a black halo around her head.

She sat on the front steps, crossed her legs, and bobbed one foot. She leaned back and lifted her face to the sky, her eyes closed as she savored the evening.

Quickly, Oba stepped from his hiding place, dodged oncoming cars, before he called out, "Excuse me, miss. Can I have a word with you?"

She sat up, lowered her eyelids, and growled in a petulant tone. "I don't know if you can or not."

"I need to know more about Clinton Brown, please. I believe the girl he's with might be my sister. Is there anything you can tell me about him or his whereabouts? Anything." He spoke too fast, and she had trouble understanding his low words. "Clinton Brown?"

She leveled a dark, malevolent gaze at him, then shook her head from side to side. "I ain't talkin' 'bout 'im. He's unfaithful. A swamp rat. He had to get out of this neighborhood—and fast. You know why. That girl, yo' sistah? Come on. Alls I can tell you, he's probably left her by now, you mark my words." She leaned back on her elbows, lifted her face to the sky again, as if the conversation was over.

"But . . . tell me. Where would a person . . . um . . . like you? Where would they go to be freed from the Southern segregation?"

She sat up, spat a quick, "Puh?!" She lectured him, "There is segregation all over, so don't kid yourself. They ain't no free state. It's the same everywhere. But I don' know." She shrugged her shoulders. "Lots of 'em goes to New York, Detroit, Ohio. Places like that. Too much snow fer me. I hate the cold. I ain't chasin' after Clinton Brown though, snow or no snow."

Oba stood ill at ease, shifting his weight. "So you can't tell me anything?"

"Not really, no. 'Cept he can't be trusted no-how. I can pretty much guarantee yo' sistah is left alone."

"Don't say that. You don't know May. She would not survive in the world. She has no experience."

"Has some if she wid' Clinton Brown."

Oba hesitated, reined in his imagination. "But is he good? Will he treat her right?"

"'Spect so. He's kind enough. But he's good looking, knows it, and has an eye fo' the wimmen."

"But there's a chance the girl isn't May?" Oba asked.

"A slim one. Look, I got things to do. Whyn't you mosey along, huh?" With that, she leaned forward, rose to her feet, and with a shrug of her shoulders, disappeared behind the faded blue door, leaving Oba to stare at the slivers of peeling paint as if it could fall off and spell out everything he needed to know.

He sighed, turned away, his hands in his pockets, his shoulders hunched, thinking of May with an excruciating ache in his chest. If she was with this man, what desperation had driven her to finally break away? And if the girl spoke the truth, there was a good chance of her life being filled with sadness, abandonment, or worse. He had to take into account, though, that he was getting his information from a spurned girlfriend, one whose heart might have been broken.

So he had a lead. A bit of information, no matter how wobbly. He would scour the state of New York, if it took the rest of his life.

His days at the garage turned into almost unbearable confinement, when the sun shone warm, when geese honked and he caught the perfect V formation of the large birds as they hurried overhead. He missed his time outdoors with the call of the mergansers on the creek, the splash of trout in gently trickling green pools. He longed for the clank of chains attached to traces, the scent of oiled leather and horsehair, standing on the cart with the reins in his hands, master of a four-horse hitch, purveyor of fields and forest, imitator of complicated bird calls.

He thought of Leonard Yoder moving his family to another Amish location, unable to live in peace knowing what had occurred on the Amstutz farm, his brethren siding with Melvin. Would things be different if the other men saw his back?

Probably not.

His wages were fair. By being frugal with food and clothing and his rent being only a fraction of most other renters' costs, he was still able to keep a small amount in a cigar box beside his bed, to which he added a few dollars every week.

But he was lonely, restless. He stayed mostly to himself, especially on the weekends, made no friends, and obsessed about May. If only he had more money, he would simply get on the bus and allow his instincts to guide him. He had saved enough to come this far and had to save again. He ate white bread and inexpensive bologna, bought bacon ends and fatty ends of ham after arguing with the butcher over on Drake Street. He ate oatmeal for breakfast, sometimes for supper, after a bologna sandwich for lunch.

Tim and Bill teased him unmercifully but in a good-natured way, never openly cruel. They loved him in their own rough way, and he appreciated their company. They were married with children, and the extent of Oba's learning never stopped, as he listened half-heartedly to the account of their daily lives.

He pumped gas, washed windshields, and kept to himself, except for a fleeting smile as he waved the occupants of automobiles with clean windshields on their way and wiped his hands on the oily rag that hung from his hip pocket, while the next car drove up. He learned about oil changes, spark plugs and carburetors, why an engine overheated, when to send a person to Tim and Bill.

But not a day went by that he did not long for the open field, the freedom of turned soil and wild blue sky filled with bird life.

One day, an old brown station wagon pulled up to the pumps, the driver rolling down his window immediately, calling out in an impertinent voice. Oba looked up and noticed the car was filled past capacity with the yellow straw hats and the black bonnets of the Amish. Children of all ages peered out from the back window, where they were stuffed like rag dolls.

Oba stood watching, pulled his cap as low as possible without arousing suspicion, then walked out as unassuming as he could muster. The Amish always did this to him, set his teeth on edge, provoked a certain wariness, brought an unwelcome mushrooming of the guilt about his clothes.

He wore English clothes, the *verboten* (forbidden) garb of the *ungehorsam* (disobedient). He was a runaway, one with a hard heart, one who had taken his own way, disregarding the wishes of his parents. Or in his case, removed himself from the regularly administered punishments of an uncle.

He recognized the round jovial face of the front-seat passenger as that of David Weaver, his full orange beard surrounding his beet-red complexion. Meanwhile, the driver—not Amish; he must have been hired—had resorted to hanging out of his window, glaring at Oba as he gesticulated with his left arm.

"Get over here. What are you waiting on? Winter?"

Oba quickened his steps.

"Hurry up! We don't have all day."

"Yessir."

"Fill it up."

"Yessir."

Should he clean the windshield? There might be a chance he would be recognized, the information carried back to Melvin. He decided against it, filled the tank, and went to the driver's side to procure the money. The man handed over a five-dollar bill with the order to bring back every penny of his change, inserting an unnecessary jab of kids being untrustworthy these days.

Oba returned with his change and stood back to allow him to drive away.

"What? I don't get a windshield wash? Come on. Get to work."

Oba nodded and did as he was told, trying to keep his face averted but with very little success. His heart skipped a few beats when David suddenly leaned his right elbow on the passenger door, following it with his enormous, shining face.

"Hey! Don't I know you? You look like someone I used to know. You're not . . . ? No, I don't think so."

The massive red beard disappeared into the interior of the car, and Oba inhaled deeply. Immediately, the gleaming face reappeared.

"I know!"

The door was pushed open, the giant man unfolding himself from the front seat. He reached Oba, grasped his hand, and pumped joyously, his demeanor entirely changed.

"You're Oba. Oba Miller. How you doing, Oba Miller?"

Oba turned away, kicked at gravel with the toe of his shoe.

"Hey. Don't be afraid of me. Salina!" he called out lustily, which brought forth his buxom wife, her face like a well-polished dinner plate, blue eyes like happy marbles surrounded by flesh, all framed with the puckered black bonnet. "Look, Salina. It's Oba. Oba that stayed with Melvin and Gertie."

"Oba! Why yes, of course. I thought sure you'd return to help Melvin out after Gertie passed away. And here you are. You'll be coming back to us, huh?"

Oba looked up, shocked. "What did you say about Gertie?"

"You don't know? Oh come on. How could you be here without knowing about Gertie?"

"I wasn't here. I didn't know."

"Well, she died, Oba. She died of a broken heart. You left the farm, and she died. Melvin said you meant so much to her, and when you left, she went downhill fast. You should think about these things, the way you've gone off into the world on your own."

"She was unwell," Oba said in clipped tones. He felt the anger rise in his body.

"That may be. But we have our arms open for you to return. Come back to us and join the church. Melvin and the boys would be so happy. You would make their life complete. He is watching for you, just the way the father watched for his prodigal son who went his own way. He ended up eating his food with the swine. That's how low he fell." The shining face was decorated with runnels of copious tears, followed by a watery smile, and a hand slick with perspiration grasping his own. "Come back to us, Oba. Give your life to the Lord."

There were so many words jammed against Oba's chest, it caused a plug, like a rockslide in a cave. He was crying, screaming inside, releasing horrible words like hornets when the mud nest is disturbed. But he could not hurt or disgust this happy couple, this truly joyous family stuffed into the station wagon, the children's faces eager with the anticipation of going fast in a real automobile.

So he nodded, accepted her plea with a blank face, eyes dark and flat, without emotion.

"We will keep praying for you, Oba. We love you and want you to be a part of our community."

He nodded again. To open his mouth would be a disaster, to allow even a portion of the boiling cauldron of his past to slip through would ruin the peaceful surface of this family's existence.

Salina turned, went to the car, her hand on the door handle.

"We're going to New York to visit cousins who have relocated in the Adirondack Mountains. We'll see some sights, I bet."

Oba looked up sharply, moved his gaze to the station wagon filled beyond the capacity of being comfortable, then allowed a weak smile, and a wave of his hand. He stood beside the gas pumps, his shoulders slumped as the station wagon lumbered off, David's massive arm still waving as they turned left and moved away.

He ate yet another bologna sandwich, touched the candy bars on his way to the garage, his mouth watering for a taste of the sweet chocolate, but he kept his vow to May. The disappearing carful of Amish on their way to New York only cemented his goal of finding her one day, when the time was right.

The heat of summer brought steaming days and miserable nights, when the town's sidewalks and brick buildings kept the heat in the rooms like an oven. Oba lay in his apartment, watching the greasy white curtain in the kitchen billow out like a young woman's skirt, only to be drawn back to whisper against the filthy screen, leaving the room as airless as before. He got up, crossed his arms in front of his chest, removed his T-shirt in one quick pull, then twisted it to wipe his face before going to the sink to immerse his whole head beneath the running water from the spigot. He shook his hair like a dog, then rubbed it dry with the T shirt before flopping back on the couch.

Why was he here in Blytheville, Arkansas, after May had left? The only lead he had been able to procure was by an unhappy young woman whose view was troubling at best. The community on McKinley Street was obviously kept in the dark when it came to Roy and Martha Brown.

The only person who might know more was Arpachshad, the questionable storyteller, the friend he was never allowed to keep. But he hadn't seem him in months.

Perhaps being here in this delta made him feel closer to finding May, as if her staunch obedience would propel her home. He would be working at the garage, and she would appear, on her way home to Melvin and the boys to fulfill the duty that meant so much to her.

He wondered about the boys' welfare for the hundredth time, wondered about their father's anger and seething frustration that always threatened to boil over.

His back was a clear testimony to the unparalleled rage which had taken power over normal anger, what should have been a commonplace frustration when things went wrong, perhaps resulting in comments of displeasure or annoyance. But this wild lashing, this discolored face, and eyes gone beyond human anger, spittle flying from his mouth—all of it was a sight branded into Oba's memory. As long as he lived on earth, his mind would be polluted with Melvin's lashes, the pain inflicted so deeply he wore it on his skin in discolored ridges. Sometimes when he was alone, he felt as if an abnormal substance floated in the blood that pumped through his heart, creating havoc with the organ's regular rhythm. His breathing became fast and shallow, the room shifted to the left, then the right, and he felt positive he was losing his mind.

No one should know about this. It was shameful to admit he had somehow contracted a disorder, as if he had inherited a bit of his uncle's craziness. That was the word. He might be crazy, bordering on the brink of turning into him. Into Melvin.

Where was God in all of this? Where had He been when his parents died? How could he call on someone who was so unpredictable?

Still . . . Who else could he call on when he needed help, especially when his own mind flew off into strange territory sometimes?

He flipped onto his back, threw an arm over his forehead, felt sick and weak with the night's heat, but he was decided again with the morning's arrival. He would go back to the overheated garage, both Tim and Bill testy as the temperatures mounted. He was here on account of May; the search for her would not end until he found her.

He imagined her large dark eyes that held a look of surprise yet an underlying lack of life and vitality, an acceptance of her lot. Or what was it that haunted him so much when he thought of her?

He felt his breathing quicken, the heartbeats in his chest chipping away at his state of mind. He got up, went to the refrigerator to find a drink of cold water, anything to occupy his accelerating mind. He drank in hurried gulps, shook his head to clear it, and felt the panic crash around him.

The apartment tightened its grip, squeezing his scarred back against his chest. The room swung to the right; the bare light bulb above him began to swing. He pulled on his T-shirt in one quick swoop, made his way to the door, fumbled desperately at the knob before making a headlong dash down the dimly lit hallway, down the stairs, and out onto the street.

He gulped in the humid night air, balled his hands into fists, and walked, not caring whether he walked away from the overheated box he called home or whether he lived or died.

He stopped after the heat of the night caused him to be drenched in sweat, his breathing coming in hurried gasps. He lifted his face to the dim yellow light from the street lamp, the mosquitoes and moths in a wild flight around it. He watched steadily as the night insects threw themselves repeatedly against the blinding heat of the light. At his feet, the dead wisps of the zapped insects lay like wheat chaff on the hot sidewalk. He shoved the toe of his shoe against them, then lifted his face again to the erratic flight of the mesmerized insects.

He stuffed his hands in his pockets, hunched his shoulders against the beat of his heart in his chest, exhaled and inhaled deeply, then sagged onto a wooden bench, his chin lowered to his chest. A stillness came over him then, a quiet calm in the same region of his agitated heart.

A voice whispered.

All he heard was, "Stop. Please stop."

He didn't know what kept him there on the wooden bench that night or why he heard the voice telling him to stop. He only knew he was grateful for the stillness, the banishment of the racing heart and shallow breath. He lifted his face to receive the deep calm, to revel in it and appreciate this unbelievable turn. He opened his eyes to find the same swarm of insects ending their lives as they continued their wild lunge against the blinding light.

And he knew.

He was like the night moths, wasting their fragile life by insisting on the brilliance of the light. He was being drawn into an unhealthy obsession by the loss of his sister, and it was getting the best of him, shoving him into an erratic state of mind.

What had sent the soothing calm? What had caused him to hear the quiet voice? It was as far removed from the feeling of losing his mind that he could imagine. A whole world apart.

It was strange, the way the stillness continued and carried him on its soft, sturdy wings as he left the wooden bench and began to walk slowly toward his apartment. When he thought of May, he thought of her in the same cushion of stillness in which he found himself. The desperation which had taken control of his life had been replaced by the assurance that she would be taken care of in the same manner he had been.

He slept a deep, dreamless slumber, in spite of the ongoing heat and damp, cloying humidity. He awoke refreshed and more than ready to face the day. He found himself whistling a low, tuneless song under his breath. With a slight bounce to his step, he greeted Tim and Bill with more than the usual grunt.

"Hey! What gives?"

"He actually spoke!"

Both of them slapped his back, jovial despite the sweltering morning, their shirts already wringing wet with an hour's work. Oba grinned back at them before picking up his wrench to begin the removal of a flat tire.

It was close to quitting time, the part of the day when they hustled to finish self-appointed tasks and worked quickly without speaking as the hands of the clock crept toward the five. Oba was sweeping with the heavy push broom, bent on delivering steel shavings, stray nuts and bolts into a pile before getting the dust pan to clean it all up.

He had a feeling of being watched. He stopped the forward thump of the broom and looked up to find Melvin Amstutz with his elbow propped against the frame of the open garage door, his hip thrust to the side with his right fist propped on it.

"Hello," he called out, in a familiar jaunty fashion, the kind of words that lilted from his mouth when the cotton weather was right.

Oba stopped, straightened, fought back the urge to flee, but refused to meet the taunt in the man's eyes.

"So . . ." Melvin waited, knowing he was jabbing Oba with the sword of his fear, that time of deadly quiet before the unleashed displeasure.

Oba fought back the accustomed urge to flee, felt the numbing anxiety mount, but forced himself to face the bearded visage in the doorway.

"So . . ." Melvin repeated the insinuation, pausing further to instill trepidation to its absolute power.

Oba felt the stillness, felt the victory of becoming very quiet deep within himself. He lifted his face, met the triumphant gaze, and it was Melvin who looked away first. Determined to retrieve the momentary loss of control, he assaulted Oba with a volley of demeaning sentences, beginning and ending with the disobedience to his authority, the utter lack of subjection to him and the church.

When he stopped, Oba nodded. "Yes, Melvin, what you are saying is true. I have disobeyed and will continue to disobey. You have never given me any reason to believe I want to live the kind of life I have lived with you. That kind of discipline is far beyond what any normal father would inflict on his son. To be beaten and whipped according to your moods was not true discipline, and you know it."

Melvin's face darkened. He took a step forward, as if to stop the flow of words coming from the nephew who retained his darkest secrets. "You have no right to speak to me in that manner."

This exchange was given in the Pennsylvania Dutch language, but Bill and Tim could sense the hostility, the absence of normal conversation. They stopped their work, laid down their wrenches, and watched as if ready to pounce. Oba was their charge, and no one would enter these doors without answering to them. They exchanged a look of unity, stepped forward.

"I do have a right. I am over eighteen years of age, I am no longer in your employ, so you have no right to stop me." His breath was coming in short, hard gasps, the stillness scattered for one moment of real fear.

"Is that right? And who gave you a home when you were destitute? Who gave you food and shelter? Who took you to church and taught you right from wrong? Who?" By now Melvin was shrieking, his face gone white with rage. He came close to Oba, his fists balled, the uncontrollable surge of anger rising.

"Whoa there. Hold up." Bill stepped forward, his hands thrust out, palms forward. "You keep this up, and we're calling the police. Don't you touch this boy."

Melvin opened his mouth, closed it, and stepped back. He turned on his heel and left, his steps quick, jaunty—the step that haunted Oba's dreams. He watched the retreating figure, his eyes never leaving the black-coated figure until he rounded a corner and disappeared.

Oba turned, let out a deep breath, and sagged against the hood of a gleaming Oldsmobile.

"Thanks," he said, his face lowered.

"We'll look out for you, boy."

A hand on his shoulder, a squeeze that said everything, and his coworkers returned to their task, leaving Oba alone with his thoughts.

He had to devise a clear plan. He felt as if he had wrung the town of Blytheville dry, removed every available nugget of information, sifted through tons of loose gravel to find one gold chip, with next to nothing the end result.

He had to move on. With bus and train fare too costly, he would try hitchhiking, a source of transportation that was both cheap and responsibility-free, except for sniffing out the unsavory characters, with which he believed he had plenty of experience after his time on the trains.

Yes, it was time to go. Time to move to New York, to be free of Melvin once and for all.

He would take the stillness with him, the place he could go when he felt the worry squeeze his living, beating heart until he could no longer breathe. He didn't have to know what the stillness was; he just had to know it was there when he needed it.

He began to walk toward home.

CHAPTER 23

S HE SAT ON THE EDGE OF HER CHAIR, CHEWING THE CUTICLE
on the side of her thumb, her knees pressed together, her heels lifted
from the surface of the stained flooring. All around her, the homeless, the hungry, the mentally handicapped, and the disfigured milled
about like a sea of sorrowful humanity, leaving her stranded on her
island of worry, anxiety, and fear.

She had nowhere to go, not a penny to her name, no one to help.
She cried out silently, lifted her arms to God, and beseeched Him to
give her answers, to help her in this awful hour of need.

She had no choice but to stay, for now, of this she was certain.
But something, something had to come up, anything to get her away
from these smells, these sad people. Her large, dark eyes followed
a balding old man with blotches of dark brown discolorations all
over his head and face, his back bent until he walked with his eyes
to the ground, his feet shuffling in scraping slides along the floor.
He was muttering darkly to himself, a fist jabbing the air in front of
him.

May tightened her knees, thrust her feet beneath the chair,
crossed her arms around her waist, and watched warily. She shrank
back even further as the old man approached her; she averted her
eyes from the sagging face that gazed at her like a begging hound.

"Missy. Oh, missy."

No, no. Don't touch me, May thought.

"Missy. I need you to find Ettie for me. She was just here a minute ago, and now I can't find her. She's not doing well." His voice rasped like old charcoal, his lower lip gleamed with saliva that hung in loose, swaying rivulets.

Suppressing a cry of disgust, she got up off the chair and moved away as swiftly as possible, turning a deaf ear to the cry of "Missy! Come back."

She went to a door marked RESTROOM and swallowed against the smell of stale excrement and aging disinfectant. She sat on the lid of the commode, hunched her shoulders, and bit her lip as tears slid down her cheeks.

She must be strong, be reasonable, and make a good decision. Did she have enough compassion to help Judy in her selfless work? She shrank back from hearing the answer she did not want to hear, the service that was perhaps God's will for her life.

Please, no.

Should she accept the offer of bus fare to her grandparents, who were likely dead by now, buried in the cold cemetery beside her parents? Or would she find the same uncaring attitude that had sent her to Melvin and Gertie in the first place?

Perhaps it was not uncaring. She remembered the phrase *ess suit yuscht net* (it doesn't suit), so she really shouldn't be thinking no one wanted them. Lives were full, relatives busy, houses overflowing with children and no extra money or food when times were lean. It was not uncommon for children to be handed to uncles or cousins, when one needed a hand on the farm or money was scarce to provide for the dozen offspring at another.

She remembered the exact location of her grandparents' farm, the small elevation in the otherwise level landscape, the group of poplar trees that stood like nervous soldiers, their branches ruffled in the dizzying breeze that sent the undersides of leaves topsy-turvy, like a glimpse of a shy child's knees when she dashed across the yard.

She remembered lacy carrot tops that felt like a caress when you thrust your face into the center, breathed in the sweet, fresh smell that was healing and forgiving when your parents were buried in the cold earth, and you hoped your soul could soon be set free to go wherever they were. The billy goat with the curly horns that spent hours butting the fence posts and getting caught in the wires between them, her child self watching with a secret hope, a sort of wild pity, that he would break through and make a delicious lunge for his freedom. The tin plates covered with peas and stewed saltine crackers, a serving of crispy chicken legs or wings, depending on how many pieces of chicken her grandmother would carve out of a fryer.

She remembered the crispy chicken leg she struggled to eat, her mind infused with the fresh sight of the heavy hatchet coming down with a dull *thup* on the proper location of the chicken's neck. The yellow eyes staring wild-eyed at the blue sky above, the last sight the chicken would ever see, followed by the head falling into the dust beside the chopping block. The wild flurry of feathers as the headless body was catapulted into the air, the wings flapping, the feet running till it lay still, the neck feathers soaked with a ring of glistening red blood.

May had enjoyed chicken corn rivel soup the next day, the small pieces of neck meat swimming innocently enough among the broth, the sight of the chicken-killing mostly forgotten. She had loved to squish the doughy rivels between her teeth, feel the comforting slide of them down her throat. Her grandmother had always served rivel soup with a side of homemade bread, rhubarb jam, and bright yellow butter that had an acrid smell, shaped into an oblong log on the blue ceramic butter dish.

All the coziness, the goodness of her grandfather's farm came alive in her memory, as she cowered in the restroom of the homeless shelter, trying to shut out the cries from the disturbed elderly and the thought of slick, drooling old lips.

"But I can't, Lord," she whispered, when fear overtook her again. "I can't stay here."

But no alternative presented itself in the coming days, so May took a deep breath, rolled up her sleeves, and went to work. Her dutiful demeanor was a godsend to the understaffed, overworked Judy, who was head of the facility and had no intention of turning anyone away.

May had a roof over her head, a decent tiny room to herself, and more than enough to eat, so she lived comfortably enough as the cold increased around her, the poor coming in from the streets as winter's icy grip threatened their lives.

Clinton stayed in her thoughts, permeated her prayers, lived in her every waking moment, but no lead or sign ever presented itself. Sometimes she felt certain he was alive and well, merely desperate to provide for her and gone to another city until he could accumulate a bit of money and come back for her.

Over and over, she imagined his homecoming, the joyous racket at the door, being lifted into those ironclad arms, her face covered in welcoming kisses. She longed to see him with a physical ache, a yearning that bordered on desperation, but every day there was nothing.

Nothing.

The doorway proved to be an entry of disappointment, the dark faces making her heart leap. This time it would be Clinton.

It never was.

She learned how to assuage the elderly's fears, learned to wipe drooling mouths, wiped noses sticky with mucus, sang to calm upset children and drunks who were coming out of a stupor. She washed dishes, clothes, and faces; dressed wounds; and cut old, thick, yellowing toenails. She swallowed the bile that rose in her throat and decided she could exchange this lowly service for food and shelter.

As winter tightened its grip, she watched the door less frequently and kept busy with everyday tasks that no longer served the purpose of repelling her. She became accustomed to the odors, the filth and smell of removing caked-on socks from half-frozen, unwashed feet.

Judy called her an angel sent from God, and May ducked her head and thought if she only knew what her body had been through, how her innocence had been taken away and never returned.

They were seated in the back of the kitchen after cleanup, each one holding a steaming mug of tea as they relished the warmth of the clanking cast-iron register. May could never hear the pinging without remembering her time with Clinton, the warm apartment filled with him. Pain crossed her face as Judy watched intently.

"You know you're thinking bad stuff now," she said, watching May's face over her cup of tea.

"No, no I'm not. I can never hear the cooling of a cast-iron heat register and not think of Clinton Brown."

Judy nodded.

"He'll be back. If he's as good as you say, he'll be back. These men have a hard time when no one will give them a job."

"I keep telling myself that, but I'm afraid he's hurt."

"Well, if he's hurt, he'd be dead by now."

"Don't say that."

Judy pointed her chin in the direction of May's stomach. "You're putting on weight."

"Am I?"

"You look it."

May ran a hand over her front without a trace of self-consciousness, merely smiled, and said she was glad. She could use some extra to keep her warm. This big rattling building was never truly warm.

"Time to stay out of the bread box," May said, laughing.

A joke was a rare occurrence with May, and Judy laughed with her, appreciating the bright tinkle.

"Bread doesn't make you fat, May. It's those day-old cookies and doughnuts we get from the bakery on Harlen Street."

"I love the sugar cookies."

"So do I."

They moved off to their separate rooms with smiles on their faces, went to bed, and slept the slumber of those who have accomplished energetic goals in the course of the day. The ice cracked and boomed on the river, the sheets shifting away, only to be caught by an even thicker section of it downstream, straggled all along the banks like huge pieces of broken glass. It began to snow during the night, hard pellets of compressed ice that roared down from the Arctic and assaulted New York with its frigid fury, erasing automobiles and pedestrians from the streets in twenty-four hours.

The shelter was jammed, slovenly derelicts huddling quietly in corners, begging to go unnoticed as they shrank into themselves. Others shed outerwear, roamed the shelter nonchalantly, demanded three hot meals, and complained about the muddy-river coffee that stank like fish.

May came upon a huddle of men, ruminating about past snow storms, ice jams the size of an ocean liner. She stopped to listen.

"Yep, them ice piles breaks up in the warm, they find anything under that stuff. Upriver, downriver, don't make no difference. That river coughs up debris. Bodies a' horses and cows, broken boats, and fifty-gallon drums, just anything."

May moved on, taking for granted that everything these men talked about was massive inflation of the truth, often fueled by cheap beer or whiskey.

When the warm spring finally descended, the forsythia burst into bloom along with clumps of purple violets along country roads. Pussy willow branches were broken off by eager children, chests bursting with pride, and presented to their mothers.

Timmy Schollhaus was only twelve years old, but when his best friend Watson accompanied him to the river, the sky was the limit. They weren't going fishing the way they did in summer; they knew spring was the time to look for washed-up treasure and who they could persuade to buy it for a nickel.

Dressed in T-shirts and denim overalls, they walked along like the little businessmen they were, shoulders squared and thumbs hooked into overalls that sagged at the waist. Timmy was the shorter of the two, with a shock of hair so red it could have been mistaken for a pumpkin from a good distance away. Watson was tall and thinner, his ambling gait keeping up with Timmy's short hurried spurts, turning from time to time to walk backwards as he spread his hands to make a point.

Timmy dashed off into a grove of trees to break off a willow switch, never meant to be presented to his mother, but to antagonize his best friend with an occasional whack on the seat of his baggy overalls.

"Cut that out, dummy."

Another good whack was delivered, followed by a hideous giggle and a dash toward the river, with Watson in pursuit, his long legs covering twice the ground of Timmy's shorter, frenzied churning. He caught him at the river's edge and hauled back on his shoulders, flinging Timmy to the ground before straddling him and delivering a few punches with the demand to cry "Uncle!"

Giggling and flailing, Timmy rolled out from under him, headed straight for the water's edge, and Watson had to let go. Either that, or roll into the river, and both knew the water was freezing cold, with bits of ice scattered along its banks. But the sun was warm, the towhees were calling, the dandelions bursting with color, and everything seemed right and good as soon as school would be over in a few months.

Timmy stopped rolling, lifted his head, and peered up at Watson, his face muddy but his eyes shining with pure glee.

"Gotcha!"

Watson pushed at his stomach with the toe of his cracked leather shoe, but Timmy was too quick, leaped to his feet, and taunted him with a forefinger hooked into each side of his mouth, crossing his eyes and letting out a screech when Watson swung halfheartedly.

Timmy moved backward, still taunting, when he tripped over a rubber boot and landed squarely on his backside. Surprised, he sat up and said, "Ow!"

"Hey, here's a boot," Watson yelled. "If we could find the other one, imagine how much we could get for it."

They both bent eagerly, but it was Timmy who yanked at the boot and found it attached to a leg. The leg turned into a whole body that was half-buried in silt and slabs of ice.

They didn't know what to do, so they didn't say anything at all, at first. They merely stood solemnly and stared at the poor person who must have fallen through the ice in early winter, and now here he was stuck in this mess by the river.

"What should we do?" Watson asked finally.

"Is he dead for sure?"

Watson nodded solemnly.

"Shouldn't we say a prayer or something?" Timmy whispered, feeling as if he had somehow drowned this man and would be taken to jail by an angry policeman who would tell him it was his fault.

"I don't know any prayers."

"I don't either."

"We could make one up."

"You go."

"No, you go."

So Timmy crossed his hands reverently and said, "God, this here is a dead man, and it wasn't our fault. Bless us and him both."

"You have to say 'Amen.'"

"Amen."

And they took off running like never before, arriving at Watson's doorstep so out of breath it took his mother a full five minutes to extract a sensible story. She then walked calmly to the telephone in the hallway and called the police.

A few days passed before the shelter got wind of the washed-up body, but by Wednesday, that was all anyone talked about. Descriptions and circumstances varied, until the police came to question any of the homeless who might have stumbled upon a clue.

May stood just inside the doorway to the kitchen, both hands clenched to her heart as she listened.

"He's black. Not too black, but certainly not white."

That was all May heard before she felt as if her chest would explode with the power of the thuds that came from her heart. Her breath came fast and shallow, but she stepped out quickly, with no thought for anyone around her.

"I . . . I . . ."

"Yes, miss?" The policeman listened attentively, his eyes kind yet in a face so impassive as if it had been cut from stone. He nodded for her to go on.

"I . . . what I want to say. I may be able to . . . um . . . help." Her voice trailed off into a whisper, so that the officer had to step closer.

The morgue was a cold, dark place, the cement walls painted a greenish blue, bare yellow light bulbs like single eyes in the ceiling creating shadow and light that lent all manner of imagining to May's overwrought mind. Her footsteps sounded as if her shoes were hollow; there was a dull roaring in her ears.

More men appeared and escorted them to heavy steel doors that swung on massive hinges, and May found herself in the presence of a corpse covered with a white cloth.

When the top of his head was revealed, when she saw the dear black curls, the elegant rise of his brown forehead, she already knew.

She covered her mouth with both hands, held back the silent scream to allow only a soft moan to escape. The men nodded to each other without a sound, but they would not forget the huge brown eyes so filled with the tragedy of her loss; those eyes haunted their nights without mercy.

She merely stood, then, nodding. Strangely in control, stalwart even. She reached out slowly, traced the cold features, ran a hand lightly over the glistening curls, then stepped back, bowed her head, and turned away.

It was final.

She would never have him again, and she must give up to what God had done. She must bow her head and admit to being an unfaithful servant, and this was the reaping of her disobedience. She had been taught to stay among the pious, to keep the *ordnung*, and to be a dutiful maid to her uncle. She had broken these vows, and so she had been punished.

Or had she?

Melvin Amstutz was not a faithful member of the Old Order Amish church, neither was he a light of Christianity to the world. She had been torn between blind obedience and escape from a life she could no longer endure, and even for a short time, God had shown her that love was possible. Even if He had taken Clinton, her existence had been warmed with his love, her life given meaning and purpose.

I have loved you, Clinton, and I will continue to love, she thought. Death has parted us, but my spirit will always love you.

She declined a ride back to the shelter but walked slowly along the cracked sidewalks with the determined green shoots of spring pushing up through them. Her head was bowed, her arms hung in loose surrender. She was a small figure in a brown skirt and a navy blue sweater darkened by tears, her hair a golden halo around her petite face.

Pigeons soared overhead, then landed on the cement fountain in the small square. Children ran in circles around harried mothers, but she walked on without seeing, her heart beating steadily but without life, without the usual warm blood that kept up movement. Her veins were filled with ice and loss and hopelessness; she was in a numbed state of being in which the world around her was obscured by total devastation.

He would never hold her or speak to her again. He could never tell her how he had come to be in the river, washed up on its unforgiving banks. Had he slipped and fallen or been brutally attacked? Or, most horrible to contemplate, had he ended his own life on a bitter note of despair?

She would never know.

It was in God's hands, she knew. It made it only marginally easier, but still. The Lord had taken, blessed be the name of the Lord.

But in the coming days, her grief was like a room without oxygen, a breath won only occasionally, her existence hovering on a deep, torn chasm in a deserted landscape. She stayed in her room until she was forced to enter the kitchen for a drink of water.

That was when Judy told her it was best for her to leave, to move on in search of her grandparents. It was Clinton that kept her here;

now she knew why he never came home, and a chapter of her life would be closed away, sealed, and preserved in her memory.

May thanked her faithful friend, accepted the five ten-dollar bills Judy handed her in a pristine white envelope, set her face to the morning sun, and walked away.

She hoisted her old suitcase up the steps of the Greyhound bus and turned her face to the brilliance of another day, another chance to make a life for herself beneath the quiet eyes of her grandparents.

If they still lived on the farm in Ohio.

And if they would take in a prodigal granddaughter.

She carried within the love of a fine honorable man . . . and the loss of him.

She knew it was the color of his skin that made life so hard, the color of his skin that drove him to desperate measures. How wrong it was. How impossible to change his circumstances in the face of such a wide divide. Why could one side be responsible for such bigotry, walking about town or in fields with the assurance they were far superior with their white skin glowing freckled in the sun? As the bus carried her away from Henderson, May pondered this until she fell asleep.

When she awoke and turned her face to the window, the sun shone, and fat, puffy clouds rode along on strong breezes that ruffled the new oak leaves on bursting tree branches and lifted the manes and tails from the heavy Belgian workhorses in the wide open fields where the plows bounced over the soil. A flurry of happy sparrows sprayed the sky with their tiny brown bodies.

And May was at peace with the deep, lasting stillness of God's love that would carry her through the days to come.

THE END.

OTHER BOOKS BY
LINDA BYLER

LIZZIE SEARCHES FOR LOVE SERIES

BOOK ONE

BOOK TWO

BOOK THREE

TRILOGY

COOKBOOK

SADIE'S MONTANA SERIES

BOOK ONE

BOOK TWO

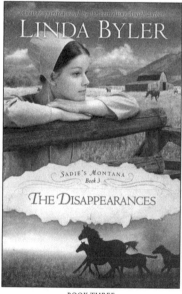

BOOK THREE

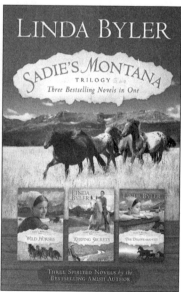

TRILOGY

Lancaster Burning Series

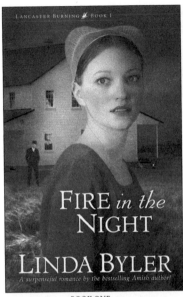

BOOK ONE

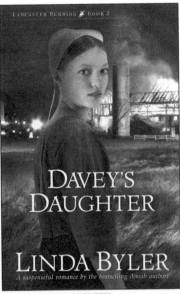

BOOK TWO

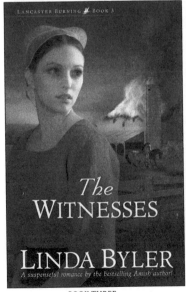

BOOK THREE

TRILOGY

BOOK ONE

BOOK TWO

BOOK THREE

TRILOGY

THE DAKOTA SERIES

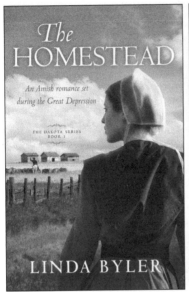

BOOK ONE

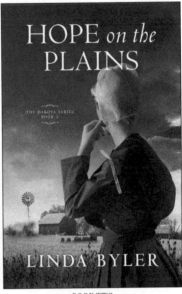

BOOK TWO

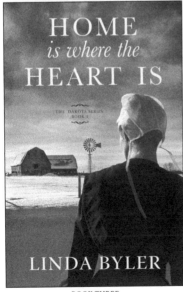

BOOK THREE

TRILOGY

CHRISTMAS NOVELLAS

THE CHRISTMAS VISITOR

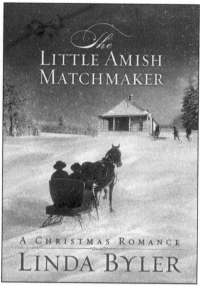

LITTLE AMISH MATCHMAKER

MARY'S CHRISTMAS GOODBYE

BECKY MEETS HER MATCH

A DOG FOR CHRISTMAS

A HORSE FOR ELSIE

THE MORE THE MERRIER

CHRISTMAS COLLECTIONS

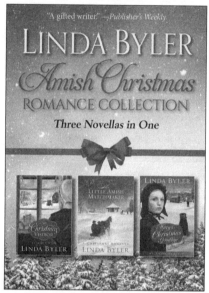

AMISH CHRISTMAS ROMANCE COLLECTION

AMISH ROMANCE AT CHRISTMASTIME

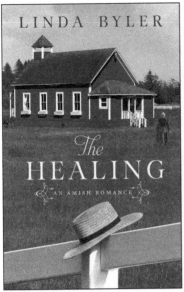

THE HEALING

A SECOND CHANCE

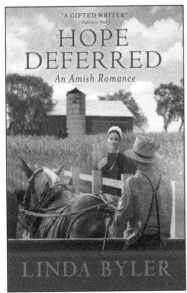

HOPE DEFERRED

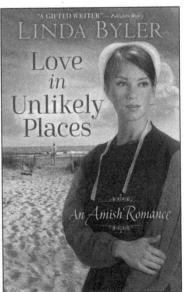

LOVE IN UNLIKELY PLACES

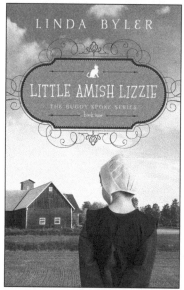

BOOK ONE

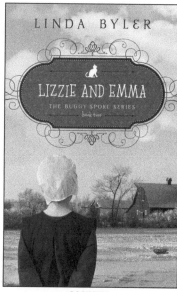

BOOK TWO

BOOK THREE

ABOUT THE AUTHOR

LINDA BYLER WAS RAISED IN AN AMISH FAMILY AND IS AN active member of the Amish church today. Growing up, Linda loved to read and write. In fact, she still does. Linda is well-known within the Amish community as a columnist for a weekly Amish newspaper. She writes all her novels by hand in notebooks.

Linda is the author of six series of novels, all set among the Amish communities of North America: Lizzie Searches for Love, Sadie's Montana, Lancaster Burning, Hester's Hunt for Home, The Dakota Series, and the Buggy Spoke Series for younger readers. Linda has also written several Christmas romances set among the Amish: *Mary's Christmas Goodbye, The Christmas Visitor, The Little Amish Matchmaker, Becky Meets Her Match, A Dog for Christmas, A Horse for Elsie,* and *The More the Merrier.* Linda has coauthored *Lizzie's Amish Cookbook: Favorite Recipes from Three Generations of Amish Cooks!*